OTHERWHERE

Margaret Wander Bonanno is author of:

Fiction

The Others (SMP, 1990)

Risks (SMP, 1989)

Strangers from the Sky (*Star Trek:* Pocket, 1987)

Dwellers in the Crucible (*Star Trek:* Pocket, 1985)

Callbacks (Seaview, 1981)

Ember Days (Seaview, 1980)

A Certain Slant of Light (Seaview, 1979)

Nonfiction

Angela Lansbury (SMP, 1987)

OTHERWHERE

Margaret Wander Bonanno

ST. MARTIN'S PRESS / NEW YORK

Design by Dawn Niles

Library of Congress Cataloging-in-Publication Data
Bonanno, Margaret Wander.
    OtherWhere : the sequel to The others / Margaret Wander
Bonanno.
        p.   cm.
    "A Thomas Dunne book."
    ISBN 0-312-06433-0
    I. Title.
PS3552.05925083   1991
813'.54—dc20   91-21580
                                                            CIP

First Edition: November 1991

10 9 8 7 6 5 4 3 2 1

For L.N., because it all began with him.

THE STORY THUS FAR . . .

CENTURY-OLD LINGRI, OFFICIAL CHRONICLER OF the Others, an advanced and peaceful island-dwelling species whose legends indicate it evolved on a far world and was "seeded" on its present world by some ancient spacefaring species not its own, tells the tale of how her kind first befriended, then were later all but annihilated by, the majority race who call themselves the People.

The People are a diverse and colorful species of many cultures, customs, languages, and religions who, despite continual war, disaster, and plague, have evolved sufficiently, by Lingri's time, to navigate the seas of their World and discover the insular but more progressive Others.

People are boisterous, warlike and superstitious, constant victims of their own fears and prejudices. Others are contemplative, nonviolent, and analytical. They are technologically advanced yet in harmony with their environment and, despite their penchant for convoluted debate, ultimately at peace with themselves. They tend, however, to homogeneity both in appearance and in thought, and to a kind of sterile sameness. The extroverted People live hard and die young; the sometimes telepathic Others are immune to most disease and can live two hundred years.

When People land on Other shores, the young Other

Lingri is aboard their flagship, having infiltrated People's society to observe their ways. Though her kind tend to disparage personal attachments, Lingri has already formed what will become a lifelong friendship with Dweneth, daughter of the People. War victim, rape victim, self-educated performer with a troupe of itinerant Players, Dweneth desires more than anything to study medicine and become a healer, a goal forbidden to women in her World. She and Lingri arrive in OtherWhere together, where Dweneth must come to terms with who and what her newfound friend truly is.

Dweneth's reaction to Others, a mixture of fear and acceptance, is typical of most People's, and when a tentative alliance is formed between the two species, Dweneth becomes one of its principal arbiters. Lingri, meanwhile, finds her life inextricably entangled with the People's; she will in time bear an Intermix son, Joreth, whom she must abandon when the alliance breaks down and the backlash begins.

For several decades, Others and People exchange knowledge and customs, and for a time the exchange benefits both. But the culture shock to a People pulled abruptly five centuries into the future by their exposure to Others proves too much. There is also Others' essential Otherness—their physical differences, their absence of law, their inability to adapt to People's religions or dietary customs, their steadfast abnegation of violence, their unattainable longevity. Lured into People's society by the People's own wishes, Others cannot become what People insist they be. The backlash begins.

Others are hunted, caged, and slaughtered. The last remnant, of which Lingri is one, is exiled upon their ruined islands. Their cities and resources destroyed, they are slowly being starved to death. When it seems that their only recourse to a death with dignity is to walk together into the sea, a sail appears on the horizon. An ancient galleon, piloted by Lingri's now grown son Joreth, leads a group of Partisans and Intermixes in rescuing the surviving Others. Among the

Intermixes is Dwiri, Dweneth's child by the Other Telepath Lerius, and Joreth's spouse. Together they will lead the Others into exile near the polar regions, where People cannot find them and they can rebuild their lives.

This prefaces all else: that there are not two but four intelligent species upon this World, for no scientist can convince me that the male of either species we call People or Others is not more alien to the female of his own species, and conversely, than to the male of the alternative species. It is a marvel that any intercourse, of body or of mind, arising out of so innately adversarial a mode, transpires at all.

—Lingri: *Chronicle*

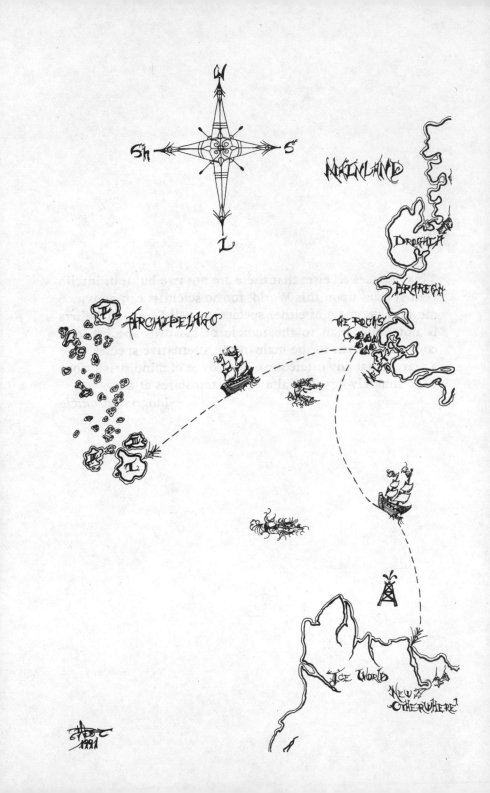

ICE WORLD?

OTHERWHERE

Excerpt: "A Nation of Administrators"
(from *Records of the Chamber: T-Y1093
WiseFrayin Philosopher recording)*

In the approximately twenty years between the time the People evidenced the theoretical capability to sail the World round and stumble upon us and the moment they actually did, the following probability factors were concluded:

- 37% probability that the encounter would result in some sort of xenophobic backlash, course and method to be determined by subcategorical breakdown.
- 8.15% probability of a reactionary isolationism, in which the People would withdraw from our Archipelago, declare it off limits, and attribute the existence of Others to folkloric or imaginary sources. This was later recalibrated against the unlikelihood of an entire species being able to keep such information secret from all of its tribal subdivisions.
- 54% probability that the People would acknowledge our existence, study our technology, and express varying degrees of desire to possess it. This category was later subdivided into probable means and methods whereby our knowledge could be disseminated. Curiously, no subcategory was proposed for what actually came to pass.
- 85% variance was calibrated for "unanticipated variables," though these were not specified.

While it was gratifying to discover the accuracy of our computations in predicting that the representatives of the People who arrived with the First Fleet would accept us, however warily, then express the desire to "know as much about [us] as we can use," to quote one delegate to the Council of the First Alliance, statistics alone could not have predicted what form this "use" would take, and this is where we failed.

Our failure was in an overdependence upon statistical probability, and a virtual absence of imagination. Our culture was replete with philosophers; an average of 11.16% of the population was registered with the Philosophers' Guild at any given time. Yet our philosophers, myself among them, were as subservient to the laws of probability as any Other. Further, philosophers had traditionally studied only phenomenology and the alter-dimensional. We ourselves required little in the way of sociological readjustment, having found the optimum sociological model for our own insular, homogeneous species, which had served us for more than a thousand years. While we knew this model would not serve the People, at least at the level of evolution whereat we encountered them, we had no true idea what would. Perhaps only the few dreamers and poets among us had an inkling, and as a society we had lost the wisdom to listen to poets and dreamers.

How then were we to know what the People wanted? We possessed no speculative literary tradition; therefore we attempted to glean what we could from the People's utopian literature. Synopsizing the frequently conflicting ideals expressed in this literature, disregarding its obligatory scenes of carnage and conquest (an additional mistake), we grafted it wholesale onto our own pragmatic model and hoped we'd got it right.

We trusted that the First Fleet, or later expeditions, would bring the best People, willing to study with us, that we might in time scatter them as leavening throughout the larger World. But few People could bear to live in OtherWhere, and those who did were reluctant to leave. The majority found our cities, for all their wonders, too untoward. Or perhaps it was we, in majority numbers, who constituted the ultimate strangeness. But clearly large numbers of People could not or would not live with us in those crucial years. Alternatively, we offered to send some of our own number to live with them, to set up places of learning on the Mainland.

"Send us your best!" we were told. "Send your teachers and your healers, your technicians and your scientists. Send everyone you can spare."

Naively, perhaps, we did this much and more. However many we sent, more were requested or even demanded. We became a nation of administrators, and there was no going back.

1

. . . and we are on our way.

How is this possible? Moments ago we were indeed on our way, to death. We began by stepping into the sea—calmly, purposefully, and without ceremony—swimming out to the point where we would be too weary to return, intending to sink and be forgotten, ending our troubles and the People's with us. Our minds were changed, our purpose diverted, by *bRi*, those winsome swimming creatures who have companioned us along our seacoasts for countless generations, and whom we heretofore presumed were less intelligent than we. Let it be a lesson to us, now that it seems we are to live.

"We" are a remnant, a tattered scattering—nine thousand four hundred thirteen survivors of a race formerly numbering one million. We are an exodus, a departure, an end and a beginning, a flotilla of fragile anythings-that-float flung wide before one ancient wooden sailing vessel across a so-far gentle sea. Our destination? A land of ice and stone, to hear it told, its precise location known only to my Intermix son Joreth and our whimsical saviors the *bRi*.

The ship appeared on a horizon until then devoid of hope. We could not take our eyes off it. It drew us. A mirage, an impossibility, at least a century old, a sail-powered galleon of a design not used since we gave the People the technology for skimmers some seventy years ago. Ancient, leaking, creaking, stripped down and laden to the gunwales with supplies for a seemingly impossible journey; if it ever had a name, this ship is nameless now. Of what nation, what registry? How did it get this far with no one noticing? No matter. It is here, and the focus of all our hope.

We foraged our desolate, run-to-ruin city for anything which was not metal and would float. Telfer windows, chamber doors, glassweave skimmer roofs upended to become boat keels, these motley flotsam are packed and ballasted with clothing, coverlets, the occasional hand tool, the last of our scant food. Everything else must be left behind, because it will not survive water damage, because there is no room. All our records, literatures, histories, once in computer microstor, were earlier destroyed. What we could, we committed to our collective eidetic memory. The rest is lost, with one exception. It shames me to mention it, but not to is to be less than truthful.

"It" is Lingri's chronicle, and I am Lingri. More than that my narrative must answer. And the less it is of "me," the more it can be of "we."

"We" are Others, survivors of genocide. Some of us died in the usual ways—tortured, beaten, torn apart by wildcurs. The majority were anonymously shot or gassed or bombed or burned. Some few, too many, were subjected to elaborate and ultimately meaningless experimentation, kept alive until they had served their keepers' purpose. Those of us who survived fled back to the Archipelago, our point of origin upon this World, though not in this universe. Not even our Telepaths can know for certain how each of our number died, though one of them, Lerius, knows all our names.

5

The fear was always with us, from the time we knew we were not alone upon the World. It was why we studied that teeming species which called itself the People, why we watched and waited, why some of us lived among the People to observe. It was why, even when the First Alliance was still forming and everything seemed for the good, our every interaction with the People was so fraught about with the potential for misunderstanding it was a wonder we dared breathe. It was why my grandmother Loriel died.

Loriel died of a misunderstanding. Or she died of a bolt from a cannonspear. It depends upon who is speaking.

Loriel was one of the most eminent scientists of her day, no little distinction among a race of scientists, and one of the first Others officially invited to the Mainland in the earliest cultural exchanges. It was her habit to swim every day, even in her two-hundredth year. Having inquired of local officials whether such was permitted from their beaches, and being told that it was, she neglected to inquire after the fine points. Unusual in a scientist, and one as thorough as Loriel, but she was of an age.

As the event was later reconstructed, she apparently rose with the dawn, walked down to the beach, slipped out of her garments and into the sea. The concept of covering the body for such an activity did not occur to her.

Envision, then, a People's child, wandering unsupervised out of one of a cluster of fishermen's huts onto a nearby jetty, where he accidentally tumbles into the sea. Picture an elderly Other—naked, long-eared, webtoed—pulling the gasping, blubbering brat out of the water in an attempt to return it to its family. What follows is a frantic mother, shrieking that her child is being snatched by a demon, a blur of running fishermen, a cannonspear of the kind still used to hunt *bRi*, and Loriel pierced to the heart. The rest is a great mind flown, a pool of virescent blood leached away into the sand, and silence.

"An accident," the People said. A "misunderstanding."

And because we were Others and not litigious, because we wished the Alliance to work for all our sakes, we made no accusations, pressed no charges, demanded no reparations. Perhaps that was our first mistake. But it would not have restored Loriel's life, and it was not our way.

We brought our cherished kinswoman's ashes home to scatter over the Archipelago, as we had done for our dead for five hundred thousand years. The Alliance endured, and for nearly seven decades there was a kind of peace. As the People came to know us better, such "accidents" were fewer.

Later, when they came to know us better than the growing Purist Party wished, nine hundred ninety-one thousand of us died, and none of these deaths were accidents.

It was not my intention to speak of death, except that I am asked, as each of us who has survived, by those who have rescued us. They need to know. They are People mostly, Partisans soulsick with what the Purists have done, not only to Others but to their own. Some few are Intermixes, like my son who, depending upon one's point of view, are either children of both species or of some third species never before limned upon this World. Torn between two thus far irreconcilable Worlds, what ambivalence haunts them none but an Intermix can know.

But they have all come from the Mainland, and know of us and our fate only what the Purists' censorship has permitted them to know, which is nothing. Hence, they ask, and I, Lingri the Chronicler, am chosen to speak. Everyone else is too busy paddling the small boats, distributing food, tending to the weak and elderly. Only Lingri, at the helm of the great ship, is free to speak, and Lingri speaks too much.

I shall speak no more of death; it is all Others have dealt in since our exile. I shall become like the sleek seagoing *bRi* who propel our small boats between their powerful bodies where our weak paddling would not prevail and think only

7

of life, only of now. With the aid of these *bRi* we will travel equator to polar region in a scant five days. This is the *bRi*'s normal migration this time of year, Jareth has explained; why should they not bring us along?

Joreth's People follow him, for they know where we are going. Others have not been so informed. Others follow him, I dare not say blindly, because any chance at life is preferable to meaningless death. Only I presume to ask our destination, and because I am his mother, Joreth does not answer.

So I speak of death, who sometimes speak so much and say so little that, assigned in exile to chronicle the events of a hundred years, I managed only twenty. Yet I speak, at the helm since morning, and it is nearly night.

I will say this and no more: nine hundred ninety-one thousand died. Nine thousand four hundred thirteen live. As does my son, as does his wife, as does—

"A daughter," Dwiri tells me with a Telepath's certainty, though it is scarce evident she is pregnant.

"A daughter," I repeat, considering my son's wife, still coming to terms with the concept that I yet have a son, much less that he has a wife, whose parentage is stranger than his own. "A daughter, whom you intend to birth in this place of ice and little else? Were it in my power, I would forbid it. Carry out your errand of mercy with our gratitude, you and my headstrong son, but then go back!"

I am breathless, a silly, disheveled scarecrow, white-haired though I am but a century old. I flap my arms, raise my voice—most unDisciplined, most unOther, and unheeded.

"Go back to what?" Dwiri wonders, her smile as unassailable as Joreth's stubbornness. It is her mother Dweneth's smile, and I know it well, for I knew Dweneth better than I know myself. I marvel at whatever web of circumstance has intertwined this being with my son. "Back to a World that would have my infant killed, for being what she is?"

"Joreth has passed for years, as apparently you have,"

I say, dismissing the prospect though I have seen enough to recognize its truth. "The child will look as much People as you do."

"Except for my eyes," Dwiri says, turning them, white-irised, away from the horizon to fix them on me.

"You can have them tinted," I offer, avoiding those eyes and the power they contain; my own past makes me wary of Telepaths, however well-intentioned. "There is a technique, or at least there was, before most of the healers died—"

"I know." Dwiri's eyes are drawn aft again, to where we have left OtherWhere behind. What must it be like for her, never to have seen this land of her heritage, except as it was destroyed? "My mother saved my foster mother's life with it, for a time."

A foster mother. I consider this. Dweneth was my own age and would have been nearly eighty when this child was born. An impossibility for People, who are not fertile past their sixties, but nothing was impossible for Dweneth Healer, the very genetic engineer who gave us the possibility of Intermixes. What questions the chronicler would ask!

"She would have done for me as well," Dwiri continues, "except that I refused. Stubbornness, I suppose. Afraid I brought little but grief to my mother's old age."

"You among Others," I reply, having been chief among them.

Dwiri says nothing to that. Is she reading my thoughts? How much did Dweneth have time to tell her daughter about her odd companion out of OtherWhere?

Every aspect of my life comes however roundabout to Dweneth. Dweneth who is dead—of old age, and peacefully, I dare hope, for she was past ninety when last we met, and People live half as long as we. Dweneth, with whom I shared a soul-thread, the only such mental link ever documented between People and anOther. Dweneth whose path crossed mine and mine hers more often and with more effect than

9

that of friend or stranger, spouse or lover or enemy else, and who, dead, leaves me severed and alone, flapping in the wind, empty, useless.

Except that I have a son, who has a wife, who bears a child, and these three raise a multiplicity of questions which I, Other-curious, must have answered. Is this enough to live for? There are also the Partisans and Intermixes, who hang upon my every word, and the last remaining Others, who also think they need me, if only to steer the ship. Therefore I steer—and argue, anOther's last indulgence, and any thinking being's last recourse in these empty times.

"You three are People, to all intents and appearances," I reason with my daughter-in-law, "and People the World needs withal. However flawed the World you left, it needs—"

"Not my daughter's life!" The voice is Dweneth's quelling argument. "You did what you had to do to save your child's life, Lingri-*al*." This voice is quieter, as Dwiri indicates Joreth making his way among the small boats in the flotilla. "Grant me the right to do as much for mine!"

I cannot argue this. I steer the great creaking ship, which sometimes courses smooth and sometimes balks beneath my hands. Twilight turns to dark and still I see them, feel them—Others, afloat on bits of planking or sheets of rigid recycle, huddled in the shells of depowered skimmers stripped of their metal to baffle scans and radar. Anyone scanning this part of the sea would read a *bRi* migration, nothing more. Oh, clever, Joreth!

Each bit of flotsam holds as many Others as it safely can, lashed fast or only clinging. We are tenacious, who swim from birth, and crest the waves with little ill-effect beyond the ever present salt and wet. Places are exchanged frequently, to keep us alert and distribute the discomfort equally. Joreth's People mingle with us, assume our rhythms, share our duress. Tentative conversations rise and

10

fall above the sound of waves and then grow still. Our exodus becomes almost festive, though we remain alert to danger.

Each makeshift vessel is flanked by a pair of *bRi*, shimmering graceful-fluked and long-maned through the darkening waters as they push the boats between them, seeming tireless. They bring us with them on their normal pole-to-pole migration because Joreth my son has asked them.

Asked them! For centuries Others interacted with *bRi*, honoring their courtesies by never making an outright request, even if lives depended on it. Yet *bRi* frequently saved our lives and we theirs, so long as the impulse came spontaneously from them. It took one shameless Intermix to change the rules. I must speak with Joreth about this, as about much else.

We sail, the weather holds, and we encounter neither threat nor obstacle—so far. Though I am not an Empath as my mother was, now that it is night I can feel the struggle among those in the boats—drenched and wind-exposed, already weakened by prolonged hunger before we left shore. There is food aplenty here, and wholesome meals steam constantly in great tureens amidships, doled out and passed hand to hand to the farthest outriders among the boats. A complex yet orderly relief system assures that at least once daily every Other may come aboard ship for a time, to be warm and dry and fed and rested before plunging on again.

Others can see in darkness, as can *bRi*; still the darkness makes us wary, and we no longer speak. No glimmer of light, no whisper of sound save the slip and splash of *bRi*-bodies reveals the presence of the thousands fanned out asea around the great ship. Each of us can sense where we are proximate to every Other; we have woven ourselves into a vast, resonating spirit-net, which we now weave about the rest—People, Intermixes, *bRi*. We are one. If any falter, too weak to continue, Others provide relief. No child nor old one is

11

left untended as we sail on. Nine thousand four hundred thirteen when we left shore, we have not lost even the weakest of that number yet.

Joreth clambers over the side from the small boats at last to relieve me at the helm. All day I have watched his progress throughout the flotilla. Easy to spot in his pirate's garb, his father's wild chestnut hair plaited and swinging nearly to his waist, boots gleaming, he leaps flamboyantly from one small boat to the next, as if this were mere adventure. He has my Other stamina and his father Redrec's deadly charm; not even Jisra Matriarch, our present leader, can resist him. Only she who bore him casts a skeptic's eye upon him, demanding that he answer.

"Tell me now and tell me truly, where are we bound?" I demand, Other-blunt and practical, refusing to yield the wheel. We have been sailing steadily Sunward, directly toward the Mainland, which is sufficient to make me uneasy. "For the sake of Others, I have a right to know."

Joreth shakes his head, his wild curls damp and flying loose from their plait.

"The less you know, the less you can tell. Still doubt me, Mother? Don't think I'll measure up? You'll have to take me at my word, as I once did you!"

Thus are the old forbiddens resurrected. He blames me for my ignorance. I did not know how to rear an Intermix child—in fairness, no one did—and mistakes were made. This does not excuse my particular errors, nor the document still outstanding which denies that Joreth is my son. A decade later, he does not understand the reasons for it. We shall have to have this out, and soon.

"Tell Jisra, then, at least. How is she to lead if she knows no more than I?"

"The Matriarch will know when she needs to know," Joreth says, embracing Dwiri, his manner softening as he does. "Have you asked her yet?"

12

"She was not ready," Dwiri answers with a Telepath's certainty.

She is more subtle than most, or else I have grown careless. Ordinarily I know when a Telepath is reading me. Not ready for what? Truth, I am ready for none of this, not least for Dwiri, who reminds me so acutely of her mother, but so young! That robust form, the frankly freckled face and redgold curls, the small, capable hands, her very smile all haunt me. Whoever said only the dead can haunt was wrong. This living incarnation of everything my lost companion desired but could never have makes me shiver as she takes my arm, helping me to sit as Joreth relieves me at the helm.

My own feebleness amazes me. Am I so old, or is it only the hunger, the long days and nights in darkness when nothing moved but my pen hands and my febrile brain? Dwiri brings me a stew of hot pulses and rice, the bowl abrim and implying endless resources. She watches over me as I eat. Some of us have difficulty remembering how.

"You've had all day and you've not asked her!" Joreth chides, teasing, willful. Asked me what?

"She was not ready!" Dwiri repeats. "Nor have I been idle the day long. There is as much to do aboard, husband, as there is afloat. Less for show and somewhat dryer, but as much!"

It pleases me to hear the way she speaks to him, brooking none of his male nonsense. If only her mother had had the knack!

"Ask me what?" I venture with my mouth full.

"We brought aboard a stasis case. WiseJisra says it holds your chronicle. Your history of People and Others. How much have you done?"

"Not enough and far too much," I answer, disposing of my empty bowl before she can take it from me. "A waste of space and paper, self-indulgent. AnOther could sleep in the space it occupies. Best throw it overboard."

I hyperbolize, of course. We dare not jettison anything

13

so obvious in our wake, to indicate that we still exist, much less where we are bound. I only mean to close the subject, but Dwiri smiles her Dweneth smile, undaunted.

"It's because it's personal, isn't it? More about my mother and you than about the World at large, and that's considered unDisciplined, unOther. Yet between you you two did more to change a World—can you call it self-indulgent to want to write it down?"

Behind the scattered flotilla, Joreth steers easily over the dark, the great ship bringing up the rear with no danger, in his hands, of running afoul of the small boats; he possesses my night-vision. He says nothing, only listens hard. This is between Dwiri and me.

"It was begun as a history of the interaction between Others and People, which resulted in our present situation," I explain, standing on my dignity; it is all I have. "That its narrow focus is on Dweneth signifies her importance to that history, as I personally witnessed it. However, it is incomplete—"

"As is history," Joreth cannot resist; he often interrupted as a child.

"Read it, as you wish," I answer Dwiri, ignoring Joreth. "But read it as it is. There was not time to finish it."

"You could finish it now," Dwiri suggests, Dwenethwinsome, mountain-moving. "Now that you have time."

"Has our unnamed destination trees, sprung miraculously through the permafrost at my behest, that I may harvest paper?" I've gone shrill, attracting Others' notice, who notice by not noticing. I do not relent. "Or have we brought computers, though we have no power source, that I may store my words there?"

"You have a voice," Joreth points out needlessly. "Voice enough, in truth, that it is the reason I am here."

His father's green eyes challenge me, out of his father's face. Intermixes invariably favor the parent from the People's side. It is true his grandfather first heard me because he

14

could not see me, though it was the Othersmell of me that first attracted blind Redrec Elder's notice. As to how Redrec Younger and I produced this son, that too has to do with voices, as with many Other things. I wonder which version of the story Joreth knows? I cannot speak of these things here and now; don't they understand?

"More self-indulgent, I would think, not to finish it," Dwiri suggests. "To leave the World as puzzled by what happened as we are. You loved my mother." She has plucked this from my mind—it lies both at the depths and near the surface—yet somehow makes it sound a question, a question I choose not to answer.

"As much as she loved you?" she persists, a Telepath and therefore rude by definition.

"How late in her life did she tell you that?" I barely ask.

"The last time I saw her. The day she died." The Telepath's white eyes tell me things I would prefer not to know. "She understood what you chose to do toward the end, and why. Perhaps if you continued with your chronicle, I too could understand."

The rest is Dweneth-voiced, in the knowledge that I can't refuse: "Tell me."

There are, as Other Histories state, four major islands in the Archipelago, practically named according to size order. The second-largest, thus named Two Greater, lies the furthest to Windward, with the remaining three clustered at the Leeward end of the Archipelago, near enough to be joined by telfer each to each. Between lie the so-named Agris and Industrials, and several hundred smaller islands.

The four Greaters also comprise the four major cities of OtherWhere; each city with its suburbs occupies the whole of its island and bears its like name.

But how to describe these cities?

The first thing visible, on approach by sea, is the perimeter wall separating each city proper from the blowing sand of its beaches. These walls are quite ancient—the youngest over a thousand years of age—more than man-high in most places, and surmounted by walkways, that one may take the sea air and enjoy the view. The walls themselves are constructed of fitted stones of myriad puzzle shapes, so intricately interlocked as to require no mortar, yet not permitting so much as a piece of paper to slip between them. The walls were built in such time, we were told, as earthquakes plagued these islands, though now the volcanoes from which the Archipelago was formed have all been "harnessed" for energy, and there are earthquakes no more.

There are no gates barring Other cities, that all may have access to them. The ways are paved in softstone, which has the appearance of multicolored glass but is soothing to the feet. Many Others are webfooted and walk chiefly unshod, and as there are no beasts of burden, travel is performed by skimmer, telfer, or on foot, and softstone renders walking a pleasure.

As Others can see in darkness, no lanterns or torches light their ways; as there is no crime in Other-Where, none need fear the dark. The foliage of a certain hybrid tree provides a soft luminescence by night, and that is all. Parks and fountains abound, to break the monotony of garden walls, for every dwelling has its garden, and every garden its wall. Others value privacy as much as they value truth.

Thus one enters anOther city and sees buildings of every description, all having in common that they are both functional and beautiful. Their facades may be rough-hewn to correspond with the landscape surrounding them or so smooth as to seem seamless, and rise to astounding heights. Even the most ancient of them sports glass windows of such clarity our factories could not begin to emulate them. Between ancient times and the present, structures in every shape and material have been wrought, some with domes and spires rivaling those in Kelibesh, some of a breathless simplicity, but each in harmony with its neighbors, so that each city, each way, is unique, yet never jarring.

As to the interiors of these faerie palaces, for as such they seemed to us . . .

2

"In the Year 1568 of the Plalan Ascendency, which Others refer to as 1025 of the Thousand-Year," I begin, seated on a coil of rope within earshot of the helm, "an entity known as the First Fleet anchored off the island One Greater, five years after three ships out of Droghia, under the command of then-Droghen Gerim, set sail on the untoward mission of navigating the World round, for the purpose of announcing to the leaders of the Fourteen Tribes of People that an alien race known as Others also dwelt upon their world.

"This First Fleet was the culmination of Droghen-Gerim's mission, though he was not aboard. Comprised of ships from the twelve tribes which kept a standing navy, it brought anywhere from twenty to two hundred delegates from each of the Fourteen Tribes to the city Droghen-Thrasim loved best in all the world. For it was Droghen-Thrasim who commanded this First Fleet.

"The Droghiad Gerim having died on his arduous journey, his former lieutenant Thrasim now ruled not only the First Fleet, but all of Droghia. Though an engineer by training and little suited to leadership, Thrasim labored mightily to—"

I break off, seeing disappointment in these faces of People and Intermix. This much was written in their own histories until the recent purges; all but the youngest are familiar with it. What more do they expect? I composed my chronicle on the supposed verge of death. Surely they do not expect me to resume so personal an account here and now?

"In the five years it took Droghen-Gerim's ships to sail the World, my mother lived in OtherWhere, the only People to do so," Dwiri says quietly.

"Indeed," I answer ingenuously.

"I wish to know about her relationship with my father."

If only answers were as simple as questions. Lerius lies in the hold among the sick and elderly; he is neither, but a Telepath, burned out before his time, as Telepaths are wont to be. It is his duty to hold the eidetic memory, where are contained the names and partial histories of all those who have died; elsewise I think he himself would no longer choose to live.

Lerius and I have a past history, more entangled and difficult to explain than his with Dweneth. When I think of how his life-threads crossed and recrossed mine, jangled, entangled, and endangered Dweneth's and mine, it is all I can do with Discipline to speak his name.

"What you will know of Lerius, you must ask of Lerius," I say.

A dangerous look flashes across Dwiri's eyes. She could rip this from my mind, but someone has taught her the rudiments of the Telepath's Discipline.

"The cities, then," Joreth suggests, perhaps with prior knowledge of what lies behind that look. "It does not seem possible that all were leveled but One Greater. Tell us how that happened."

"Without understanding what went before and why, you cannot understand how," I answer, wanting very much to leave, to go below, though sleep is far from me. "Others

19

have lived these many years with death and more death. Grant us some reprieve! For myself, I will speak no more of death!''

"It's all the same, meseems, birth and death," Dweneth had confided to me shyly on the day Droghen-Gerim's three ships set sail around the World. "Having witnessed both beneath your healers' tutelage, I conclude they are merely passages, from there to here and back to there again, wherever 'there' may be. Having encountered Others, whom the priests who taught me my religion could not have dreamed of, I don't know what to think anymore."

She let her hand trail along the seawall as we walked; I kept anOther's silence and listened. It served her need to form her thoughts aloud, and my own curiosity.

"Birth and death I've witnessed all my life." Her eyes were very far away. "Violent and horrible mostly, and oftimes close together. Women dying in childbed; babies stillborn or born only to die. But that's in my World, never here. You're all so perfect."

"Hardly perfect," I had to interject.

"Even so, I think I shall never understand you."

"You have not been here long," I offered.

Droghen-Gerim's ships had cast off only that morning. The brash Droghiad himself, restored to health by Other healing, waved from the foredeck to an assemblage far more somber than he was accustomed to. Flanking him, his austere lieutenant Thrasim and Renna the Huntress Queen saw no banners, heard neither music nor cheering crowds upon the quayside. A proper committee of Matriarchs and Wise-Ones stood as silent witnesses to the departure, but only Dweneth waved.

Doubtless Others watched and read on vid and infonet, solemnly contemplating this moment in history, the outcome of which could not be predicted, but only Dweneth and I and an orderly file of schoolchildren with their tutor stayed to watch the sails over the horizon. Once certain they were no longer visible to Droghen or his crew, the Matriarchs and WiseOnes turned as one and returned to the City to resume their daily tasks. OtherWhere must continue to function as it had for more than a thousand years, for at least a few years more.

Dweneth and I sat on the ancient perimeter wall for a long time without speaking. She swung her legs idly as she did whenever she was lost in thought, But thinking what? I wondered. Perhaps she regretted her choice to remain, lone vibrant People's spirit, whelmed about by aloof, distant Others. She had sailed with Droghen for the adventure, abandoning her father and her Players' life without a second thought. In OtherWhere she had found the fulfillment of a dream. Everything she saw and heard enchanted her, particularly our children.

" . . . Thus planetary curvature ensures that the ship's hull will disappear from our line of sight first, to be followed by the combined mass of mast and sail," the tutor at the quayside droned, while her charges, solemn three-year-olds, listened avidly, jotting notes on their portaslates for their prephysics course. "Fortuitously, the day is quite clear, and visibility subsequently unlimited. Neither mist nor fog therefore becloud our perception or impede our study. . . ."

"Neither mist nor fog dare becloud Otherthought or Otherstudy," I remarked dryly near Dweneth's ear. "Their linear clarity are so pure as to render them quite colorless."

"Oh, hush!" Dweneth chided me, embracing the angular colorlessness of OtherWhere after the tumult and squalor she had left behind.

The tutor and her charges moved purposefully through the portal into the City, single file like a brood of seabirds, though far less engaging. No doubt they were intent upon perusing some additional phenomenon with equal thoroughness but just as little sense of wonder.

Had it been so very long since I was one of them?

Rather, I never was—not the manner of Otherchild who followed dutifully, listening attentively, emulating my peers. Unkempt, easily distractible, I had been awkward to the degree that my elders ironically theorized I must possess my own unique law of gravity.

"Lingri-la, have you transcribed today's theorem, or has your preoccupation with gathering beach stones so diverted you . . . ?"

"Lingri-la, while the physical senses are deemed valid means of data gathering, is it strictly necessary that you taste and smell everything?"

"Lingri-la, try not to stumble overmuch."

"Lingri-la, mind the flowers when you pull the weeds."

"Lingri-la . . ."

I had never been so orderly, so ordinary, as these.

"They're so young!" Dweneth marveled, jumping down from the wall to watch the last of the children vanish through the portal and back into the City. "No wonder you're all so clever, when your formal learning begins at such an early age!"

Dweneth's own education had been a haphazard of Players' stories learned by rote, and teaching herself to read from roadsigns and a handful of old books. Now OtherWhere would rectify that.

"I've been accepted by the hospice," she had told me gleefully the night before. "I'm going to be a healer!"

Did she think it so simple? She could not know what price would be exacted, from her and Others. She had spent the night in untroubled slumber. I was summoned by the Chamber.

Scarce had Droghen's ships arrived on our horizon than they became the impetus for something which should have been established long before: a single locus for the exhaustive study of every possible permutation of Others' interaction with People. If I have not mentioned it sufficiently before, let me reiterate: Others would as lief debate as breathe.

Heretofore this debate-without-end had officially transpired in several places, principally in the Council, where the Matriarchs had since before my birth expended more time and energy upon People-watching than upon the no longer challenging governance of a homogeneous nation of Others, but also in the science halls and laboratories, the libraries and Archives, the gymnasia and gardens, on the four Greaters and the Agris and the Industrials, in the Observatory until recently governed by my maternal grandmother Loriel, among the global scattering of us known as Monitors and, for all I knew, at every gathering of Others to share a meal or harvest a crop or attend a lecture or engage in any of the myriad Other communal activities which had transpired since the day before I was born. Only when the ships had actually dropped anchor in our harbor was it deemed necessary that all this brainstorming be focused in one central place.

Everyone on One Greater knew the purpose of the featureless structure thrown up with great haste but no less thoroughness in the suburbs well beyond the Citadel. No official statement was ever issued, no rumor ever countenanced, yet we knew. And when we were summoned, we appeared.

I found my way at midnight to a structure whose squat decahedral shape might suggest a granary or warehouse. Clearly none of the People scattered about the City from Droghen's ships was meant to notice it was there.

Inside, past scanners which only the practiced eye could see, were bare, well-lit corridors and a lingering odor of new-poured thermocrete. A ubiquitous comm-hum suggested that the real work had already begun.

Every entry led to a single ten-sided high-domed room, replete with commscreens and microfiles and their attendant technicians. Three steps led to a table, also decahedral, beneath the apex of the central dome. Each side of this table was fitted with a screen, a modem, and an identipad. There were no chairs, no single place to sit and be comfortable in the entire structure. The implication was clear: we were past the time when we might be comfortable, in any wise.

The concept was Other, yet it was not; it was that *not* which troubled me. Urgency had colored our thinking for a generation, without degenerating into this contained hysteria. Those few Others about the table I knew from different contexts; even identically clad in the drab jumpsuit which was to be the Chamber uniform, they were as out of place as I.

My only assurance of normalcy was that a debate, the Debate, was already in progress as I entered.

There were five present: my grandmother Loriel, my former teacher Rau, WiseFrayin Philosopher, who was currently Matriarch, the physicist Govin, and one more my contemporary whom I did not know. As I joined them this too struck me as strange: Others traditionally transacted official business in groups of ten; the tenth was usually a Telepath who served as focus. There were only six here, and no Telepaths. Were times so desperate?

"The concern being that, using our mathematics, they would better calibrate the angle of projectile firing for greater accuracy in war," Loriel was saying, anxiety in her voice. I had never known my grandmother to be anxious about anything before. Charts of Kelibesh and holos of tribesmen in indigenous costume, complete with their ubiquitous firearms, graced the wall screens. Frayin and the Others listened gravely. "As to the potential for using our science to make neutron weapons and beyond . . ." My grandmother, nearing her two-hundredth year, had to pause for breath. "How are we to reconcile the sharing of our knowledge with the uses they will make of it?"

" 'Will'?" WiseFrayin interjected, her soft contralto

24

voice grown softer still. "We know this not for certain, WiseLoriel. Soliah? Your opinion?"

Soliah was the fifth, the one I did not know. Bedecked in the very costumes featured on the screens about us, she was also tattooed, Tawa-style, on all visible parts of her body. Had I not known there were but three females on Droghen's ships, I would have been convinced this exotic personage was People. For Soliah was what I had been, a Monitor, and one so skilled she had infiltrated a Tawan harem, becoming chief concubine, and second only to the caliph's wife. Hardly a role I could or would have aspired to, but apparently it had served her.

"I concur, WiseFrayin, there is no certainty." She caught my eye as she said this, equally curious about me. "The hill tribes, being an admixture of Tawa and Kelibek, owing to years of intertribal bride-rape, are unpredictable in entirely different ways than city or desert dwellers, each of whom have their own traditions and taboos. It is also significant to note that their mathematical evolution outdistances ours at a similar level of development. They will, for example, arrive at the calculus within two centuries independently of us."

Further, I wanted to say, though I had not yet been acknowledged, any Lamorak tribesman knows that if you fire an arrow in an upward arc its range is quite different from one loosed in a direct line. Calculus, indeed!

"Two centuries," Frayin mused, "where it took us twelve! Yet one more variable we must document before we can so much as breathe the same air they breathe." She addressed Loriel. "Based upon what little concrete knowledge we possess, WiseLoriel, juxtaposed against how much there is yet to learn, I should not think absolutes acceptable, particularly not from thee."

Loriel looked momentarily abashed. "One grows old, and perhaps precipitous."

"Perhaps so." Frayin dismissed it, giving her attention

to Rau, who thus far had not spoken. "We will need a closer study of Tawa and Kelibesh. Mathematical specialists particularly, and a liaison with those Monitors still abroad."

"We will see to it," Rau said, indicating himself and Soliah. "Preparations are already under way. I leave on the morrow, following Droghen's departure. Soliah will follow after."

Soliah acquiesced with a gesture, well aware of the difference between duty and choice. Dismissed, Rau passed me with a quizzical look, in which I could read no clue as to my summons here. Enough was enough.

"And I, WiseOnes?" I presumed to speak out of turn. "I have already answered a summons from the Telepathy. Now I find I am further summoned here."

Frayin seemed only then to notice me. "Lingri-*ala*, wellcome."

"May I presume that I am called here, like Soliah, to return to the Mainland as Monitor? After the Telepathy releases me, of course." The silence which greeted this was deafening. The Telepathy's business with me was an embarrassment to many Others, a thing better not spoken of aloud. But since when had Lingri observed protocol? "I know not what else you want of me, unless it has to do with Dweneth."

There was a murmur from the heretofore silent Govin, always the voice of dissent.

"As you come directly to the point . . ." Frayin gathered herself. "To reiterate for the record and for those assembled what you, Lingri-*ala*, already know: For the first time in our history, one has come among us from the People. The one has asked to remain with us and study our ways, and in particular to become a healer, though the rest of her People leave us, with a strong possibility that they will not return."

I waited.

"Understand," Frayin went on, "much is at risk here. The one will be the first of her kind to live entirely with

26

Others, with no recourse to her own kind for an indeterminate period. Should she become disaffected with her tenure here, should her People fail to return, should, in short, any event preclude the optimal outcome of her request that she become a healer so that she might proliferate her healing as our emissary among her People . . ."

Frayin left the thought unfinished. The commscreens on the table and about the room were rampant with probability statistics. My mathematical skills had not improved with age; I read as much as I could decipher:

A 32-percent probability that shipwreck, disease, mutiny, or war would prevent these particular ships from making the return voyage.

A 48-percent probability that if they did return, this-Droghen would not be in command of them.

An 18-percent probability that this particular group of People would alter their thinking about the benefits of interacting with Others and attempt to disavow our existence in spite of what their own sailors had witnessed.

A 13.5-percent probability that they would return with reinforcements in an attempt to invade us.

"And the temporal parameters?" I asked.

Loriel touched a keypad, reflexively reaching her spare hand to the nape of her neck, where there ought to have been a cascade of silver hair. She had cut it short over a year ago in preparation for her work on UnderSea, a project designed to hide Others before the People came. UnderSea was abandoned when they came too soon, with Lingri leading them.

"Five point six one years, with a variance of seven point one percent," she answered me. "The figures are mine. Accurate, of course."

"Of course." It was as near to our old familiar irony as I was to earn from her. "WiseFrayin, understand that I will assist Dweneth in adjusting to OtherWhere, no matter how long it takes her People to return. Say not that I do this for friendship, which is too unOther, but for the soul-thread."

A glance which was not a glance passed among those present. I had brought out into the open this topic, which unsettled them all.

A soul-thread, simply explained, is a mental link between one person and anOther, a kind of resonance along a common frequency, confirming what our philosophers refer to as the Continuum of the All, but also exclusive to the two it joined. Traditionally the realm only of Telepaths and extremely well-attuned bonded couples, soul-threads are as little discussed in Disciplined company as sex or money were among well-mannered People. And never, to anyone's knowledge, had anOther shared a soul-thread with People.

Logic suggested that this might be nothing more than a lack of proximity, hence an absence of opportunity. But one school of thought had it that, because People had no Telepaths, their brains were fundamentally different from ours, hence any form of mental linkage was impossible.

Imagine the astonishment of Others in general—and the Telepathy in particular, in the person of Lerius—to discover even as Droghen's boats ground onto the sands of Other shores, that Lingri Inept, least likely of Others, shared a soul-thread with this wild-haired motley-clad Player maid Dweneth. Lerius had been first dumbfounded, then fascinated, and had arranged for the Telepathy to summon me to their Enclave for protracted study. Where the Council or the Telepathy summoned, Others obeyed. But Lerius held no jurisdiction over Dweneth.

Neither did the Chamber.

"Suppose the one does return to her World as our harbinger?" Frayin was saying. "We have no assurance she will not use her newfound skills for harm. A healer can as easily kill as heal."

"Suppose I stayed?" Dweneth had asked me only hours before, clear-eyed, contemplating her future. "Dare I tell you I don't care if Droghen's ships ever come back? I'd have to spend my life here. Not so bad a prospect. You and I could be together, unless you're assigned to go back, and without the Tribes' agreement, you'd be as stuck here. Trapped forever in OtherWhere? Not the worst of fates. We could rear our children together, grow old together. I suppose your kind does that sort of thing as much as mine?''

''We do,'' I answered carefully, ''though not quite as does yours.''

What seemed a simple matter to her had not occurred to me until now. She could know nothing of our mating customs thus far, and biology dictated I was to outlive her by at least one hundred years. The soul-thread made no allowance for any of this.

''What would you say if . . .'' Dweneth's voice trailed off; I saw her blush. ''What I mean is . . . I was wondering . . . Surely if we're to live and work together, form alliances—could People marry anOther?''

The soul-thread jangled stridently, a warning.

''Perhaps such will be possible, in time. But, as you say, first alliances must be formed. Exchanges of cultures and ideas, commerce—''

''I'm in love with Lerius!'' Dweneth blurted, then clapped her hand over her mouth as if she had not meant to let the words out.

''You cannot know that,'' I began. They had met but once, and she had barely spoken.

''But I do! Just as I knew when first I saw you we'd be friends for life. When his mind touched mine . . . I *knew*.''

''The neophyte's first encounter with a Telepath is always strange, and can be mistaken for many things,'' I began, to temper her rapture, thinking of my own first encounter, at the age of nine, with Lerius. Since that time I was never entirely sure his presence had left my mind.

''I've never felt so *at one* with any man before,'' Dweneth said with an eerie sort of certainty. ''When he reached into my mind that day we made the landing, I

29

thought me, here is the one male in all the World who could cure me of what men have done to me, and teach me to love the race again."

She looked at me as if what she was about to say next was my fault. "Yet the Council dictates the Telepathy is the one aspect of Others forbidden to People. Why?"

"Telepaths are formidable beings, even to Others," I explained. "In ancient times, before we mastered Discipline, they were our most feared warriors, for what physical weapon could stand against power-of-mind? Do you recall the Marketfest where we first met, and the slaughter where you saved my life?"

Dweneth frowned, remembering. "That was a Kwengii raid."

"Do you recall the Zanti beggar who sang the dirge that triggered it all?"

"Recall him? If the Kwengii hadn't killed him, I might have! Not to know better with a town full of swaggering Kwengii than to toy with People's fears!"

"That 'Zanti' was anOther and a Telepath," I told her. "A renegade who never should have left OtherWhere. The Marketfest massacre was the result of a single Telepath's power-of-mind."

Dweneth thought this over long and hard.

"Lerius . . ." she said at last, having difficulty with the name. Her yearning for him radiated like a fever down the soul-thread. What she said was true, as I understood love— and Others' fear of it. "Lerius would never do such things."

"What Telepaths can do—will do—in proximity to un-trained People's minds is not known. Studies must be made." Beginning with me, I thought but could not tell her. "All this will be made clear to you in your time with us."

She was not listening.

"WiseLoriel says the Telepathy holds some special claim on you." Her manner was watchful. "Has it to do with me?"

"In part it has to do with something Lerius and I experienced when I was but nine years of age," I began, remembering my body as well as my mind pulled into his presence, and how we bespoke the Old Ones.

"And the rest?"

"I am not free to answer that."

"Ah!" Dweneth said. "Thus by not answering, you answer. This is to be the first barrier between us. The first example that, soul-thread or no, People are People and Others are—well, Others. Suppose I said I could bear that, if only you'd bring me to this Lerius, present me to him? I exonerate you of anything that happens, for you know me by the soul-thread, and know I mean no harm."

"Nor does Lerius intend harm to you. Nevertheless . . . Forgive me, but I cannot."

"I see," Dweneth said lightly, though I wondered if she did.

" . . . A healer can kill as easily as heal." Here in the Chamber, Frayin was still speaking.

"If this was of concern," I reasoned, "why did the hospice accept Dweneth as an apprentice?"

"Because of thee, and the soul-thread!" It was the first time gruff Govin spoke. Again, a glance which was not a glance passed about the company.

"I see," I replied, sounding much like Dweneth—and like Dweneth, I was beginning to see far more than I might desire. "You hoped to keep her here, while Lerius and the Telepathy poked and probed at me, for while you have no jurisdiction over Dweneth, it were better to have her nearby. Pity her aptitudes alone could not have been the arbiter!"

"She is People!" Govin protested, as if it ought to be self-evident. How were People's aptitudes to be measured against ours after all?

It came to me then what they wanted of me. Just as in my childhood, I had been subjected to endless experimenta-

31

tion as a result of my joining with Lerius, so now in my adulthood I was to be made the model for Other/People intercourse. I gathered my thoughts in a place which owned no commscreens streaming endless statistics around ten-sided walls, where nothing clicked or hummed or smelled of thermocrete.

"WiseOnes," I said formally, to make it official. "What do you want of me?"

It was Frayin, as Matriarch, who as formally answered. "Much like what the Telepathy requires of you."

It was as I thought. Lerius had summoned me to the Enclave to study the phenomenon of the soul-thread. Until Dweneth's revelation, I had assumed that this was all. What if he shared her infatuation? Was it possible? What did a Telepath, existing simultaneously on all levels of time, understand of love? And what had any of this to do with me?

"The Telepathy holds the prior claim," I said.

"As we are aware," Frayin acknowledged. "However, when they have done with you—"

"—if it is within a single lifetime."

"Even so."

Soliah and I left the Chamber together; the Others would continue their research or debate until the hour before dawn. We had all to make ourselves presentable to see Droghen's ships away.

As my elder, Soliah spoke first. "Strange what we do in the name of Others."

"Indeed," I answered warily.

". . . And yet we do it, because we are Others."

Her broken fingers grasp the steaming bowl I bring belowdecks; her sloe eyes glow with gratitude in the semi-dark. The twining tattoos drawn down her cheeks are crossed with scars, as if someone has tried to remove them, and not painlessly. Her spine was crushed in the extermination camps, and she somehow escaped. Yet Soliah walks with difficulty and can no longer swim. She must remain below with the sick and elderly. Only her mind is as sharp as in her youth.

"We were younger then," I venture, helping her sit upright so she can eat.

It is the first time I have been below, having made myself useful with rigging and sail and whatever else needs doing above by one who long ago earned a brief and counterfeit living as a ship's boy. The glory of menial tasks is that they free the mind.

Mine has been feverish, knitting past to present, wondering about the true nature of our destination. Islands near the Windward polar cap, my son has said; I know of no such islands. Our course thus far has not been to Windward at all, but straight to Sunward. If we keep on we will hit the Mainland, somewhere too near Mantuul. This cannot be Joreth's intention. Jisra Matriarch, as the one in charge, has gone to ask.

As our first night asea bleeds into dawn, she has gone to confront our erstwhile pilot in his cabin. I go below, bearing food for those too weak to fetch it for themselves. Let it not be said that I put Jisra up to anything.

Dim forms are visible down the length of the galleon's keel, distributed on their makeshift pallets between crates of supplies and foodstuffs, piled to the rafters in the gloom. A cluster of children plays some fervid, whispered word game in the central aisle. Further on, someone coughs; someone else breathes with difficulty. Soliah indicates the children with her eyes.

"The young fare best. All they needed was food and sleep and freedom from the Purists' sentence of death. The healers will release them above in the morning. But we will lose two old ones before the dawn."

"Krayal and Thera," I answer, hearing their presences fading down the common soul-net. There is no mystery in

33

the way anOther dies, when that death comes at the proper time.

"It is truly a continuum," Dweneth had remarked that morning on the beach, the day the ships left. "Birth and death, all one, and death so natural as I've observed it here. Your old ones put me in mind of flermoths, that when they die simply blow away to dust on the next passing breeze. It's as if it's meant to be."

"An interesting analogy," I had offered dryly. " 'Postulate: AnOther is like unto a flermoth. Analyze and specify.' "

Dweneth had been idly skipping stones across the water as we walked, shading her eyes each time she threw to count the number of times each stone skipped. Now she made a face at me and laughed.

"I believe you're developing a sense of humor. You know that wasn't what I meant."

She thrust the last stone into my hand expectantly.

And if I tell thee I desire her also? Lerius's mind had found mine, echoing. *What will thee?*

The concept of a Telepath desiring anything was beyond my comprehension. Most had to be reminded of the necessity of food and sleep; their matings served only to answer biological necessity and the need to replicate more Telepaths. Lerius's question frankly puzzled me.

And I, Lerius answered what I did not need to speak. *Yet thee accepts without question the soul-thread between her and thee. Why not this?*

"Our soul-thread is formed out of shared experience." I insisted on speaking aloud, even knowing he could read me before I drew breath. "What possible commonality have thee and she?"

The commonality of the All, Lerius answers.

I wanted to scream at him, but I was Other, Disciplined.

34

I could only surmise what would happen if he permitted the joining he and Dweneth mutually desired; Lerius did not need to surmise: he knew.

Most assuredly, her death. And, most likely, mine.

Dweneth thrust the last stone into my hand expectantly. I studied it, reluctant to do what she wanted.

"Basalt," I ruminated, turning its texture between my fingers. "Igneosedimentary, and quite dense. Doubtless formed by the volcanos comprising the backbone of the Archipelago. This would make its age approximately—"

"Oh, *throw* the bloody thing! Go on!"

It went against my nature. What if it struck a fish or, worse, a *bRi*? The latter, I knew, were not feeding close to shore this time of year. And it seemed important, for reasons I did not fully understand, that I try. Imitating Dweneth's motion, I flicked my wrist and threw. The stone skipped twice further than any of hers, to my immediate regret.

"Show-off!" Dweneth muttered, and stalked away up the beach, past the old ones sweeping the tideline free of seadrift, stopping at the flower borders just inside the main portal.

"What are these called?" she huffed, pointing, breathless from the pace or only angry. "And these?"

"The twining ones are *kressha*. The border is comprised of sea-pinks and *gli*."

"Sea-pinks I have seen, but never these two." Her voice was strangled, as if she could barely control it. Anger radiated from her, jangled the soul-thread. Anger at herself, at me, or only at whatever perversity made Others twice as strong as People? "Are they hybrids, like the light-trees, or are they found only here?"

There was more than botany at stake here.

"They are not hybrids but grow wild, yet only on our Archipelago. Their genetic structure resembles no flora ex-

35

tant elsewhere on the World, and they cannot be cross-pollinated with indigenous species. We have tried.

"One theory has it that Others brought them with us, inadvertently, as pollen beneath our nails or in our hair, from wherever we first originated. They grow best in sandy soil, suggesting that our homeworld may have been largely desert. Perhaps on that world, Others are no stronger than People."

Dweneth exhaled sharply, as if she had been holding her breath all this time. Perhaps she had. Her anger was mastered.

"I'm sorry, Dearheart! It's just that everything you do, even skipping stones—is there anything anOther can't do well?"

Despite my characteristic Other reluctance to be touched, I let her take my arm then, and we walked together along the softstone ways.

"But it's all about me, isn't it?" she said, after we had walked some way in silence. Shadows played on us from the silent telfer cars gliding above; lizards trilled in the shrubbery by a plashing fountain. "No consideration for you at all, Lingri-one. Fancy being jealous of someone who's about to be walled up in a Telepath's Enclave, will she, nill she. Oh, irony! The very thing I'd give my eyes for is the very thing you must do out of duty. How long will they keep you?"

"I cannot say. Telepaths owe no homage to time."

"How ever shall I manage without you?" She stopped to tuck her cobble-trailing skirts up, to better keep pace with me in my more practical Othergarb. "Sorry! There I go again. Let's not think about it. Let's think of when they let you go, and I've got my healer's pass, and we go back to roving the World together. That's what you want, isn't it?"

"Perhaps. But I have Other obligations first." I told her about the Chamber.

"But even they can't keep you forever. What hold have they, when every Monitor else is free? What about what you want?"

"What I want . . ." Admittedly, it was an extraordinary concept, for one whose life thus far had been determined by skillscans, Discipline, and duty. "Is what will best serve Others," I finished.

"Oh, rot!" Dweneth cried, her trained Player's voice rebounding off the garden walls. "We've a soul-thread, remember. I *know!*" Her face took on a watchful look, as if once more she was coming to understand things she had rather not. "Besides, I thought this Monitor business was only a kind of apprenticeship. Like soldiering. You do your stint and then you're free. Is being anOther only duty? Responsibility, obligation, what-to-do-when-the-People-come? What about you, Lingri, yourself alone? *What about what you want?*"

There was no answer I could give her, without revealing overmuch. We were almost at the hospice gate, where I would have to leave her with her questions unanswered. She came to a dead halt in the center of the way. Several Others passed us, pretending not to notice this public display.

"What aren't you telling me?" she asked narrowly, her hand lingering upon my arm to stay me.

"Perhaps I will be better able to answer you when I leave the Enclave."

Neither of us knew that it would take a year.

Excerpt: "On How the Greaters Died"
(Eidetic Fragment, as Preserved by the Telepathy;
Incorporated as Oral History into WiseLingri's *Chronicle:* T-Y1100)

When the People's Purist Praesidium had completed its work of slaughter on the Mainland, fewer than half the population of Others remained, who fled to the Archipelago to be exiled there. The debate then was as to whether or not we had the right to defend this remnant, here in our own place, and in what manner. Even the most cautious of WiseOnes and Matriarchs began to reconsider. Provisional permission was granted the Telepathy to repair to Two Greater and fend however they might.

Seven hundred forty Telepaths, excluding some few who held that in conscience they could not participate in any form of fending, positioned themselves throughout that city, mostly on the Sunward shores, from where attack planes would most likely be seen when they made their first approach. In hindsight, the child among them should not have been there at all, not only because she was too young to speak for the disposition of her own life, but because she was largely untrained. Little is more volatile than the untrained telepathic mind.

Two Greater's nonTelepaths, including the Dissenters, were evacuated to Leeward, distributing themselves by lottery among the Lessers and Industrials. Seven hundred thirty-nine Disciplined telepathic minds gathered on the Continuum to await the anticipated attack, along with a Telepath's child of five years, held in her parents' arms. As the first wave of bombers *neared, the intent was only to create a mind-surge which would confuse the pilots, cause them to doubt their instruments, and return to the Mainland with their bombs undropped. Therefore the Telepaths projected an image into their approaching minds of a great, impenetrable dome, which covered all of the city.*

Initially the illusion was successful, as the first wave of planes flew over the supposed dome, then swung away. Only when a perspicacious navigator recalibrated his instruments and confirmed that the dome was a mirage did the planes circle, returning for a second run.

This time the pilots found no island at all where one was supposed to be, only empty ocean. What seemed to be Two Greater appeared in a mist some kilometers to SunWindward, and this time the pilots' instruments confirmed it. Telepaths could not move an island, but their combined kinetic skills could alter a dial or two.

No longer able to trust their instruments, the flyers attacked the "ghost" island, dropping payloads which harmed no more than fish. Sustained long enough, the mirage might have succeeded, save that a child is a child, and even a Telepath's child can succumb to fear. The continuous shrieking forays of the planes, the thunder of their bombs destroying a city which did not exist shattered whatever small Discipline she knew. Her thoughts shrilled outward, uncontrolled—to home on vulnerable People's minds, to pierce and destroy.

First one plane veered and crashed, then a second. A third caught the wing of a fourth, and both went down. Their crews were dead already, their fragile People's minds imploded, life's-blood streaming from their ears.

Seven hundred thirty-nine Telepaths rallied to contain the child's terror, but too late. Young as she

39

was, she knew what she had done. She extinguished her mind like a candle flame. Her parents followed. The Telepaths dropped their shields, the mirage city vanished, and the true one reappeared. The surviving bombers swung about to finish what they'd started. This time, none prevented them.

3

A word about Telepaths:

Approximately one Other in ten evidences a genetic predisposition toward true telepathy, though each of us possesses some degree of ability in one or more of the seven recognized telepathic categories. I myself test on the low end of the spectrum, being able to shield, but not impenetrably, to receive only from a trained Telepath and, rarely and with unpredictable results, to send. While a true Telepath can send precise and complex thoughts to any Other or group of Others, often over great distances, the most I have ever been able to manage is a manner of crude, inchoate scream.

Having discovered in ancient times an inverse correlation between the suppression of external emotion and an enhancement of the powers of the Inscape, most Telepaths are now among the most Disciplined of Others. This has not always been so. Every ancient warlord owned his own lavishly kept Telepath, to be used in probing an enemy's mind with varying degrees of proficiency and ruthlessness. Many Telepaths became warlords themselves, for they possessed the most powerful weapons. Mind-rape is still a thing more feared by Others than death.

Our most cherished, sheltered citizenry—founders of the Disciplines, preservers of the Way, guardians of the Continuum which joins all Others in a single, subliminal soulnet, able at one time, it is said, to commune even with the dead—Telepaths nevertheless evoke in nonTelepaths an ambivalance not unlike that which People have always had toward Others. Call it a lack of common perspective, but we both fear and envy them, inasmuch as we can do either within Discipline.

Rapt in realms of pure thought, Telepaths needed the rest of us to feed and care for them, if nothing else. In return, they served as focus for any weighty gathering of Matriarchs or WiseOnes. But the connection was always tenuous, governed by no external law or dictate but strictly by Telepath's reasons, which could not be explained in words. Lacking their multidimensional perspective, few nonTelepaths ever truly know what a Telepath is thinking, and rare are those among us who are entirely comfortable in their presence.

To be summoned to an Enclave, for whatever reason, was to be visited with both apprehension and curiosity.

I was no less curious than any Other.

As I placed my hand in the portal recess of the Enclave's enclosing wall, I found it already encoded to admit me. The portal slid silently open and as silently closed behind me, leaving me in a darkness not even Other eyes could penetrate, and an equal silence. There was also neither taste nor odor beyond the expected filtered air which characterized most Other interiors. My fingers found featureless walls, traditionally constructed in half circles within half circles, each opening in a variant and unpredictable direction. But, not knowing how far one had to go to find an opening, one gained no purchase.

Further, to explore unbidden was to invite danger. In ancient times, Enclaves were defended by trapdoors and walls which swung open onto chambers full of poisoned

42

spikes. Surely such artifacts were no longer extant, but one did not take the risk. No nonTelepath ever saw the extent and complexity of an Enclave until the Purists' bombs breached the walls, exposing all privacy.

Having entered, I waited. Lerius's voice touched my mind.

What is this Dweneth, that she is of such importance to thee?

"The ancient poets of both our species speak of the one who is the Other half of one's soul," I said aloud, following my own voice into the darkness, cautious step by cautious step, always most glib when I was most uncertain. There was a silence, even in my mind. I stood quite still.

Unacceptable. Try again.

"Unacceptable to whom?" I demanded, aware of more than one Telepath presence tickling sticky-fingered about the edges of my mind. "If it is my answer, then it is acceptable. You are a Telepath; therefore you both know and do not know. I had hoped we would assist each Other. I had also hoped for privacy."

Done!

The intrusive presences receded. Lerius's shields were sufficient to keep them away, even the most experienced ones.

Soft lights came up, bathing the gaunt, ethereal kneeling figure in further ephemering light. Telepaths in trance tend to blur about the edges, but Lerius seemed translucent. He gestured me to come and kneel beside him and, sensing my acquiescence, touched the fingers of one hand to the side of my face. Images swirled and sparked between us, reflected in his white-irised eyes.

While I was in crossover to the People's side, I had observed with what rituals of shyness, shame, and brazen flaunting People conducted their sexual encounters. Others, whose mating urge need not be answered until well into adulthood, attached a like ambivalence only to intercourse of mind. Thus the power of Telepaths—to at once lay bare the mind's nakedness and to offer self-knowledge, which was both pain and delight.

And I was hardly virgin.

Open to me, Lerius thought, and my memories were his:

Two figures and a war*graax* hiding in an abandoned granary against a night of blood and fire; Dweneth's gift for sweet talk getting all three past a murderous town guard. . . .

Two figures clinging to a cliffside, then swimming the frigid torrent below, though only I could swim. . . .

One figure tumbling amid the *bRi* in a hurricane-ridden sea, while the second shouted her name from a ship's rail, One Greater on the horizon. . . .

"Memories!" I said aloud, pulling my mind back as Lerius withdrew his hand. "Surface things. Hers bred of a People's compassion, mine of anOther's Discipline. No more than either of us would do for any in like distress. The poets speak of more—"

Patience! Lerius all but shouted, and I understood it was not only me, not only the objective curiosity of the soul-thread. He had told me truth: he desired Dweneth as much as she desired him, and somehow I was to be the one who went between.

Open to me! he thought again, this time more urgently.

I hesitated. "And if I refuse? How do I know this is not some betrayal—of Dweneth's trust, if nothing else, and what she perceives as mating custom? I will not betray her!"

I am asking you to save her.

I rose to leave. "What rot is this, to borrow her turn of phrase? Save her from what? From thee?"

Envision . . .

Again he touched his hand to my face, only this time it was I who shared *his* memories, if such they could be called. Is it memory, to recall something which has not yet transpired? My feeble mind tried to assimilate the multitemporal

44

plane where Telepaths exist, and could not. How was I to distinguish true future from possible future? Only one thing I saw, which made me blanch.

Dweneth, daring a joining with Lerius, instantly destroyed. Lerius followed soon thereafter.

"Why is it given to thee, then?" I asked, tears streaming down my face. Whose tears—mine or Dweneth's? I had not wept since infancy. "How can it be given to either of you to desire most what will destroy most?"

Unknown. It is why I summoned thee. I need. I need! As she does. Do thou be our go-between.

Perhaps it was only the thought that a Telepath, any Telepath, could *need* anything, which decided me. Perhaps it was only that vision of Dweneth destroyed, and the desire to do anything, offer anything, to prevent that.

"What shall I do?" I asked, already knowing.

Open to me. In exchange, I will offer you delight. . . .

The lure was irresistable. To give one's mind over totally, free of all responsibility, to have the privilege merely to *be*—I knelt, surrendered, opened. . . .

And nearly lost myself. Yet I could not have done elsewise.

It is dawn of our second day out of OtherWhere as I haul myself up the belowdecks ladder, empty crockery in my hands. I am aware of a sudden course change. Even lacking Othersense, I would feel it tugging at the ancient, creaking galleon, slacking the sails, straining the wheel. Yesterday was a breathless flight Sunwindward/Sunward, as fast as sail and *bRi* could take us. Now we veer hard to Leeward, and our pace slackens. The mainsail flaps, seeking the crosswinds; crew scramble to trim it. I would join them, but Jisra is suddenly beside me.

"Wash your face, Lingri-one, and repair with me to our pilot's cabin," she commands tersely. "He has a greater truth to tell us today than yesterday."

45

"At once, WiseJisra."

I am unkempt as usual, and reminded none too subtly. Jisra is not the youngest Matriarch ever to represent us, but the burden rests overheavy on her, with so many of her elders gone. Let her bully me if it helps.

Perfunctorily groomed, I am the last to enter Joreth's un-slept-in cabin. Soliah is already there, having dragged herself or been carried up from belowdecks. There are three lesser Matriarchs, and Jisra.

Joreth is unrolling charts—antiquities, by their look, if one does not look too closely. Easier to smuggle out seeming museum pieces than something overtly newer, but though close scrutiny proves these are hand-drawn, they also possess a close-calibrated accuracy and, I see almost at once, any number of topographical features not shown on People's maps. People were too busy killing us in recent years to finish charting all their World.

The maps feature not Windward, where Joreth told us we were bound, but Leeward.

"The less anyone knew yesterday, the better," he is explaining, spreading the charts on the table which is between us, a kind of bulwark. "I can inform you now that there is an area far to Leeward, a network of fjords quite near the pole. . . ."

He trails off, looks at Jisra like a chastened child, full of rationalizations. Jisra is his contemporary, but her authority commands his respect, or at least his alibi.

"Go on." Jisra indicates nothing by her tone or face.

Joreth continues uneasily. "There was a serious danger of our being intercepted on the first run. We are most vulnerable to detection and attack at either end of our journey"— he stabs a finger, here at the Archipelago far behind us, there at an expanse of open FarLeeward sea—" and I thought if any of our number strayed and were captured—"

"We would yield to questioning, thus betraying all who have arranged our escape." Jisra's tone is lofty, almost pa-

46

tronizing. "Did you think us so weak, or only ungrateful?"

"I was thinking of the children," Joreth reasons. Only I know that he's blushing.

"Who would die before they talked. Go on."

Has Joreth ever faced down six Others at once? Probably not since the orals for his first degree, and those Others were far more receptive to his words than these. His eyes scan each of us in turn, to see if we accept his reasoning. How well can he read Other masks, after ten years away from us? He grasps the table edges for strength, exhales.

"All right. We change course here, for a run close to the lava fields Shadoward of Melet." He points. "Barren rock, treacherous seas, even *bRi* won't go there. We'll rest there overnight. WiseJisra, trust me!" She was on the verge of interrupting. "You're going to suggest we keep on through the dark, but what you don't see *here*"—he jabs the map— "is kept up here." A finger taps his temple. "Shipping runs, patrol planes, currents and weather patterns this time of year. Plus a fairly recent reading of the Purist Praesidium's plan, for what they are still calling 'the end of Others.' I won't even address the weariness of your numbers—exhaustion, exposure, the need for food and dry and rest. Have you, WiseJisra, access to all these variables?"

"Currents and weather patterns, yes," she replies. "And the healers have apprised me how much longer we can continue at this pace. As to the rest, no. We will rely on your judgment. You anticipate fog this time of year?"

Joreth grins at her, triumphant. "Exactly! It should cover us for a day, a night, and a day, until we have to make our final run."

Jisra confers with the Matriarchs. "And once we reach the open sea?" she asks. "Prevailing winds will dissipate the fog, leaving us exposed—"

"To any passing plane or, worse, the oilships," Joreth acknowledges, pointing to his charts again. "Three nations claim oil rights around the Leeward pole, and we have pin-

47

pointed each of their stationary rigs. There are also ice floes, all through here." His tapered fingers sweep an area. Where has he acquired all this knowledge, my sheltered musician's son? "There's very little passage in between, but we've one long moonless night, and the guidance of the *bRi*." He shrugs. "The only chance we have. Hence the chance we'll have to take."

Jisra and the Others nod as one, accepting. What alternative do they have?

"And our destination?" Jisra's final question would have been my first.

To answer it requires a more detailed map. Joreth unrolls it, revealing a topography of narrow, intricate fjords winding toward an ice-free bay.

"What miraculous current is it which keeps the inlet open in such climate?" It is the first I've spoken.

Joreth's grin is for me this time; I find it has too many teeth in it.

"Actually, it's an active volcano, and a network of hot springs. They've carved a system of caverns throughout these cliffs, with a modulated interior temperature. With adequate supplies, we could live there forever. People think it nothing but unbroken ice clear to the pole; they've never bothered to explore it."

One of the Matriarchs, a botanist, has found Joreth's charts particularly fascinating. "I would need to know the extent of these caverns, WiseJisra, Joreth-*ala*. The salinity of the water, its algal content. We will require sources of light, particularly in the dark season. But it may be possible, with the seed grain we have salvaged, and some spores, to harvest crops within a year."

This, after shelter, has been our chief concern. How is a race of vegetarians to subsist in a polar region?

"That was part of our plan." Joreth has everyone's attention again. "Though for the first year, *bRi* will act as couriers to our suppliers on the Mainland—"

" 'Suppliers'?" Jisra's eyebrows rise. "Will you further endanger your People on our behalf?"

"My People have volunteered to serve on our behalf." So Joreth is both Other and People now, acknowledging both his heritages, I note. Within a moment he will deny both or neither, as the situation suits him. "We will need to be supplied from outside until the first harvest. Unless you will turn flesh-eaters."

This is out of the question, for physical if not moral reasons. Most Others are literally allergic to animal flesh. Jisra knows that Joreth knows this. She will acquiesce to the need for a supply route—again, because she has no alternative.

Joreth's grin could warm a cavern of its own. He has won us over, become the center of attention and approval. His craving for that has not altered since he was a boy.

His father, as I recall, never outgrew it at all.

"Well, Mother?" he says when the Others are gone. I am helping him reroll his charts. No one else will see him yawn, or lean against a wall strut too weary to stand upright. " 'Who will be the first to trust?' " Not too weary to indulge in sarcasm, or the quoting of old aphorisms.

"I was not aware you were so well-versed in geography," I counter dryly. "Though I think you did not draw the charts."

"Oh, Dwiri's the geologist, not I. Top of her class, in fact, until one of her professors noticed her eyes. Only in your world does a Telepath have the luxury of being just a Telepath."

"You speak of her professors. Is that where you met, at a university?"

Joreth laughs bitterly. "No, we met in a sewer tunnel, actually. Both on the run, but in opposite directions. We literally bumped heads."

I wait. He will explain this if he wants to. He cocks an eyebrow at me expectantly.

"Do you want to hear the story?"

"Do you wish to tell it?"

He does not cover the yawn this time. He flops onto his bunk, motioning me to sit. I take the desk stool, to be at his level, but not too close. Still I do not understand his thoughts toward me. Am I beloved mother, loathed betrayer, or something in between? Who will be the first to trust?

"Dwiri was running from one of the general roundups once her eyes gave her away. I was running because of the Tapeworm Controversy. Do you know of it?"

My own situation had been less than comfortable six years ago but, yes, I knew of it.

"The Purists' computer files on place of birth and blood type were breached in 1637 P.A." I say by way of an answer. "A tapeworm or virus program was introduced to delete all files relative to Others and/or Intermixes. It was about eighty-five percent effective before it was discovered and neutralized. It may have bought time for thousands. Its perpetrators, naturally, have been under death sentence since."

"Exactly." Joreth yawns.

It is a good thing I am sitting down. "You?"

"And a few Others." Yawn. "I was on the music faculty at Agladon, a deliberate plant for over a year, in the hope of accomplishing this. Musician in residence, that kind of thing. Mostly, I suspect, because of who my father was, but never mind. At any rate, you know my blood tests 'pure,' so it was my job to remain above suspicion and gain the access codes so that Others could get into the infonets. I was the gatekeeper, the lookout. We accomplished it all in a single night. Rather exhiliarating, actually. First 'real-life' adventure I'd ever had."

He yawns again, flings one long arm up over his heavy-lidded eyes. Thus he used to sleep when he was a child.

"Naturally, we didn't wait around to see who would be questioned. The constant pressure of having to make nice on

50

the job was getting to me anyway. So I ran. Would have been running still, if not for Dwiri.''

With that he is asleep. I want to go to him, tuck the coverlet about him, touch his face. I do not, cannot. He has told me his tale as if I were a stranger, and I am. A trusted stranger, to be sure, but not a parent. I saw to that ten years ago.

And this, my stranger-son, has doubtless saved my life and a host of Others' with his tapeworms. Something tells me he will not accept my gratitude for this. There are so many things we cannot speak of. Yet.

I leave him in his cabin. My disorientation is not only fatigue. What am I to do now? I go below, not certain if I am intent on sleep, or seeking Dwiri, to question her. The image of her running into my son in a sewer tunnel both entrances and amazes me. She is a Telepath. Did she know who he was and where to find him?

Telepaths do nothing by accident. They hold past and future in their minds; their only dilemma is in distinguishing them in the waking World. Little wonder they spend so much of their lives in trance. Or did, when they had the luxury of being only Telepaths.

To our knowledge, only four remain. There is Lerius; the Savant Tisra, once focus of One Greater's Enclave; my young companion Gayat, keeper of the keeper of the chronicle; and Dwiri. The rest died when Two Greater was leveled, or took their own lives after.

Telepaths! At once the bane of our existence, and our soul.

Open to me, Lerius thought, and I did so.

Healers' descriptions of those in deepest trance are extant; there are no secrets here. They describe a body more than comatose, a pulse which beats but once an hour, flesh chill and lifeless to the touch. If I were thus, I still do not recall.

51

Did I eat or sleep, and sleeping, did I dream? Did my heart, my bowels function? Did I breathe? Such things were unimportant where I was.

For eight decades I have pondered the experience, but attempts at description fail even the poet, devolve down into sketch and fragment—inaccurate, inadequate, inconclusive, incomplete. Eight decades later I have scant words; when first my mind was returned to me, I had no words at all.

Formless, labile, attenuated to the edge of being, pulled willingly into a knowledge which subsumed me, cradled me, then gave me back, washed up onto the shores of my own unlinked consciousness, I could feel nothing, think nothing save the ebb of ecstasies I had known but knew no longer. Returned to the boundaries of my own being, I lacked even the memory of memories, for what I knew as truth one moment was transformed into a contradictory but as valid truth the next.

Two things remained to me: Dweneth and a soul-thread which transcended even death, and Lerius's link, through me, with her whom he desired but could not have.

There are those who will at least question, if not condemn, my choice. Once more I possessed what Dweneth desired but could not have, while at the same time I myself did not desire it. But what were my alternatives? Perhaps I thought by offering Lerius my knowledge of Dweneth, he would be content. Certainly I hoped to help him resist the temptation to go to her. In him I sensed a desire, equal to his desire for her, that she be free to choose without him. I, then, was go-between, balance mechanism, that which in our tradition holds two opposing forces at bay, lest they annihilate.

The worst of it was keeping what I had done from Dweneth.

Floating to the surface of the lighter trances, I would sense her, hear her, coaxing, bullying, all but pulling me by the roots of my hair, leading me by sheer act of will down the soul-thread to the realm of light.

I had entered the Enclave with the night, emerged with dawn. A year had passed in the interim. Without Dweneth's insistence, I wonder if I should ever have returned.

Enjoying yourself? It's an addiction, I can see that, as surely as if you poured it in your veins. What is it that you do there, you and he, that I cannot be part of? Come out of there and be, else I'll come in and get you in spite of danger. . . . It's an addiction, I can see. . . .

Throughout this diatribe, I could feel Lerius's laughter. Laughter! Something could delight a Telepath in the here and now, if only one People's fire and determination.

Telepaths! If I had learned anything from them, I no longer remembered what it was. Teaching my legs to walk again, I left the Enclave, regretting no single moment of that yearlong night, but grateful it was over.

Dweneth glanced up from her microscope as if I had been gone a moment, not a year. "You look like last week's shit!"

"Thank you," I croaked. My voice was hoarse, unused for months. Or perhaps I had used it and overused it in giving voice to my ecstasies, howling like a mad thing. My eyes had been prepared for all things to be stranger after so long turned within, but was this Dweneth?

Her transformation was complete. Othergarb and Other-manner cloaked her person equally. The former freed her limbs of cumbersome skirts and stays and petticoats; the latter circumscribed her movements, rendering them less wild, more dignified. Her once expressive face, with its danc-ing eyes and mouth that pouted, grimaced, smiled by turns, was well-schooled to Other-mask. She had mastered Other-tongue with barely a touch of an accent.

Apprentice healer she might be, I reminded myself, fighting back a great disquiet, but she was still a Player maid. I had seen her don skins in a Lamorak camp and become more Lamorak than Renna the Huntress Queen. I had watched her play the comedies when I knew her heart was bleeding.

Who are you today? The answer I got was no answer at all.

"I've passed premed." She addressed her instrument, changing slides, methodical. "In less than the year you've spent lolling about the Enclave, if you're interested. Tomorrow I'm off to observe a Survival camp. Can't say when I'll be back." She went on before I could say anything, though I do not know what I might have said. "Wise Rau and Soliah report from the Mainland that Droghen's ships have passed safely down the coast from Hraregh to Plalas without inciting the Melet, and now have Mantuul ships in their train."

She coded a rack of slides, setting them in stasis for later processing, scowled at me over the eyepiece of the microscope, letting the mask slip. "I don't suppose any of that's of interest to you now!"

"I had not heard," I answered, my voice more like itself. I wondered if Rau had regrown his beard.

"Not where you were, no, you wouldn't have!" Dweneth accused me, slamming a drawer shut, rattling slides and retorts, her Othermask dropped entirely and revealing rage. "Wouldn't hear, wouldn't listen! Wouldn't be with me when I needed you. Flaunting your ability to be with Lerius in that way, when I cannot. I no longer know you. You're a stranger!"

And you? I ventured. The soul-thread was silent, shielded at her end. When and how had she mastered shielding?

"I went after you, you know." She had started a fresh batch of slides, and gave them most of her attention. "I was worried; it had gone on too long. At first I only went to the portal, to ask after you. But I didn't like the answers I was getting—or rather, wasn't getting. So I asked if I could volunteer as an attendant."

54

I had not known this, had not even sensed it. Lerius must have been aware. How much else had he kept from me?

"They were wary of me at first, and kept me mostly to the gardens. Ah, the gardens! Never a leaf out of place, none but the beneficial insects, and never any weeds! The way each twig and branch, each flower, rock, and bit of moss is worked into the harmony of the whole. . . ."

Lost in her own rhapsody, she let the slides slip from her fingers. Her curses fell sharper than the splintering glass.

"Shit and shit again!" She had lapsed into Hraregh; there were no "barnyard words" in Othertongue. Together we gathered the pieces from the floor, being careful our hands did not touch.

"Was it only I you came to see?" I ventured.

Dweneth blushed. "You at first, yes, but . . . Well, damn, the point is I never got anywhere near Himself, so my intentions hardly matter. And the one time I did get near enough to get a glimpse of you . . . "

She dumped her share of the glass in the disposal, dusted her hands, clutched her hair at the temples, grimaced. "I was forbidden to enter the inner places, but being People and innately devious—"

"You do not mean that."

"SavantTisra did! Far be it from the Savant of the Enclave to say as much, but it flashed across her mind before I could shield it. I'm a very good receiver, did you know? Mostly it has to do with starting with no shields whatsoever—"

"I know."

That stopped her.

"Explain."

"It is the very nature of the problem. Lerius, the day of the landing, barely touched your mind with his, more out of a Telepath's curiosity than any malicious intent. The result was startling, the discovery of a compatible soul, but incom-

55

patibly inaccessible because People cannot shield against a Telepath."

Her amber eyes took on a coldness I had not thought they could possess.

"So that's it, then. My entire life's to be overshadowed by an accident, a fluke. A Telepath's curiosity. Damn him! Damn all Telepaths, damn all men! I—"

She stopped herself, tugged at her hair again. "Else you're lying to me. Else it's all some Other's trick to hang together against we poor simple People, laughing at how gullible we are. How many plays have I performed, replete with love triangles, and always the best friend stealing the lover away? How do I know it's not something as simple as that?"

I held out my hands. Impossible to say anything. If I dared "Who will be the first to trust?" she would have struck me.

She took my hands then, squeezed them hard. The cold look vanished from her eyes.

"All right, then. That's what I thought. Let no male come between us, ever. The world is full of men, but I'm given only one Lingri."

She sighed, began to put her work away.

"What is it like?" Her voice went childlike, wistful. She clasped her hands idly in her lap, her tidying half finished. "I've lain alone in bed anight, imagining you two intertwining soul and mind, telling myself if I love you I will not begrudge you such pleasure. Telling myself it is some Other thing, and not erotic, and I've no right to be jealous. But how can it not be, how can I not be? Among my People, mere bodies' intertwining is sung of as some higher thing, though my experience has been quite the opposite. Yet to do it with the mind—is it erotic?"

Sexually dormant as I was, the question frankly baffled me. "I cannot say. Except to reiterate that minds and souls have no gender."

"So you keep reminding me." She went back to her tidying; I tried to help. "What a puzzlement you Others are. No physical passions till you're in your thirties, yet with such passions of mind! It's what you do instead, I guess. But you! Gone a year, and not even aware of it. Such passivity, from you of all—it seems excessive. It's an addiction, I can see that, as sure as if you poured it in your veins. . . . "

The familiarity of those words was chilling. "You said you sought me at the Enclave. Did you speak those words to me when you did?"

Dweneth gave me a blank look. "I never said a word. I barely had time to draw breath, seeing you lying there— dead, I thought, not breathing, no color any living thing ought to be—before SavantTisra descended on me and threw me out."

Only then did she seem to discover a last batch of slides that needed coding; she always thought more clearly, I recalled, when her hands were busy.

"I was so frightened. I thought they'd killed you. I can't trust Others, still; you're the only one I know well!"

Again she seemed to be addressing the microscope. From time to time a large drop of moisture slipped along her eyelashes; she caught it on her forefinger, wiped it on her lab smock absently.

"And so I was totally alone in a land of strangers, for most of a year. Not even knowing it was to be a year. It might have been forever."

"I heard you in my mind," I ventured, keeping my distance. Touching was not innate to my species; I had had to learn. If I touched her now she might fly apart. "Your voice in my mind was what led me out. I would have come."

"But I didn't know that!" she cried plaintively, more tears slipping over her eyelashes. "So all I had was an entire year of holding inside all the things I wanted to tell you, ask you, share with you. An entire year without seeing a smile or hearing melody. Oh, kindness aplenty, and instruction to a surfeit, and gentleness even from your menfolk, if remoteness can be gentle. But no laughter, no japery, no noisy children's play. Never a voice raised in anger or in glee. Only your infants laugh. What happens to the rest of you, and is it worth it? One thousand twenty-one years of peace, but at what cost?"

She banished a final tear to the fabric of her smock. "Did you know, when I first came here, I often sang or hummed when I was at my work? I did the same in my world, if you recall."

"I do."

"No one ever *says* it isn't proper. No one ever says a thing. I'd simply be aware of eyes and know I'd broken yet one more propriety. I doubt I'll ever learn them all, but it might have been easier, were you here."

"I am here now," I offered.

"Until the Chamber wants you!" She sighed, put her slides away. "Duty first, personal considerations later. You are anOther, after all. Promise me something?"

"Anything."

She broke down entirely then. I took her in my arms. The storm was one we'd weathered before, and it did not last long.

"It's the way you say that. 'Anything'! No questions, no qualifiers. Well, it's this: the soul-thread. You've said before either of us could sever it anytime we want, then take it up again. If I asked you sometime in the future, to sever it for a while—I swear to you I'd take it up again as soon as I was able."

Something told me what this was about. Something told me not to ask. I nodded.

"I will. So long as you will do the same for me."

"Anything!" she answered, seeming quite relieved.

Dweneth gave herself entirely to her studies, I gave myself to the Chamber. One day she simply asked me to sever the thread; I did so, and did not see her for some days, days when the Chamber seemed particularly to demand my attention. Dweneth returned and we resumed the thread, no explanations offered, none needed. I thought at the time she seemed drawn and distracted, but we did not speak of it. We took up the joined threads of our lives where we had left them that day on the beach, before I entered the Enclave, neither of us addressing what lay unexamined between us.

Barely five years from the time they had departed, as Loriel had predicted, Droghen's ships, now leading an entity which called itself the First Fleet, returned to Other shores.

The young Telepath Gayat is suddenly beside me. Where am I? I have drifted all over the great ship, and find myself at the aft rail. My eyes, turned within, have not seen what they have been staring at all this time. It seems much of my life is to be bound up with sailing ships.

"What is it?" I ask Gayat vaguely. His unlined face bears that importuning look which characterizes all his dealings with nonTelepaths. Poor lad, he must spend far more of his life with us than with his own kind!

"I am sent to tell you," he breathes hastily. "Lerius is in communion with his child. He wanted you to know."

I accept this. No need for a chronicle of my life, once Lerius tells Dwiri of the role I played between Dweneth and him. Well, no matter.

"Send to WiseLerius: My gratitude for his consideration," I reply.

For a moment I think Gayat will do that from here, sending a mind-flash to Lerius belowdecks, then hover about me for his Telepath's reasons. I most especially need to be alone. For once his instincts coincide with mine, and he is gone.

And we have stopped. The galleon, the small boats clustering around her, stragglers gathering in, has come to a full stop. Where are we?

The rocks off Melet, Joreth said. So these are they.

We have come about before what appears to be an endless forest of sea-washed rock, much of it bow-high or even higher. Some millions of years ago, volcanos spewed these miles of bubbling effluvia from the bottom of a tortured, boiling sea. Cooled to twisted, igneo-fantastic shapes, the resultant basalt plain has since been relentlessly reclaimed by a relentless sea. Pounding, grinding, eroding inlets into freestanding shapes, it has produced these massive monoliths, slick-surfaced and shining, streaming kelp and foaming spume, a labyrinth, a maze in which to conceal ourselves until the morrow.

The many small boatlings have already begun to spirit themselves within the rock forest; I see their denizens clambering upon the rocks in search of kelp to supplement our diet, and sunwarmed crevices in which to rest. The great ship's sails are furled to make it less conspicuous from the air, though the masts are plainly visible even in this baffling place.

It is near sunset, and Joreth will have us remain here until dawn, when the *bRi* confirm there will be fog, all down the coast past Melet to the open sea. *bRi* mistrust the rock forest; it has too many hidden reefs. They have left us and gone to feed further out. Will they remember to return or, being *bRi* and easily diverted, abandon us for some new pursuit?

"Shall we position sentries?" I hear Jisra call to Joreth, who is making his way from rock to rock, apparently to fetch me.

"That's been taken care of!" he calls back, reassuring. I see no sentry, but perhaps that is the point. I join my son on a rock not too far from the great ship, and as yet unclaimed by Others.

"Is it safe?" Joreth asks as soon as he joins me. "Dwiri's intercourse with Telepaths thus far has been limited to her foster mother. What she and Lerius are doing—is it safe?"

60

"As safe as anything to do with Telepaths," I answer. "A foster mother? She also mentioned this."

"Practicalities." Joreth shakes his shaggy head, stretches out on the rock, tilts his face up toward the last rays of the sun. "Dweneth was too old to bear her. Couldn't you figure that out?"

"I can figure none of this out. I am still coming to terms with the fact that she whom I knew better than I know myself could keep this one great secret from me."

"Life is full of secrets," Joreth offers. "But for the present, we have earned the right to lie beneath the sun again!"

He sprawls back against the rock with his arm flung over his eyes, and I think him asleep again, until he begins idly to whistle. The song he chooses is an old one.

"You are out of tune," I chide him, sitting cross-legged, too weary to sleep. "And must you choose that song above all?"

He breaks off, neither rising nor moving his arm. His voice is muffled, taunting. "Does it bother you?"

"I am anOther—"

"Impervious to bother. All right, then!" He whistles it again, then in a low voice begins to sing. I did not think anyone knew the words but Redrec.

"Did your father teach you that?" I ask, a tight grasp on my Discipline. "Or did he publish it finally, though he promised me he wouldn't?"

Joreth props himself on one elbow.

"No one knows the words but me. And you, I suppose, since he wrote them for you. More's the pity. It could be the most simply beautiful thing he ever wrote. He's still credited with the melody, of course, and it earned him a pretty penny in royalties all his life. But the words were better not published, considering the times. No point in linking himself with anOther, for my sake more than his. But the words . . . the words are haunting."

"Some of us have had our fill of haunting!" I reply,

61

finding a rock of my own, out of earshot of Joreth's whistling.

Redrec wrote the song for me. He called it "Lingri's Air." I begged him not to.

"Name it something else," I pleaded, long before I had become a household word, or the emblem of a thing which must be hounded unto death, but already, after my years with the Chamber, possessed of anOther's awareness that I would in time be both. Redrec and I were newly reconciled after yet one more separation; I thought it meant he'd heed me. " 'Air for anOther,' if you must, or rather give it no name at all."

"I name it for the one I love, though she does not love me." He almost sang it; his elegant baritone innately suggested singing. Lolling against the pianoforte, which was his instrument of choice this week, he plucked the melody lazily with one hand, while his green eyes laughed at me. "Let me name her for the World, that all may know I love her."

"And because the name can be no Other's while I live, and will know it's mine."

"I've always thought that clever of your kind." Redrec spun round on the bench, inspired suddenly to try the tune two-handed, scowling over a chord change. "Unlike we foolish People, who saddle our offspring with 'Redrec Younger' as if begging supplantation. No son of mine will ever have my name!"

"Nor will you have sons, or daughters for that matter," I tweaked him, "so long as you linger with Lingri."

He stopped playing to laugh out loud. "No wonder I love you—see with what facility you do that? 'Linger with Lingri.' It sings! What a partnership we could make, in all senses, still. Unless, of course, I write my own words. Hmm . . . ." He fingered the keys anew, his long body languid, mischief in his eyes. "Let all the world know the pleasures I have known in you. . . . "

"You wouldn't," I said, knowing he would. "Redrec, I beseech you . . . "

Wickedly, ignoring me, he sang:

> "Cresting like a wave—oh!
> Crying like the sea
> a wave, a gull,
> a sob, a lull,
> Then clings she fast to me—oh!
> No Other, only me—oh! . . . "

He turned back to me, grinning, feral. "There are ways to stop my mouth, meseems you know. Tricks the People's women can only hope to learn from you. Be mine again, and none will ever hear the words. Elsewise:

> She opens like the sky—oh!
> Streams o'er me like warm rain
> cleansing, bathing,
> soothing, saving,
> She nurtures only me—oh!
> No Other, only me—oh!"

"Blackmail!" I said as he took me in his arms. In truth, the time was upon me again—he had planned it thus—and I wanted him as much as he wanted me.

"If you like," he teased, his lips atingle against mine. "Mmm—whatever works!"

And because I did know techniques the People's women could not guess at, I took him and took him until he was exhausted. He slept like a stone, to waken humming,

> "No Other, only me—oh! . . . "

"What Do Others Do?"
[from a children's nursery rhyme]

What do Others do?
They hardly ever do.
They think and scheme
Debate and dream
And leave the work to
    you.

How do Others say Hello?
They don't exactly do.
They nod and bow
Don't touch, that's how
And ne'er, How do you do?

What do Others eat?
It's amazing what they do.
No fish nor meat
They think a treat
But grass, and seaweed too.

What do Others know?
Whate'er they think they
    do.
Us they would teach
But what they preach
Sets what we know askew.

How do Others pray?
They're much too proud to
    do.

No church have they
No psalms to say
No god, but "All" in lieu.

How do Others love? you
    ask.
They never, ever do.
Nor ever sigh
Ane much less cry
Too faithless to be true.

How do Others say
    Farewell?
They sort of halfway do.
Their words are sweet
As: "Go in peace,"
But cold their faces, too.

What do we need Others
    for?
I wonder if we do.
To heal our sick
Make watches tick
Then vanish once they do.

4

The morning brings fog, as Joreth promised. Thick roiling walls of white enclose us, surround my chosen rock; soft droplets caress my face to waken me. Voices, ephemeral as mind-voices, carom off nothingness, distorted, as we gather what we own, erase our presence here before we journey on. Will Othersense be sufficient to hold us together in this?

I find Joreth on his rock, his arm still flung over his face as if he has not moved since I left him. I intend to leave him yet again, to join those in the small boats. Rowing serves better than arguing at this point.

Dwiri is suddenly beside me. I had not heard her climb the rock, or has she simply appeared?

"Are you well?" I presume to touch her, grip her arm, recognizing that greenish hue which visits those in telepathic trances.

"I have been better," she admits. "My father was as gentle as he could be, but . . . My powers are nothing to his. Perhaps it is only maturity, or being an Intermix. Perhaps I know less about my own kind than I thought." She hesitates. "What you did for my mother—"

"We will speak of that a different time." I release her, gather myself to be off. "Don't wake Joreth until I'm gone."

She nods, agreeing. "Krayal and Thera died last night. Jisra has seen to the partial rites. She said to tell you."

I acknowledge this with no surprise; we all knew they were dying. There can be no gathering for the rue passage ceremony, no cremation; there is neither time nor place. We can only weight the bodies and leave them to the waves, with apologies to the *bRi*. Never before have we buried our dead, either in land or in water, but always burned them, cleanly and completely. In ancient times we offered them to the volcanos, not to propitiate any god, but because it was efficient. On an island world, land is for the living.

Today expediency rules. We do not permit ourselves to think of the hundreds of thousands of Other bodies still unrited and doubtless unburied on the Mainland. Our number is now nine thousand four hundred eleven.

The *bRi* have not forgotten us, which is a boon. They return as if summoned, well fed and playful, stirring up the water with their long snouts, displacing tendrils of fog with their energy, seeking out unerringly whatever bit of flotsam they chose to guide when we began our journey. Two half grown males frolic about a glassweave floatible, a skimmer roof overturned, adapted with rope handholds and lined with waterproofs. A girl of about thirteen years and two smaller boys have journeyed this way from the beginning. The elder boy beckons me toward them as I leap from rock to rock; he grasps my hands that I may come aboard without undue rocking.

Are these siblings, I wonder, or kinless scatterlings brought together by the solidarity of youth? It is improper to ask, even of children; if they wish me to know they will tell me.

"I am Peria," the girl says, and points to each boy in turn, the elder first. "This one is Yarel, this one is Aloyi. It

66

would honor us to share our boat with WiseLingri Chronicler."

"As it would honor me to share it with you, WisePeria,"
I answer with equal solemnity; the Lingri I know best is
seldom as wise as any child. "But only if you tell me what
I may offer in return."

The three commune with their eyes, not speaking. Orphans, I surmise; their caution indicates it.

"This one"—Peria indicates Aloyi—"would have you
tell us where we're going. Only WiseOnes and *bRi* seem to
know, and none of us can *bRi*-speak."

This youngest one is barely six. Who knows what horros his solemn-staring eyes have seen, what fears his apt
young mind encompasses? I extend one hand, palm upward;
he extends his own above it, palm down. We do not quite
touch, yet an energy passes between us. Thus have Other
elders offered children comfort since the Thousand-Year.
Small Aloyi's taut body shudders with a single breath as I
absorb his tension and he grows calm.

"Yarel and you think differently." I do not ask Peria so
much as tell her.

"None of us can shield, WiseLingri. Nor have we experienced Survival, or the trial-by-pain. If we should be separated from the Others, lost or captured . . ."

Her voice trails off, and I wonder how long she has
sustained this mask of courage to spare the younger ones. I
offer her my alternate hand, still holding the first above
Aloyi's in the comfort gesture; she returns the gesture, extending it to Yarel, who extends his to Aloyi. Thus we form
a circle in the lolloping boat, and even the *bRi* grow still,
receiving resonances.

"We thought it preferable not to be too well informed as
to our destination," Peria finishes.

"I see."

This is how we must rear our children in these times,
unschooled in the learning their ancestors knew for genera-

tions, yet overskilled in furtiveness, to ensure their own survival. Can we somehow teach them freedom once this ordeal is past?

"Be assured, none of you shall be harmed as long as I am here."

The three commune again and nod as one.

"Know also that where we are bound is a place far less fearsome than our latitude and heading might indicate," I say. "All will be well, once we reach there."

"Will it be like OtherWhere?" small Aloyi pipes up. Yarel looks as if this were his thought as well but, the elder by some two years, he is much too Disciplined to speak.

"Not the OtherWhere that you have known," I answer, wondering whether he remembers tranquil once-Other-Where, or only the OtherWhere of lingering hunger and death. "But the best that we can give."

The sea is choppy hereabouts, lifting our precarious flotsam boats on intemperate greasy swells and slamming them down again, though there is no wind. A humid stillness about the air is what lends it so readily to fog. While bRi continue to move the boats effortlessly between them and provide their bodies' warmth to add to ours, we are far from comfortable. Though Others do not succumb to seasickness, the People with us are not as uniformly fortunate; their intermittent retching embarrasses them as much as it discomfits us. Lastly, there is the danger of capsizing our marginally seaworthy boats.

Peria and Yarel lash themselves to one side of our floatible as Aloyi and I balance their weight on our side. Tying the small one to me by a waist sash, I secure one wrist to the nearest handhold. If we do capsize, I will learn if I am still the swimmer I once was. We will have to remain secured this way for as long as the swells endure.

Voices surround us in the fog, as boats near and pass or fall behind, depending on the current and the speed of individual *bRi*. Still the chronicler, I cannot help but listen. What I hear surprises me.

Others are weaving speak-nets, to overlayer the soul-net which has held us together thus far. Everything stored in our collective eidetic memory in the final months is valid fuel for discourse. Mathematics, history, physics, semantics, philosophy, and any topic ever deemed debatable reverberate around us in the air. The Partisans and Intermixes add their welcome thoughts and questions to the texture of the weave, strengthening and enhancing it, for it was always true that People and Others together were stronger than the sum of their two parts.

And everywhere throughout this complex spoken fabric, stubborn and relentless in its battered cadence and paltry poesy, Lingri's chronicle gleams defiant.

They are taking my poor words, having committed them to memory, and weaving them into the net, above the waves, enduring. The sweetest voice is Peria's. Spellbound, I listen.

"It is said we are not alone here in the bowl of the sky. There are those among our WiseOnes who from their studies have extrapolated certain precise and complex data which indicate that the conditions which support life on the World can be duplicated on approximately forty thousand of the estimated billions of worlds in our part of the universe. . . . ."

There is silence, Peria's last words swallowed by the fog. No sound but the plash of boats and *bRi*. Surely the collective memory holds more history than this?

No one asks me to continue, but I do.

"Droghen's ships are returned," Dweneth told me softly. Was I the last in the City to be so informed?

The newly qualified healer had come personally to fetch me from the Chamber. The City was about its diurnal business, as if every dawn brought People's ships to harbor. Only

69

the slightest air of urgency wafted up the fresh-washed ways from harborward, settling round the Citadel. Something lured us to the harbor first, where Droghen's three ships lay at anchor, though not quite as they had five years before. Ragged, limping, badly weathered, they were not alone. With them was a vast and polymorphous fleet, extending out beyond the limits of UnderSea, flying the standards of all the Fourteen Tribes.

"Even Kwengiis—can you imagine?" Dweneth breathed beside me, her words a vapor on the morning air. Her amber eyes shone with contained excitement. The soul-thread hummed. I seemed to hear Lerius breathing beside me. Dweneth had not been this open with me since the Chamber claimed me four years before. Was the Telepath there, through me, watching her vicariously? "Kwengiis here, and peacefully, though bracketed about by Wertha and Lamorak, and forbidden grog or firearms. Still, Thrasim tells me there was blood shed along the way. Llellaar braggarts against a trio of Dyrmen with knives, Thrasim says."

"Thrasim is well?"

We had turned in tandem toward the Citadel along the empty ways. No People were afoot, and only crew were on the ships, goggling at what they saw ashore; whoever else had come would have been escorted to the Council.

"Aye," Dweneth said, skipping childlike along the soft-stone despite her Othergarb and healer's sigil. Her tongue had relearned People's intonations as well. "The priestly one returns, though weathered weary and not entirely whole. There's none else here I know. Renna was the first they dropped ashore five years ago. Doubtless she's back in Lamora, spreading fantastic tales!"

"And Droghen?"

"Thrasim took a musketball in Tawa," Dweneth went on, telling the tale in her own time, her mind skipping over topics as her small feet skipped over cobblestones. "He favors the left leg, and I promised him a session under regen once the talking's done. He could scarce believe I was healer-made this soon. Oh, and Droghen's dead."

She stopped skipping to watch me sidelong, wondering would I react. How long had she known the brash and charismatic Droghiad was dead? They had been close once, in a quarrelsome, bullying way. I thought I saw through Dweneth's careful mask that she was somewhat shaken.

"Aren't you going to ask me how?"

I waited till we'd climbed the steps of the Citadel. "Very well, how?"

"Philandering, how else?"

Her voice was pitched deliberately loud in the corridors, to rattle the Citadel's intricate acoustics and announce to all that we were coming. Calculatedly People, calculatedly rude. But a greater noise, in fourteen tongues, already issued from the Council chambers, swallowing hers.

"Dallying with a merchant's marriageable daughter while he was supposed to be playing the Great Peacebringer in Tawa," Dweneth went on anyway. "He might have offered for her legitimately, only her father would have wanted her made queen. Instead, our Droghen dresses like a beggar and goes climbing garden trellises. Spoils the wench's market value, and gets himself shot withal. That's how Thrasim took the musketball, trying to save his master's hide if not his pride. Such a waste! Childlike and foolish, we People, after all!"

She sailed into the gallery as if prepared to present herself to the throng below, announcing herself by simple red-gold contrast to drabber Other selves as clearly People. She caught herself and ducked behind a pillar at the last moment, hand over her mouth in amazement at what she saw below.

Surely no such diversity of People had been gathered in one place since the Plalan Ascendancy had enslaved half the known World over a millenium before, parading their exotic

71

captives in chains through their capital. Never before had the representatives of all the Fourteen Tribes been met freely and as equals in one place at one time. Ironic that the event should transpire first in OtherWhere.

The role of Matriarch had again come round to Frayin, who held the Chair with such centered calm as indicated to the most unschooled outWorlder that she was leader, yet:

"No crown nor scepter do we see! And a woman withal!" the multitude cried in their babble of tongues, agreeing upon little else, even to where they should sit or stand in the Council chamber and in what precedence, but as one in their outrage at how we greeted them. There were some women among the Lamorak, but these were all. "What mockery is this?"

They milled and jostled, crowding the Council with a press of overheated bodies, frantically gesticulating in their need to understand and be understood. Only the barest sense of a guest's propriety in a foreign principality kept Mantuul from attacking Melet, Kwengiis from drawing sword out of habit upon Hraregh, Lamorak from biting Llellaar by the ears, or Tawa and Dyr from laying odds and taking bets on outcomes all.

Few Others chose to attend in the gallery, preferring to keep their distance and observe on infonet, as the Council had advised that not too many of us gather in one place, to alarm our guests. The sheer volume of noise in the Council, I observed, was causing no few of the Matriarchs actual physical distress. I dared not think what the cumulative assault of gaudy native dress and intermingled odors, the stamp of boots and jangle of armor and decorative bells and bangles must have been on those for whom until this moment the Fourteen Tribes had been but an encyclopedic abstract, safely distanced, not reeking of sweat and beer and onions and the attared musk of butchered animals. Nor did encyclopediae smear handprints on walls, spit on heretofore immaculate floors, and all talk simultaneously.

Yet Frayin, plain-garbed and wearing no badge of office, simply held the Chair as Thrasim led his charges in. The new Droghiad greeted her and the assembled Matriarchs. Frayin acknowledged but made no further move. Her stillness, her waiting posture and their own curiosity soon reduced the throng to uneasy silence. With that, Frayin motioned to each of fourteen interpreters to translate for her; she would speak only in Othertongue, to show no favoritism.

The exchange took all that day and far into the night, by which time most of the delegates were stupefied, half slumbering in their seats and on the floor. Food and drink were brought at intervals, and frequent announcements made that the honored guests were free to retire at any time they wished, either to chambers provided for them or to their own ships, where transcripts of the proceedings would be supplied for them. But none trusted his fellows enough to retire, so all stayed, and suffered for it.

Frayin's message was brief, and not dissimilar in content from that which my mother Jeijinn had delivered to a far smaller band of Droghians five years earlier. The purpose of this Council, Frayin stated, was to formulate an agreement upon our future interactions with the People. We desired nothing from them but to learn their ways and to be respected in ours. In exchange we would offer them whatever knowledge we had which they might find of value in the betterment of their lives and well-being.

Further, the delegates were free to avail themselves of everything our Archipelago offered, provided they remained within our laws. As this coincided with the most primitive tribal ethos, there was little murmur at the restriction itself, once these laws were made clear to them. What caused the controversy was the People's suspicion of us for freely offering such largesse.

*　*　*

73

Nor does Joreth understand it to this day.

"Why give them all your knowledge at once?" He has been quick to find me in the vast flotilla, perhaps only back-tracking the chronicle as it fans out along the weave-net. He rows a borrowed boat alone, not calling on the *bRi*. "Why not raise their level of understanding gradually, to coincide with the number of centuries it took you to attain such progress?"

Them and *you*, I note. Joreth has divorced himself from both species this time, or perhaps only from the elder, ruin-causing generation; he and his would have done differently, of course.

"We were too honest to do elsewise," I reply. "Nor could we countenance the waste of life, either from medical or philosophical ignorance, that would have resulted had we held back. Once discovered, we deemed it necessary to open our hearts."

"And look at where it's got you—where it's got us all!" He waves one hand and almost loses an oar, unable for all his strength to keep up with a pair of *bRi* at normal speed. I stroke the larger of the pair and trill to him; he slows to let Joreth catch up.

"Shall I remind you that it was the accusation of the very opposite—that we were holding back, hoarding knowledge and progress to ourselves, much less the secret of a longer life—which gave the Purists rise?"

Joreth shrugs, doubtful. "How long do you intend to stay out here in the wet?"

"As long as I am needed," I say softly. Small Aloyi nestles close to me, asleep. If I leave him, he will be cold.

Joreth starts to say something else, stops. "When it's your next turn to come aboard, I'd like to speak with you."

He rows on. Our *bRi* pick up speed once more, and Joreth disappears in fog.

At midnight of that first night, out of simple pity, WiseFra-yin adjourned the meeting, having wordlessly made the point that she and hers, having neither supped nor rested, could have endured indefinitely. Incredulous, the grumbling delegates and their entourages were amply housed in simple guest quarters, in which most of our fearful gadgetry had been removed, that they might rest themselves. Their ordeal, and ours, was just beginning.

"What is the general import of their talk?" Jeijinn Matriarch inquired. "I have monitored the proceedings meticulously, yet I confess to some confusion."

"So you might, Mother. Confusion is the dominant theme. Anything else is difficult to ascertain."

" 'Difficult to ascertain.' " WiseJeijinn was not sparing in her irony. "You were once Monitor. Try."

Jeijinn had summoned me to her apartments, where she had been sequestered since the ships were sighted, the only Matriarch unable to attend this Council of the Fourteen Tribes in person. My mother was an Empath, most rare of Others, who could feel any thinking being's emotions as if they were her own. Quite safe among Disciplined Others, she was at great risk when in proximity to too many People. She had watched every moment of the Council's proceedings, from Thrasim's landing to the final adjournment. Yet she hoped I would concise the matter for her.

"I am still a Monitor," I reminded her, with a permissible trace of pride. "And my assessment is that these People cannot overcome their own confusion sufficient to formulate a unified thesis of their wants or needs. Recall, please, that they have never before acted as one People, and the stresses of the long sea voyage have not improved their mood. Further, they are still not entirely convinced that we exist."

Jeijinn was incredulous. "How can this be? We are here. Incontrovertible evidence."

I drew upon what little I had learned in crossover, which I had been submitting to the Chamber in constant permutations since.

75

"Each of their religions encompasses some spirit world whose messengers can appear in this realm for either good or ill."

"So they think us either angels or demons." Jeijinn's grasp was always immediate. "Can they not touch us, accept our corporeality? Accept us as some heretofore unknown fifteenth tribe?"

"They cannot trust their senses," I offered. "And our technology is too advanced for us to be one with them. They cannot comprehend that the mere absence of war and disease has made this possible. Further, we appear different. Our behavior and mores are markedly different. Therefore we cannot be of this World."

"Your grandmother will be pleased to hear that!" The Legat's Parallel/Liiki's Dilemma debate was an ancient one between them. "WiseFrayin requires each Matriarch's recommendation. I shall submit that we select among this—horde—only those like Thrasim who can accept our reality and conciliate with us."

"An interesting suggestion, WiseJeijinn. Provided each tribe is assured of equal representation. How you are to overcome an intertribal jealousy which has endured for centuries—"

Jeijinn raised one hand to silence me, harking to some inner voice. "Someone is near. One of *them*, and in great pain. . . ."

I too listened, though I was no Empath.

"Are you certain? The healers have cautioned that even at this distance some resonance from all these many People might reach you."

"And so it has, since they arrived. I have been under autosedation since Thrasim's feet touched land, but this is different!" She clutched my arm, most unlike her, and her fingernails dug deep. "One voice, one solitary soul, and suffering—oh!"

I had watched transfixed the night then-Droghen or-

76

dered his sailors flogged for causing havoc in our City, and Jeijinn's body had broken out in bloody weals for every blow struck on the ships. It was the first I knew my mother was an Empath. She had always been more distant than Others even in her parenting; only then did I understand why. But even under such suffering she had never uttered a sound. Now she clamped her hands over her fluted Other ears and cried out.

"He . . . oh, find him . . . somewhere near . . . oh!"

She moved stiff-legged from room to room while I searched, following her resonance to find him.

He never knew parents, or tribe, or point of origin. All attempts to reach that portion of his past resulted in a blank, years missing, his mind blocked even from our Telepaths, as if the memory patterns had been burned away. Antigen scans suggested he was likely the product of the Gleris prison camps, whose orphanages reared mostly thieves and prostitutes. This child had been both.

Political prisoners in Gleris either died in the camps or were reconditioned to slave labor in the surrounding countryside, never permitted to return to their homes in the cities. Children who were conceived in the camps—a not infrequent occurrence despite the supposed segregation of the sexes, for obvious pregnancy earned a female prisoner better food and softer labor, at least until the child was born—were taken at birth and consigned to the orphanages, to be "reconditioned" in spite of their "bad blood."

Fed on gruel and flour water, most had the good grace to spare taxpayer expense and die. Those few who lived were physically stunted, emotionally twisted, savage, surviving any way they could. The less deformed were frequently purchased as sex-sellers.

I turned his wrist to find the mark, hidden beneath several layers of grime. Pity Jeijinn's delicate nostrils, much less her

77

empathy; this child stank. I hauled him out of the impossibly small space beneath a wardrobe where he had squeezed himself, having heard our voices while he foraged for something recognizable to eat or steal. I held him firmly.

How often have I had reason to berate myself for being less than gentle with him? At the time I deemed abruptness something he would better understand.

"None will harm you. What are you called?" I ventured first in Intertribal trade patois, then in every tongue I knew.

There was no response. Even his eyes remained uniformly widened, not with ignorance but with fear. He did not struggle but merely pulled backward with nearly as much strength as I pulled forward, resisting, giving no quarter while he assessed the situation for any means of escape.

"What could bring a child to such condition?" Jeijinn breathed. No matter how much she learned of People, she could not assimilate this.

"His society breeds such 'throwaways' as by-products of social or political upheaval," I said tersely, still holding his eyes with mine while I answered Jeijinn. "He is an orphan, doubtless escaped from the ships. By the mark, a sex-seller. By the bulges in his pockets, a thief. By his callused hands, crewmember, cabin boy, and plaything. By all of these, a survivor, and by the way he resists us, quite intelligent."

"Astonishing!" Jeijinn had her empathy under control by now, though what she saw and heard had immobilized her.

"Until someone misses him, there can be no harm in feeding him," I suggested.

Jeijinn gathered herself and went to program the servitor, while I tried to expand my acquaintance with our charge.

Still holding him firmly by the wrists, I sat on the floor to show him I was his equal. He flinched slightly but did not lessen his resistance. His eyes stayed wide with fear, and he had wet himself. Despite the wizened ancient face and the stunted body no bigger than a normal six-year-old's, I judged him to be about eight years, and well able to understand me.

"I am called Lingri, and I know you understand me," I said carefully in Hraregh. By his cast of face and coloring and what remained recognizable of his ragged garb, I judged him to be at least part Llellaar, though an amulet to ward off plague indicated he had spent some time in Hraregh. "None will harm you. We will feed you and provide for your needs, but you must help us."

He exhaled rancidly, his chest full of rales. Verminous and phlegmy, he was ateem with any number of things which ought to have killed him. Whatever else he was, he was stubborn. His teeth were loose and broken, but no less effective, as I learned when he lunged to sink them into my arm.

"No!" I said sharply in Llellaar, the only word I knew in that tongue. Did I only imagine his eyes grew wider? He recoiled, and I released his wrists, certain I could intercept him if he ran.

Jeijinn brought him porridge, which he sniffed suspiciously and rejected, growling, until I ate some first. He snatched it from me, gulped it down, and vomited almost at once. Jeijinn had to turn away as he scooped the vomit off the floor and reswallowed it, desperate as a wildcur.

"We've questioned everyone, down to the lowest swabbie," Thrasim reported gravely, studying the boy, while Dweneth and a Llellaaran aide fussed over him by turns. "No one will claim him."

"How is this possible?" Jeijinn wondered. She and Thrasim had early reached a mutual respect the first time he was in OtherWhere; they spoke as equals always. "I do not understand."

Thrasim sighed, not for the first time embarrassed for his People.

"None wishes to admit that such abuse could take place

aboard a ship bound for OtherWhere, much less that such abuses are chronic in our society. Therefore, it can only be that the boy does not exist. No People will claim him. I suppose that makes him yours."

Jeijinn raised her hands helplessly. "We will of course provide for him, but how are we to keep him?"

The subject of this discourse, still nameless, though newly fed and washed and clothed, injected with antibiotics and multivitamins, hunkered glowering in one corner of the guest quarters, as far from Others as he could. Dweneth completed her examination, put up her medkit, and glanced sidelong at me.

Now it begins!

"WiseJeijinn," she said smartly, "he will need prolonged care. His pleurisy's old and well entrenched. Add to that pneumonia, two venereal conditions, suppurating rectal lesions, rotted teeth, several chronic intestinal complaints, lice, scabies, and any disease that dirt and hunger nourish."

"I know." Jeijinn studied her hands in her lap to still their trembling. "Why is he mute? There is no organic cause."

"No, none that I can find." Dweneth scowled. For all her healer's training, she was not used to Empaths. "Something's frightened him out of voice, maybe only life as he perceives it. He can speak, but he won't."

"How many like him are there?" Jeijinn addressed the question to no one in particular. She had discovered a chasm between what could be studied about People and what they truly were, which stymied her.

"Countless thousands," Thrasim replied gently, concerned for her concern. "Even in my own land, I fear. Yet one more reason why I cannot remain here long." He sighed again, this time for himself. "What about the boy?"

"We will do what we can," Jeijinn replied with sudden resolve. "Dweneth Healer, advise the hospice that I will bring him shortly. For now, leave us, please."

"WiseJeijinn, I would not advise . . ." Dweneth began. Jeijinn ignored her.

It was I who led Dweneth, Thrasim, and the Llellaar out, so only I saw Jeijinn touch the boy. I could not close the door quickly enough to muffle both their screams.

Succinctly, the boy remained with Jeijinn, who in fact adopted him, creating a precedent for a wider social program which was one of the fruits of the First Alliance. But I run ahead of myself, and the boy's story is not mine to tell. He has told it himself repeatedly, though it changes each time he tells it.

Upon Jeijinn's recommendation, seconded by several Matriarchs and supported by the findings of the Chamber, no few of which were mine, ten representatives of each tribe were selected to remain and form with Others the Pact Between the Two, of which all history texts spoke eloquently until quite recently. It was to take those one hundred forty People and an equal number of Matriarchs a full decade to formulate the basis of the First Alliance, and decades more to refine, reshape, and reform it. This is not to say that intercourse between Others and People did not ensue in the meantime.

Among those sailing back to the Mainland was the new Droghiad Thrasim, torn by duty from his beloved Other-Where for a second time. He knew his destiny lay in Droghia, and there was a fervor in him to return and bring what he had learned from us to the governing of his People.

"If Redrec can be found," I began as we took our farewells for the second time in five years on the quay. My thoughts in those five years had frequently flown toward the so-named Halfman who had taught me music, in despite that Others had abandoned this most wondrous art a thousand years before my birth. "Say to him that Lingri sends regards."

81

"I shall find him!" Thrasim promised, exuberant with departure, "and deport his sorry carcass here to entertain you all—"

"And to mitigate his blindness," I reminded him, having ascertained from the healers that this could be done.

"—or I'll know the reason why!" Thrasim finished warmly, his pale hair lifted by the breeze. "What further message shall I bring him from ye?"

"That, as I cannot come to him, he must needs come to me."

We spoke no more of this. There were no more Monitors on the Mainland; even Rau and Soliah had been recalled. In the interim while the ships returned to spread the word of the First Alliance, no Other would venture off the Archipelago except those who went with Dweneth.

Thrasim was bringing the new-fledged healer and a contingent of handpicked Others to establish two experimental hospices in the geographically opposite and traditionally enmitous lands of Droghia and Kelibesh. Healing, it had been decided, was what People needed most. When word of the wonders of these two hospices spread beyond the borders of their two lands, all People would desire like benefit, and their newfound health would be best evidence of what Others offered.

Dweneth and her healers had gone aboard earlier. She and I had said our farewells in private the night before.

"I couldn't bear to break down in front of everybody," she explained. "Let me not be accused of public blubbering in OtherWhere. Besides, it makes my nose red! Not like Omila, who could weep buckets and never lose her looks!" She misted over in spite of herself. "I think this must be the hardest moment of my life!"

"We have the soul-thread," I suggested.

"Do we? I've been so cold with you! So torn between you and Lerius and the entire tangle. It's true, isn't it, that you gave your life to the Chamber because of me?"

"I *give* my life to the Chamber out of my duty as a Monitor," I began.

"Answer me!" she warned.

"Who told you this?" I countered instead.

"One of my fellow healers let it slip, accidentally-on-purpose. I was furious for days."

"I know," I said, remembering sparks of static prickling down the soul-thread. "What I do not understand is why."

Dweneth sighed, her face working. "Duty and Discipline, never any questions. If ever I came to hate your kind, it would be for your honesty. Now I am bound, out of duty and Discipline, to give my life to my People as a healer. Which is what I would have done anyway, but it's the burden of it—damn the lot of you, anyway! There, I'm crying; are you satisfied?" She wiped her eyes with the heel of her hand. "Why do I love you, Lingri-one? All you ever do is make me cry. Now I go off into the World, while you remain here in your velvet cage—"

"Will I, nill I. Now it is you who have but do not want what I want but cannot have."

"Duty first, personal considerations later," Dweneth sighed, gathering up the last of her belongings. "Look after Lerius in my absence. We all know it's better I forget him, but good luck! Will the soul-thread work at a distance, do you suppose, after all the neglect we've given it?"

"Try."

We clasped our four hands; she closed her eyes. I held off Lerius's inquisitive mind with my own. This much was my privacy, at least.

What are you thinking? she thought to me.

That wherever you are, I will know you by this.

If ever you need me, for whatever reason . . .

If ever I can be of use to you . . .

Yes . . .

"Don't open your eyes!" she cried, letting go my hands. I heard her scrabbling about in a last noisy effort to collect her things and knew she was gone by the coldness in the room.

Betimes the next morning her bright head would appear among the milling throng about the decks of Thrasim's ship. Her bright laughter rang out in her delight at being back among her own kind, but there was a sadness to it. I thought I saw her embrace one of Thrasim's officers, a Player's caress, offhand and meaningless. And yet . . . She had been long without the People's warmth. When I queried the soulthread, I found it as ever toward me. And Lerius was silent at his end. Anything else was a matter for Dweneth's privacy.

The First Fleet departed, the Pact Between the Two in working order; it was my place to lose myself once more to work. No Other dared prognosticate about what transpired beyond the horizon. If the First Alliance failed, and more than once in that formative decade did it seem it might, no Other would venture beyond the Archipelago, no People, except perhaps in aggression, return to us again.

Calm prevailed throughout the Archipelago, though none but the remotest solitaries failed to watch the infonets and visicomm to learn what transpired in the Council daily. Calm was the only Disciplined response to that over which one had no control. Calm was my mode as well, for I had much to do.

In addition to further duties toward the Chamber and anOther's daily regimen of study, meditation, exercise, my chief occupation became the mastery of every iota of Other literature extant in the Archives. Imagine my surprise to find some of my own poems preserved among the ancient works, as being the only contemporary examples! Loriel took full responsibility for that, a glimmer in her eye.

Having mastered all our literatures, I took it upon myself to learn as much of People's as I could while still confined to the Archipelago. Thus did I pester every one of the

84

delegates to share with me his songs and tales and legends, which I then catalogued. Some few books and scrolls had been brought aboard the ships, and these were lent me for my study. And though there were no true musicians among the delegates in OtherWhere, no few of these delegates could sing, or thought they could, and frequently regaled me with their favorite songs, which seemed to ease their homesickness. Such drunken-sounding caterwauling, all in the absence of intoxicants, had surely never sounded on our shores before.

Optimally, at some time in those years I should also have acquired a bondmate. I did not.

Not unexpectedly, Lerius remained silent once Dweneth had departed. It was I who on occasion sought him out, to reassure myself he was not reaching for her from a world away.

When there was time to spare, I visited with Jeijinn and my newly acquired sibling.

Other healing cured his body and, as much as it could, restored his soul. He evolved from a feral, cornered creature to a nearly normal People's child, intelligent and curious, although he never laughed.

Jeijinn's empathic communion taught him trust, and in time he flourished, drinking in knowledge as if it were sunlight. No field of study was alien to him once he learned to read. Skillscans indicated his best talents lay in sociology, psychology, and political science. If he stayed in Other-Where—and thus he seemed to wish, for he never willingly went near any of the People—it was hoped he would become a Matriarch some day, perhaps even an ambassador, if the First Alliance held.

He grew straight and whole and, aside from dark memories which always lingered just beyond his reach, waking him screaming from the deepest sleep, only one thing troubled him. He wanted more than anything to be an Other.

"Shall I have ears like yours, WiseJeijinn?" was one of the first full sentences he uttered in his reedy, piping voice once he retaught himself to speak. "Surely wisdom makes them grow so elegant, and I am learning to be wise."

"So you are," Jeijinn would answer, a marvel to watch in her devotion. My mother the Empath had heretofore subscribed to absolute egalitarianism; to see her so committed to a single individual was quite fascinating. "But your ears are People's, and thus will remain."

Again the boy would ask, "And what about my toes? If I swim every day with WiseLoriel, shall I have webtoes like hers?"

"You will not," Jeijinn would say—a little sadly, I thought.

The boy received each negative answer as if it were a blow. In time his eyes grew veiled and, I thought, dangerous.

"Glory in what you are, Dzu," Jeijinn would say, sensing the danger but uncertain how to address it, "for you are glorious!"

"What was the boy's true name?"

It is the question I have dreaded most, asked me by a grizzled Dyrman, accompanying three Others in one of the few boats I can distinguish in the fog. Yarel and Aloyi listen wide-eyed, as Peria ceases to repeat my words. Like all those who have been passing my words along the living infonet, she yields to the uncanny silence.

The Dyrman is the first of the full-People to address me; the rest have thus far been speaking of me among themselves with a kind of disquieting awe. Now no one speaks at all. Silence, and the plash of boats and *bRi*. If I do not answer the Dyrman's question, the silence will endure.

"What was the boy's true name?" the Dyrman repeats patiently.

"Dzu was the name he told us, once he found his

86

voice," I answer carefully. "His full name was Dzugash, though we always called him Dzu."

"There was only one who bore that name!" the Dyrman says, spitting into the sea. "Cursed be it, for all eternity! Your story must be false, for Dzugash the Demagogue was never reared by Others!"

"There was only one Dzugash," I confirm and contradict at once, "and he was reared by Others."

The Dyrman shakes his head; his boat retreats into the fog. My last words carry down the story-net. I must continue.

It is not our intention to govern you, nor to intervene, advise, arbitrate, or assist in your governance of yourselves, unless you ask us. Asking us, you must be assured that we will neither intervene, advise, arbitrate, nor assist in any way which will give one tribe precedence or advantage over its fellows. It is our penultimate hope that all People will in time unite into a single entity, our ultimate hope that this entity will include us as a fifteenth tribe in the harmonious government of a world.

To that end, we will treat only with those tribes who so invite us, and whose customs do not violate our Discipline. Therefore we will not treat with slaveholders, nor with those who traffic in slaves. We will not treat with those who make war, either wholesale or by invasion, usurpation, espionage, or internal revolution. We will not treat with those who kill, whether that killing take the form of execution of criminals, genocide, or exposure of infants at birth, or any form in which any person's life is untimely curtailed.

We will not treat with those who torture, maim, rape, kidnap, or elsewise hold against their will any persons, either in the name of personal or national advantage. We will not treat with those who abuse or exploit the helpless and disenfranchised, or with those who exercise prejudice against any person owing to differences of ethnic origin, nor religious or philosophical belief. There is more, but this is the beginning. . . .

Free your slaves and we will provide devices which

will do their work, improving both your lives and theirs. Give us your unwanted, whether prisoners or indigents, and we will show you ways to make their lives meaningful. Bear only the offspring you desire, for our healers will instruct you in ways that this may be done. This, too, is only the beginning.

In exchange, bring to us your scholars, your philosophers, your artists, artisans, poets and musicians, that they may brighten our lives and expand our understanding. This is all we ask of you.

We do not suggest that the transition will be without suffering, inconvenience, or bewilderment. We simply state our terms for interaction. You the People must decide if they are worth the cost. You must make the choice.

5

Did I follow the proceedings of the Council as assiduously as Others? I confess I did not. What beset either side at any given moment concerned me less than how soon both would reach some basis of agreement, so that I might return to Droghia.

For Redrec was not getting any younger; if I was to bring him to OtherWhere it would have to be soon. And now-Droghen Thrasim, once returned to his land, was never heard from more. The simple radio interlink established to keep the delegates in communication with their fourteen separate nations brought out of Droghia only uneasy rumors of war.

Not invasion by any outside hostile force—which was of considerable relief to the delegates, who might have found it necessary to enact like hostilities within the very Council chamber—but some internal strife beset that usually most peaceful land. Nothing more specific could be learned, and in addition to their ordinary homesickness, for all the delegates were homesick, the Droghians were particularly disturbed.

Part of the Matriarchs' plan had been to utilize that homesickness. The more the representatives of the Fourteen Tribes hungered for their homelands, the sooner they would stop their petty squabbling and come to terms.

Having personal acquaintance with People from at least six of the Fourteen Tribes, I knew how likely it was that this would transpire in anything less than a decade. I blocked these trivialities from my consciousness, the better to concentrate upon my work. Still, the Council's proceedings reached me will I, nill I.

"Suppose, then," I would hear some delegate dogging a WiseOne down the corridors, "suppose we allow you to give us these—these things-that-make-the-wheels-move—"

"Engines," the WiseOne would reply.

"Engines, just so. We've realized that half our factury workers and all but domestic slaves will no longer be needed!"

"Precisely," the WiseOne would respond, not understanding why this caused distress. "And with the extra revenues provided by upgraded manufacture, you could free the remaining slaves and pay them wages for their service."

"But don't you see?" the delegate would cry. "Half our work force would be idle, with no work to do!"

"And thus be free for study, recreation, and to spend time with their offspring, as opposed to setting four-year-olds to work beside their elders in the facturies." Even the Wise-One would stop here, seeing blank incomprehension on the delegate's face. "Where is it written that all but the ruling class must labor dawn to dusk?"

"Excepting on the seventh day!" a second delegate would pipe up. "Why it's right there in the holy Writ. How can you not know this? Perhaps you are not as wise as you pretend to be."

Every aspect of our interaction was a problem. Some wanted no part of Others, wanted us apart on our Archipelago so that they might pretend we did not exist. Still,

91

they could not give the remaining tribes the advantage of our acquaintance by returning home. Thus, despising us, they stayed. Some tribal spokesmen wanted to purchase our women for brides, so simple was their understanding. All were suspicious of us in some degree, and the bickering went on.

"But we and Droghia are traditionally enemies," Kelibek's chief representative would carp. Behind him, nerve-shot without their swords, the Kwengii delegation swore and leaned in to overhear. "If you give to them, you cannot give to us, or contrariwise."

"Why not?" a Matriarch would ask, and the Kelibek would throw up his hands in despair, while the Kwengii roared with laughter.

"An exchange of children? Yours to live among us, ours to live with you?" The Melet, island dwellers, had expressed some interest, but Plalas was aghast. "Never, not even for a year! But supposing we had waifs and throwaways that we could not feed . . ."

He would not finish his thought, much less mention Dzu's name, but there had been discussion of taking orphans off the hands of all the tribes.

"This also can be discussed," the Matriarch would reply, somewhat relieved, for the logistics of settling Other children, unsupervised and in the minority, upon the Mainland had been offered in the hope of building a generation without prejudice, but it was deemed too soon.

"What are you hiding from us?" some would ask. "Why can't we meet personally with the Telepathy?" It was the only thing we had forbidden them. And, most often, "Why do your histories lie? You cannot have been peaceful for a thousand years!"

"Well, now. Say you managed to cure all our agues and plagues, as your healers say you can, and soon we live to be as old as you . . ."

92

Loriel and I, passing through the hospice, watched two WiseOnes exchange glances above the head of a crabbed Zanti being treated for advanced arthritis.

"That is not precisely what we said," the first one answered. "Once most contagions and dietary illnesses are eliminated, and genetics improved—"

"Yes, yes!" the Zanti said impatiently, flexing a shoulder that heretofore he had been unable to move.

"You would reach People's optimal life span, whatever that might be," the second WiseOne finished.

"Fine, then!" the Zanti said sarcastically. "We're hip-deep in old People, and no one to take care of them. By the same token, if all our children live, we'll be eyeball-deep in offspring."

"Do you observe such a state in OtherWhere?" the first WiseOne asked calmly.

"No, of course not." The Zanti left the treatment room with a spring in his step. "But that's because you have so few children."

"As might you," the second WiseOne suggested as the three walked on together.

There ensued, I am told, a three-hour debate about contraception and its specific prohibition by all the laws known to Zanti gods and mortals both, though exposure of unwanted infants, particularly in an evil-omened year, was quite acceptable.

"Ask me what the Plalan delegation said when I explained our lack of monetary standard," Loriel said wryly, as if it were a joke. It wasn't. "Or what I told Tawa and Kwengiis when they decided the best thing to do was to enlist our aid in conquering the Hillpast Wastes and turning them into a prison farm."

The whole was a barely controlled chaos. I was grateful to have the Chamber to escape to, though even that was temporary. I must continue to gather songs and literatures, including those of a burly, bearded Kwengii warrior, reduced

93

to tears and maudlin versifying because he had not seen his wives and children for more than a year.

" 'Tis different if I'm asea or fighting with me brethren 'gainst some enemy ashore," he sobbed, wiping his eyes on the ragged edges of his waist-length beard. "But here I'm only one o' ten and can't speak to half of 'em because we're cross-mate families."

"Aye," I would reply in his tongue, pretending not to notice his tears for fear of shaming him. "I do understand ye, man."

"But here there's naught for me to do only talk and argue, hardly man's work, and everything I'm hearing says there'll be no need for my kind once this Alliance thing is done."

"Why say ye that?"

He snuffled lustily. "Oh, hear it: engines and facturies and exchange of goods. Naught for a warrior to do but gut fish or grow posies, once it's done. I've killed a hundred in my day. What shall I do once Others teach us peace?"

If only we could, and so easily! I thought. "Having killed a hundred, why not save a hundred?" was what I said.

He dried his eyes, which were small and red and beady. "Now ye're talking nonsense. Begging your pardon, this being your land, but what are ye on about?"

"There will always be enemies to fight," I suggested. "Flood and fire and earthquake and storm. Places where strength and skill are needed still. Orphans and fendless women to protect. Peace will hardly come at once."

"That's good to hear!" the Kwengii roared. "Thank ye, Lingri-one, for cheering me with that thought!"

"Indeed," I said, masking irony. "Now, will ye sing me 'Gurrd's Battle Song' once more, to see I've got it right?"

He cleared his throat, twisted his mustaches back, and struck a heroic pose.

" 'Tis better done with ale," he suggested winningly.

"No matter," I replied, setting my recorder; there was

94

as yet no ale in OtherWhere, at least not legitimately. "I'll trust to your skills and the timbre of your voice. Go on!"

Thus flattered, he roared me full seventeen verses before his Werthan neighbors began pounding the walls to complain.

The delegates quarreled, cheated, bootlegged, fought with table knives, brought mayhem in their train. Somehow the final draft of the Concordance of the First Alliance was ratified and committed to microstor on 11TasEth T-Y1035. A single hardcopy was too large for one person to carry unassisted. The delegates, haggard but rejoicing, left for home.

The fine points of the Concordance mattered not to me. On 12TasEth, permission to Monitors finally granted, I powered up my own personal skimmer and set course for the Mainland.

The Chamber's conclusion was that coastal regions would be most quickly affected by Others' influence, and their indigenous cultures most radically altered. Therefore, despite my curiosity about what transpired further to Windward, I set course first for Hraregh, setting the skimmer down in the very wood where Rau and I had come ashore on my first crossover.

Duty first, personal considerations later.

I don't need you to tell me that. How fare you?

Busy, Dweneth would answer, then be gone. In the opposite corner of my mind, I would hear Lerius:

Tell her my thoughts go with her whenever yours do. Tell her—

Enough! This is our privacy.

The next season was spent collecting Hraregh songs and sagas, retracing the steps of my earlier journey, though at considerably better speed.

This was to be the pattern of my lifetime. Announced in a town square or village anywhere from Melet to Tawa to Wertha, my request would be a simple one:

"Tell me your best stories."

If my recording devices made the local People uneasy, I would simply listen as they spoke or sang, memorizing word and gesture and intonation, and music if there were any, all to be written down later, stored in memory before they were lost in the onslaught of technology.

Often People would ask me for a tale of my own in return, and as I had the night Dweneth first thrust her grandmother's singstick into my hand, I sang of OtherWhere. My stories would be passed along from People to People, and I would find them repeated back to me, altered to suit the culture and the era, years and latitudes away. In time, with universal access to visicomm, even the children no longer stared at me.

Decades later, the Purists were to point to this as cultural pollution. I saw it as mere fair exchange.

From Hraregh, I set my course for Droghia, full fifteen years after I had left it. Despite the rumors and the silence, I must know what had become of Redrec.

This was not the Droghia I had left behind. Its stolid burghers' houses still hunkered in the back streets, cheek by jowl with elder wattle dwellings teetering two or three storys high before crumbling into disrepair, but the waterfront gleamed with glass-fronted skyrises of distinctly Other design. Steel bridges usurped where stone had formerly arched across canals. Telfer pylons loomed and vanished too sharply around curves above the winding streets, their cabled spans too loosely strung, and no gondolas to traverse them. As the harbor ferry made fast I could see that many of the skyrises stood half finished, their jutting girders bleeding rust, tumbled piles of broken town houses lying crumbled at their feet.

Droghen-Thrasim's name had not been spoken hereabouts for five years. None would tell me why, but glared at my Other face and garb whenever I inquired.

I would have walked to the Great House, had I not been

set upon by jitney drivers so desperate to attend debarking ferry passengers that I chose the poorest-looking, if only to keep the peace. Hungry he might be, but not too hungry to give me an odd look when I spoke my destination.

What remained of the palace of the Droghiads was whatever in oversize structures of a certain era would not succumb to fire—essentially a charred and roofless gutted hulk. I sought the glassless casements of what had been Redrec's apartments, thinking to find someone to tell me where he had gone. Surely the reactionaries who had killed Thrasim had not killed the Halfman as well in their frenzy? Not only was he innocent of any political charge, but Redrec was too resourceful to be caught.

Courtyard after courtyard was weed-grown and deserted, mocking my echoing footsteps. None ventured willingly within the environs of the Great House. None would tell me the location of the healers' hospice set up by Dweneth and the Others, if it still existed. Dweneth, I knew by the soul-thread, was elsewhere. Any I questioned in the streets glanced first at my face and ears, then scuttled furtively away. I must try Redrec's older haunts. A sinister whispering followed me down the streets of the Old City.

"Other, Other, cursed Other, go back, back where ye came . . . spoiler, desecrator, go back!" they hissed from alley and casement, and more than once a stone flew past my Other ear.

The cellar inn where Redrec used to play was largely unchanged, though its wizened landlord had been replaced by a burly youngster tending the scant patronage. There was a pallor over everything, more than its being underground. The very oil lamps seemed to pale, and more than once I heard the hacking cough of plague.

"Yer kind's not welcome here since Droghen-Thrasim died!" the youngling growled, daring the name in his urgency to be rid of me, wary for all his size, for he'd heard that even anOther as unprepossessing as I could prove inordinately strong.

"Nor will I linger," I replied evenly, "so you tell me where I might find Redrec Musician, who used to play here when I came here last."

"He never did, and ye never were!" a toothless old one spat at me, though behind him stood the cut-down chair, the cut-down table by the hearth, with its set-in notch for Redrec's crutches, untouched as if a kind of shrine. Following my glance, he corrected himself. "Anyways, *ye* weren't. It's longer Redrec wasn't here than that we've known of your kind, and wisht we never had!"

"Redrec was Regent in Droghen-Gerim's absence, this I know," I began, but they turned their backs on me, and I ceased to exist.

My last recourse would be the UnderCity, where Redrec had had his haunts whenever he was out of favor with the Droghiad. Had the new landlord been amenable, I might have found my way through his cellar to the sewers and the catacombs; now I must go through the streets once more, despite the threat of danger, to find further entrances that I knew. Pulling up the hood of my travel cloak, lengthening my stride and giving it swagger, I might guise both Otherness and gender, either of which were a danger on the streets of Droghia.

Deep in the UnderCity, I found the vast arena out of Plalan times which housed the ancient Hydraulus, the towering water-engined pipe organ that Redrec used to play. If he were living, I would find him here, else find those who knew him.

But the Hydraulus lay in ruins, smashed first and later burned, nothing but wreckage. My fears for Redrec increased. None would dare do this while he lived.

"Over his dead body, ordinarily. Except he wasn't here!"

Had my Other ears betrayed me, or was this man's step

softer than soft, that he might surprise me first with voice? I whirled, my hood falling, revealing my double vulnerability.

Whirled to find him yet some steps away, at the far end of one of the tunnels whose acoustics lent him a voice far preceding his person. Now I heard the scuffle of slippered feet on stone, and took his measure.

He was scarce a lad, sixteen at most, but with voice as deep as any man's, and far deeper in fact than most. I knew that voice. Moreover, I knew that face, though it belonged to a different man, far older, born to walk crabwise and no taller than the average person's belt. Further, the man I knew had scalded, blinded eyes, not these clear green orbs which took my measure as I took his.

"Where was your father when they destroyed the Hydraulus?" I asked, as if to recognize Redrec's son were the most natural thing. I had meant to re-cover my head, but refrained.

"He was already dead, you see, or else they wouldn't have had the nerve," the boy began, flippant, bitter, stopping himself with a too familiar Redrec scowl. "How do you know my father, much less that I'm his son? Unless—" He answered his own question, with something like surprise: "Of course. You are Lingri."

"I am. Nor did I know until this moment that Redrec had a son."

The words came automatically as I struggled with my thoughts. Was I shocked to know Redrec dead? The odds had been against him. He was nearly forty when I knew him. Between his many afflictions and the temper of the times, he would be well past an average People's life span were he here.

"How did he die?"

The boy's answer startled me: "Of pox, how else? The strange new kind brought up from Tawa, what with all the to-and-fro since Thrasim's return from OtherWhere. There

99

had been cautious trade atween us down the years, but nothing like the traffic there was once Droghia heard about Others and their ways. It's what brought Droghen-Thrasim to his end, this insistence on everything being new and Otherfashion. Damn Others, damn you all! Why did you ever come here? Why can't you leave us be?"

"I think you've got that wrong," I began. He lunged to strike me; I was not where he thought me when he got there.

"Sidestep me, will you?" he roared in his father's voice. "Damn all of you and your Other tricks! Droghen-Gerim should have loosed his cannons on you before he went ashore! Else told us he'd found dragons so we'd never venture o'er the edge. Oh, *damn*—my father's dead. . . ."

He wiped a fine linen sleeve across his eyes; fatherless he might be, but prosperous.

"The pox was unforeseen," I ventured quietly; he did not attack me further. "Perhaps Others were its catalyst, but not its blame. I came to seek your father. If you could tell me how he died . . ."

He snuffled lustily, exhaled, grew calmer. "He always said your voice was beautiful. He never said how it could persuade. Sit you down!"

He cleared charred wood and organ guts from a part of the floor, ensconcing himself in the very corner where I'd huddled beneath the Hydraulus's assault so long ago. I sat near him, but not too near.

"You were scarce an infant when I knew him," I began.

"And you didn't think him capable of such?" The lad's tone was suddenly affable, as if by some sea change we'd become fast friends. "Redrec may have lacked legs and eyes, but the rest of him worked fine, thank you. There was also that in him which brought out the mother in some women, and he left no few mothers in his wake. However many children he got, I was the only one bequeathed his name and gifts."

"Then you are also called Redrec?" It was a strange

custom People had, to name a child for someone still living.

"Redrec Younger—oh, aye!" he answered sourly. "It's lain heavily on me all my life, even though I started music far earlier than he. And though he's dead I still can't be just Redrec. For such a small man, he casts relentless shadows!"

"I shall call you simply Redrec, if you like."

He eyed me warily. "Can you do so without thinking of my father?"

"No," I answered truthfully.

"Well, then!"

We sat, the silence punctuated by his sometime sniffling. Teeming passions roiled in this young one, as easily read as if exuded from his skin.

"Could you not choose a different name for yourself, at least as it pertains to your music?"

"I thought you wanted to know how he died?" he countered sharply.

He waited in the silence, undisturbed by it, his shaggy head lolled back against the ashy wall, his strong hands resting on his drawn-up knees. Not anOther's hands, too knotted and hairy at the knuckles, but as beautiful as his father's had been. The glass green eyes assessed me; the beardless face seemed feral.

"How old are you?"

"Too old to tolerate impertinence," I countered, aware of what he was thinking.

His laugh was short, lost in his scowl.

"How my father died . . ." He almost hummed it. Dirge for a dead musician. "I said of pox. That's only partly true. The rest has to do with a broken heart. He was not young— five and fifty had he lived out the year—yet he survived Thrasim's 'reforms' and Brok the Fat's insurrection, and called upon old favors owed by both sides to keep him and his fed and under protection even after Thrasim died and there were reprisals. But he no longer composed, no longer played, and the heart went out of him. All the talk of Other-

Where, when Thrasim took the First Seat and the healers came. The only one he waited for was you.''

''I was unwillingly detained—''

'' 'If Lingri can, she'll come for me,' he'd say. 'She'll bring me to play my music, and to show me OtherWhere.' I was a boy, and ignorant, and demanded to know how he would see OtherWhere when he had no eyes. He'd cuff me and roar, 'You're the one who can't see, but you will! If Lingri can, or Rau'—that was anOther name he used, though he never said who it might be, as he did with you—'if either can, they'll come for me.' ''

He dabbed his eyes on his sleeve again, though the gesture seemed too delicate this time. ''You never came, and so he died.''

''I was detained,'' I said again, knowing I could not have explained to him by what.

''Did you love him?'' The lad sat up, as abrupt as his question, his hand uninvited on my knee. He was only a boy; it was a boyish gesture. I tried not to interpret it elsewise.

''Love? I am anOther.''

''And Others do not practice love,'' he finished. ''So I've heard. It doesn't answer to the fact that he loved you.''

This information gave me pause. ''Did he tell you that?''

''Not exactly.''

''Then you cannot know it. You were an infant when he knew me, and People frequently embroider cold memory with might-have-been. If Redrec ever spoke to you of me—''

''*I* am Redrec!'' His father's roar.

''So you are,'' I acquiesced, gathering myself; I had overstayed my welcome. ''And yet you're not. If perhaps your father found something of value in me—''

''And you in him!''

I had begun to retreat down the catacombs; he followed. I turned to return his shout.

"More than you can know!" I answered vehemently. "And I would have returned for him, to bring him to us for healing, and for what he could teach Others—"

"Others, always Others! You're no different than the rest of them—talk alike, act alike, think alike. Wooden puppets all!"

"How little you understand!" I breathed, on my way.

He ran after, turned me by the shoulders. "Teach me?"

My, he's pretty! Dweneth would have said then.

Go away! I would have answered.

And suddenly I knew this charming, disarming manchild for what he was—a court-reared musical prodigy, every woman's pet, fondled and doted on, accustomed to his own way. Except where they needed callus to pluck strings, his hands were inordinately soft. He had never yet met female he could not persuade. Until today. And who were his current patrons in these unstable times?

"No," I countered. "Rather, you teach me. What happened here in Droghia?"

He shrugged, clasped his hands behind him coyly, and we walked.

Would that Droghen-Thrasim had stayed in OtherWhere, at least long enough to study less of our architecture and more of our social philosophy. Returning to Droghia, he set about at once implementing the changes which would bring about his downfall.

Buildings were the answer, Thrasim thought. Or, as he put it, "The superiority of a culture is a direct function of its plumbing." Given free rein and unlimited funds, he might have razed all of Droghia at once, rebuilding it with mushrooming skyrises of Other design in place of what native artisans had wrought down the centuries. Open People's eyes to wide, glassed windows and limitless vistas, open their lungs to warm, fresh-processed air and their faces to bright slanting sunlight, Thrasim thought, let them stand tall in high-ceilinged chambers instead of stooping in low-slung hovels, let them turn a tap to find water and touch a switch to have light, and one would as easily turn their souls to peace and touch their minds with progress.

He had so embraced the trappings of OtherWhere, forgetting he and his were People, that he neglected to consider the most fundamental thing: no Other would discard that which was old, traditional, and cherished merely for that which was new. Had he been less impatient, Droghen-Thrasim might have been hailed as a hero.

When Droghian masons refused to labor on the skyrises, Thrasim imported laborers and artisans from Tawa and highwalkers from Dyr and Zanti. The result was resentment and unemployment in his own land and families separated in the lands these men came from, the men themselves thrown abruptly into the midst of customs and language they did not know, among People who hated them. And those from Tawa brought the plague.

Other healers would subsequently determine that a mutated intestinal parasite, content to dwell innocuously in Tawan guts for generations, played havoc when it met with Dyr and Droghians. Ironically, it was the overcrowding and open latrines in the work camps—the very conditions Thrasim sought to eradicate in his architect's fantasy—which encouraged the spread of the disease.

The city dwellers were too debilitated to rise up against their obsessive leader; their government too decimated to raise a quorum to depose him. It took Brok the Fat, Brok the Brigand King, Brok Dain'sSon and Dweneth's brother, exiled to the swamps of Hraregh by Thrasim's predecessor and plotting like a spider all these years, to gather his constituency of swamp and sewer rats and seize the day.

A further irony: Brok's ego was so great he had never trained a successor; perhaps he thought that he would live forever. When his massive weight and the strain of the long march caused him to literally burst asunder on the highroad overlooking Droghia Harbor, his horde went berserk and rushed the city at random, carving their way in pillage and rapine, burning the Great House with Thrasim in it before they too were stopped.

They had brought with them a swamp pox which, while it had always taken its toll in infants and old ones in the swamp, found new virulence when nurtured on city food and, once more, overcrowding. Swamp rat and sewer rat perished alike, along with whoever in Droghia had survived the Tawan plague, including Redrec Elder.

An instant aristocracy rose up among the wealthiest burghers, and these appointed an Acting Governor, who ruled a nation understandably isolationist with regard to Others.

"Some flocked to religion, some to greater hedonisms," Redrec Younger finished, his attention on the cobbles where we walked beneath the sky, in a part of the city unknown to me but redolent of the waterfront. "But even as the temples filled, the Filaret himself turned poxed and died. So much for religion! And the revelers found their servant class fled up the canals to the countryside, else bashing their betters' heads in, that they might share the reveling. But it's hard to debauch day and night with no one to clean up after you!"

His eyes phospored briefly, too old for his face, as if he himself had witnessed if not participated in such debaucheries. He walked gingerly, as if sick from drink. Where had he been the night before?

"And through all this, the musician survives unscathed?" He did not answer. "Had you kin to protect as well? Your mother?"

"My mother was a servile in then-Droghen's house." He seized my arm for emphasis. "She bore me, then she died. Common enough. But her servile status spared my neck when Brok's horde came roaring through. And my father was owed favors by both sides. I survived. The rest was using my wits, my looks, and being a better musician even than my father!''

He swaggered when he said it, an overlarge, pretty boy who might someday make a man, but shallow and soft-bodied, never tested physically nor mentally. Except that I must know whatever information he could give me, for it was as much my duty to record his music as any peasant's lay or sultan's eunuch's love song, I would have left him then.

"I am, you know," he declared. "Far better."

I had not said aloud I doubted him. He stood swaggering in midstreet, while I would have preferred to seek shelter. More than one passerby's fingers itched to pick up stones on seeing me.

"Already I've mastered every instrument he played, and several more besides. And I've written far more than he had at my age. His own fault, truth, for driving me."

He pulled me into a nearby alley, as if we were lovers at some tryst, and he more drunk with words than wine could make him.

"He drove me, night and day. I think I was barely out of swaddling clothes before he propped me upright at the keyboard to do scales. 'Play!' he would roar, and 'Again, again!' no matter how many hours already spent on it. No matter that my head ached and my back was bowed with pain. 'Nothing matters but the music!' he would shout, and crack me between the shoulders whenever my attention lagged."

There were many forms of child abuse, I thought as he babbled drunkenly on, though the side of Redrec Elder I had known did not allow for this. Yet People were so compli-cated, and rarely what they seemed. There was a plea for pity in this man-child's voice, a pout on his pretty-ugly face, as if by now any female with a heart would have patted him and lavished him with sympathy. When I only listened and said nothing, he scowled his Redrec scowl at me, sighed piteously, and went on.

"Even when Droghen-Gerim made him Regent, you'd think it might have slowed him, but no. By then he'd further plans for me. I was not only to practice, I was to perform.

"He ordered suits made up in miniature of what the finest gentlemen wore, and had my face painted as any lady might envy—except, says he, 'Ugly is as ugly does, and you're your father's whelp for that!' He'd even feel my face, because he could not see it, to be certain the paint was there. Thus powdered and perfumed and all in lace and fripperies, I would perform nightly, having practiced all the day, for all of then-Droghen's court and the wealthier salons. Petted, fondled, asleep on my feet, or so stuffed with sweetmeats that my head spun round. This was how I grew up."

"Did your father never see to the rest of your education?" It was all I could think of to ask.

"I can read words, though not as facilely as notation, and know some mathematics, but nothing to teach me of the world or get me to university." He snorted. "Except I major in the arts of love, for I learned those early on. My father taught me that, too!"

Poor baby! Dweneth would have said at this point.

Enough! I would have answered.

"Did he also teach you self-pity? For while I never encountered it in him, it seems that you have mastered it!"

He cocked an eyebrow at me, as if contemplating what I might do if he tried to hit me again.

"How well d'you think you knew him? You're probably the only thing female he never laid, and only because he sensed somehow you're Other. I hear tell your kind don't fuck till well past thirty. Is that true?"

He said it just to wound, was not interested in my answer. His own troubles took precedence.

"For as long as I can remember: 'Practice, practice!' all the day, and the sound of him grunting and sweating with

107

some doxey in the night. We shared the same rooms, and I'd watch and learn, and soon the burgher's wives and daughters were petting and teaching me. There was one likely lass, twelve years to my eight . . ."

The reminiscence made him gentle, and he ceased to clutch at my shoulders, touched his two soft hands to the sides of my face instead. Before I could pull away, it triggered something in me, nonTelepath though I was, and I saw his damaged childhood whole, a whirling stew of colors, harsh voices and harsher laughter, lights, torchieres too bright for sleepless eyes, noises shrieking into overweary ears. I felt the ache of fingers too long cramped in playing position, felt the cramp work up my arms and shoulders, down my back and legs, up my neck and head, throbbing, heard the purr and coo of woman-voices, cloying painted faces, clinging scents and fabrics, cool hands suddenly fevered, touching, stroking, rousing . . . tittering and leaving unfulfilled and frustrated . . . felt my small boy-legs pulled out from behind a satin divan while hands brushed me off and shoved me toward the crowded bustling salon that I might perform as well on keyboard as on cushions. I became the precocious, pampered poppet, a caged, bewildered, indoor thing, blinking any time he saw the sun.

Small wonder I had found him loitering in the shade of catacombs, comtemplating the ruin of his father's work.

He pulled his hands away, yet their burning imprint stayed. I swayed beneath the brunt of unaccustomed insight. Had he any idea what had happened?

More important, had I?

He was talking again, oblivious to my state.

" . . . And yet, I loved it, love it still. Practice daily hours longer than I need, as if he's still standing over me and I can never shake his shadow. Yet I love it. Love the adulation, the openness it evokes in women. Like a drug, like sex, but only the best kind—subtle, yet passionate." He glowered at me. "Do you understand any of this at all?"

108

"More than you can know!" I breathed, suddenly uneasy in his presence.

He touched my face again, this time only fingers lightly holding my chin. There was no overspill of consciousness.

"Why are your eyes sea-color?" His voice grew boyish, wondering. "I thought all Other eyes were black or brown?"

"Most are," I acknowledged, "for it has been determined that we arise from a limited gene pool whose parameters did not include the emergence of a recessive gene for eye color until we had been on your World some half million years."

He released me roughly, shook his head, disgusted. "You're supposed to blush and fuss and stammer 'Why, what a flatterer you are!' " he said, pouting, his voice a cutting falsetto. It dropped back into his own deep register: "You can't all be as passionless as they say! Two things I know completely, Lingri-one, and they are music and women."

With that he tried clumsily to embrace me; I held him out at arms' length, my strength surprising him. "You're scarce a boy."

"Who has had no boyhood." He took his hands from me, held them out in plea. "Would it melt you if I told you I was in the catacombs because I knew you would be there?"

"I was not aware that People boasted Telepaths!" I answered, slipping past him to indicate the interview was over. Its repercussions were just beginning.

In truth, I thought never to see him more. With his father dead, there was nothing to keep me in Droghia. Yet I could not shake free of that brief spark of empathy that had passed between us. Even as I hurried from him, it recurred in echoes. I had seen his boyhood, now I heard his music, no different than I thought it would be—cloying, winsome, meant to please, changing with the wind. Images superceded my vision as I stumbled down darkening streets grown fur-

109

ther dangerous, finding my way downharbor by sheer Othersense.

*"Patriotic tunes as well," I heard him say, saw him
swing idly about on a stool before an ornate keyboard, powdered and brocaded, plucking melodies with one languid
hand, his auditors unseen. "Change the words, depending on
who's in power, save the melody for economy's sake. Thus
both sides think I'm brilliant. Listen. . . ."*

His audience tittered. A wave of nausea passed over me.
Half blind, I clung to a crumbling seawall, fighting for each
breath. The symptoms were familiar, though I had never
experienced them before. The only problem was, it was too
soon.

According to my innate cycle, I should have had a year
or more to answer the mating urge. Yet clearly it was upon
me. What was I to do now?

My biorythmic patterns had been awry since my first
crossover; the healers with all of their sophisticated tests and
instruments had been unable to determine when my first
mating cycle would occur. This made it virtually impossible
for me to bond until the time came, and I had been advised
to return home after Hraregh. Nevertheless, I had gone to
Droghia in search of Redrec, thinking I still had time.

No matter, so far. My skimmer, retrieved from outharbor where I'd berthed it, set on autopilot, since I could not
trust my senses, would have me back at One Greater before
morning. While my less than dignified scramble to the
healer's hospice to request a readout of immediately available bondmates was not the usual Disciplined way of doing
things, I was not Lingri Inept for nothing. Undignified I
might be, but not in any danger, yet.

Other biology dictated: the first cycle of the mating urge
must be answered, or the Other died. There were no excep-
tions.

Expediency, then. Wrapping myself in my travel cloak
against a sudden chill, I waited for the next harbor ferry to

110

take me to my skimmer, masking my urgency. My symptoms were under control, thus far.

I remembered when Dweneth first came upon the file during her studies. Horrified, she had summoned me. She had the file up on her screen when I arrived:

> . . . impossible to separate physical from psychotic symptoms once the urge goes too long unanswered, for they manifest themselves simultaneously, the physical exacerbating the psychotic, and transversely, until the time has passed.
>
> Clinical symptoms include acute pyrexia, hypertension, pulse rates in excess of 500, genital engorgement, convulsions, violent hallucinogenic psychosis, severe neurasthenia, opisthotonos, nephritic and intracranial hemorrhage, and death usually by cardiac occlusion.
>
> Symptoms may endure for as long as seven days with no recourse to effective medication or sedation. The victim must be kept under full restraint, for as long as voluntary movement is possible, she can cause the death of anyone in her path, unwillingly and with no cognizance of her actions. Nothing further can be done except to wait for the inevitable. . . .

Dweneth's face was ashen, her eyes dead at the center. "What can I do?" I asked immediately.

"Erase some knowledge from my mind?" she wondered aloud softly. "Give me back my ignorance?"

"The realm of Telepaths," I offered, watching her grimace, "not mine."

"Horrible!" she breathed. "Truly horrible! The healers

111

tried to warn me before they gave me the access code, but I would be adamant. How was I to treat Others without knowing everything? Now I wish I didn't. I had no idea! Small wonder you wrap yourselves in Disciplines, with this to rule your lives."

"There was a time when this was so," I said, "when it affected every aspect of Other life, and in fact the female principle may have evolved directly from its adverse effects, in that the female of an unrequited bonded pair may sometimes, though rarely, survive where the male will not. However, an unbonded female will inevitably succumb. This was often used as a weapon in the ancient days. Warlords frequently amassed harems, leaving opposing tribes bereft of females in order that unbonded males would die. Nor were all the warlords male. But those days are past, and computational parameters can track each individual's cycle, making bonding more precise and foolproof. . . ."

I stopped. Dweneth was wearing one of those pained looks, which reduced me, however belatedly, to silence.

"All right, the past is past," she answered bleakly. "But still, each of you must go through life knowing that *that* hangs over you if you're not circumspect. Small wonder you bond for pragmatic reasons and have abandoned love! You'll forgive my parochialism for finding it horrible!"

She tugged at the hair at her temples, getting a grip on herself. "What People would do with it if they knew! They could kill you with it, horribly, every one!"

"Not least of an infinity of means," I suggested, "and less practical than most. It would necessitate holding us like zoo specimens to wait out each individual's seven-to-ten-year cycle. The cost in feeding us alone—!"

"And you can joke about it!"

"I must 'joke,' if you will, because it is there. I face the necessity of the mating urge, as does any Other. Sometimes irony is the only response." More than the soul-thread told

112

me of her concern. "Worry not. I shall be bonded long before I need concern myself."

Aboard the harbor ferry out of Droghia, I had sufficient focus to call upon the soul-thread. It answered with some minor discord, nothing critical.

How fare you? I inquired of it.

Busy, came the accustomed answer, followed by a kind of mental scowl. *What's wrong?*

I must ask you to release me, for a time, I answered, reminding her of our mutual agreement.

Certainly, but—

I shut down the thread at my end, while I still had time.

"Sank!" the harbormaster reported when I went to fetch my skimmer. It could only have been sabotage; his smirk confirmed it. There were no Others, no Other skimmers. The radio link established during the First Alliance had been dismantled. I was trapped in Droghia.

There were no *bRi* offshore this time of year; I could not have swum the entire distance with them in this condition if there were. A hired boat would take five weeks; I would be dead in one. There was no recourse but to hide myself, lock myself away where none would ever find me, and so die.

To the catacombs, then, as far below as I could go. A length of rope or chain to bind me, some water for the first onset of fever, before delirium set in. None must see me enter; none would see me leave.

The furthest person from my mind was Redrec.

"He *found* you? How?"

I have answered Joreth's summons to the pilot's cabin, and this is his response to what I tell him of his father. Doubtless my description of the mating urge disquiets him; he is pacing in these close quarters, his head a hair'sbreadth from the ceiling.

113

"He found you!" he says again. "Never mind how; I do not need to know. I see it clear."

"I think not," I say, breathless from reliving my narrative, even after all this time. "You scarcely know the beginning."

"It's clear!" he shouts, against some tumult begun outside—hurried footsteps, a pounding on the door. Joreth pays no heed. "You raped him, else he raped you. I see no third alternative!"

"And you were born of miracle forty years after?" My voice is acid.

"Much can be forgiven in forty years!" my son replies, who is scarce five and twenty. Already diverted by duty, he is undoing the doorlatch.

"Moment!" he calls to those beyond, then finishes with me: "Else some bond of secrecy. He does not reveal what he knows of Other mating, and you reward him with a son."

"Who has such a high opinion of himself—" I begin, but the door is open, and half a dozen Partisans pour in.

"Arrows, flaming arrows out of the fog. Melet outriggers, near as we can tell."

As if to confirm the tale, a spate of flaming arrows leaps at us over the gunwales; one lodges in the doorframe, not too far from my head. Sharp vicious phantoms, heard before they're seen—do they attack the big ship only, or are they playing havoc with the boatlings? We hear cries, but cannot identify them in the fog. Hardly Others, who would not cry out so. What then?

Melet arrows indeed, I confirm, left behind to study the configuration of the feathers as Joreth and his Partisans scramble into some course of action. Melet arrows which are not coated in flaming pitch sometimes hold poison. Does Joreth know this? How am I to find him in this fog?

The Melet were once a warrior People, who retained the panoply of war while deciding not to fight. It was Mantuu's belief that they were an offshoot of their own race interbred with Zanti, for their features resembled both, but studies of their ancient island religion and the employment of isotope dating relative to artifacts indicated that they were more likely the parent race which spawned the latter two.

Their island World, with its simple life-style and conversely complex religious structure—a culture which possessed an advanced calculus and an inordinately accurate astronomy, yet whose fibercloth-clad indigenes had developed neither wheel nor engine, fed themselves upon a simple grain agriculture and what could be harvested from the sea with net and outrigger—nurtured a race which stayed content on a vast archipelago, much as Others did on theirs, until the Droughts.

From 1545 to 1548 P.A., no rain fell in Melet, and the islanders came ashore in Mantuu seeking aid. Mantuu's response was war against the "infidels," who by their lights threatened an already bloated and dying theocracy. The wars ensued for a generation, with Melet seizing coastal lands solely to have access to freshwater springs, and Mantuu periodically gathering enough of a mercenary force to drive them back into the sea. When Droghen-Gerim sailed the straits between the two realms in the year 1562 P.A. on his mission out of OtherWhere, he faced an arrow to the throat from the Shadoward side and a musketball in the belly from the Sunward. Only the fact that neither side had ever seen a Droghian ship so far to Leeward gave them pause, and Droghen-Gerim, master of surprise, passed safely between the two.

The news of Others brought a temporary truce, for Mantuu's ships could not leave harbor to journey to OtherWhere and see the wonders for themselves without Melet outriggers to give them escort. For the journey, at least, the fighting ceased. When, further, Others taught Melet the art of desalinating their ever available seas for the needed fresh water, providing incidentally a lucrative trade in salt to the inlanders of Lamora and Dyr, the islanders, whose astronomy could easily countenance outworlders such as we, and whose immediate problem was now solved, withdrew from Mantuul lands, once more content.

The effect of Others on Mantuu was less salutary. Already an inflexible society founded upon a fixed, erroneous idea, it found its theocentric, flat-World view irrefutably shattered by Others' very existence. Those Mantuul chieftans who came to OtherWhere at Droghen's bidding departed hollow-eyed and shaken; if Others existed, their theology was wrong, and that simply could not be. Muttering into the dark, dispersed upon the wind, preyed upon in their weakness by their Plalan neighbors, Mantuul society virtually ceased to exist. Its wiser citizens claimed refuge elsewhere, allowing themselves to be absorbed into the dominant culture. The majority stayed to work their stone-poor wind-scoured land, mumbling the old prayers to a cold clay god, awaiting salvation after death. Their surviving children grew wild in the hills, and it was there that the seeds of Purism first flourished.

Melet had only profited from their knowledge of Others, and had no cause to loathe us.

6

. . . until now.

I make my way forward through the fog despite the arrows, which fly less frequently, at least where I am standing. The hue and cry have given way almost to silence, out of which a single voice declaims. Male, People, elderly, Melet-cadenced, confirming the origin of the arrows; I cannot clearly hear what he is saying. The fog seems to be lifting, revealing myriad shapes in the water below. Our many clustered boatlings are being held at bay by Melet outriggers.

Ancient war canoes, by their size and decoration, ships of exile by their decrepitude and the starveling look of their nearly all-male crews. What brings Melet this far to Windward? Nearer, I can hear the old man clear.

'' . . . and 'punge this curse from out our waters, that has poisoned our fish and makes our young men forget the old rites, cursed Others!'' He finishes with a flourish of his ropy, wizened spear arm, a trained orator, crack-voiced but still able to carry above a crowd. The ''dragon mark'' down one side of his neck identifies him. For all that the World has altered, Dzilbak the Dragon still rules in Melet, if this is Melet represented here. Perhaps if I can speak to him, out of old times, or instruct Jisra Matriarch, who of a sudden is beside me, we can defuse this situation with no one hurt.

"What shall we do, Lingri-*ala?*" the Matriarch whispers urgently, deferential to my age despite her office. "Instruct me what to do!"

"First watch and listen, WiseJisra," I reply, listening myself as the old man begins a new harangue. "This may not rest in Other hands."

For Dwiri has moved to the forward rail and dares to answer the Melet chief. Her lyric voice is not as loud as Dzilbak's, but it carries to his ears and to his Jemadar's.

"The Jemadar will inform Lord Dzilbak that if he offer proof of Others' poisoning the fish, he may take whatever action he deem necessary . . ."

Who taught her to speak Melet? I wonder, much less to know that commoner never speaks directly to a Melet chief, but to his Jemadar, so that the old man may have time to digest her words before giving his answer back?

" . . . else we suggest that his words are like a fog upon the sea, obscuring what is truly there, and as such we take no offense from them, but do not heed them either."

Call the old man a liar to his face? Be careful, Dwiri-one! I attempt to send this to her, not daring speech. Jisra, who knows no Melet, instinctively stiffens at my side.

Dzilbak seems not to know he is dealing with a Telepath. Perhaps his old eyes cannot see Dwiri's white ones in the fog. I try to send Dwiri everything I know of Melet, only to find she is shielding against me. She is reading Dzilbak's thoughts and has no time for mine.

The old man's prolonged silence signifies contempt. Undaunted, Dwiri answers it.

"We further suggest to Lord Dzilbak that while his time is his own and he is free to squander it in silence, the one who speaks is young and, failing all else, she will outlive him."

Incredibly, the old man chuckles, impressed with Dwiri's cleverness. She has managed simultaneously to pay homage to his age and take him to task for his rudeness. He is shouting again, asking Dwiri if she is young enough to outlive the flight of an arrow? Hearing this, Joreth and some of his Partisans move to surround Dwiri, but she waves them off, watching wry amusement ripple among the men in the outriggers for all their air of desperate grimness. Melet cherish games almost as much as life. Inventors of many of the board games and games of chance the People thrive upon, they are creators too of "think games," which are evolved and stored in the mind and played out in shouted challenges from boat to boat as Melet travel.

But skilled though they are, no People should play mind games with Telepaths.

"Lord Dzilbak insists his quarrel is with Mantuul and Others," Dwiri continues when the amusement has run its course. "How then will he kill me?"

"Clearly you are not Mantuul," Dzilbak's Jemadar answers after some consultation. "But if you are not Other, why do you travel with them?"

"Ask Lord Dzilbak if I should rather travel with Melet, who fire first and ask questions later, and whose grievance is clear in their faces even when they do not speak its true nature?"

There is a stir and controversy among the outriggers. Jisra uses the confusion to suggest to Dwiri that she invite the leaders aboard for a consultation. Shouting that he will not treat with Others, Dzilbak accepts the invitation only when it comes from Dwiri's lips. He and his retinue at last come aboard the great ship under a banner of truce. Only then do they tell their tale of woe.

It begins, as most things do, in extreme simplicity, culminating in the kind of complex chaos only People can create.

Say it begins some years ago, when the first desalination plants donated by Others begin to show signs of wear. Melet lacks the parts to fix them, having been content to allow Others to see to their manufacture and repair. Say this is a time when Others are restricted in their travels, and the Purists' genocide has begun. Say the Droughts return to haunt the Melet, and their incursions on what is left of Mantuu are renewed.

History repeats itself, with variations, most of these originating with the Purists. Melet males leave the islands, partly to seek work, partly to seek Otherlore and to learn how to repair their own machinery. Purists accuse them as "Other-lovers" and descend upon Melet islands, killing their firstborn, depriving the survivors of water. The surviving Melet, bitterness in their hearts, have no choice but to leave their islands, hating Others, bound they know not where.

Long before he mentions water, Dzilbak and his People are offered fresh from our supply, and food as well; being Melet, they accept only the water, and only so much as they need. Jisra sees to those in the outriggers, and soon all are refreshed.

"Surely these are not all Lord Dzilbak's People?" Dwiri asks solemnly, when the old man finishes declaiming at last. The corners of his mouth are caked and dry, his rheumy eyes half open; clearly he is ill.

"Stars' mercy, no!" the Jemadar replies. "Lord Dzilbak wishes you to know that those you see are only some of us. The rest"—he gestures—"wait beyond the fog, to know if we have vanquished you and seized your ship and goods."

"Which obviously you have not." For the first time Dwiri turns her white eyes full on the Jemadar; I hear him gasp. "If I tell Lord Dzilbak that we too are in exile, what will he do?"

Our status should surprise no one who knows of World

120

events. Yet there is renewed conference, carried on in whispers between the Dragon and his Jemadar, with sometime calculations from lesser advisors in the retinue.

"How do you read this, Lingri-one?" Jisra ventures, rapt and helpless, as Dzilbak will speak to no Other. Joreth has joined us and is listening also.

"I can only surmise that they are weighing our fate against their own," I reply, noting how Dzilbak now stares openly at Dwiri, as if staring at a ghost. "What decision they will reach I cannot know; it is long since I have traveled among Melet."

"When was that?" Joreth asks, surprised, whispering as are we all.

I will not satisfy him. "A question for you first, one I have asked before and not had answered: have you weapons aboard?"

Again he does not answer, merely shakes his head and indicates the Jemadar, who has begun to speak again.

"My Lord Dzilbak has arrived at a decision, and it is this. . . ." This Jemadar always speaks in measured, even tones. No foreknowledge of his lord's intent bleeds over into his speech. The man intrigues me; neither old nor young, iron-haired as many Melet are in middle age, his sharp-featured face a study in almost Other dignity.

"If we let you pass," he is saying, "we seal our own doom and possibly your own, for if we do not seize your ship, we lack the strength and resource to continue our own journey to some safe shore. Thus, we die. Further, should we sail far enough to encounter friendly People, why should we not parlay our knowledge of your whereabouts for food and precious water and our own survival? Lord Dzilbak sees no alternative but that one of us must die."

Joreth stirs at that, about to slip below. I grope for his arm to stay him, too late. Discarding dignity, I seize his ankle; anything to stay him.

"No farther!" I hiss into his nearer ear, drawing myself

121

up to stand beside him, his arm now in my grip. If we disturb the conference, no matter; I am preventing greater disturbance hereafter. "Before you take a further step, remind yourself of this: who taught you fending?"

He seems amused. "Why, you did—no, wait, don't do this now. Fend against me, in front of *these?* How do you know where I'm going?"

"It takes no Telepath to know your mind!" I release his arm, and he goes nowhere. Dwiri is speaking.

"I ask Lord Dzilbak: in the Losers' Game, which is the stronger, two exiled forces opposing, or both joined together?"

The Dragon's silence is eloquent this time. His rheumy eyes still scan Dwiri's determined face. Only she and I know whose lineaments he seeks there. Amazingly, he does not relay his next thought to the Jemadar, but stares direct at Dwiri and grunts: So?

"We know of a place, alien to us both. Harsh of climate, but elsewise free of enemies," Dwiri says softly. "Come with us. Join us, that we all may live."

A most extraordinary thing happens. Dzilbak rises shakily to his feet, waving off his retinue. He approaches Dwiri, squatting before her like a commoner, and speaks.

"Who are you who dares to speak to the Dragon so brashly, and whose face is it you wear?"

"Her name was Dweneth," Dwiri answers simply, "I am her child."

Dzilbak nods, his curiosity satisfied. It is to Dweneth that he owes his life.

During the Drought Wars, the males of both sides agreed upon one thing: a woman raped by the enemy was defiled; a child born of rape was to be stoned to death along with its mother. Odd how two disparate cultures, sprung from the same root but holding no single thing else in common, could arrive simultaneously at such a conclusion, but these were People. Trust Dweneth to try to put things right.

"They'd come to me under cover of night, some having walked so far their feet were bleeding, most near collapse from duress and fear. I couldn't save them all!"

Her tale was months past and a hemisphere away, yet fresh to her as she told it.

"There was one village where all the males had fled out of cowardice, leaving the women and children. Every female from eight to eighty fell victim to the Mantuu mercenaries when they came. When the men returned, the women were turned out upon the road. Some leapt from the sea cliffs, some dragged themselves off into the woods to birth and die, leaving their infants to the heljacks."

I listened; it was my role. She swept her tumult of curls back from her harried face, clutching her temples as she did to calm herself.

"We'd been told the war was over; I was only passing through. On my way to Dyr, in fact, for Cwala's youngest's coming-of-age rite, for which I never did arrive. I doubt Cwala's forgiven me to this day. But stay I did, sheltering those who came to me—some as young as twelve—birthing their babies in secret, smuggling them out to foster families, some even to OtherWhere. I had a foreigner's immunity, you see, and Melet respect healers. But there were no resources to feed them all, and the arrivals never seemed to end. So when I yanked this last one free after a daylong labor—he was a breach birth, if you please, cauled and jaundiced, with the cord wrapped round his neck and scrawny as a rail fowl—I flipped the cord up over his head and there it was. The birthmark, or dragon's-mark, as Melet call it. It meant he was god-touched, and destined to be king. I felt inspired."

" 'And it came to pass that the flame-haired one, named Healer, beloved of Xcha despite her outland birth, did mount

123

the steps of the Pyramid to challenge the Judges, the Dragon in her arms,' " I recited, and she gawked at me.

"What? How . . . ?"

I showed her one of the countless cassettes in my kit.

"Scarce a year ago, and already you are legend. Melet's chief harper sang it for me at the Harvest festival, in honor of Others 'for bringing the waters back to Melet.' It had nothing to do with me."

"So much for cultural integrity!" Dweneth snorted, embarrassed and pleased at once. "It wasn't half so grand while it was happening!"

I reached for my recorder. "Tell me your version, then, and I shall incorporate the two."

She snatched at the recorder, shutting it off. "For your ears only, and that's enough of it. Let them repeat it till they wear the corners off it and mayhap they'll forget my name."

"I doubt they will, but go on."

"For one thing, he was colicky, and his mother had no milk. Further, he pissed all over me before we'd got halfway to town. I was seeking a wet-nurse foremost, but when I found myself in the Street of the Pyramid of Judges—well, what would you have done? I climbed the steps, bluffed my way past the guards, who were gawking at my tits and wondering was the brat mine, and sailed straight up to the Judges' Banc with the squalling hellion in my arms. It was then I remembered that I'd been reared a Player maid."

I said no word, envisioning it. Did I see her blush?

"I'll admit I camped it. Raised him up above my head where they could not miss the dragon's-mark, and shouted out his story loud enough to bring eavesdroppers from the halls. If this were the result of rape, I demanded, how dared they stone the rest?

"I took an awful chance, I see that now," she admitted with a sigh. "After all, they might have killed him."

"And you."

Dweneth shrugged. "But as it was, ancient omen out-

124

weighed more recent prejudice. He was god-touched, destined to be king, and that's what saved him."

"And in saving him, you saved countless like him," I concluded. She never tired of touting my accomplishments; let me do as much for her.

Again she shrugged. "And Others saved all of Melet, with a simple saline filter! Take that line of reasoning to its fullest extent, and you could as easily say Others destroyed Mantuu by refusing to vanish when the Mantuul chiefs yelled 'Boo!' Instrumentality, as your grandmother would have said." She sighed, grown teary-eyed with the burden of it. "Oh, how I do miss Loriel!"

"And so you made a king and saved a kingdom," I said when her silence had gone on too long. "What happened after that?"

She waved a hand, dismissed it: I don't want to talk about it! "I had to leave!" she answered all the same. "Slip away like a felon and nearly drown—I've little skill with boats! But there were rumors of honors and gold and ceremonies, and a kind of benevolent captivity for the Great Healer thereafter. They'd never have let me breathe!"

She breathed deeply then, as if she feared she might have forgotten how.

"My sources tell me Dzilbak's growing like a dragon. That he walked at nine months and spoke full paragraphs at a year. Tell me I can't pick a Melet king!"

" 'Deliverer of Kings, Healer of a Kingdom,' " I tweaked her out of the harper's song.

"Oh, give me strength!" she pleaded. "Don't *you* start!"

I relate this morsel of ancient history to WiseJisra as Dwiri and the Melet continue to confer. If she is to be our emissary from hereon, Jisra needs to know. Someone speaks my name, if only in my mind, and I turn to find Dwiri risen from the

125

meet circle to sweep past me, anxious to speak with me alone. Jisra goes to take her place.

"I had to get away from there!" Dwiri hisses as I steady her, safe in Joreth's cabin. "People wear me out. They sicken me! These silly, petty games they play with life! 'One of us must die,' this Jemadar dares say, as if it were so simple! Let me live with Others, or alone!"

"Yet you managed splendidly," I point out, holding her by the shoulders until she regains her strength. "Dweneth would be pleased to know her offspring is a diplomat."

"Nothing to it, with a race whose minds are so accessible!" she sneers, shaking me off. She turns on me. "She faked that 'dragon's-mark,' in case you'd like to know. Sulfuric acid poured on a newborn's neck—small wonder he cried so much! Don't think my mother the saint the histories painted her!"

Whether it is true or not, it oddly pleases me; if I were not Other, I would laugh. Dweneth's spirit tweaks me still, even from beyond death. Not merely Deliverer of Kings, but Creator of Kings—ah, Dweneth!

"Tell me Dzilbak objects to being king!" I chide this arrogant, untried Telepath. "He wears the burden well, and elsewise would have died. The ruse, if such it was, saved hundreds."

"While preying upon the primitive superstitions of a backward race!"

"Backward? Their astronomy rivaled Others', and without a telescope. Would you prefer they die as a race than live in backwardness?" I am breathless again; this brat would try anOther's patience. "On a more immediate topic, Dwiri Telepath, what will Dzilbak do?"

She seems amazed at my ingenuousness. "Why, accompany us, of course. Having heard my reasoning, how could he not?"

Even as she says it, we can hear the Jemadar announce it.

* * *

Fog yields to drizzle laced with sleet; Dzilbak's bare-chested warriors shiver stoically in their grass cloaks, reluctantly accepting extra garments from us. Together ship, outriggers, and boatlings take the heading the Jemadar indicates; we cannot help but note that the *bRi* have abandoned us again. Is this only whim, or ancient memory of a time when Melet preyed on them for food?

"Is there food enough?" Jisra wonders, in command of details now that Dwiri has managed the grandiose part and retired. "What of shelter for a People accustomed to more tropic clime? What shall we do if either prove inadequate?"

"If you don't mind that we eat fish, we'll manage," Dzilbak wheezes beside her at the rail, strangely merry, addressing Jisra as an equal. His merriness has good cause; his People are beginning to materialize out of the dissipating fog.

The untrained eye would see only vast extensive mats of indigenous tropical reeds, undulating flotsam, matted and tangled, trailing flowered streamers. A natural form, one would think, some extraneous sargassum originating on nearby islands, rocking with the swells, common enough in these parts that sailors dread its tendrils fouling the rudders, but never any People-made thing.

But the Jemadar, with Jisra's permission, raises Dzilbak's standard on the maintree, and suddenly the reed mats come alive. First a young one's face, then several more, then women's faces and a horde of children's peer out of what seems only piled refuse in the center of each sometimes ship-long reed mat. A ululating cry sets up, rejoicing.

The mats stretch almost to the horizon. There are nearly as many of Dzilbak's People as of ours.

The old man climbs spryly down to the nearest outrigger to harangue his own with the news of our alliance. The practicalities are just beginning.

Melet will fish for their own sustenance, and the question of cold seems not to trouble them. Our greatest difficulty will be speed. Without the *bRi*, how shall we move these reed mats any faster than the current?

"The *bRi* will return," Joreth says, as confident of them as Dwiri was of Melet. "But we must know the weather. Where is Peria?"

The child is our most reliable weather reader, and she is soon aboard, handed gently up by the Melet who, once they learn her function, treat her with awe. Even Others, who have seen it done for millenia, watch solemnly as Peria takes her readings. She must taste the wind and listen to the air, measure the humidity with her flesh; her willowy small frame becomes a living barometer. At length she closes her eyes and listens, opens them finally with unsettling news.

"Storms, Joreth-*al*," she reports, and we can see them in her eyes. "A true blizzard, with violent winds and extensive drifts of sleet and snow. There is also much free-floating ice before the fjords. The galleon by itself might weather it, but these . . ." She everts her hands in eloquent Othergesture to indicate the mats and boatlings.

"What is your recommendation, WisePeria?" Jisra asks solemnly.

"I know little of sailing, and less of People's tolerance for extreme weather, Jisra Matriarch," the child replies. "Yet, were it possible, we should remain passive. Lash together and ride out the storm. This is my opinion."

Jisra confers with Joreth. "Will this not bring us into the open sea too near daybreak?"

Joreth muses over this but does not answer until Peria is safely out of earshot.

"We'd be naked in the full of day for our final run to the fjords," he begins, then laughs bitterly. " 'Run'? How shall we move at all with this floating flotsam? We'll be helpless to anything that passes from the air."

"Only if you harbor some sentimental and unDisciplined attachment to your sailing ship," an unfamiliar voice suggests.

Once he had completed his duty as translator for the Dragon, no one expected the Jemadar to speak more, much less to use the words of Other Discipline. Joreth frowns.

"What's that supposed to mean?" My son was never noted for his manners.

"Observe," the Jemadar says, and gestures to an outrigger below.

In a twinkling the canoe has slipped beneath the reed mat like a child beneath a coverlet. Two women and a half-grown boy scramble gleefully out of the center of the mat, straw bits and flowers in their hair, to lift the further edge and lap it over the nearest of our boatlings, hiding it as well.

Soon every mat dweller has done the same. The effect is quite extraordinary. Nothing can be seen but an endless sea of reeds, their trailing ends deceptively concealing baited fish lures, which the women occasionally free of the catch as we drift. Even Joreth is impressed.

"How long can they remain like that?"

"Indefinitely," the Jemadar replies, as at his next signal all emerge from their hiding places, the People laughing at their accomplishment. "It is actually quite warm beneath. How do you suppose we got this far?"

Only the great ship stands out, tree-tall, undisguisable.

"All our supplies are aboard," Joreth protests the unvoiced question. "Our books and chronicles, and what survives of record."

The Jemadar shrugs eloquently: which is more important, things or People?

"We shall see" is all Joreth will say.

With each outrigger and every boatling protected beneath a mat and the big ship turned to meet the wind, we may yet survive the nearing storm. The wind picks up; the great ship creaks, anticipating. We have much work to do.

129

The wind howls unceasingly somewhere above our heads. Peria, Yarel, Aloyi, and I shelter beneath a reed mat, which also houses an extended Melet family of eight. It is warm here in this manner of low tent with ocean for a floor. An occasional trickle of melted snow seeps through the seams where two mats join, but overall we could hardly be more comfortable on land.

At first I played the translator as we twelve shared a hurried meal, calling upon the little bit of Melet I once knew. Out of deference for my age or only my halting, weary tongue, the Melet elders have dismissed me, commanding that I rest. The youngsters continue to exchange facile lexicons with the flexibility of their kind while we adults doze.

I lie beneath a grass cloak at one end of a Melet outrigger, fitting my bony frame to its sheltering contours. The canoe rocks; I doze and dream of Redrec.

"You raped him," is Joreth's conclusion, "else he raped you. There is no third alternative."

A parent's privacy is predicated upon how much her grown son thinks he needs to know.

"He died a drunk!" my son accused me as I prepared to descend to the Melet canoe below. "Unfulfilled, embittered . . ."

Must he presume to wrest some explanation from me in the midst of wind and snow? His face was livid in the roaring dark; Joreth had always lacked a sense of time or place.

"He always drank," I answered softly; let him catch my words above the wind. "It was his way. Though never to excess, I think, until he met me. Is that what you must hear, my son? Then hear it! Hear too that it is my fault, if you like, but leave it there and leave me here—in peace!"

The onset of a blizzard is no time to try explaining the impossibility of the life Redrec and I shared, the however many years of love and loathing interlayered one on one, intertwined so tightly that the knot could never be untied, and neither could sever it. How can I explain what I do not understand myself?

"You've never asked me how he died!" Joreth continues, straining over the rail to be heard. Does he think one or both of us will not survive this, that he needs to do this now?

"Which means I do not care? Or that there has not been time?" I shout back. The outrigger beneath me rocks dangerously; the warrior it belongs to waits, inordinately patient, for me to finish babbling to this madman on the deck above in our rasping, fricative-riddled tongue. "Perhaps I only do not wish to know!"

I grasp the edge of the mat beside the warrior and nod to him, dismissing my son. Let me, Joreth, son too young to comprehend, cherish the image of the whole man I once knew, rather than confront the broken spirit who was Redrec at the end. How much of what he became truly is my fault, and how much only circumstance and Redrec?

.

In the deepest regions of the Droghian catacombs, I walled myself about in total darkness and prepared. Bones among bones, once the fever finished with me, I would not be found for centuries, if at all, and then be indistinguishable from the bones about me, save that they were tucked up neatly in their sacred niches while I would lie twisted and obscene upon the floor. Say to the curious that I was dislodged and shaken loose by the thunder of machinery during Droghen-Thrasim's building craze. These were the few rational thoughts which lingered as the fever claimed me. Awash in a lake of flickering green flame, I burned.

With the fever came pain, indescribable, beginning in the joints and inner organs. Simultaneously, hallucinations—lurid, sexual, fantastic and bizarre. Small wonder Others preferred to meditate, arbitrate, and argue, to study, research, analyze, debate, and contemplate, to labor in any wise rather than confront this fixed, unmanageable, unalter-

131

able aspect of our nature. Small wonder we avoided it, fought it, until we must submit or die.

Telepaths, it is said, are given to know their own impending deaths; the rest of us are seldom quite so fortunate. Yet I had Othersense to apprise me of the passage of time, and a textbook memory to assure me that my symptoms progressed precisely as they ought. Given this, I knew I had six days and several hours more to live.

But how much longer would I know I was alive?

His voice cut through my fevered dreams, slaking them while it also fanned the flames.

"Well, well, well!"

At first I thought him fond hallucination, for I had not yet learned to affix that voice to this hale and upright personage I saw framed against the sudden light. The light was torchlight, blinding, quickly shaded by his hand. The personage was Redrec, kneeling over me, young and alive.

Redrec, virile, eager, more than willing to assuage my difficulty once he intuited its nature, even if it killed him in the process.

His hands were fire on my face, his fingers tracing flame along my breasts, his whispered kisses liquid in my Other ears. How had he found me, how?

"You left a trail that phosphored in my brain," he whispered between kisses. "When we touched, I *saw* you, as much as you saw me. I could not but follow you."

As I had seen him in my mind, so I saw him seeing me, understanding what I was, where I had gone and why. As he trailed lambent kisses down my breasts and up my thighs, he learned me, learning Others, taking on my plight as if it were his own. Instinctively, I tried to stop him.

"Danger . . . " I tried to warn, tried to push him back while I longed to cling to him. My tongue thickened, speech became impossible. "Grave danger, Redrec, for you. . . . "

He closed my mouth with kisses, prying my rigid fingers

132

from his chest and trailing his tongue along each one, pushing at me where I tried to push him back. I could not resist. I wanted life; Redrec wanted me. Let it substitute for bonding, until the time had passed. I would free him after that.

Blind with fever, I could not trust my flesh, which told me it was naked to his touch, as he to mine. He had made a kind of bed of our spread cloaks upon the chill stone floor. He touched, I thrilled, and felt him thrill as well, through me. When we joined we both cried out, he as if I burned him.

"Seagod's mercy, you're on fire!" he cried, withdrawing quickly, but further tantalized by what he felt. He entered again and we reached together, more and more, until he was exhausted and I healed. The fever ebbed, leaving helpless trembling in my limbs, but I would live.

Then it was I who tended him, caressing his pale, hirsute body with fingers lacking feeling, straightening limbs tumbled insensate into sleep, cradling his tousled head on a pillowed shirt, covering him with an overlapping cloak.

He had brought candles as well as the torch, and by their light I found my own clothes. Not rent and scattered in haste as I had thought, but neatly folded and with no fastener damaged. He had removed them with the greatest care and tenderness before he mated me—mated in the true sense, fitting himself to me and me to him in spite of my condition.

"Two things I know completely, Lingri-one, and they are music and women," he had said. But what did it truly mean?

Our minds had touched and he had followed me—for pity's sake, or only because female was female to his adolescent's need? Either way, I owed him my life.

Shivering more from recent nearness to death than from physical cold, I dressed and slipped beneath the cloak beside him, careful not to touch his manchild's body, though I could feel his heat.

I woke to his tongue exploring my lips, and my named whispered.

"Lingri?"

I sat upright, full of explanations. "Redrec—"

"You could not have been virgin, to love like *that!*" he said in awe. "I have never felt the like! I'll not ask you who the Others were—assuming they were Others—only what further skills you know that we may try. At once, if you like."

He leaned on one elbow, touched my hair. I scrambled to my feet.

"Redrec, what you—what we . . . experienced, was a physiological symptom, nothing more. By rights it should have been met by a bonded Other. It was a passion bred of the need to mate, a necessity of my Other blood."

"Whatever it was, it was lovely!" he mused, shaking off the cloak, standing easily against the guttering candlelight, secure in his pallid nakedness. "Whatever the details, whatever you may call it, let us do it again, for I love it. As I love you."

"You love the passion," I demurred. "The awareness of the Other's mind. You cannot love me."

"You're shy," he said, misunderstanding, suddenly all tenderness. His hands were on my face, which had grown cold. "Embarrassed by what happened. Mayhap you were a virgin, and I was rude. Mayhap such passion frightens you. I understand."

"You cannot, you do not—"

Once again he silenced me with kisses; I stirred within, a remnant of the fever lingering, but held myself and did not respond.

"I see," he said, taking his hands away. He searched for his clothes, began to dress. "I was crude to talk of Others. You're offended. Now that your fever's cooled, I can wait until you want it again."

"You do not understand," I said, extinguishing all but a single candle. "This thing might have killed you. Even now it binds us in ways you cannot comprehend, and I must somehow set you free."

"You could grow me with this mind-touch thing. I felt it in your mind."

"As a flower can be forced to bloom in Freezeseason, by keeping it indoors?" It was one of the things I most feared. "No, Redrec-one. You must grow yourself."

"Or we could grow together. You're frigid when you're not with me."

"Oh, manchild with the ego of a boy! 'Frigid'! How simple it seems to you! That which cannot be acted upon is better deferred until it can." He started to speak, I stopped him with a gesture. "Answer me this: would you, could you, wait seven years more to do this again?"

"Well, no, but—"

"There you are!"

He had brought me to his rooms, where we had a kind of supper, more because he needed it than I. In the aftermath of fever, I did not wish to eat. An evening, a night, and most of a day had been consumed by my fever and our passion.

Our passion, no denying it. But I had done a reckless, reprehensible thing, and now must answer for it.

What about what you want . . . what you want? Dweneth-in-my-mind resounded, the old insoluable argument.

"Who is Dweneth?" Redrec asked suddenly, gobbling down a good meat pie while I battled nausea. He had a courtier's manners, and wiped gravy on his frilled sleeves, decked out as he was for performance later at the Acting Governor's request.

"Who is Dweneth?" he asked again, as if I had not heard him. How many tendrils of my mind still clung to his?

"A—friend," I said. "Why do you ask?"

"Not anOther?"

"No." I all but smiled.

135

He wiped his mouth, poured more wine.

"When you—when we—came the first time, I thought I'd reached the deepest part of you. It scared me. We came again, and I went deeper, but each time sensed there was some further depth where I could not go. In one of these I found two names. Dwenth was one; Lerius the Other, I think."

"Indeed," I answered. "There are many layers of an-Other's mind you cannot share. These were but the sentinels. There are some so deep you could not get out again."

He drank the wine and poured some more. How much did he drink, I wondered, and how often?

"We came again, and I went deeper. Again, and deeper still, until I thought I'd never surface, never get out the way I'd entered. Your body, yes, but your mind more capturing, and yet—"

"Be grateful for your youth and your naivete!" I snapped, shamed again at how uncontrolled I had been, how far I had let this go. "Else I might have killed you!"

That stopped him, as it stopped me. If he was frightened, so was I: he by the prospect of his own death by such means, I by my sudden, excessive candor. Was this still the fever, which made me so free with the forbidden? Dweneth, as usual, had been right. What could unscrupulous People make of this if they knew?

Redrec sipped his wine slowly this time, considering.

"Meaning Othersex is that insatiable? Whew!" He pretended to examine his person carefully; the wine had made his eyes glaze. "Well, so what? I'm here, with all parts functioning, though some are a little sore. What of you, my Lingri-one? Some parts raw from unaccustomed exercise?"

He wanted me to strike him; I stopped him with a glare.

"Be angry, Lingri, do," he taunted, winsome as a puppy. Most women would find him irresistible in this mood; he could not believe I didn't. "How I would love to see your rage. It would be magnificent!"

"If I am angry, it is with myself, and you will never see it!"

"It's my father, isn't it?" he demanded out of nowhere. "Whenever you say or think my youth—'manchild,' 'puppy,' 'boy'–it's Redrec Elder that you're thinking of. Say you never loved him, and I'll tell you Others lie."

"That is not what stops me here. Nor did I love him as you understand the term."

"Yet you loved him, as anOther can," he persisted.

Had he found his father's presence interwoven in my consciousness, in one of those layers breached before he found Dweneth, Lerius, all those I held dear? Did he persist in misunderstanding what his father had been to me? Yet one more reason why I could not bond with this manchild in any wise. Our mind-touch was fading; I could feel it being torn loose, tendril by tendril, by his growing rage.

"Would that I could rip him from your mind!" he shouted suddenly. "How do I rip him from your mind?"

He had reached across to grasp my temples, squeezing, as if to crush his father's memory out of me, or only crack my skull. I fended lightly, sending him just out of arm's reach, but it did not stop him.

" 'Redrec, Redrec,' " he chanted, as if imitating me, some me he had never heard, for I had never spoken thus. Tears were running down his face. "Thus you cried out in your passion, but it was *he*, not I you savored. . . . "

Redrec! I wanted to send down the fading mind-touch, but thought the better of it.

" . . . not the first of his castoffs I've had—it was how I learned. But you were special. . . . wanted you to be my own . . . rip him from your mind, your body, scrape him off your skin—"

He tried to score me with his nails. Again I fended, harder. He struck the wall where it ended beneath a sloping roof, bumping his head. How badly had I hurt him?

"Golden skin . . . " he murmured, shaking his head to

137

clear his vision, wiping his eyes, clutching his arm where I'd grasped it. My strength did not surprise him, after what he and I had done. "Otherskin is golden. Soft to touch, and warm. Hard to believe what's under it's not blood but ice."

"Redrec," I began. "Your father—"

Something crashed behind me in a scattering of glass. A paving stone had flown through the casement, narrowly missing us both. A second followed, and Redrec's name was shouted from below. Knocking glass shards from the splintered window frame, he showed himself to the several persons in the street below.

"What's amiss?" he bellowed in his father's voice.

"Ye've anOther up there. We seen yer bring her in. Turn her over to us and ye'll not get hurt!"

"Brok'smen," he whispered aside to me. "Don't know yet the war is over.

"How dare you challenge me?" he roared back. "Break my windows, disturb my neighbors—do you not know who I am?"

"Aye, Redrec'sSon," came the answer; I could feel him wince. "Don't matter who ye are; ye've broke the law. 'Consorting wi' Others,' it says clear. Hand her over or we'll come up to get her!"

"Hold on!" I heard him laugh. "Let me get her dressed first!"

He closed the shattered casement on their ribald laughter, turning to me with a shrug.

"Have to preserve my reputation, no matter what it does to yours. Here, then."

He touched a panel built into a cupboard, and it opened to a rope ladder leading down to darkness and the chill dank air of catacombs. Like his father, Redrec knew the Under-City well. He saw my face and laughed.

"Did you think I'd hand you over to them? What, then?"

"Perhaps better you did than proliferate a fiction."

138

"A 'fiction'? Oho, still playing the virgin? Who then was it that I fucked but yesterday?"

"Not I, apparently," I answered coolly, "for by your word, I was busy fucking your father."

He took my arm, gently this time. "Crude again. I'm sorry. But you see the influence you have on me. How much I need you. But for now we've no time for niceties. This passage will take you, by what means you'll have to figure out, to the old granaries back of the Great House. From there you'll doubtless encounter sentries. Tell them to bring you to the Acting Governor, and show them this." He removed one silver earring, set it in my ear. "Tell the Governor to see you're better dressed. Don't want to show me up when I perform tonight."

"What of them?" I nodded toward the casement.

He shrugged. "They'll grow impatient, then storm up. I'll tell them you used sorcery to fly above the rooftops."

"Sophistry and further fictions," I began as he held the ladder.

He kissed my forehead, furtive. "If it saves both our carcasses. They'll not harm me; I still have some charm left, but not enough for both of us. Go!"

Excerpt: Testimony of Lingri Monitor in Closed
Council
(Code 161514611818: T-Y1042, sealed file)

Healer: *Finally, based upon physical symptoms as described by the Subject, and evidence of medscans upon
her return to One Greater, we conclude that her testimony is accurate. Given the advanced state of the
Throes, in propinquity with a cooperative male of an
equally sentient and, as it happens, primitively empathic species, the events the Subject describes would
almost invariably have occurred as she describes them.*

Adjudicator: *Statisticians have provided us with a permutational variable of .4711 on either side of the curve
of the actual event, which we deem acceptable. Let the
record so indicate. Healer, your summation?*

Healer: *We conclude that since the Subject acted
within Discipline, given the circumstances, and she
could not have anticipated the arrival of the male, she
sustains no culpability for the event. Further, in that
she attempted to warn the subject male of his danger
suggests her behavior within the Throes to have been
exemplary.*

Adjudicator: *As a matter of record, had the male not
been as sexually responsive as he proved, what might
have been the parameters of the outcome?*

XenoSociologist: *(interjecting) Their males do prove re-
markably resilient in this regard, at least in youth.*

Adjudicator: *Granted. But for the sake of accuracy?*

Healer: (consulting compuscreen) Depending upon the depth of the Throes, possibilities range from a potentially fatal exhaustion of the male to subsummation of the Subject by the fever, to direct homicidal impact directed toward the male, resulting from intracranial hemmorhage and the Subject's subsequent insanity.

XenoSociologist: That is, of course, neglecting to consider the historical aggressiveness of the male of this particular species, who would reasonably be expected to defend himself from such attack, with possible homicidal impact upon the Subject.

Adjudicator: Therefore one may conclude that the event was minimally traumatic to both participants, as well as to their respective cultures. Let us now to the events which follow. Lingri-ala, with deference to the discomfiture with which this testimony may have visited you thus far, we must inquire of you why you chose the particular course of action you did next, as opposed to several alternatives which might have seemed more desirable.

Lingri: Having made my escape from Redrec's chambers by his aid, I might logically have kept on going, fleeing Droghia as I was and however I might. But as it seemed to me, within the context of the time and place, so abrupt an action might have proved more detrimental than the one I chose.

Adjudicator: Please explain.

Lingri: Had I thus vanished into the night, I might have been rendered, in Redrec's young and ingenuous mind, as a Woman of Mystery, a recurring figure in the popular romances of that country, whose inevitable return

141

to the Lover is requisite to the narrative line of the genre. Succinctly, it was my intention to sever my connection with Redrec as thoroughly as possible, thus giving him no cause to anticipate my return. Further, as my original purpose in Droghia was to record as much of its literature as I could, and this purpose had been largely unfulfilled when the mating urge overtook me, and as I interpreted the political climate in light of Droghen-Thrasim's overthrow, I assumed there would be no further opportunity, beyond that night. Therefore, I followed Redrec's instructions, and remained, that I might finish all which I had begun.

7

Droghia's Acting Governor wore a face I knew, though it was her raucous laughter I knew first.

"So he's giving away his earrings, is he?" Renna fondled the one I'd presented to her in one plumpish, gone-soft hand. "I'll have you know I gave him these. Enameled 'em myself, back when I was still a starving artist. There's gratitude, giving it to you!"

The Huntress Queen had always looked askance at me, sensing something alien long before she knew. Not even Mantuul loathed Others as much as she.

"Some of my patrons, now," she wheezed, resettling her soft backside on the cushions of a singed and salvaged First Seat, while I remembered the wiry hunter who would sling one leg over the arm of the Second Seat when she was Droghen-Gerim's mistress, and who could ride a *guravek* bareback for weeks, "are far kinder to the 'vek-greased waif who called herself the Queen of Lamora and earned her meat with shortbow and betimes with paintbrush. Aren't ye?"

She fluttered her free hand at those assembled, Droghia's surviving wealthy elite, who paid her desultory court here in someone's borrowed mansion, if only because her hunters had manpower and skill enough to cow the likes of Brok'smen.

"It's these have made me Acting Governor, until my eldest's reached majority."

I had seen Renna's eldest male child skulking about the place, a bearish lad with his mother's manners, about Redrec's age. So this was to be the next Droghiad, with Renna pulling his strings? Such an alliance between Lamora and Droghia would seal the borders of both nations against Others completely.

"The lad presumes too much!" Renna informed me confidentially, meaning Redrec, handing me back the earring. "Well enough, I'll let you through the borders, but not because of him! Say it's because I'm sick at the sight of you, or perhaps because I owe Dweneth one. How is she keeping in your alien country? Have you turned her into one of you yet?"

"She is no longer in OtherWhere, nor has been for ten years," I answered. "Once she became a healer, she went to Kelibesh, to establish a hospice the mirror image of the one you and her brother Brok between you shut down here in Droghia."

"And you've not seen her since?" Renna stared at me, owlish, whether at the thought of her fellow ragamuffin wearing the dignity of a healer, or at the separation of a friendship she'd always resented for supplanting, as she thought, her own. "How came you—"

Her question was lost in a great uproar from the antechamber, where applause and stamping and cries of "Redrec, Redrec!" let us know the cause. Renna pulled me to her with one red-nailed, flaccid hand.

"The tide turns at thirteen-hour," she whispered rancidly. "See you're on the canals by then, I don't care what boat. If the sun finds ye this side of the border, I'll not be responsible!"

"Understood," I answered. Redrec was among us.

* * *

He was resplendent, his hair done in ringlets to his shoulders, his new-shaved face as fresh as any girl's. He flirted, clowned, lapped up the adulation as he played—four instruments by turns, and also conducted a small chamber orchestra and a soprano he had handpicked himself. I wondered if he'd picked her for her singing.

I recalled the pallid music once played in the Great House, usurped by the soaring, glorious sounds that Redrec Elder had brought back from his UnderCity exile. What I heard this night was neither pallid nor did it soar; it was the shallow, facile output of a keen natural talent suffocating beneath indolent artifice, exactly as I'd heard it in Redrec's mind.

Nevertheless, I recorded every piece, my ubiquitous Other recorder hidden in a pocket of the gaudy formal frock Renna's wardrobers had found for me, my ubiquitous Other ears equally hidden by a lacy hairnet that was all the rage. The gown was a good brocade, but neither new nor clean, and reeked of its previous, unwashed wearer; the hairnet teemed with lice. The evening's entertainment was little better in its trend toward tawdry decadence.

Redrec pointedly caught my eye at every interstice; when he changed instruments, for instance, or when one needed tuning. At least he did not speak to me or draw the crowd's attention toward me. I returned his gaze evenly; having said I would attend his performance, I would, but nothing more.

Was I not supposed to recognize it when he substituted one of his father's keyboard compositions for his own? While I might not know this particular piece, the style was unmistakable. Seeing that I knew it, Redrec ducked his head and blushed, deliberately misplaying several bars, to his audience's dismay. Poor boy, he meant well, but he was not his father. And as it had once long ago, Redrec Elder's music still

145

could make me weep. Easing through the press of bodies, I left the salon to seek the night air on a balcony.

Redrec found me, as I knew he would; some fading resonance of our joining lingered still, bitter, rueful. He did not yet know how deeply he was wounded by what we'd done; what I was about to do next would wound him further, and he would feel it at once. There was no alternative. Better he should hate me than think he still could love me, still believe his love could turn my distance into something else.

"What did you think of my performance?" He was flushed and breathless, soaked through with sweat. "Be honest, now; you can't hurt me, Lingri-one."

An unfortunate choice of words. I gathered myself and faced him.

"I thought . . . nothing of it. It inspired no thoughts that I can share with you."

He grimaced, clamped his jaw, regained control, narrowed his eyes and nodded.

"I see. Try to insult me, think it'll get rid of me. Not so easily gotten rid of. Try again."

"Redrec, hear me: if I had been my conscious self and not subsumed by fever when you found me in the catacombs, I would not have chosen you. It was not I you joined with. It was a fever, an impulse to survive."

"But we were joined before that!" he cried. "When I touched you, on the street!"

"The onset of the fever, nothing more."

"Am I so undesirable?" Incredulous and plaintive.

"No. It is only that I am so undesiring."

He thought that over. "I saved your life."

"For which you have my lifelong gratitude."

"That's pat. And cruel."

"And Other."

"That too." He hung his head. I could feel him grope for words; his roiling emotions buffeted me. Would that I could offer him comfort! I had not comfort to give.

146

The salon, deprived of its entertainment, had begun to search him out, demanding an encore. Failing to find him, the throng broke up into smaller groups of revelers, some of whom began to disport themselves in pairs or threesomes on the grounds beneath our balcony. Distracted by this drunken erotic play, perhaps intent on joining it, Redrec hunched his shoulders suddenly, looked at me, stricken.

"It's no, then, isn't it? Just no. No comfort, no compromise, no explanation?"

"There is anOther explanation, but I suspect you would not accept it."

He drew me to the balcony rail, insisting that I see the revelers, and whispered in my ear. "Am I the first People to bed anOther? Suppose I told of what I've learned?"

His sheer cruelty caused the resonance between us to snap violently; we both felt the pain. He gasped. The crowd's clamor rose from within the salon again, calling Redrec's name. Distracted, he released me, turned to go.

"Will you stay for the second half?"

"Renna wants me out of Droghia."

"Will you at least say good-bye?"

"No."

"No again." He shrugged, a People's gesture, signifying ambivalence, a People's malady. The night's activities drew him in and he was gone. Why was I visited with such sadness?

Up the canals and roundabout to Werthaland—let it not be said I left a trail that Renna could follow—I journeyed afoot for the better part of a year to record the last vestiges of an oral tradition already losing vitality to the printed page, as this once preliterate People acquired Droghia's cast-off handpresses and learned to use them. One of the few of Thrasim's improvements to survive him was the use of electricity, and Droghia was to advance from roller presses to laser printers to microstor before the last authentic Werthan speakbard

147

died. Redrec's latest compositions, laser-printed and translated into fourteen languages including Othertongue, though no less mediocre for their wider proliferation, would taunt me from music shop windows in Zanti only a few years after we had parted.

Contacts in Wertha got me safe passage through the volcano gates into a truce-bound Kwengiis, where Others sojourned freely and in substantial numbers throughout this formerly savage state. In fairness, Kwengiis had had its own parliament even before the Plalan Ascendancy, and its laws for freemen were among the most fair the People knew. But the Kwengii were among the eldest slaveholders, and preyed on any People they thought they might conquer, until they encountered Others.

The First Alliance was clear in the matter of slavery; the Kwengii, ever fascinated with machinery, craved trade with Others enough to set their slaves free. By the time I arrived in Kwengiis, Other trade flourished there, and Other ways were gradually being grafted, however peculiarly, onto Kwengii society.

Thrasim had not been the only one to carry a brainful of ideas out of OtherWhere. Other technology had begun to trickle beyond our Archipelago between the fingers of all the People who returned to the Mainland, excepting Mantuul. By the time of the First Alliance, it was being received with varying degrees of receptivity by eleven tribes of People.

While Others desired no material goods from any of the tribes, it was necessary to Kwengii pride that a somewhat complex form of barter ensue.

What Kwengiis wanted from us was largely gadgetry to improve the material quality of their lives. Disparaging our medicine, for they believed the weak and sick should die, dismissing our lore and learning as "soft scholars' stuff," they scrabbled like greedy children for anything which could improve trade, transportation, mining, or domestic life. They also required our expertise in building the necessary devices, and our presence to assist in running them. For our part, we were as much concerned with ensuring that these things served as engines for peace and prosperity, and that they harmed no one. We took our fee in service.

Thus, Kwengii mine owners turned to harvesting metals with machinery instead of men, returning the land, under our supervision, to its pristine state when they were done. Kwengii cartwrights turned to building skimmers and, while we accepted it, however barbaric, as their way, consigned their draft beasts to wholesale butchery. Kwengii housewives now had automated servitors to clean their dwellings and do their laundry and kitchen chores. In exchange, Kwengiis "donated" its slaves and indentured serviles to us in OtherWhere.

The benefit was the abolition of slavery in Kwengiis. The detriment was a deluge of weeping, disoriented kitchen drudges, chimney sweeps, mine serfs, and stableboys arriving by sail in steerage, for they were terrified of skimmers, in a land where they knew not what doom awaited them. Resettling these lost ones, where we could, among their own People proved a bureaucratic nightmare. Thereafter we specified that all we would accept from Kwengiis were exchange students and cultural liaisons. The deluge became a trickle, then dried up. Few Kwengii could be comfortable, they said, among a nation of grass-eaters.

But Others settled easily enough in Kwengiis, some to keep the machinery running, some because they found this cold, clear, harshly mountained land and its uncompromising People amenable. Lavished with gifts of gems and beaten gold, we secretly reinvested these in a fund for the education of miners' children, in celebration of the fact that gold and jewels need no longer be harvested by the breath and blood of back-bent, consumptive People.

Kwengiis was one of the more successful outcomes of the Alliance. Adaptation did not progress smoothly in any land, but staggered forward, blundered about and halfway back where it had come from, only to start up again. In Wertha, *graax*carts still lumbered along rutted, unpaved roads; more than once I rode in one carrying a perfectly functional skimmerpak mounted at the rear as a kind of ornament or talisman, but never used to power anything. In Llellaar, computers and commphones were held as objects of worship, for who else but gods could send voices and data invisibly over great distances? Later, when Others tried to turn the running of power sources over to native maintenance and the turbines failed, Llellaar's commphones were relegated to duty as doorstops and flower vases.

In Zanti, only the Emperor's kin were permitted access to infovid until a popular revolt resulted in the overthrow of the ruling class and a vidscreen in every common room. In Dyr, effigies of Others were added to the godforest, until a group of Matriarchs made a personal visit to discourage this, though Othercult flourishes in the deeper recesses of the Dyrmind even today.

All our calculations and preparations proved inadequate to every individual case. We would have had to interview every individual among the People in order to know what each one wanted. As it was, we did what we could.

In Kwengiis I acquired a new skimmer to replace the one mysteriously sunk in Droghia and flew overland to Gleris, above the Hillpast Wastes. I had never been this far inland before, and marveled at the barrenness of the place. Easy to understand why People dreaded it, though far to SunLeeward, even that was changing. Tawa, under Other guidance, had begun limited desert irrigation, to increase their arable land and decrease their dependence upon sometimes unpredictable neighbors. It would be some years before they expanded beyond the parameters Others recommended, to run head-on into a similar project out of Dyr. The dispute, as most People's disputes by that time, would be untangled only under Other diplomatic auspices.

Given freedom, I would have preferred to stop in Llellaar to see Dweneth before making my way to Gleris; soulthread or no, too much time had passed us. But the Council assigned me to Gleris, owing to extraordinary events there. In an effort to better their relationship with Others, Gleris had abolished its centuries-old system of prison camps. Freed inmates were flooding the countryside, returning to the cities. Objectively, this was glorious news. Subjectively, it meant that the sometimes multigenerational gulag songs were about to become extinct. The Monitor, the chronicler, knew where her duty lay.

The blizzard has ended. It is morning, brilliant, crystalline morning, aching in its beauty. We emerge from beneath our reed mats, Other, Partisan, Intermix, and Melet, unkempt and groggy, to air that knifes the lungs and dissipates precious body heat when we exhale.

Analysis of *kressha* and *gli*flowers, the two species of flora which, until People transported samples to the Mainland, grew only in OtherWhere, indicates that they are best suited to a desert environment. While they grew adequately in OtherWhere's temperate climes, they only truly flourished when as an experiment we transplanted them as nitrate fixers in the sands of the Hillpast Wastes, with their contrast of torrid days and frigid nights, where little else would grow.

The analogy is obvious. If Other flora flourish under extremes of hot and cold, then so should Others. Usually we do, being impervious to high temperatures which will prostrate most People and tolerant of cold for longer periods. However, add dampness to the cold and we have difficulty.

Therefore there is an added danger for us in this part of the World. We cannot remain immobile in this cold. And there is more.

We have drifted in among a field of ice floes. They range in size from man-high fragments to literal floating moun-

151

tains of sheer, implacable metal-hard ice. They hide us from aggressors, but also from one anOther. Are we all here, or have some been separated in the storm? And where is Joreth's galleon? I ask the *bRi*.

The two adolescent males who have escorted us thus far are gone; an adult female swims near enough for me to call. I do, hoping I will not have to get into the water with her. She is in her element here; I am not.

"*bRi*-friend," I trill the near-call, leaving it to her whether she will answer. She is a young adult and pregnant with what I surmise is her first calf. Perhaps I can use this as our common ground. Let me remember all the skills I once possessed in communing with these whimsical creatures. Let me be mindful as well of what they have suffered at the hands of People, as brutal as what has befallen us. "*bRi*-friend . . . "

She executes a half roll toward me, floats supine to study me with her small, laughing eyes. She trills.

"Sssspeakk."

"*bRi*-friend, soon mother . . . " I try to slow my pace. It is cold and I am anxious, but *bRi* will not be hurried. "*bRi*-friend, felicitations. How soon do you calve?"

Peria and Aloyi listen respectfully, pulling straw from their hair after their night in the reed mats. Yarel is not with them. The Melet family which has sheltered us emerges from their nest of leaves and reeds, amused and intrigued by the apparent whistling gibberish I utter.

"Ssoonn," the *bRi* answers, pleased that I observe the amenities. "Moontime next. Thee calf has?"

"Long ago," I tell her. This is the opening I need. "My son-spouse is with calf, and I cannot hear my podkin. Are they here? Do your podkin know?"

Of course they know; *bRi* can far-call from pole to pole. But I must observe the courtesies, and give her opportunity to take pride in her species' skills.

"Yesss," she whistles, then sounds just below the sur-

face, listening. "All your podkin near. Two-species podkin."
She nods her domed head toward the Melet, puzzled.
"Many-pods. Two-species. Why?"

"Keep us hunter-safe," I tell her. This she and her kind
can understand, though perhaps she wonders, as she swim
away, who hunts the hunters.

A scrambling on the nearest ice floe reveals young Yarel
and a Melet female perhaps a year or two his elder. They
come over the top of the floe and slide agilely down the sheer
face and clamber back into the boat.

"We went to see from up there, Lingri-*al*," Yarel reports.
His hands and his companion's are bloody and chilblained;
the contrast between blood colors has never seemed more
vivid. "All the boats and reed mats are hidden within this ice
field, even the galleon. And the ice stretches as far as eye can
see. WiseJoreth says we'll use it as a shield until we make
the final run. Heading LeeSunLeeward fifteen degrees, he
said to tell you. Mellia and I will serve as runners."

His companion is lanky and tall for her age; her callused
hands and feet indicate she is of a tree-climber clan, adept at
harvesting the fruits of the hundred varieties of palm native
to her lost land and as agile as anOther. I bind up her hands
as well as Yarel's, and find some manner of warmer yet
limb-freeing garment for each.

"Be aware that there is danger, Yarel-*la*," I caution,
"and not only from above. Ice floes make sharp cracking
sounds before they split or upend themselves."

Several booming reports afar off underscore my words.
Yarel and Mellia nod solemnly.

"We will be careful, Lingri-*al*."

We are arrived. There was not time to write or speak or even
think once we cleared the ice field and, abandoning the reed
mats, brought the Melet into our small boats for the final
run. Stringing boats and outriggers loosely together in a continuous long strand, two *bRi* to each vessel, the great ship

153

flanked by six *bRi* to a side, we made the final moonless run across open sea to reach the fjords.

Nights are longer this close to the pole, and it was dark before we had finished a hurried midday meal, still hidden by the ice floes. Total darkness provided the optimum condition for concealment, while also adding to the cold.

No matter. Navigating a complex pattern past the oil rigs, rowing more to keep warm than to assist the powerful *bRi*, we were fortunate not to be seen by any ship or plane and so passed on. An incredibly cold wind drove us before it, an uncannily warm sea current slipped beneath us. Dwiri and her cohorts among People's geologists have done their research well.

There have been no casualties, only minor cases of exposure and general discomfort among us all. Only once were we truly in danger, and that from Joreth's unsteady temper.

An oil rig's searchlight caught a Melet outrigger in its beam, and there was some commotion aboard the rig. Alarm klaxons blared eerily across the open water, and we dared not move as figures scurried along catwalks and searchlights flashed everywhere in the waters about us. We dared only drift with the current, hoping chance would cause the beams to miss us. Except, of course, for the galleon, which stood out like a stand of trees even with its sails furled.

Dzilbak's Jemadar was heard to make some snide remark about foolish attachment to things as large as sailing ships, but it was Jisra who saw Joreth go below, presumably to some hidden arms chest. She stopped him with a pistol in his hand.

"What will you?"

"Only take the light out!" my son swore, as activity on the oil rig intensified. "No one's harmed if I take out the light!"

"But no Discipline is served either!" Jisra insisted, her hand like iron on his arm. "How explain a random shot fired from out of an empty sea? You will have the whole of their arsenal out in force in moments, a distress call on their radio after that.''

She was right, of course, and Joreth calmed himself, ashamed, though there was renewed tension as the rig's master dispatched a flitter to scan the area about the rig. By then Joreth had gathered his wits and brought the ship about far enough to Sunward of the rig so that the flitter missed it. We drifted on, shivering in our immobility, until the rig and its noise were far enough behind us for the *bRi* to resume. Only I saw Jisra go below with two strong Others, to weight the arms chest and hurl it into the sea.

We rowed, forced ourselves to eat our cold, savorless rations, if only to keep our strength up. With the sunless morning, our hands stiff on our makeshift oars, we reached the fjords.

bRi have no reason to enter here. They abandon us with no more than a flutter of flukes and are gone, having no use for either gratitude or farewells. We may never see them more. Now we must row in earnest, for there will be only a few hours of light given us to navigate this narrow pass between two sheer mountain walls, carved by this very sea in a time before time, its twists and turns seemingly leading to dead ends and futility. More than once a small boat grinds against some dark hidden rock or shallow; the outriggers cannot pass until their pontoons are removed. This may prove a perfect hiding place once we achieve it, for who could possibly know that we are here?

From dawn until midmorning we row in awed silence, reluctant to give voice and risk rockfalls within these crags which we can touch on either hand. The air is cold and colorless, but the sea is pellucid and warm enough to raise a soft steam about us; there are volcanos near. We are no longer as beset by cold.

The first boatlings have passed on a head around the curve under Dwiri's guidance, to make camp before full

155

darkness; there are several turns now between us and them, and we can no longer see or hear them. We in the middle have been entrusted to transport those sick and elderly once sheltered in the hold of the great ship, which is too wide and deep of draft to enter the fjords. For its exemplary service, we can only offer it burial at sea.

Heavy-laden, we in the middle boats move with extreme care, water lapping over the prows betimes. Behind us we can hear the sound of axes hollowly stoving in the sides of the great ship to scuttle her. Anything salvageable, any trace of who last sailed on her, has been removed. Should anyone by some remote chance find her on the bottom decades or centuries hence, they will think her a casualty of some far earlier time, some People's ship abandoned in a plague or war.

It is a necessary falsehood, but no easier for Joreth to bear. When last seen he was weeping shamelessly, swinging a double-headed ax in his soft musician's hands, wiping sweat and tears on his billowing pirate's sleeves.

Peria's small boat now holds eight: she, Yarel, Aloyi and I, Mellia and two from the Melet reed mat, and an old one from the ship. We no longer row at all, merely jostle in the momentum of the boatlings fore and aft, letting that momentum carry us.

One final sharp turn, the pass so narrow that the rock walls join above us, blocking out the sky, then our way opens to an inlet and a bay, a snow-covered shoreline, the ragged edges of a glacier, and a broken-looking mountain face honeycombed with caverns. There are no small boats before us. Footprints despoil the snowfield, leading toward the caves. Those who arrived before us have carried everything—boats, outriggers, and everything they held—inside the mountain.

Beyond this cloven, rambling hill, taller peaks jut up in close formation; two of these smoke desultorily. How stable are their inner cores? Only time will answer. This must serve as safe haven for now.

Carrying our own small boat, while two Melet males make a kind of litter for the old one, we choose a cavern entrance. What wonders lie within!

Some entrances are shallow and large enough to walk upright; some require a half crouch down branching, narrow tunnels. Some, the children have discovered, can only be entered on hands and knees, with considerable wriggling. All lead into a spacious, cathedral-ceilinged cavern, glowing with a warm, natural light. Whatever the chemical properties of this translucent stone, Lingri nonscientist can no longer remember, but the effect is of a grand salle larger than long-ago Droghia's, larger than anything the Plalan Ascendancy once boasted, lighted with a light to rival a thousand torches, and naturally warmed.

Arctic cold suffuses air and soil outside; only the ocean current retains its uncanny warmth, causing fantastic ice formations to drip off the edge of the glacial shelf and plash into the sea. Here inside, a natural warmth pulses audibly from the heart of the mountain. The children, ever more daring empiricists than their elders, shed layers of protective clothing as they have already begun to shed the ethnic differences between Others, Melet, Partisans, and Intermixes, and begin a joint expedition to explore their new environs.

This central chamber branches off in uncounted directions. Tunnels, alcoves, chambers, streams of both hot mineral water and cold glacial waters weave and interweave a natural habitat of dimensions sufficient to shelter many times our number. One could not have designed a better underWorld. Only the addition of an ultrasonic field is necessary, cobbled together from the oddest spare parts, to ward off predators, though surveys indicate there are no large animals here. We will make more permanent alterations as the need arises. Once we have all arrived and deposited boats and baggage on the central cavern floor, a delegation is dispatched outside to erase all traces of us from the snow. This done, Jisra speaks.

"People, Others, Intermixes: let us all partake of food and rest until twelve-hour!" Her sweet young voice resonates from these walls almost as perfectly as it once did in the labyrinthine confines of the Citadel. "Thereafter we will require a census of our number, and representatives therefrom, to begin to formulate our future."

Dzilbak's People gravitate toward one end of the cavern, not precisely shutting Others out, but enclosing themselves in. They gather in their offspring who, having found a spring-fed pool, had freed themselves of the last of their clothing and joined their Other counterparts in a swim.

Others, moving as one, begin to set up a rudimentary survival camp, as we each did in our own however-long-ago Survival Year.

The tradition of the Survival Year was yet one more Other custom People could not understand. Why coerce our children into living under such primitive conditions when our technology had eliminated the need?

It was the very elimination of the need which drove us, lest we grow soft with urban living. Let no one of us become so dependent upon conveniences that she could not survive without them. Hence we sent our ten-year-olds into the wild, to teach them Survival.

There were two phases, solitary and social, each designed to teach its own set of values. During the first each child was assigned to her own small outisland for a period of one hundred days, to fend and forage for herself. Each island was remote enough to afford complete isolation; each was prescreened to determine that there was at least one source of fresh water, and sufficient food and shelter for those resourceful enough to find and utilize them. Pretraining for Survival began in infant school.

Each child brought with her only the clothing she wore

and a small, sharp knife adequate for cutting plant stalks. Everything else must be garnered from the environment, and the Alimentary Discipline was to be observed at all times.

Our Archipelago contained no predators dangerous to Others save the occasional poisonous snake. If there were dangers, they arose from carelessness. Rockslides, quicksand, strong ocean undertows, and no few poisonous plants lay in wait for the unwary. Training had been rigorous beforehand, but not all contingencies could be foreseen.

Most Other children had never been totally alone until this time. Nurtured in a society where every child was desired and planned for and, with our innate seven-to-ten-year mating cycle, reared individually, in the company of elders who taught respect by treating all as equal and by peers who challenged without competing, provided with every manner of physical comfort and intellectual stimulation, free to choose solitude or company as we wished, we lived in danger only of a great complacency. Thus the necessity of Survival Year.

Many Survivors kept journals in which they recorded rhapsodic meditations resulting from their first solitary communion with their own souls; my own journal had been the first place where I recorded my errant poetry. No Other was untouched by the glory and the terror of being the only living thing extant in a darkness replete with stars. No child emerged from this first phase unchanged.

In truth, some few did not survive, but none had died within my memory. Some bore physical scars which could be removed upon return to the cities, or preserved as a reminder of one's own fallibility. Some were so altered in soul that they became lifelong Solitaries after. But Other society allowed for all these variations and was the stronger for them.

Solitude teaches self-reliance; social intercourse, community. Survival's second phase was societal. For two hundred days following the first phase, Other children who had mastered solitude were consigned to communities of ten on further untamed outislands, in order to master the cooperative skills necessary to any functional social structure.

Selection was random, with no allowance for leadership qualities or compatibility factors, the rationale being that one could not always choose compatible partners in life. Telepaths intermingled with nonTelepaths, science-track students with less defined intellects like mine. Ten children were simply relegated to an unfurnished thermoconcrete dormitory, lacking any amenity including running water, and given a tract of land marginally suited to agriculture. Seed grain and vegetable seedlings were provided, along with rations sufficient for one growing season. Whatever else we required we must provide ourselves, with no recourse to adult assistance, for two hundred days, at the end of which the harvest must be gathered before Stormseason.

Some of the most inventive devices sprang from this second Survival phase, for everything from cooking pots to irrigation implements to the grass mats we slept on and the reed sandals on our feet had to be provided by our own ingenuity and our newly callused hands. Personal differences were either set aside or worn away against the constant abrasion of Others, for if the crop was poor or the storms came too soon, all survived or perished equally. Penalties were stringent upon any community where some thrived while Others suffered. Those who survived the second phase, which held dangers unforeseen and in a sense greater than those of the first phase, emerged no longer children.

"And so we are second-phase Survivors yet again," Soliah observes as we labor side by side, collecting every garment not presently on anOther's back, to be processed through our primitive but efficient communal laundry. "I am grown too old for this!"

"Indeed," I concur, noting how the Melet, drifted from their own tight-knit camp to watch us, marvel at our effi-

160

ciency, when they thought to find us spoiled by our own technology.

Compared to true Survival, this cave existence possesses a degree of luxury. Where it differs is that, unlike Survival, there is no hope of rescue after two hundred days. We must live here as if this is to be our place forever, or at least until we are discovered and hunted down once more.

Thus we set about constructing a communal kitchen, laundry, waste disposal, all of which may be modified or abandoned once we are able to choose individual living quarters among the myriad grottoes and cavelets but which are now essential. An infirmary, with its scant pharmacopoeia, a central administrative locus or Council, a spacious grotto set aside for a school, all are shaped and concretized before any one of us presumes to any extended rest. Once we do sleep, it is by turns, with some awake at all times to check the perimeter, mind the smallest children, and keep the soup pot bubbling.

Peria and Aloyi have in a manner adopted me, needing an adult presence, though by our standards Peria is some three years adult. Yarel seems content to stay with Mellia's kin, who have raised no objection. I have not seen Joreth since I left him to the destruction of his beloved ship, and Dwiri is with Lerius.

Aloyi brings me food before he himself will eat; I bathe him in the warm springs, salve his scrapes and chilblains, hold him until he sleeps. While I rock him, Peria combs and braids my hair.

"You and WiseSoliah were speaking of Survival Year," she begins tentatively. Something in the child's past has made her choose her slightest phrases with great caution.

"Yes," I say to encourage her.

"I am three years past the time but have not undergone it."

"Have you not?" I wonder. "Surely your experience has encompassed greater tests."

161

Her hands falter at the braiding. "I had not thought of it in quite that way."

Ever the chronicler, I call upon a magical incantation, the one that Dweneth taught me: "Tell me."

My parents were stationed in Pikola in Plalas before I was born. My father was administrator for the Transportation Ministry, my mother chief engineer in the major solarkinetics laboratory. Both resigned their posts and made arrangements to leave the province when the first Purist Laws were passed in that country, less than one hundred days before my birth. I was born at home on the day of the Victory Marches, because Others by then were barred from receiving treatment at the very hospices they had helped to establish in that land.

For a time we lived unmolested on an agristation near the Dyr border, the object being to flee across the border if the situation worsened, since we could not gain access to the coast without the proper travel permits, which of course we could not obtain. As long as my parents took jobs no one else wanted, we were allowed to live. They worked by turns at the irrigation plant or in the cane fields—jobs which had been eliminated by automation, until the Laws returned them to hand labor.

I remember how they would come home covered with soot from the burnt cane, with horrible slashes on their arms and legs from the cutting. We had a small two-room allotment cottage on the plantation, and I was allowed to attend the station school. There were . . . some incidents of abuse, mostly verbal, but sometimes physical. I was the only Other child there.

As to the scar on my neck—they tried to cut my ears off. I was able to fend . . . there were only six of them . . . but afterward I was not allowed to return to school. My father schooled me at home thereafter; he had kept his small personal comp so that he could administer my skillscans. In addition to my natural proclivity for weather reading, I showed aptitudes in linguistics and biochemistry. All futile under the circumstances, of course. Someone reported the comp, and it was confiscated. My father was severely punished.

Some who do not understand the circumstances of the time will ask why my parents never attempted to slip over the border and escape to OtherWhere. At that time, for every Other who was known to escape, ten more were executed as retribution. When it was seen that there was no way out, my parents gave themselves up to the outstation overseer, declaring themselves "dangerous state criminals." If he made a citizen's arrest, he would be greatly rewarded. In exchange he swore to smuggle me out, as I was not registered on any infonet. Teachers could be bribed, my fellow students frightened into silence. No one else knew I existed, so no one would be executed in my place.

I do not remember all the details of my escape. I was drugged and, I believe, kept as a kind of "pet" aboard a pleasure ship. Somehow I was taken off by Others with some bRi. I know only that I am here, and alive.

Yarel will tell you, if you press him, that he was born in Werthaland, near the glaciers, where his parents were paleobiologists; it's why he's used to ice. He will not tell you that he watched his mother die at the hands of bounty hunters, or that his father succumbed in the death camps. He himself was sheltered by a worker's family, who got him aboard a refugee train.

Aloyi remembers no past. The only life he knows

*is the tunnels of the Citadel. If he wakens screaming, it
is because he still hears the bombs.*

*We have not been reared as Others, nor have we
been permitted to live as People. We have not undergone Survival, yet we survive . . . .*

8

"Lingri?"

"Yes, Dzu."

He was the first of the People to undergo Survival Year, making the rite of passage despite his lesser physical strength and the psychic scars which were still healing. Thereafter, considering himself an adult, he never employed the traditional forms of address. Jeijinn offered no explanation, grateful that this once catatonic child had progressed so far in so brief a time and exempting him, perhaps, because he was People.

For my part, I was never comfortable with honorifics when they were addressed to me, and therefore saw no point in demanding these formulae from my adopted sibling. This single stubborn idiosyncrasy in an elsewise decorous and Disciplined youngster was hardly worthy of rebuke. Dzu remembered his honorifics in the presence of WiseOnes, and that sufficed. Therefore, between him and me, it remained until the last:

"Lingri?"

"Yes, Dzu."

"When you were Monitor, did you encounter many like me?"

"Like you in what way?" I remember temporizing, surmising by the hard look in the dark eyes behind the careful mask that he was testing me. "You are yourself, Dzu, and as such not quite like anyone else."

It was a ritual Other response, a deference to each individual's uniqueness, but Dzu was having none of it. It was his need always to question everything, test everyone. Nor was he the first to find Lingri lacking.

"Do you hate me, Lingri, for that I am made your sibling?"

Hate was the primal factor in Dzu's life, the one concept he could understand in all its dimensions. All his questions arose from it. Loriel, Jeijinn, and I, among countless Others, had labored to teach him its mirror side, but still he questioned from it.

"I hate no one, Dzu. It is my honor to have you as a sibling, and to watch you flourish."

"But I make Jeijinn suffer." He had never called her Mother; the term meant nothing to him. "Don't you hate me for that?"

"I cannot hate you for the choices Jeijinn makes."

The healers had wanted to take Dzu from Jeijinn, to treat his many physical and psychic hurts in some clinical context. Jeijinn had refused, calling upon the healers only when her own empathic gift failed. It cost her much, and Dzu, as he grew older, learned to manipulate her through her empathy. Jeijinn accepted Dzu's pain, thinking that if it became hers, it would no longer be his. That Dzu chose to take advantage of this was his choice; that Jeijinn chose to accept it was hers. It was not my place to speak, nor would my mother have listened if I had. In my observation, Dzu throve on the exchange. As for Jeijinn, her compassion for People was no longer detached, and she was far less cold.

"Surely you must hate me for taking your place," Dzu ventured, watching me with his haunted eyes.

"You cannot take my place, Dzu, for it is mine and you have yours. You cannot harm me. I only wonder why you wish to."

"Loriel dotes on me!" he boasted.

"Indeed." I would hardly attribute anything so fatuous as doting to my formidable grandmother, though I had noted how she lavished as much attention on his childhood as she had on mine. "Then cherish this, for Loriel dotes on few."

I presumed to touch him, laying my hand gently on his taut, bony shoulder. He shrugged it off, knocking my wrist aside, coldly furious.

"Suppose I said I hated *you?*"

I folded my hands into my sleeves to indicate that I would not further encroach upon his space.

"That is of course your privilege, but again I wonder why."

Dzu folded his own arms tight across his small body, coiled with tension. Jeijinn could relieve him with a touch. Dweneth, were she here, would take him in her arms and hold him close until the tension left him. He would accept neither from me. His brownblack eyes, dark as any Other's, flashed at me as he considered how much he would dare.

"Were there many like me in Hraregh?" He demanded again, returning to his first course.

"Like you in what way?" I reiterated; enough of temporizing.

"Many maltreated, abused, sick and suffering, exploited as I was. Slaves and sex-sellers." He bit off his words, staccato, as if to thrust them from him, hurl them at me. "You were in Hraregh. You saw. You must have!"

"There were many such in Hraregh," I responded, mindful of a Marketfest, a horde of Kwengii and a night of slaughter.

"And you saw them!" Dzu accused me, his tight reedy

168

voice gone deadly monotone. "Day by day you counted them, 'observed' them like a dutiful Monitor, and did nothing!"

" 'It is the duty of the Monitor—' " I began.

" 'To intervene not in the People's way.' " Dzu cut me off. "That's all to change now, Jeijinn says. There's to be an Alliance. No more sex slaves if the People want what Others offer. No more child labor, no abuse."

"That is now, not then, and only because People have sought out Others of their own volition," I explained patiently, knowing he knew this, intellectually at least. "Prior to that, as you are aware, neither I nor any Monitor could intervene."

"Monitors, no. But Rau says you are the Unlikely Candidate!" Dzu cried. "You alone could break the rules!"

"No, Dzu, I could not. Only now, if there is to be a First Alliance, can such as you and I labor together . . . ."

I stopped. I was not reaching him.

"Lingri?" He was breathing hard, trying to regain his Discipline.

"Yes, Dzu."

"If you had known me in Hraregh . . . would you have passed me by?"

You had not been born yet, I wanted to reply, but that was not his question. Nor could I be less than truthful.

"Yes."

Dzu's face did not change. "I *do* hate you!"

Though I remained in OtherWhere a full seven years more, Dzu never spoke to me again in all that time. I had been tested and found wanting. Shortly after his Survival Year, Dzu left for Three Greater to pursue his university studies, leaving word under the privacy laws that I was not to have access to his commcode. After Loriel's death he abandoned his studies and became a Solitary. He was still a Solitary when the Alliance permitted me to return to the Mainland.

169

There Dzu haunted me by his absence, for there were no longer those like him in the streets of Hraregh. Child-labor laws, universal schooling, improved housing and medical facilities had rid the land of its underage indentured serviles and sex-sellers, presumably forever, but certainly for as long as Hraregh chose to interact with Others.

Dzu haunted me in Gleris, where I attempted to trace his origins through the endless empty way stations of the prison gulag, finding it impossible. In Gleris one carried one's history with one out of the camps, else had it destroyed in the general conflagration following the liberation. Neither guards nor administrators were ever found alive; those the freed prisoners did not hang immediately dressed themselves in prison garb, disfigured their faces, and blended into the mass exodus upon the dust-choked roads, indistinguishable from their victims.

I was never more useless than in Gleris. The place wanted healers, psychologists, social workers, grave- and latrine-diggers more than it wanted a literary archivist. I learned to conduct my research from the business end of a shovel. Someone had to help to bury the dead.

"We dare not wound the Mother with your excavating machinery," a Gleran scholar, weak and wasted from his long imprisonment, told me. He would lean on his shovel wheezing after only a few minutes' work, his protective mask dangling uselessly about his neck. The stench of unburied corpses in the Thaw was overpowering. "So we must dig by hand, and offer a chant of expiation with each third shovelful."

I had already recorded most of Ziyar's incantations, wondering why a People with such deference for an inanimate land could have so little regard for their own living.

"But you are a scholar, Ziyar," I said from behind my own mask. People's germs generally did not affect us, but the Others present wore the masks as an example, to stem the

170

spread of typhus, dysentery, and assorted contagions. "Surely you do not believe your Worldmother will exact retribution for so necessary an activity as burying your dead?"

"My People do." He stopped to cough, wiping bloody froth on a bit of rag he kept tucked up one sleeve. "They have believed so for two hundred generations. In time, they will possibly outgrow it, but not now. And as my People believe, so I must believe."

I was constrained to stop whenever he did, so as not to remind him of his weakness, though I might have accomplished twice as much without him. Still, these were his People we were burying, including his own wife, and Ziyar would not retire to the field hospice until his shift was done.

"In time," he went on, wheezing, "under the new order, many things may change. Your kind tell us there are riches buried in Worldmother's womb, metals and gems which would make us flourish. Possibly some things will change." He swung his shovel at a horde of rats already chewing at the waiting corpses. "But cremation? Never!"

It was the ultimate Gleran taboo to reduce to anonymous ashes a body which would be needed in the afterlife. The worst fear any Gleran possessed, on being assigned to the work camps, was not lifelong imprisonment or starvation, not torture or even death, but the certainty that in death his body was no longer his own and would surely be burned, denying him salvation.

Other pragmatism had pleaded the cause of disease prevention and labor saving in vain. The very thought of burning these rat-chewed, bloated corpses set my scholarly companion to trembling.

"Ziyar?" I asked to divert him. "What was your crime?"

"Ah!" he said, resuming work, still whispering his incantation with each third shovelful. "The most irredeemable of all: curiosity."

171

"Please explain," I prompted.

"It is forbidden—was forbidden, under the old law—any but government workers to learn any language except our own Gleran tongue, much less to possess books or manuscripts in any alien tongue. But I was a scholar. How was I to curb my curiosity about what People learned and spoke about beyond our borders?"

He stopped to rest and cough again, seeming with a great efficiency of movement to arrange to do both simultaneously. This time it was not froth but fresh blood which stained his bit of rag.

"Curiosity," he gasped at last, tucking the rag away. "I lived in a coastal city, where trader ships from Kelibesh frequently made harbor. I struck up a friendship with the captain of one of them: he taught me to play *sksha*. Many a long night we would play; I usually lost, but it was stimulating. When he sailed, he gave me the gift of an illuminated scroll from his land. An antique, he told me. A collection of children's tales, quite harmless. My wife made the error of showing it to a neighbor.

"The secret police declared it was a spy's codebook. Why else would anyone possess such a thing? I was accused of passing secrets; what secrets or to whom was never specified. There was no trial. My wife . . . " He faltered. "My wife chose to join me in my exile. She might have changed her name, made a new life. I was legally dead. . . ."

He coughed and wept at once. I led him away as our relief shift arrived.

"I have been of little service to you!" he gasped from his cot in the field hospice. Other healers, supplemented by those of his own People strong enough to work, tended to him. "You ask about the gulag songs, and I speak of religious taboos and curiosity."

"All these things have value, WiseZiyar," I assured him, earning a glare from a healer for being in the way.

"When you are well, I will require your assistance on the final translation."

He clutched at me.

"I shall never be well! Even when we are released, we die, but never mind. The gulag songs, yes, you asked me . . ." Whatever sedative he had been administered began to take effect. "Go to the camps, wherever there are walls still standing. Within the cellblocks, in the latrines and the solitary pens . . . inscriptions, poems, prayers, curses, last testaments. Find them; they are yours. Our legacy of pain and despair, in language sometimes most sublime."

He sat up on his cot, to the healer's dismay, shook his head, found a last burst of clarity, still clutching my sleeve.

"*The Hunger Cycle.* Nine hundred seventy verses, of which I once knew twenty. Begun in the Zlovis camps, smuggled out on the flesh of the inner arm in crude tattoos . . ."

He succumbed to coughing and at last to sleep.

"Nine hundred seventy verses!" I marveled, moving out of the tent; the healers had had their fill of me.

There was considerable excitement among the gravediggers when I returned.

"We think we may have found one of your kind."

They pointed to one of a row of corpses already laid in the mass grave Ziyar and I had dug, about to be covered over.

AnOther, here and unaccounted for? Impossible, unless there was some Monitor still unrecalled this long after the Alliance. I climbed down into the grave to get a closer look. My pulse quickened. It was Rau.

My Teacher. Author of the Unlikely Candidate, in all respects. Dead in a Gleran mass grave. How?

"Once a Monitor, always a Monitor," Rau had always said. He among all was least able to stay long in OtherWhere, his curiosity ever luring him back to the Mainland whether the Council wanted him there or not. He had been the last recalled from Kelibesh, where he had worked his way from

173

galley slave to caliph's advisor in the interim before the Alliance. Afterward, he had gone over again. What had brought him to Gleris, and why had he died?

Rau had been a self-healer, able if allowed time to recover from the gravest tortures. This was one reason why he had made the study of People's methods of torture his life's work.

"If the smallest fraction of the energy and ingenuity they invest in giving pain were more positively utilized . . ." He would shrug elaborately, unable to go on.

Apparently whoever had worked on him in Gleris had not given him sufficient time to heal. His wounds were among the most grievous I had ever seen. And I must see, for I must bear witness.

"Come away," the gravediggers said not ungently, their voices as hollow as their eyes. "We have lived with death and will see to him, not you who neither kill nor mourn."

They knew little enough of Others to mistake my lack of outward grief for something like the indifference to life or death Gleran inmates evidenced after long internment. They could not know the measure of my grief, or that it would take years—and Redrec's music—before I could weep for Rau.

I never learned why Rau died, though I did find his final legacy. It was of all things a poem, scratched on the wall of a Z-camp which was to be demolished within the hour. I had not known he had the gift. Even in death, Rau could surprise me.

As for the scholar Ziyar, though the healers were able to treat his malnutrition and cure his consumption, he died within a month of gaining freedom, as he had said he would.

Perhaps it must be reiterated: it is not that Others have no passions, but rather that we have passions so violent we have perforce learned not to give them rein. The cost is often great.

174

I was ordered back to OtherWhere for extraordinary leave following the events in Gleris, and also to give an account of my actions in Droghia, and of why I was not yet bonded. In truth, the summons gratified me: I had never so longed for the tranquility of my own kind. But something tugged along the too-long-silent soul-thread, and I answered it. It drew me to Plalas and, once more, to the shadow of a prison.

"Oh, go away!" Dweneth greeted me, shaking the bars of her cell in frustration, her face turned away. "Don't look at me! Who asked you to come here?"

"You did."

The gaoler locked the door behind me, and shambled muttering away.

"So I must have, though I swear I don't remember!" Dweneth sighed, plumping down on the straw-strewn shelf which did duty as a bed. She offered me the backless stool which was the cell's only movable furnishing. "That's what comes of having too much time to think. When I'm busy I haven't the leisure to send you stray distress calls." She ducked her head to avoid my eyes, scratching her scalp with both hands. "Don't get too close. The bedstraw's lousy. I'm crawling with them!"

"Lice have no taste for Otherblood," I answered, nevertheless staying where I was. Clearly she did not want me to see how she had aged. How could I have stayed away for thirteen years? "We shall have you freed presently. I have logged a writ with the Governor, which will take the requisite time. I am curious: what was your crime?"

"Saving lives, that's all!" she grumped, tilting her face up for the first time, curious. "Who's 'we'?"

"Plalas has a pact with Others for communications technology, agronomy, education, and healing." I scanned her face as I spoke. She was thirty-eight, my own age, but middle-aged for People. There were traces of silver in the redgold

175

hair, fine lines scored the flesh about her eyes. Laugh lines, People called them, though Dweneth was not laughing. "In exchange, they were to have abolished this primitive penal system for a more progressive—"

"They still drink out of pewter goblets and line their roofs with lead!" Dweneth snorted. "You expect progress from a dying gene pool?"

"Their progress has been uneven, their motivations frequently irrational," I admitted. "Lead poisoning? A distinct possibility, and one which no Other has considered. You must file a report once we get you out of here. As to 'saving lives,' perhaps if you were more specific . . . "

"Aye, lead poisoning," she echoed me, still scratching, both hands buried in her curls. "The entire nation suffers from it to some degree. Don't tell me it was Dyr invasions or the Mantuul religious wars which destroyed the Plalan Ascendancy. It was pure stupidity!"

"I would not presume to tell you anything of People's history." I needed to keep her talking, partly for the sound of her voice after so long, partly for a plan already hatching. "Go on."

"I don't want to go on!" she cried, springing to her feet. "Don't go Other on me, not now. Don't you dare chill me out with your eminently Disciplined manner and your careful questions! They're going to burn me for a witch on the morrow, I haven't seen you in thirteen years, I can't even touch you I'm so full of bugs, and you sit here playing the barrister! Go on be damned!"

"Are you quite finished?" I asked calmly; it annoyed her when I did so. "Sit you down and stop shouting. They shall not burn you, and I am not leaving until you are free. But I must know why they have brought you here."

She narrowed her eyes at me, sat down, stopped scratching. "You're up to something, aren't you? Tell me."

"When the time comes." I moved from the hard stool to the straw pallet beside her. "Now, explanations."

176

She sighed, leaned back against the cold stone wall. "Have you ever wondered why the Plalan aristocracy are called the Blue Fingers?"

"I confess I have not considered it a burning question."

"It's the lead. It's their principal resource, and it permeates their lives. They eat off pewter plate and drink from pewter cups. They line their roofs and coffins with it, then build their cemeteries too near the streams and pollute the groundwater. Their blood teems with it, hence the cyanosis in their fingertips. A third of their infants are stillborn, a third of those who live are brain-damaged. 'God-touched' they call it, thinking it confers a kind of sainthood. Of the adults who live, most succumb to a manner of dementia in middle age; they're vegetables before they're truly old. It's a kind of mass insanity, because they will not see it.

"Well!" She tucked her knees up to her chest, wrapped her arms around them, tried not to yawn. "My healers and I introduced chelation therapy: an injection regimen to strip the toxins out of the bloodstream, megavitamins to counteract—"

"I am familiar with the technique," I interjected, earning a sour look.

"Of course you are! Others taught it to me. It was fine as long as I worked on the adults, but when I started injecting the unborn in the womb—well, this was deemed witchcraft! A generation born with normal brains and normal-colored fingers, robbed of their god-touch—for that I'm due to burn. Have I aged so badly? Do I really look so old?"

"Not old enough to burn."

We talked the night through. She told me of her thirteen years of travels, setting up hospices, healing, a stay with the Zanti mystics, her excapades in Mantuul, which produced Dzilbak the Dragon-marked.

"You did not seek my help then."

177

She yawned. "I didn't seem to need it. I'm all right as long as I can move around; there's always some way out. Pent up, I tend to panic. Besides, I called you then. You were shielding."

Shielding, indeed. I was deep in a Droghian catacomb, consumed with mating fever.

"You should have been bonded later that year," Dweneth said slowly, realizing. "It came too soon. You were on the Mainland. Something happened, for you are not bonded yet." I acknowledged this, not wondering how she knew. "Yet you're still alive. Tell me."

I told her about Redrec.

"Yet you left him? How, *Why?* If he saved your life, and is so infatuated with you—"

"That is why. He was a child. And People. I had no desire to be a test case for interspecial relations."

"Coward!" was Dweneth's opinion. "There have been some Intermix bondings, I'm told. And you enjoyed him, while you had him?"

"It is over," I answered stiffly, "and I wish to discuss it no further. And you?"

Dweneth blushed. "Let's say I'm no longer afraid of men. Now it's more that *they*'re afraid of me."

"Go on," I prompted.

"Damn you!" she yawned. It had been early evening when the gaoler let me in; it was past midnight now. "I'd rather sleep, now you've assured me I won't be barbecued. What influence have you with the gaoler, that he hasn't thrown you out?"

" 'She who asks the question—' "

" 'Must be prepared to accept the answer,' " she finished the aphorism for me, her head on my shoulder, half asleep.

"As to men . . ." she sighed after some moments. "The first was a lieutenant on one of Thrasim's ships. You see

178

how bad I am? Scarce out of sight of OtherWhere before I was in his bunk, eager to try out if I was truly cured by Other healing. I hear there's much afoot in OtherWhere, and not only in healing. Student exchange, surgical instruments adapted to better serve People, research on gene splicing and longevity. Think I've served enough time in the field? Think I might ask permanent residence, now I've repaid my debt and sworn off men?''

"How so?" I prompted. "After only one?"

She yawned again; her eyes were closed. It was important to my plan that she be lulled to sleep ere dawn.

"First the sailor. Then a widowed merchant with six kids. After him an itinerant herbalist, then a magician who knew my father—was he before or after the apothecary's clerk? At any rate, nine men in as many years, and then I gave it up. Enlightened Era of Peace or no, men haven't altered overmuch, at least not the ones I've met. They want bed and someone to pick up after them, that's all. 'If I wanted an Other I'd wed one,' they tell me when I try to talk philosophy or even tell them how my day's been. To hell with them all. I was the one wanted anOther and could not have him. Wanted a child as well, though by now I am too old.''

"You are yet fertile," I pointed out. "Under new techniques Others have developed, you could have twenty years or more yet. There is still time."

"Cwala's a grandmother several times over," she murmured. "Under the old ways, I should be too."

"Under the old ways, you would likely be dead by now. There are new ways now."

"If only you had been a male. . . . " She was very near sleep. "Pity Changers can only alter in one direction. . . . "

She slept. It was then I slipped the manacle about both our wrists.

Other technology had recently developed an extraordinary alloy which did not read as metal under People's crude

179

scanners. Flexible, decorative, it had served me as a bracelet, unremarked when I was body-searched. Now it joined my wrist to Dweneth's, and People's tools could not cut through it without injuring one or both of us. Only my personal code could loose it. If Plalas meant to burn Dweneth, it must as well burn me. And the violent death of anOther at Plalan hands would terminate our Alliance.

The sky was lightening. I also slept.

The trial was a formality, the writ from the Governor hardly necessary. My bracelet, with its implication of Othermind behind it, was the deciding factor. It created sufficient controversy, bought enough time, for a delegation of Other administrators, in the company of the Chief Representative of the Plalan Central Committee, to arrive upon my summons and turn that backwater gaol inside out. Changes were in order forthwith. A great clanging of bars and cheering among freed prisoners echoed about the compound.

Still linked to me, Dweneth stood in the courtyard, blinking and disheveled in the sunlight. Not dissimilarly had I tasted freedom when she and Redrec Elder rescued me from a gang of kidnappers in Droghia half our lives ago. Three times had Dweneth saved my life; now three times had I hers.

I decoded the bracelet and it snapped free.

"Even?" I offered her my outstretched palm, in a gesture I had learned of People's children in a brigands' camp in Hraregh. It took her a moment to comprehend.

"What are you on about? Not the kidnappers, after all this time?"

"Just so. You said I should never be able to repay you for that."

"And so you wait decades to rub my nose in it!" Cross, she slapped my palm with hers. "Even! I swear you're like a child. And mind you, I'll get you back eventually!" She grabbed my hand and pulled me out through the courtyard toward a passing tramcar. "Come—I want a bath."

We ran for the tram, I more often dragging Dweneth, who never had my stamina.

"Pity," she huffed once we had swung aboard, "pity you always catch me helpless. You've never seen me at my work. I'm *good* there!"

" 'Dweneth Healer who, instructed by Others, did in Zanti in the year 1574 P.A. established a clinic for the cure of childhood illness, which in time eliminated measles and dysentary, chief killers of infants in that land,' " I recited, taking advantage of her shortness of breath. " 'Dweneth Healer, so-named Dain'sDaughter, founder of the contraceptive distribution programs in Tawa and Kelibesh: Dweneth Healer, who in the wake of the floods which killed a thousand in Llellaar, coordinated relief efforts which—' "

"Oh, enough!" she spat, finding breath again. "I mean you've never seen me, *been* with me, worked by my side. We have lost too many years apart, and I will not tolerate it longer. We remain together from hereon, whatever else we do."

"Perhaps," I temporized, having yet to answer the summons to OtherWhere, yet to answer for my actions in Droghia, yet to learn what the Chamber, the Telepathy, the Matriarchy, or all three might want of me this time.

"Don't 'perhaps' me!" Dweneth warned as the tram left us off at the hospice gates, where her healers had kept an anxious night-long vigil.

Her staff and patients, Others and People alike, clustered around her, eager to touch and be certain she was whole. A horde of children of all sizes, sick and well, danced about her, chanting "Dwen-eth! Dwen-eth!" as the crowds had done for the Player maid once long ago. Some of the stronger People swept her up from the cobbles onto their shoulders.

"Put me down! Put me down at once before you all need

181

debugging!" she demanded, clutching at her dignity. "Clear off, now, all of you, and get you back to work!"

She was laughing, breathless, flushed. Her eyes shone; she was ageless.

"I'm serious! Off with you! But not before you thank the one responsible, at least!"

I had gone unnoticed in the tumult. Now a path seemed to clear about me, as all of them stood to one side of the grand foyer of the hospice to let us pass.

"My friends, this is Lingri." Dweneth's practiced voice resounded off the vaulted ceiling. "She who is my Other half, and the better part of myself."

Dweneth's Grenni hospice was a special, cherished place, an oasis of health in a dying land. Overcrowded, with makeshift cots end to end in corridors and People clustered waiting in the courtyards in all weathers, it nevertheless shone as an example of what enlightened healing could be, once People accepted it. And Dweneth was its lodestar.

Children followed her everywhere as she made her rounds. Those ambulatory and well enough scrambled about her down the halls and through the gardens. Other-style gardens, I noted at once, maintained by staff and patients alike, forming a special kind of breeze-blown therapy. Those too sick to leave their beds followed her with their eyes, drew her with their piping voices and eager, clutching hands, touching, patting, clinging, basking in her presence. No infant cried but it was comforted, no minor hurt went unattended, no small face went uncaressed. She changed their dressings, read and sang to them in her practiced voice, rocked them to sleep, held them if they were dying, gave to them all.

"Reduce by half the medication for yon Witrin," she would instruct an aide. "And Clya goes home tomorrow, with a provision for one more session of regen in the morning. Her mother may stay with her overnight. Oh, and

Sinak's not to have any more greenfruit, no matter how he begs. It makes him fart, and we can't have that!"

She would glare at the miscreant in question who, verging on death a week ago, now burst into giggles and rolled delightedly on the floor in perfect, gleeful health.

Dweneth gave them little pieces of her heart. In exchange they adored her.

"They're all mine, yet none of mine," she would say wistfully when she had the leisure to sit and watch them. "I suppose it's selfish to want one of my own body, when I could adopt so many who have no one. And is a child ever really anyone's, even if we bear them? Or are they only ours to nurture, then let go?"

She squeezed my hand, her eyes closed to keep them from betraying her.

"It's all I want—that and Lerius. And one precludes the Other. Does it seem too much to ask?" She shook the mood off against my silence. "Self-pity—ugh! Enough! You're duty-bound for OtherWhere."

"I have not told you that."

"You don't need to. I know, remember? May I come with you?"

"Need you ask? I have wondered why you never went back without me."

"Because—" She caught her breath. "without you, I wasn't sure I could trust myself. Or Lerius."

"I never told you this and, having no one else to tell it to, I've kept it secret all these years. . . . "

We were in a skimmer back to OtherWhere, cruising barely above the surface spray of gleaming emerald rollers in the mildest weather. Far different from our first tumultuous arrival in the land of my birth. I kept my eyes on the controls, that she might be freer to talk.

" . . . but all the men I've slept with since, though

183

they've touched every part of me, could never touch me as he has, who has never touched me. . . ."

"I lied to you about the Enclave. Yes, I went to inquire after you, but that was only part of it. I needed to get close to him, regardless of the danger. I told you SavantTisra taught me how to shield, but not because I begged her, not exactly. It was she who demanded it of me, after she caught me lurking about, sending to Lerius with all my might, sufficient to distract him from his lofty meditations. Rather like a flea disturbing the sublime thoughts of a war*graax!*" she added bitterly. "I think it frightened Tisra that a nonOther could send so strongly, and it puzzled her that Lerius would respond. You and your damned mating cycles! She wouldn't have recognized unmitigated sexual desire— mine, I mean; who knows what Lerius desires?—if she fell over it.

" 'Very well,' says I, 'I'll practice shielding, on one condition: bring me to Lerius first. Let happen what will happen. I will accept the consequences.'

"Well, my position was ambiguous. Ordinary People were forbidden contact with Telepaths, but I'd been granted special leave to study with the healers; perhaps I was the exception. To this day I think Tisra hoped I'd simply be burned up by it. Perhaps she even saw as much in her own time-that-isn't-time. One less troublesome outWorlder to contend with! But she sent me away that first time, instructing me to return within a year. That was why I asked you to sever our soul-thread that first time.

"I never faltered in my purpose, and when the year was up, I returned. Tisra led me into the presence.

"I swear I almost wet myself, I was so scared. And when he turned those white eyes full on me! Even if I had not known how to send, I think my mind would have screamed then. It was like being impaled, dissected, turned inside out. Agony, but glorious at the same time. I never wanted it to end.

"I offered myself to him shamelessly, body, mind, and soul, as I've never to any man, all the while thinking 'If he denies me, what will I do? Kill myself? Not hardly. It's not in my nature, having survived this far. But what?' And then the answer came, not from me, but from him.

" 'You will survive,' he answered in my mind. It was like orgasms, I guess. Bells and fireworks—we'll you're the poet, not I. It was like nothing else I'd ever known. 'You are what you are, as I am what I am. Therefore we can never be as you desire.

" 'Think you,' he went on—my knees had given out by then; it was all I could do to keep from writhing on the floor. 'Think you what would happen if we joined in any wise.' He shielded after that, leaving me to work it out. I don't know how long it took—a year, a breath?—but then it came to me in a single image, like a cold wind through my soul. Well, I'd always known it would kill me, but now I truly *knew*. And not only me, but him. It was his last thought. 'I could not bear it, that I had destroyed thee.' "

For an hour by my timesense we did not speak. Dweneth studied her small healers' hands or stared out at the forward horizon, as if to pull One Greater up over it by sheer longing. I banked the skimmer slightly to Leeward, adjusted the navcon, took weather readings, listened to the prevailing wind buffeting us betimes. When she had lolled her head back against the headrest for so long I thought her sleeping, Dweneth cleared her throat.

"It might have been easier if he did not desire me as well. I might never have erased him from my soul, but it would have made the leaving bearable. What perverse creation has made us this way, wanting most what we cannot have? If he had cared nothing for me, I might have shouted 'Take me, once, even if it destroy me,' but knowing it would destroy him too . . . " Again she studied her hands, sniffed, forced her voice to steady. "Perverse! The only way to prove

185

our love is never to consummate it. Does this make sense to you?"

"That a thing exists does not necessitate that it 'make sense' to us at our present level of understanding," I offered lamely. "Perhaps it would have been better for you to share this with me at the time."

" 'A sorrow shared is half a sorrow'? That's one Other aphorism I'm afraid I can't accept. You had troubles enough of your own. I'm only telling you now because we're going back. Because I need your help."

"What do you wish me to do?"

"Never ask for qualifiers, do you?" Dweneth mused. "Someday I'll simply say 'Die for me,' and all you'll ask is how and when. The shadow side of that being that I suppose I must have the courage to do the same for you."

"It need never come to that."

" 'Only a Telepath can know the future, and then not always so,' " she reminded me. "Reduced to speaking in aphorisms—we must be nearly there!"

We traveled awhile in silence.

"Help me!" she pleaded suddenly. "Help me to stay away from him. I'm not sure I can trust myself."

"I will do what I can," I promised. "We are near. One Greater harborside at twelve degrees, mark."

Dweneth squinted against the sunlight on the waves. "Other eyes! I see nothing. What's it like there now? I hear it's overrun with People, excepting of course for Two Greater. How are your parents?"

"My last communication was some time ago," I confessed. Commstations were everywhere on the Mainland now, but not to be used for the frivolity of personal communication, except in emergencies. "But I understand Evere is as always, lost in his work. He does not own a personal comm, having no use for it. Jeijinn teaches now, when the Council does not require her. Sociology and Otherhistory for select exchange students on Three Greater."

186

"Da's dead, you know."

"Yes," I said.

"What 'yes'? Yes, you knew, or yes, you've just now learned it?"

"Yes, I knew. It was mid-Thaw, three years ago, the twelfth day of the second month, when he had his first attack. He lingered until the fifteenth day and died in his sleep in your arms." I waited a suitable moment of mourning. "I grieve with thee. I would have come, but I was skimmerless and between canal locks in Wertha."

"Damn that soul-thread!" Dweneth sighed, exasperated. "How much of my mourning did you share?"

"As much as you would permit yourself."

She dabbed her eyes. "I didn't mourn long, strangely. It wasn't as if he wasn't old. His heart just couldn't tolerate Others. He feared for the future of live Cirque and Players once every citizen had his own vidscreen. He couldn't foresee the next step. I mourned more for myself, I remember, for he was better out of it. Oh, and he said to tell you he always knew you were a ringer."

"Indeed."

"A pity about Rau." I had told her in the Plalan gaol. Her thoughts turned to the living. "Dzu must be quite grown now."

"He has passed twenty-two years, if he still counts them," I said off her alarmed look. "He became a Solitary after Loriel's death. None have seen him since."

The leader natural-born will always be surrounded by those who envy him what has been his from birth. This same leader, no matter how meticulous his efforts to preserve the truth of his origins, will perforce be the victim of repeated falsehoods, and slanders meant to denigrate his roots, belittle his achievements, make him out a liar, and undermine the message of salvation he brings to his People.

There are those who will say that my birth mother was a whore, that she spawned me in a prison camp solely to have better food and easier work for herself, little caring what happened to me once I was born. But how can this be, when there were no such forced labor camps until the accursed Others came among us?

There are those who will claim they are survivors of such camps, from a time before the verminous Others were allowed to make their foul incursions into our midst. But can they offer proof? Do records exist, photographs even, or anything beyond these impostors' specious claims?

In the city of Dver there exists a complete record of my true parentage. Let any true citizen who disputes it offer proof to the contrary!

Most vicious and slanderous of all accusations against the leader is the atrocious lie which says that what I am is the result of my having personally been harbored, healed, and schooled by these same parasitic Others! As if Others ever harbored, healed, or schooled anyone except their own pernicious breed! While everyone is aware of the secret laboratories in OtherWhere, to which People's children were abducted and held for experiments and blood rites too heinous to be re-counted here, and while the known victims of these horrors will always have this leader's most profound sympathy and any monetary compensation for their sufferings which the budget can encompass, so long as they testify to the truth, let it be known from my own pen: I was never one of them.

There are those who will remark that my manner and personal habits are those of anOther. There are those who will claim that even my writing style and use of rhetoric are Other-influenced. There are those who will point to my fluency in Othertongue as some spurious proof. Can it be that they are ignorant of the saying, "First study the enemy, the better to destroy him"? To those who hurl the ultimate insult that I "argue like anOther"—these I spit upon! They dare not make such accusations to my face.

There is the ever present rumor that my psychic powers are the result of study with Telepaths. There is the fanciful tale of my being fostered by an Empath—as if such really existed. Some will even dare to give that self-claimed Empath's name. Propaganda, all of it, designed by my enemies to discredit me. Let them know that my blood is red and tests pure: I am People through and through.

Finally, let me challenge my accusers with a single question: If I owe so much to Others, why is it my primary goal and driving purpose to obliterate them all?

9

"I did not think I could ever forgive them for her death. It took me many years of Solitude before I understood. Those who killed Loriel were but tools; the power was mine. Her death was my responsibility, because I had given them the power, by permitting myself to care."

"Dzu?"

"Yes, Lingri."

"This argument makes no sense."

"It is my argument and my sense!" His brownblack eyes flashed dangerously. "It harms no Other, and it serves me."

What manner of adult had Dzugash become? Physically he was as flawless as Other healing could render him, following upon the damage inflicted in his youth. He would always be undersize, always plagued by intestinal ailments, always sterile, perhaps impotent as well; his early years as a malnourished sex-seller had wrought too much devastation for even our healers to remedy completely. Fine-boned and never robust, he created a presence out of sheer intensity. In later years, People said, his very entrance into a room could move the walls back.

His mind was brilliant, his tongue agile, his voice beautiful; to say he was manipulative was to understate. There was something in those burning eyes and that wan, bloodless face which People could not resist. Few could detect the depth of his spirit's wounds.

When Loriel died, he had thrown himself into a kind of passion, abandoning his studies and retreating to the realm of the Solitaries, to whom no law applied. Choosing one of the smallest outislands upon which to live his primitive, beachcombing life, he had spent those years in brooding reveries, staring out over an ever changing sea with unchanging hate. Though no living soul was permitted near him by our privacy laws, Jeijinn knew his mood.

Still joined to him in empathy, my mother could feel Dzu's pain even from his Solitude. She had asked him for her sake to return for a time, to teach with her on Three Greater, in the hope that in the company of Others he would work his pain through at last.

By the time Dweneth and I sought him out at the Academy, there was no youth left in him. Weathered, bone thin, his dark hair sunbleached and already streaked with gray though he was only twenty-two, Dzu was less of substance than of phlogiston.

"If you so hate People, why have you come back to teach them?" Dweneth challenged him at once.

Even her welcome presence had warmed him only briefly; the spark of hope she kindled in his opaque eyes extinguished almost at once.

"Because I owe the debt to Others, to make People understand!" he answered bleakly. "If they can leave their stupidity at the feet of one who once was one of them, it may save one Other's life!"

The Academy at Three Greater, where both Dzu and Jeijinn taught, was host to a cross section of all the eleven tribes still active in the Alliance. Wearing their various translating devices, for very few had mastered Othertongue, they

191

drifted from course to course. Dzu's was a popular one; his words drew People, his voice mesmerized. More than one female student removed the translator as she sat transfixed by him, more fascinated by the voice than by the subject matter, though even in translation Dzu was mesmerizing.

"The Disciplines, it may be said, had their initial impetus from the Telepaths, though quite by accident. . . ."

Neither exceptionally deep nor resonant, Dzu's voice nevertheless possessed an extraordinary tonal range; he would use it in time to bully, incite, shame, and inflame an entire People. For the moment, it had reached Dweneth and me above and through the babble and murmur of People's voices and Othervoices percolating throughout the Academy compound, long before we reached the small side garden where Dzu chose to teach. Settling ourselves on one of the farther benches, Dweneth and I, though we knew the content of Dzu's narrative as well as he, found ourselves as caught up by his words as the most ingenuous of People.

" . . . While power-of-mind had theretofore frequently been employed as weapon, and Telepaths were often kept lavishly by warlords where they did not become warlords themselves, it was discovered that a blow struck in anger was considerably weaker than one aimed deliberately and in cold blood. There was formulated a theory of an inverse correlation between the suppression of emotion and the heightening of telepathy, and from this arises the entire Theory of the Disciplines. . . ."

There was no effort to slow down, to simplify, to leave open the possibility for questions. Whatever his students' aptitudes, they must pull themselves up to Dzu's level or be lost.

"He's grown arrogant enough!" was Dweneth's whispered opinion. He could not have heard, yet I saw him take note of us, curious.

"It would be simplistic to suggest that emotion exists as a form of energy to be diverted, channeled, and focused into power-of-mind, else all Others and perhaps even some People could, by simple self-control, teach themselves to be Telepaths," Dzu went on, staring at Dweneth and me intently enough to cause a stirring among his auditors. It was short-lived; his voice and presence pulled them back. "But it is fact that if one forms an inner quiet, removes oneself from anger, fear, brooding, and sorrow, as well as the more 'positive' emotions, one gains access to the Inscape, the interior labyrinth of one's own mind, and there may learn the possibility of reaching out to Other minds and, ultimately, to the interconnectedness of all minds, of All Mind."

"Speaking from personal experience?" Dweneth muttered to me; for once it was my pleasure to shush her. I had the same questions, but I would ask them of Dzu.

" . . . Thus what was first used as weapon became the psychological pattern for a civilization, and a tool for first internal, then external, peace. One cannot but wonder if this evolution cannot be duplicated elsewhere. . . . "

" 'One who once was one of them'?" Dweneth repeated Dzu's words as we walked in the almost deserted garden afterward. Half hidden by a pillar, a trio of his students lingered; young, female, daughters no doubt of visiting dignitaries, obviously infatuated with their remote, ascetic teacher, they tittered behind their hands. Laughter was no longer so untoward a sound in OtherWhere as it had once been. Dzu ignored the threesome. "If you are no longer People, Dzu, what are you?"

"I don't mean literally!" His lip curled despite his Discipline. "Even if I could replace my blood drop by drop, my genes and history doom me. But philosophically, I denounce them all; I am no longer one of them!"

The tittering girls overheard, and scattered like frightened birds. Dweneth slid me a warning look; I said nothing.

"And yet you teach them," she goaded him. "Do they begin to suspect how much you hate them?"

193

"I am too Disciplined to let it show!" Dzu said grandly. "They think I say it only to challenge them, to take the part of Others. If they knew how I despised them!"

"And this is Disciplined?" Dweneth persisted. "This serves Loriel in her death?" Dzu did not answer. "Very well, you can't speak to me; I'm People, after all. Explain it then to yon Lingri, for she is of what you wish to be."

"If Lingri wants to speak to me, she will," Dzu answered, at his most charming; only I saw him wince at the "what you wish to be."

"Lingri is not certain you will hear her," I replied, unsoftened by his charm. "You did not the last time she spoke."

"That was years ago. I was a boy."

"Were you? Ever?" I wondered. "Then answer me this: how do you preach against such unDiscipline as hatred even as you practice it?"

"It is not hatred, Lingri-one, don't you see?" His hands were on my shoulders, winningly. He was just my height; his eyes burned into mine so that even I was almost moved. "It is what gives me focus, purpose. It is that with which I hope to remake myself."

"Now he sounds like a Telepath!" Dweneth snorted, not meaning it as a compliment. Nevertheless, Dzu chose to take it that way.

"I thank you," he said grandly. "The Enclave has instructed me well."

I saw Dweneth's face tighten; there was envy in her eyes. "You are permitted in the Enclave? At what level do you study?"

"Is that not for my own privacy?" Dzu's voice was arch. How much of Dweneth's history did he know? Knowing Dzu, he would know as much as the privacy laws allowed. "How am I to teach what I do not know? When Jeijinn lured me back from my island, I resumed my former studies. History, xenology—oh, that was irony! To study the 'alien psy-

chology' of my own breed, from the perspective of anOther!
Yet, truth, I found People completely alien by then, having
become as Other as I can."

Now it was his face which tightened, holding back old
pain and new. Denouncing People, unable to be Other, what
was he, truly?

"History, psychology, sociology; all the things the
'scans said I would flourish in. And so I do, in a clinical,
detached fashion. I am a breathing commscreen: I absorb, I
give back, I am untouched. But to teach of the Telepathy, I
must needs study there. That's only logical."

"And in studying there, you have learned nothing!"
Dweneth challenged him.

"I have learned," Dzu said coldly, "this much: That
the female is more attuned than the male in this realm, and
I suspect she is learning to be in the larger World as well!"
He was shaking with ancient fury now, his Disciplines abandoned. "Neither you nor Jeijinn could leave me to my Solitude. What more do you want of me?"

"He's mad, you know." Dweneth shared this diagnosis with
Jeijinn as well as me. "It's like a crack run through the whole
of his nature. All he really understands, even now, is how to
hate."

"Do you think I am not aware of this?" Jeijinn asked.

The rapport between Dweneth and my mother had always been instantaneous and strong; if Jeijinn had any
doubts about the Player maid turned healer, they had to do
with why she persisted in associating herself with her way-
ward, bondless daughter.

"Everything Dzu feels I feel as well," Jeijinn said now,
"however much I contain my empathy. My own mother's
death was less to me than to Dzu. Loriel was of an age; her
time was due of natural causes if not of violence, and her life
was full. Yet Dzu was inconsolable. But what are any of us
to do? Otherlore provides no answer to obsessive hatred.

195

Even the Telepaths lack answers. I welcome your advice!"

Jeijinn had received us in her offices at the Academy, which served her in her dual role of educator and administrative consultant. Our arrival had coincided with the tumultuous departure of a contingent of Werthans protesting the abolition of lunatic asylums in their lands.

"All well and good ye cured 'em!" their elder-mother was saying as Jeijinn escorted her and her entourage to the door. "One of 'em was me own granddaughter, as used to scream and tear her clothes and eat her own filth till yer healers came and give her the medicine. But what are we to do with 'em now?"

Dweneth and I had sidled in past this harried, gesticulating group to wait in the antechamber, where a servitor went silently about its task of tidying; if Jeijinn had an obsession, it was for order.

"Once ye cured 'em all and let 'em loose on the town and countryside, they fair flooded the place," a younger Werthan explained when the elder-mother ran out of breath. Jeijinn by now had shepherded them out into the hall. "Them as could work took our jobs 'cause they worked for cheaper. The rest just lay about the roads and squares abegging. Ye've got to take 'em off our hands, as ye did with Kwengiis' lot!"

"That we will not do," Jeijinn said firmly. "For 'Kwengiis' lot' were of differing tribes brought into Kwengiis against their will. They were not kin of the very People who would be rid of them. Do you set the beggars to work in rebuilding the asylums with the funds we will provide you. Some can become private dwellings, which those who build them may have without stipend in return for their labor. Transform the larger areas into some manner of farmers market and craft shops, where all can display their wares and turn a living. If this be not practical, consult the Archives for alternative solutions, but these persons are your responsibility, and as such must remain."

With such pragmatic advice did she lead them in the direction of the telfer which would bring them to the proper archive and set them, and herself, free of this particular problem. Returning, my now one-hundred-forty-odd-year-old mother actually seemed winded.

"Thus are the 'lunatics' freed and the sane rendered lunatic!" she breathed ironically, permitting herself a moment of weakness in the doorway before joining us. "You see what trivia they ply the breadth of the Great Sea to bring to us? Comm messages won't suffice; they still don't trust their reality. No, they must present their petitions in person lest some dissenting group get our ear first. They trouble us like children, until we are grown as petulant as they."

She sighed and sat with us. The servitor sidled up to her, its tensor arm producing a hypo held at ready.

"mmmedicationnnn . . . " it hummed blandly, awaiting Jeijinn's consent.

"Proceed," she acquiesced. The hypo pressurized against her inner forearm; I saw Dweneth scowl. Jeijinn sighed again. "Servitor: tea and accoutrements, then dismissed."

Humming, it wheeled off to comply, but Dweneth intercepted it, examining the hypo.

"*Cleramon*, WiseJeijinn? In what dosage?"

"Thirteen units, bihourly. I know it is too much. But it is the only way I can function among People."

"And I suppose you're the only one who can do what you do?" Dweneth presumed to be familiar; Jeijinn permitted it. "By rights, Jeijinn-*al*, you should not be near People at all."

"Which is why I am the only Matriarch who cannot leave the Archipelago!" Jeijinn lifted her hands in a gesture of helplessness as the servitor arrived with the tea. "How many Others do you see about you? As many as you see People? When you arrived on One Greater yestermorn, did you find it much changed?"

There could be no denying that we had. OtherWhere was still OtherWhere in its esthetic, in its order and tranquility, yet these were underlayered now with People's many voices, timbres, colorations, idiosyncrasies. People crowded the ways, as if at a perpetual Marketfest. Special housing had had to be constructed on all of the Greaters excepting Two to accommodate different tribal life-styles. Shops had sprung up run by People catering to People, importing or synthing wares and delicacies not usually available in OtherWhere. Food synthers could now synthesize animal flesh for their cuisine, which we were told tasted "almost like the real thing."

Before the advent of People, the Council chambers had been the only place where Others gathered in large numbers. Now crowds of People attended nonviolent sporting events, operatic and musical performances—I had scanned the public notices as soon as I arrived, dreading to find Redrec's name among those performing; I had not—even Players. Dweneth had happened upon her old traveling companion Omila who, somehow overcoming her aversion to Others— or was it only me she loathed?—was full of gossip about everyone on the Mainland Players' circuit.

True, this was still OtherWhere, but in the virtual absence of Others. Only the very old, the very young, Telepaths and Solitaries, and sufficient Matriarchs to run the Council remained. Only Two Greater, Windwardmost of the Archipelago, remained exclusively Other. There a group calling themselves Dissenters had emigrated in protest following the First Alliance.

Some few were Matriarchs like Govin, some WiseOnes like my former nemesis Chior. I might have noted the seeds of this in Chior's earlier attempt to lure me away from People when first I brought them to our realm. Many were Telepaths or Empaths like Jeijinn who could not bear to be in direct contact with People for any length of time. But most were ordinary Others who, while they acknowledged the inevitability of People in our midst, could not live with it in practice.

An ancient Other aphorism has it, "One Other comprises an opinion. Two Others become a debate. Three or more Others are an insoluable syllogism." Thus Dissenters were within our Discipline, though they made the rest of us uneasy.

Thus even as People were fragmented into fourteen tribes, only eleven of whom currently accepted us, and each of these under varying degrees of mental and emotional stress, so Others were divided among themselves. As long as the Dissenters remained apart on Two Greater, this did not pose a problem—yet. And the presence of increasing numbers of People lent the rest of our realm a festive, sometimes unsettling carnival atmosphere it had never owned before, not even in the barbaric times before the Thousand-Year.

"Such diversity can only be for the good, we tell ourselves. At the same time we wonder: has our world changed more radically than the People's?"

Jeijinn held her teacup in hands which had developed a slight tremor. Again Dweneth slid me one of her cautionary looks.

"Eighteen years ago, Dweneth-*ala*, when your People first arrived here," my mother went on, "the most advanced of your cultures was full six centuries behind us in technological development. That gap is closing daily, and it is estimated that by the time the First Alliance comes up for renewal some six point seven nine one years hence, the gap will no longer exist at all. This is, however, not as auspicious as it would seem."

My mother set the teacup down, falling back into the style of oratory which had held me spellbound when I was a child observing her in Council.

"One essential thing which the First Alliance failed to accomplish was the establishment of a World entity, a supratribal governance where all could seek arbitration for domestic and intertribal disputes. At the time of the First Alliance, you may recall, WiseAccolon Matriarch proposed that Others not be coequal with People but comprise a fifteenth tribe, in order to expedite this planetary government. Even this did not satisfy the People.

"Georgraphy was the first sticking point. What nation was to have the prestige, and the potential for control, of having the Governance domiciled on its soil? OtherWhere was out of the question as yielding Others too much power, but none of the Fourteen Tribes would yield on the issue, nor establish some neutral point on unclaimed land. Even now, when it is feasible to operate a decentralized Governance by means of infonet, with delegates never actually meeting in one central locus but carrying on their business by comm, the Tribes refuse. Who will run the power sources? How can it be ensured that no one tribe earns more 'net time than its fellows, or that Others, whose technology it is, will not dominate the whole?"

Jeijinn paused, letting her words sink in.

"The alternative is the barely controlled chaos you observe, with Others invariably being called in as arbitrators of the least dispute. We become more intricately interwoven into People's internal affairs daily. This simultaneously yields us more and less power, for while we are now the coequals Accolon wished us to avoid becoming, we also have little time for our own needs.

"In order for the Alliance to function, more Others must dwell on the Mainland than can remain here. This was never what we intended. Optimally, we should have set up the function of those advances People desired, then withdrawn. But the People insist we stay. So we do, in ever increasing numbers. Even Evere has been persuaded out of his hermitage into crossover."

Jeijinn addressed this last to me. I considered the implications of a demand so great it could persuade my reclusive father to leave his commscreen.

"The Melet Wars," I answered.

"Just so." Jeijinn poured more tea. " 'Brushfires,' your teacher Rau would have called them. I always wondered where he learned his terminology. But this is the primary function of Others now: to extinguish People's brushfires. The Werthan delegation is a prime example, as I need not tell two who labor on the front lines, so to speak."

"Indeed," Dweneth interjected solemnly, though I could see by her eyes that she wanted to burst into giggles. *Wait*, she telegraphed to me, *until I add the tale of Dzilbak the Dragon-marked to the infonets!*

Jeijinn indicated her deskcomm, where a plethora of cases scrolled automatically into the memory from Worldwide.

" 'A petition by the Chandlers' Union of Hraregh'," she read, " 'to stop the construction of electrical plants in the outer provinces, for if all citizens have electricity, what hope is there for candlemakers?' 'A request from the Oligarchy of Melet, in that as their sworn enemy Mantuul does not believe in Others, Others should aid them not only in the area of desalination, so generously overseen by WiseEvere, but in military aid as well.' Imagine! Have all our words of peace meant nothing? 'A motion before the Council this very afternoon'—proposed by a Matriarch, if you will—'that a combined work of Others and People be initiated toward spaceflight, with the prospect of orbital colony stations within two decades. Accusations by the People that we have the theoretical capability'—and so we have; spaceflight trajectories were Liiki's province before I was born—'but that Others deliberately withhold it'—and so we do, until we solve the problems on the World below. I am only grateful Loriel did not live to hear this much!"

She touched the power toggle; the screen went blank,

though the memory would continue to store each petition as they came in, seemingly without end.

"And yet," Jeijinn concluded, "the principal complaint of the majority of People is that we do too much. The dichotomy grows daily between those who cry 'More, give us more!' and those who lament that we 'leave them no challenges for themselves'."

Dweneth had her fingers on Jeijinn's pulse. The servitor, having returned punctually in two hours' time, hovered nearby, humming patiently. Dweneth looked at me and shook her head.

"A leave of absence, Jeijinn-*al*," she suggested. "Perhaps on Two Greater, as far from People as you can go."

"There is much yet to be done . . ." Jeijinn protested.

"By an overworked Matriarch in her advancing years, grown querulous with overmedication?" Dweneth's voice dripped sarcasm. "Is this efficient? Is it Disciplined?"

Jeijinn raised one eyebrow. " 'Querulous'? Perhaps you are right. Doubtless someone among the Matriarchs, returned from the Mainland, could replace me temporarily . . . But what of Dzu?"

"Bring him with you," Dweneth suggested. "If he so loathes People, doubtless the Dissenters will cherish him."

Jeijinn gave her an odd look. "He did not tell you? No, he would not. That is Dzu. He requested a place among the Dissenters, long ago."

"And?"

"Denied, of course. If the Dissenters' purpose is to separate themselves from People, how are they to welcome one of the People into their midst?"

"Lingri?"

"Yes, Dzu."

"Is it only biology which makes anOther—the color of one's blood, the pace of one's heart? Can Other philosophy

202

not encompass the possibility of anOther soul trapped in a People's body? What does it mean to be anOther?"

"Perhaps it begins with the ability to master hatred," I suggested.

"You have not lived what I have lived!" he flared. "No Other has! What do you know of hatred?"

"Only that it harms you far more than those you hate."

"Only because I will it so!" He had had his back to me; now he turned to face me for the first time. I could see his jaw clench, his back stiffen, though his fine-boned hands stayed lax, deceptive. "I am dangerous, Lingri-one: mark me! If I should ever leave the safety of OtherWhere and return to People, there is no telling what havoc I could wreak! I begged for haven on Two Greater, so that I would do no harm. Haven for myself, safety for the World. Why do they deny it me?"

"What reasons did they give you?" He did not answer me. I thought of those Dissenters I knew personally, close-minded Govin, soft-handed Chior. Bigots—was it possible? Even Others were not without such flaws. "Perhaps it is only that you represent a living paradox. Their logic cannot encompass People who wish to be Other. It is their weakness, Dzu, not yours."

"Then I belong nowhere!" Dzu cried.

"Or everywhere." I thought of how his anguish would affect Jeijinn, and tried to calm him. "Dzu, hear me as one who knows: the Unlikely Candidate is free to choose her own way."

"Poets' words!" he sneered. "I know your story! Babbling in tongues with Lerius when you were a child. But you were free to choose what you became thereafter. What choice have I?"

"Within the parameters of your skills, all the choice there is."

"An academic, teaching those he hates!" He sneered at

himself now. "A Solitary as the only choice to keep from going mad? Neither People nor Other, without place—"

"Except the place you choose."

He approached me then, his manner suddenly fervid, desperately confidential.

"Even as Others subdivide themselves into Diversers and Dissenters, People subdivide themselves as well. The time will come when the Fourteen Tribes are only memory, when more primeval drives supercede ethnic differences. There will in the end be two entities only: those who call themselves OneWorlders and, opposed to them, the Ethnocentrics. There will be wars, wars in which no Other can in conscience participate, and their neutrality will be interpreted as betrayal by both sides. Out of this tumult—I can see it clear—will arise a third entity which will inadvertently emulate the Dissenters in their desire to be People alone and separate. These will eclipse all violence heretofore wrought upon this World, with a violence so cataclysmic . . . "

He staggered beneath the weight of his vision and I caught him, mindful of Dweneth's assessment that he was already mad.

"Dzu!" I held him by the shoulders; he had gone limp, slack-jawed, glaze-eyed, all charisma, all personality leached out of him by a kind of trance. "You have seen this for yourself?"

He shook me off, clutched his forehead as if it pained him.

"Not a vision. Not a Telepath's dream. I *know!* The 'scans always credited me with extraordinary gifts in political science, and Jeijinn has schooled me well. I *see*, as if it were already written down; history, not future." He caught my look, recovered himself. "You think me mad, don't you?"

"Not mad. Suffering, certainly, and in need of aid. You must not keep this knowledge to yourself."

He pulled away from me, putting the room's distance between us. "With whom am I to share it? The Chamber will not hear me, nor the Council. How can I have a Telepath's insight into the future? I am People, after all!"

"If some Other were to speak for you," I began, wondering why Jeijinn at least had not done so.

"No!" he said. Unqualified, unexplained, simply no.

"Then if you wish to look upon life as a duty, your duty is clear," I said after a long moment.

"Is it?" Dzu arched his eyebrows at me. "Then explain it for my simple People's mind, for I don't see it."

"You must return to your People, using your knowledge and your skills, in order to prevent this future which you see with such clarity."

"Return to 'my' People, whom I loathe—"

"To make the way smooth for Others, whom you honor. Dzu"—I will never know what made me ask this—"have you ever bonded?"

He recoiled as if I'd struck him, though the image is not precise. I could have struck him, could have mortally wounded him, and he would not have recoiled so. This was Dzu.

"Bonded, I? Again I ask: with whom? One of the People's vacuous daughters, who flutter about and would cling to me like limpets except that I consistently repel them? I can't abide their meat-eaters' stench, much less the emptiness of their minds! And if I am not Other enough to live among Dissenters, how dare I so much as touch the shadow of anOther female?"

"Dzu—"

"I exaggerate, of course. No Other female would condescend to notice if I stood full in her shadow. But you see what I mean."

"Dzu . . ." Permutations were scrolling through my mind. Legally Dzu and I were siblings, though as far as possible from consanguineous. The Council had absolved me of culpability in the matter of Redrec and, though he was young, Dzu was in fact two years Redrec's elder. Yet, were these reasons to offer what I offered next?

"I will bond with you, if you will have me."

At first his response was only prolonged silence. Then, for the first of three times ever, I heard him laugh.

"Is this the Continuum which speaks through you? Some convoluted Other plan to take two Unlikely Candidates out of the path of normal Other ways? Or am I so obviously in need of your charity? Lingri, I shall not even thank you. There is no one for me, no one!"

"Forgive me," I said, "but grant me one thing more."

"I shall consider it." This was the old Dzu now, the arrogant, charismatic Dzu, his voice arch, his manner lofty.

"Do you remember what you once asked me about the sex-sellers of Hraregh?"

"I remember everything," he answered coldly.

"Grant me the right to ask you the same question. If you had been Monitor, what would you have done?"

"I would have done everything I could to save them!" he answered fervidly, becoming some Dzu who had lived before any Other knew him, before the hunger and abuse, if ever such a Dzu existed. This Dzu endured but a moment, incandesced, and vanished. "Even disregarding Discipline, everything!"

"I see," I said. "Yet you will not do so now?"

He scowled. "Explain."

"How many children do you condemn to die in the conflagration you foresee?"

I persuaded him of nothing that day, nor in the many days which followed, yet I did persist. Circumstance was to keep me in OtherWhere for some time, and I continued to challenge Dzu. My only indication that I was reaching him was that he did not return to Solitude.

I do not know for certain if it was my argument which

206

finally swayed him or only something he himself foresaw—
his later writings were rife with references to his "destiny"—nevertheless I remain convinced that it was I, Lingri,
who persuaded Dzugash the Pure to return to the world of
People.

To my everlasting regret.

"For myself, I have never subscribed to the theory of one
man as destiny. . . . "

The voice is not one I recognize at first, having heard it
more usually as the instrument of someone else, specifically
the Dragon Dzilbak. For it is Dzilbak's Jemadar who speaks
to me beside the hot spring in our communal cavern in this
world of ice, decades and latitudes removed from my memories of Dzu. I have been desultorily continuing my chronicle,
as a kind of recitation during the single rest period we allow
ourselves between the many things we have to do.

"It seems to me," the Jemadar says, "having lived
among leaders all my life, that any individual's ability to
move a People is only as strong as that People's predisposition to be moved. What say you, Lingri Chronicler?"

"I think, Jemadar, that Lingri Chronicler has become
superfluous now that Others are to live; therefore she is not
entitled to an opinion."

"He's flirting with you," is my daughter-in-law's opinion. We have lived in this place of fire and ice for ninety-
three days precisely and there have been extensive changes,
one of which is that Dwiri at last looks pregnant. She also
spends less time with the Telepathy. "Nothing wrong with
that, of course. In fact, it might do you both some good. He's
very lonely."

"While I am supportive of continued intercourse between Melet and Others, Dwiri-*la*," I answer dryly, "I dare-
say it need not begin and end with me!" Dwiri's words lend
me caution. I have learned through long experience how

207

difficult it is to detach a male's attention once it becomes affixed to one.

Yet I value the presence of this Jemadar, whose designation has become his name, by Melet custom. Thus he will always be He Who Goes Between until he dies. I find him sensitive, knowledgeable, gratifying to listen to. Alas, he is also recently widowed in the Mantuul incursions, and disdainful of the choices among the women of his kind.

"I am past one hundred years," I tell him bluntly from the start, as if my too-white hair cannot speak for me.

"Thus younger for one of your kind than I am for mine," he answers smoothly, smiling with his eyes, though his face is lined with sadness. Thus the diplomat, this Jemadar. "Quite acceptable, in a friend or in a mate."

Yet he is wise enough to understand I do not share his interest and derives whatever he can from our exchange of dialogue, which is stimulating. Now he wants to know, having followed my chronicle down our new-wrought story-nets, whether I really hold myself responsible for what Dzu ultimately became.

"I know this much, Jemadar," I answer: "That few People before or since, few Others for that matter, possessed in any degree the aptitude Dzu had, for either good or ill."

Perhaps I should explain about the story-nets.

Since our arrival in this realm of ice and fire some ninety-three days ago, Others have begun to share their personal histories, with the intention of preserving each person's uniqueness in the eidetic memory, until such time as it can be committed to more permanent physical record.

Succinctly: ten Others form an age-chain in which the eldest relates her life history to the one next to her in age, who commits the tale to the mnemonic Discipline, in which all of us are trained from childhood.

Each Other commits to memory the exact words of her next elder even as she relates her own tale to the next

208

younger. Then the youngest entrusts her tale to the eldest, completing the chain. Thereafter each member of the chain reiterates her portion of the chain to the eldest who, having the strongest mnemonic, commits all ten to reinforced memory, forming a ten-chain.

Each evening, as we gather from the separate tasks and places we have assigned ourselves, we attend the recitation of a new ten-chain; our listening, combined with what any one of us may know about the individual spoken of, reinforces the communal memory. Thereafter one of our last Telepaths commits the ten-chain to the eidetic Discipline intact.

In time, each of the Telepaths will have absorbed one quarter of the nine thousand four hundred eleven individual histories which remain. It is hoped that before SavantTisra dies, her portion of the mnemonic can be written down. If we are to be the last of our kind, we shall not go unrecorded.

Thus have I set aside my ragtag chronicle in its physical form, all tags and scraps and media, to write down Tisra's words each evening as she speaks. As if by miracle, one of our relief parcels from the Zanti on the Mainland contained several reams of quality paper and a quantity of pens. My own unworthy tale is hereby relegated to the trivial, pulled out of me in snatches by the curious, such as this Jemadar. Our new life-style gives us too much else to do.

Nine thousand four hundred eleven Others, approximately fourteen hundred Melet, twenty-three Partisans, and fourteen Intermixes could not overlong inhabit that single large chamber where we made camp when we first arrived. The Melet went exploring on the following day, taking with them those Partisans who were not immediately returning, bRi-led, to the Mainland to oversee the supply routes which have kept us fed and clothed and in paper thus far.

The Melet found a series of caverns within a smaller mountain, as well as a fresh-running inlet where they might fish. Thus were we first divided into two distinct settlements. Melet come to visit us on occasion, and one Other, the youngster Yarel, has been more or less adopted by them as a possible future bondmate for the orphaned Mellia. Our only consistent messenger from the second settlement is the ubiquitous Jemadar, He Who Goes Between. I trust it is not only to speak with me.

As for this Other settlement, this New OtherWhere, its central locus is still the cathedral-ceilinged chamber with its spring-fed pool, which we now call the New Citadel. Here our remnant Matriarchy holds its Council, here the necessarily communal activities of communication and food distribution endure, here we all gather betimes to partake of the salubrious effects of the pool. But for all things else, we are scattered everywhere throughout the heart of the mountain, seeking privacy as Others will, though we can gather as one upon the proper signal.

The mountain is a maze of tunnels, chambers, grottoes, cavelets, cold springs, hot springs, steam vents, labyrinths and spiraling natural stairways; People would get lost here, but we rely on Othersense. Families and individuals, and makeshift units such as the one I share with Peria and Aloyi, have chosen their dwelling places and begun to personalize them.

The grotto I share with the children contains three distinct chambers and opens to one of several paths leading to the greenhouses. A cold clear spring trickles into a natural catch basin a few paces from our door. My central chamber, irregularly shaped, yields a sleeping shelf, a ceiling high enough to stand, and any number of small crevices in which to store things, including a disused chronicle.

Aloyi's chamber sports a shabby but colorful Zanti blanket and a collection of lightstones harvested from the deepest caves, glowing softly in the dark. Peria's chamber features a Plalan story tapestry and a Droghian lute, which she had begun to learn to play. Only my own place is virtually barren, "a nun's cell," Jemadar calls it, who has been here only once.

The reason is simple: I am here only to sleep, and that but seldom. My waking hours are spent as any Other's, doing laundry, rowing the supply boats, *bRi*-speaking, writing down Tisra's words. Then there is my luxury—the greenhouses.

The Windwardmost face of our mountain is sheathed in a glacier as much as a mile thick in places, but of such clear, pristine ice as to be quite translucent even through this depth. The further beauty is that this face of the mountain, much like the one which faces the fjords where we entered, opens out into a series of small interlinked caves which, completely covered by this ice wall, are invisible from the outside but, from within, form sun-brightened natural growing places for our crops.

The temperature within the mountain, owing to the hot springs, falls into a somewhat humid but evenly temperate range perfect for agriculture. Meltwater from the interior of the glacier provides irrigation, and Otherlabor has harvested the richest soils.

When we first arrived, the nights were longer than the days; now the reverse is happening. Between our mountain and Melet's there is an open plain, where the ice already begins to melt. Rich volcanic soil nourishes an incredible variety of mosses, herbs, and flowers with which in time we will supplement our diet and our pharmacopoeia. For now, we concentrate on the greenhouses, where our very breath and excrement provide welcome nutrients.

The concentrated carbon monoxide exuded by over nine thousand beings, combined with spores somehow miraculously intact on our clothing after our tumultuous sea voyage, resulted in growths of moss on previously barren cave walls within the first thirty days. Now it nurtures the seeds and spores WiseAguisel the botanist has had smuggled

211

in, and countless seedlings flourish. We expect to be self-sufficient within a year.

Meanwhile a manner of *bRi*-caravan sustains us, depositing its loads of food and clothing at the mouth of the fjords for us to ferry in further. Upon occasion a parcel will contain incredible luxuries: the aforementioned paper and pens, old-style paper books, sheet music and even the occasional musical instrument or two, decorative holos, and, more practically, electronic components and items which are beyond my nonscientific comprehension, though I recognize their ultimate purpose: to construct a solar power plant which will render us completely self-sustaining.

It is not that we are ungrateful for what the Zanti and their Partisans continue to do for us; it is our very gratitude which strives to end the smuggling, for the longer it continues the greater the risk of detection. We will add no more People's lives to our debt. Further, it behooves us to regain our technology, if only to construct a radio receiver and learn what transpires in the World we have left behind.

It has been as full a day as most. I have been running one of the supply boats up the fjord; I often accompany the rowers anyway, because I speak the purest *bRi*, but we are frequently shorthanded, so I row. The afternoon occupies me in the greenhouses, repotting countless fragile seedlings. Covered with dirt, I seek refuge in the hot spring, and the luxury of a swim before consigning myself a stint of recopying Tisra's ten-chains.

I surface to find Jemadar sitting on the moss-covered bank contemplating me, his arms clasped about his knees. Having removed his outer cloak on entering the caverns, he wears only his ornate sandals-of-office and the typical Melet male's loincloth. Yet he is overdressed for swimming, as Others practice it. I step from the water, deliberate in covering myself. It is not nakedness itself which shames, but the

212

glance it earns from those who are not Others. This Jemadar's glance is entirely too warm.

"I've been hearing tales of you," he begins pleasantly enough, inviting me to sit beside him. "Tales of Lingri Monitor which stretch back eight decades or more."

"What tales, and told by whom?" I counter, also pleasantly, sitting across from him on the bank so that our conversation may be private but not intimate.

"Your son, among Others. An interesting hybrid, your Joreth. I have not met an Intermix before. Would all your children have looked like him?"

"All my children would have resembled their fathers, assuming their fathers were People. That is past. What do you really want, Jemadar?"

"You are direct!" he jokes, but then his face clouds. "I am told you knew the Hated One. That you were once his instructor in a way, even some manner of kin. I don't understand this."

"I know no one by that name," I temporize. Ah, Dzu, when will it end?

"Call him what you will," Jemadar allows, "Dzugash the Pure, Dzugash the Demagogue. Patriarch of the People's Purist Party. Dzugash the Genocide. Is it true?"

"I knew Dzugash as a child, yes. He was reared in OtherWhere from the age of eight; instructed by Others, myself and Lerius among them; adopted by my mother Jeijinn. Other-reared and Other-instructed, no matter what he later preached."

The Jemadar is at a loss for words; he studies the decorative work on his sandals, traces similar patterns in the moss with his fingertips.

"How is it then," he says at last, his lined face troubled, "that he could become what he later did?"

"Ask anOther to explain a People's heart?" I demand archly. "You are the diplomat, Jemadar, not I. Others taught

213

Dzu to overcome his hatred of his own People. We could not know we were teaching him to hate us."

"I hear more than your words, Lingri-one," Jemadar offers gently. "Is it possible you blame yourself for some of it?"

"Not blame, Jemadar," I answer, clear-eyed. "Rather, I accept the responsibility. The first implies the possibility of atonement. The second does not."

"That's all you'll get from her, Jemadar!" Joreth is among us, already stepping out of his clothes. "Evasions, inversions, Other chop-logic. Expect no more!"

Our former ship's captain has long since resigned his post in deference to the Council and resumed his previous occupation. When each evening's story-chain has ended, Joreth and what musicians he can find among Others and Intermixes provide an interlude to soothe us off to either the close or the opening of our day, for in this place of half-year days and half-year nights, we choose our own natural rhythms.

"What I might expect," Jemadar says thoughtfully, "is anOther offspring's characteristic respect for his parent."

Joreth swims the length of the pool twice before he answers, "Lingri is not my parent. I've a document which says so!"

I rise to my full middling height, causing the unfortunate Jemadar to scramble to his feet out of Melet courtesy, the while he struggles to understand what Joreth has just said. Nor do I enlighten him, but rather lock eyes with my son. I will not have my privacy toyed with before outWorlders.

" 'Fair for fair'?" I challenge Joreth, who loses his easy grin at the ritual words. He pulls himself from the pool to tower over me.

" 'State what terms,' " He answers the ancient ritual.

"Total truth," I answer. "Then silence."

Excerpt: "Key Voices of the New Age, Part III: Redrec
           of Droghia"
           by Licho d'Gleris
           (from *Musical Notes*, vol. 20, no. 6 [Bask
           1637 P.A.])

                                              [pre-Censored]

   *When one examines the oddly contradictory adult
evolution of this former child prodigy, one discovers
two distinct phases: before and after the age of twenty-
four.*

   *Let us suppose that Redrec's "prodigy period" ends
with the death of his father, the dwarf genius Redrec
Elder, when Redrec the Younger was not quite sixteen.
As a prodigy, under the hand of that unfortunately
unrecorded by undisputed "giant in a small package,"
as his contemporaries have called him, Redrec
Younger's composition was copious, but not original.
Rather, it was his playing which dazzled.*

   *Upon the death of his father, easily the greatest
influence upon his young life, he began to compose in
earnest. Larger pieces, bravura pieces, operas and symphonies in place of the operettas, concertos, and popular songs which earlier had emerged from his pen like
clockwork beneath his father's heavy hand now poured
from him like a very deluge. But again, of what quality?*

   *He was certainly the most popular composer of his
day. With the miraculous advances in printing and
communication, his works were soon extant in all of
the fourteen lands of the Known World. But while his
works were bigger, more grandiose, more crowd-pleas-
ing, there is no indication that, without the fame of his
earlier success, he would have lasted much beyond his*

early twenties without "burning out," in the popular imagination if not in actual output.

But something happened to him before the age of twenty-five which slammed the door firmly on this phase, while simultaneously hurling open the portals of the next. Without his signature on the sheet music, it is doubtful even the most meticulous musicologist could recognize these compositions as the work of that same Redrec d'Droghia who went before.

Was it only the advent of new instruments and new techniques as a result of [CENSORED]? Was it, as some more romantic theorists have put forth, "the result of a broken heart"? Whatever it was, the change was radical and immediate, and upon it Redrec built until his death in 1606 P.A. at the age of seventy-nine.

All that is known for certain is that he traveled extensively in his middle twenties, having signed for a tour first with the Concert Orchestra of LamorDroghia, and later as soloist with the Pan-Shadoward Ensemble.

Something he experienced in those years changed his life. Was it truly some long-lost or unobtainable love object, some shattering love affair which lent his music a new maturity, a heartrending poignancy in place of his once facile but superficial stylistic turn? Whatever it was which gave his voice, as Farho was to describe it in the Regon Symphony, a "towering melancholy," it transformed the simpering boy-composer into a genius who overshadowed even his own father. . . .

Finally, the long-lost–love theory is either refuted or reinforced by Redrec's later life, for the number of women who claimed to have known him intimately was legion. There was even a son, Joreth, born when his father was nearly sixty. A promising young musician in his own right before being declared a State Criminal, Joreth's mother's identity was never revealed. "Dead!" the elderly Redrec would tell any interviewer who *raised the question, and the fact that he raised the boy himself led to speculation that she had been some sweet young thing, seduced by the famed composer old enough to be her grandfather, who died tragically in childbirth. Was she the subject of the unfinished song, found among Redrec's papers following his death, entitled simply "To the Lost"?*

10

"Dislove me because I do not *feel?*" Redrec was incredulous. "And this from anOther? It makes no sense!"

Since my return to OtherWhere I had almost daily scanned the performance notices, run on the infonets Other-fashion as well as pasted up on waysides as they were in People's lands, finding nearly every People's virtuoso but Redrec passing through the Greaters on a World tour. Only now, nearly seven years to the day since we had parted, did he turn up, and not in the expected way.

Other food synthers had finally, at least according to Dweneth's finicking standards, managed to produce a passable Werthan ale, along with stronger spirits. While Others did occasionally imbibe these curious alien concoctions, they had no effect on us, hence they existed in OtherWhere largely for visiting People's pleasure. This did not, of course, sanction public intoxication.

Nevertheless, more than one People's tavern had sprung up in the environs of One Greater's original harbor. Though most travelers arrived by skimmer now, the harbor endured as a symbolic first landing place. Hence People newly arrived and reluctant to plunge headlong into the strange, bright-faceted City before them lingered here. It was such a group which accosted me on my way to the beach for an evening *bRi*-swim.

Free swimming, Other-fashion, had become increasingly problematical of late. Visiting People seemed equally divided into those who accepted nude swimming and had learned to join us, those who found scandal in the very idea, and those who gathered on the beaches to gawk and leer. Mindful of what had happened to Loriel, Others tended to avoid these last by swimming only from the Lessers, or at night.

To hone my *bRi*-skills and because I liked to swim, I frequented the beaches almost nightly except in Stormsea-son, and had never encountered difficulty before. This one night some dozen beery-breathed outWorld males material-ized out of shadow to surround me, blocking either progress or retreat. Should Lingri Inept be required to fend in her own land? Oh, how the infonets would treasure that!

"What difficulty, Goodmen?" I inquired in Intertribal, seeing several tribes represented in their garb and faces. Meanwhile I readied myself, in the event words proved insufficient. "Is the way not free to all who walk it?"

"That be 'er?" a Lamorak growled over his shoulder at one in Droghian garb, nudging him sharply. I had not expected either tribe represented here while Renna and her kin ruled.

"Aye, sounds like!"

The Droghian elbowed his way to the forefront as his fellows melted back into the inn with a curious glance or two behind. I did not relax my fending stance. There was no mistaking that voice.

"Redrec."

"Lingri."

He tried to embrace me, succeeded in kissing me full on

219

the mouth before I held him off. Either he was quick or I was careless. His grin still had too many teeth in it.

"It's been sheer hell to get here. I hope I'm on time?"

No point in pretending not to comprehend him; he would only repeat his question at the top of his lungs till it was answered.

"Are we grown so barbarous that we must discuss this subject in public? Is that why you've come here?"

He took my arm, leading me into the dim-lit inn while I marveled, as I always did with Redrec, at how easily I let myself be led. His long frame had filled in; there was muscle in his once-lax arm. Physically, at least, the boy was now a man.

"Officially, I am here on a special permit to perform with the Ensemble, which is featuring my newer works," he explained, choosing a table and signaling for two mugs of ale without bothering to consult me. "It's the only way a Lamor-Droghian can travel currently, by request. However, even that's about to change."

His tone grew confidential. "Dame Renna's son may not be the brightest, but he's figured out how much the two nations are missing in not dealing with Others. There's a hefty black market in Other goods by way of Wertha and Kwengiis—"Some of which you might know of at firsthand, I thought but did not say—"which is slowly ruining the economy. There's talk in the Diet of a split with Lamora if the ruling party won't see sense. So it's likely you'll have Lamora and Droghia back in your Second Alliance where you lost 'em to your First."

My ears took in his words the while my eyes took in his person. His eyes danced green as bottle glass, his pretty-ugly face had grown true Redrec-ugly, and the trimmed and perfumed beard he lately sported made him more than ever his father's son. I kept these thoughts to myself as well.

"But what does a musician care for politics, except where they get in the way of his freedom?" He wiped foam from his mustache. "I wanted to see OtherWhere, to see how it measured up to hearsay. And there's nothing as irresistible as a fresh audience for my music. But I also wanted to be sure I got here for your next cycle."

Had my last departure taught him nothing?

"As to that last, perhaps you have come for nothing. What if I am already bonded to anOther?"

"You aren't. Your eyes wouldn't rove over me with such pleasure if you were. I've learned that about Others. Never mind their faces; watch their eyes. At least this time you can't say I'm too young."

I said nothing. He had not been lonely these seven years; I knew. Nor would he be faithful even if we were to bond. This I also knew, as I knew Redrec. What, then, was the point?

"There are medications," the psych-healer informed me when I had sought remedy at the hospice, "as there are meditations. Either will suppress any cycle except the first, though at great physical and psychic cost. But why?"

She knew why, and had asked me merely as a formality. All of my contemporaries were already bonded at least once. While I was within my rights to seek a partner from the next-younger group, this would complicate first-bonding for females of that group, particularly now that unbonded females currently outnumbered available males. This was yet one more unforeseen dimension of our relationship with People.

"For whatever reason, there is a trend toward Intermix marriages, and these new-fashioned bondings tend to be more Other male/People's woman than the turnabout," Dweneth explained.

"Curious. To what do you attribute this?"

It was to influence her near future, as her Grenni hospice had been awarded a grant to establish a clinic for the study of genetics, particularly the possibility of gene splicing

221

to enable Others and People to have Intermix offspring. Everyone from botanists to nuclear biologists seemed to be dabbling in genetics of late.

"So far all they've managed are several blight-resistant grains, and a heljack with the disposition of a lap-pet," Dweneth reported from her reading on the science 'nets, "but People seem to take longer. What interests me more is the disease-control potential; it's why I asked for the grant originally. Then again, I should probably be treating vitamin deficiencies in Gleris, where I'm needed. Best I take what I'm offered and stop complaining. As to why our women choose Other males more than the turnabout?" She shrugged, as if it did not apply so poignantly to her personally. "Beats me. Imagine only wanting it once every seven to ten years! Obviously no redblood male will stand still for that. Oh, we all know Others *can* as often as they wish, but only *must* when the cycle's upon them. And since most of you are so preoccupied with Other matters you never think about it until you must—am I right?"

"Not entirely."

"Well, anyway, I can't tell you why Other males choose us—some of us—but it's obvious why our women choose them. Rockets and fireworks on a set schedule, and no pleading in between. And no fear of getting pregnant. Quality in place of quantity? As near as possible to perfect sex, some call it. Not that I'll ever know!"

In our several years on OtherWhere we had both been busy, Dweneth in study and research on the newest techniques in her field, I in a project of ever growing proportions: a cataloguing of all People's literatures, past and present, literate and preliterate, Before Others and After Others, in all the People's languages and our own. A staff of twenty linguists aided me, yet the work was all-consuming. Only Dweneth served on occasion to drag me out of doors and into something which was not work. This night it was to be Redrec's OtherWhere premiere.

These restful years in OtherWhere had been somewhat kinder to Dweneth than her years on the Mainland, save that the constant strain of being near Lerius yet not near took its toll.

"Is there no alternative for you?" I had asked, already knowing the answer.

"None," she had answered bleakly. The years had given her an introspective look. "Nor for him. He suppresses his cycles now, as Telepaths can. He's had no mate since I became his nonmate."

"And this is healthy?"

"No more nor less than you suppressing your next cycle with drugs because you're too stubborn to accept what you're offered!" she retorted, eyeing the figure Redrec cut, preening backstage in his formal finery. "You could do worse."

"Worse than a perfumed musician, a hothouse flower with manicured hands, who lacks the courage to confront me formally but slithers into OtherWhere like the smuggler he no doubt is as well? Perhaps I do not wish to do worse. Perhaps I do not wish to 'do' at all!"

"That's the part I don't understand," Dweneth said as we took our seats. "The time is almost upon you—and don't tell me elsewise; you grow more irritable by the day—yet you haven't bonded with anOther. You do want him."

I did not answer.

"Look you," she persisted, "ask for perfection in the male of any species and you're doomed to disappointment. But yon Redrec's gifted enough, different surely from any Other male, if that's your objective, and certainly pleasing to the eye. Pleasing to the Other senses too, to hear you tell it. Not to mention that he saved your life."

"If we are not to mention it, let us not mention it," I answered irritably. "Do you find him so desirable? He is yours!"

"Except it's you he wants," she answered as the lights

223

went down. I hoped that this would silence her; it did not. "Perverse! Not to be redundant, but what about what you want? You *do* want him. And he wants you. What is it in Others, and Lingri in particular, which denies yourselves what you desire most? And what right have you to deny it him?"

The "him" in question stepped out onto the stage then, silencing my companion's feverish whispers in an uproar of applause.

Of all the People's arts welcomed in OtherWhere, only music must by its nature be prescreened for Other audiences. My own experience with the Hydraulus beneath Redrec Elder's hands had countless precedents in our ancient history and in Monitors' reports. Something about the Other nervous system rendered us emotionally susceptible to certain kinds of music.

No such danger from Redrec's compositions, I recall thinking as the opening strains of his first keyboard work—conducted by the composer-soloist himself; Redrec was nothing if not versatile—resonated reminiscent of his earlier works. True, there was some evidence of growth, of newer techniques mastered under teachers who were not his father, yet he remained Redrec, more concerned that his audience love him than that his music transcend. Imagine his surprise, I thought, to find Others' appreciation less than effusive.

For myself, I began to thread a path within his complex, artful melodies, pleasant and flower-strewn, upon which to wend down certain seldom explored reaches of my mind. . . .

To awaken, as if from trance, and find the concert hall emptied for the intermission, and Dweneth's eyes upon me, her pupils dilated like a Telepath's. She had followed me at least partway down the soul-thread. What did she see that I could not?

"Beware this!" she cautioned me, exuding irony. "Be-

224

ware Redrec. He represents chaos, and all that is unOther. He will render you shy, uncertain, uneasy with your passions and your drives. He will grow you, and you him. Joining with him will be no Monitor's aloof exercise, but true commitment, loss of control. This frightens you."

"Indeed." As my mind was open to her, I could be no less than truthful. "By your own words, People's males want only whores and servants. Which shall I be?"

"Redrec has come back for you. Is it possible he loves you?"

"That is as may be, and I have no control over it. But I do not love him."

"How can you be sure?"

This gave me pause, and I considered it. Some few musicians had returned to the stage to move music stands and tune their instruments. I watched them.

"Truth, do you love anyone?" Dweneth would not relent. "By the soul-thread, I know that you love me, though it is beyond you to say the words. How can anOther tell? You seal yourselves about in Disciplines and your duty to the Continuum. Are these not dimensions of love?"

"Then by your definition I should love all People, not only Redrec."

"And so you do, in a generic, objective way." She sighed, withdrew back into her own space; Others and People were returning to the hall. "Yet when one individual personally dares love you back, you falter. If not Redrec, who? Will you remain unbonded all your life? Transform it into duty, then, if you find that more palatable. He saved your life. You owe him something!"

"Whatever I may owe him—" I began, but the entr'acte was over; there were too many ears. I fixed my attention on the stage. Let Dweneth whisper as she would; I had come to listen to the music.

To my detriment. The exuberant young composer leapt

up to the podium to renewed applause and with a flourish began to conduct his newest symphony.

This was a new Redrec, an older Redrec, a Redrec still possessed of his fawning idiosyncrasies but verging on some hinted-at grandeur. This music began to touch upon transcendance, and thus it was my undoing.

Dweneth told me later that I wept. For myself, I do not recall.

Love him¿ It must have jangled down the soul-thread; I saw Dweneth start. *So I may. But if I do, is it not as dangerous as what you desire with Lerius¿ Bonding with anOther is no trivial thing. What right have I to determine the course of his young life¿*

Dweneth gawked at me, struggling to hold back the words which decorum dictated she must not speak, but outrage said she must. Forced to contain herself until the symphony was over, she rose with the applause and all but dragged me out into the foyer ahead of the crowd.

"How *dare* you!" she blustered. "While you live, every life you brush against you impact on. Be a Solitary else! Look what you've done to the course of my life! Everything I am now is because of you!"

"Oh, spare me!" I answered, my Discipline edged with exasperation. I strode away, she followed; I turned on her. "What you are is who you are. Mine was but a minor instrumentality."

"Will you listen to yourself!" she shouted. We had begun to quarrel like children, forgetting time and place. "Follow your own reasoning, Lingri apt-named Inept! If I am what I am, then so are we all, including Redrec. Let your 'minor instrumentality' do for him what it has done for me!"

Our quarrel had taken us away from the crowd, down obscure back corridors. Dweneth I think intended to storm away, to make some grandiose Player's exit. Instead she found herself in collision with the sweating boy-composer, who, breathless from his several curtain calls, had been on his way to the tiring rooms when he came up against our noise and chaos.

"Oh!" Dweneth gasped, instantly recovering herself. "Meister Redrec, well played!"

His eyes danced over her; he would not be Redrec if they had not.

"I thank you, fair one. Who . . . ?"

"A friend of a friend!" she snapped, stepping quickly aside to reveal me.

"I see!" Redrec frowned, clearly not seeing at all.

Dweneth was right and I was near the time. My blood pounded in my ears, my hands shook. A subtle fever had ensued some days ago. Noises startled me, silence brought me near to weeping; I had lost all taste for food. The touch of the lightest fabric against my flesh was irritating; I burned.

There were medications and meditations; I had availed myself of neither. I had scrolled through the files of unbonded males and remained indifferent. In not choosing, had I chosen?

There was a clamor from the concert hall, clamor in the the tiring rooms, People's clamor, demanding the presence of the heroic young composer. Heedless, he stood before us, wiping perspiration from his beard, puzzlement creasing his Redrec-ugly face. He held out his hands in a receptive gesture, hands which trembled from the effort of performance. He seemed content to wait out whatever scenario Dweneth and I chose to play.

Dweneth touched my shoulder, breathed into my ear, "For my sake, Old Stick, if not for him or thee. I deserve to see you happy. Mayhap someday a godchild or two for me to cuddle . . ."

She could not finish. It always came around to children.

"Perhaps, Dweneth Healer," I said, trying to make light of it, "that is more your realm than mine!"

"You do your share!" she whispered, squeezing my shoulder hard. "Grenni and I will do ours!"

She all but shoved me in Redrec's direction and was gone. She would be skimming over the Great Sea to the Mainland and her duty within the hour. I was alone with Redrec.

"I promise nothing," I cautioned him.

He shrugged. "Have I asked for more?"

He was the musician, and I became the music.

We were harmony. We sang, we swam, we soared, become both dancer and the dance. We burned and culminated, tumbled into sleep, awoke to incandesce again. In two days' time the music died.

"When do you next perform?" I murmured when at last it seemed a time for conversation. The uneasiness had woken me, though my body lay at rest, my head in the hollow of his shoulder, my hair flung about his chest like seakelp.

"I don't," Redrec yawned. The tendrils of his mind still joined with mine were as untroubled as his body. What was it that troubled me? I sat up and frowned at him.

"You did not journey this far, with an entire ensemble, for one performance!"

"I didn't say that exactly."

He avoided my eyes, eluded my touch, slipped out of my embrace and found a shirt, stood staring out the shuttered casement into a sunset burning into the sea. When he could bear the accusation in my silence no longer he faced me.

"Well, does it make sense to you that there'd be such a long hiatus between performances? When I didn't show up for yesterday's rehearsals they knew I'd gone missing, and Varazdin's covered for me, though he's not as good on the viol pieces. 'Meister Redrec's gone on one of his benders,' they'll say; I'm famous for them. There'll be some gloating from those as had opening night ducats and much grumbling

228

from those as did not, but believe it or not it works to my good. Crowds will double wherever I'm bound next."

"Why did you do this?" I asked slowly, already guessing at the answer. Not for me? The first night would have been sufficient; it had been his idea, not mine, to leave One Greater entirely for one of the Lessers and linger these two days more. "Do you care so little about your art?"

"What?" Half his attention was on the food synther by now. "Well, mostly for you, for the state you were in—there was that. Seagod, I'm hungry! Is there nothing here but the fodder your kind eat? Help me with this, will you?"

There was a saying in more than one People's land, especially in the places women gathered: "Half the children born are men, but all men born are children." Indeed.

"I will reprogram it for you presently," I said, holding fast to my Discipline, "after you have answered me."

"Answered you what?" He feigned annoyance, but my tone was cold enough to stay him. He sat on the bed beside me. "All right, yes, I insisted on this journey to the Lessers— that is what you call them? imagine, our very own island! might one stay forever, I wonder?—partly for the state you were in. Nor do I recall you arguing it. For I tell you, Lingri-love, there's no woman can love like anOther can, and I remembered that.

"But it's also within my right. Let them carp! They'll get their money back if they want it; the Ensemble's insured to cover it. I will play when I choose to play. I'll not be enslaved by anyone or anything! That is an artist's temperament!"

"Or a child's bad manners." Drained of passion, I sat as still and cold as stone in the fading light.

"I don't expect you to understand—"

"Because I am anOther," I finished for him, "hence lacking an artist's temperament. That is reserved alone for Meister Redrec."

"Don't put words in my mouth, though I know you're

capable!" He smiled his most disarming smile. "I'm not forgetting you're a poet. But poetry's such a solitary art. You can put it aside whenever you choose—"

"Do you think so?"

"—but when one is at the mercy of the public, as I am . . ." He shrugged and could not finish. "Anyway, it's done, two days ago. Even if you send me away now, it cannot be remedied."

While he talked I had felt the tendrils of his mind withdrawing from mine and had made no effort to hold them. We were completely separate now.

"You feel . . . nothing . . . do you?" I asked slowly. "Not for your music, not for any living thing. It's all opportunity, adulation, sensual gratification without true passion. People accuse Others of lacking passion—how little they understand! Few of us could be as cold as you!"

"Cold?" His hands were on my arms, caressing. "Was I cold last night, or yesterday? Was I cold the first time we—" I did not physically move, but he sensed how far removed I was and took away his hands.

"You—truly—feel nothing," I said. "You are hollow, sad. I grieve for you."

His face contorted violently, he leapt up and stalked away from me. "Don't say that. Don't you *ever* say that!" he shouted, raising clouds of birds from the trees in the forecourt; they had never heard shouting before. "How *dare* you say that? You don't know!"

"Don't I?"

It stopped him; he could not deny it. His eyes scanned the corners of the room as if for meaning as his mind reached back across these several days to find . . . emptiness. Sexual exhaustion, yes, but nothingness beyond. I had given him all I had. He had given me release from my cycle, nothing more. He had nothing more to give.

"Circumstance!" he tried to excuse it. "We've never formally bonded, not by my People's custom nor yours. And

230

look at where we've loved. Cold catacomb floors and some-one's borrowed summerhouse. If we had some permanence . . . I have a house, given me by Renna's clan, upcanal from Droghia. Not a palace, but with rooms enough. It's empty, not a stick of furniture. I've never had time to fill it."

"Fill it with what?" I asked rhetorically, not interested in the answer. I had not thought I could feel such pity for the emptiness of him.

"Oh, don't go profound on me!" he pleaded, his grand voice cracking. "Lingri, I love you! I want—"

"What do you want? To play me as you play your music? This is not love, but trivialization!"

"And you, of course, cannot love me."

"What is there in you to love? The gaudy outer man or the emptiness within? Fill that emptiness with something, if only feeling."

"So you dislove me because I do not *feel?*" he cried, incredulous. "And this from anOther? It makes no sense!"

I gathered myself and moved at last, this airy chamber stifling me. I had to get away. Weak from mating, by rights I should have rested, but duty, something, drove me.

"You do not love me," I told Redrec slowly. "You love no one, excepting possibly Redrec. You wish to own me, to display me on your arm as some manner of conquest. 'Mei-ster Redrec is so great a star he can even capture the heart of anOther!' I will not be that Other! You say you will not be enslaved? Well, nor will I. Go, while we are both free."

"Go where?" he asked dismally. It was as if he had truly expected to take me with him when he left. It had never occurred to him that I would refuse. "Shall you summon me in seven years?"

"No."

"You said that the last time."

"So I did. Nor did I summon you. It was you who came for me."

"May I at least do as much again in seven years?"

231

"Perhaps."

"What 'perhaps'? I need an answer!"

With an effort I came to him, when I would rather put as much distance between us as possible. Touching my hand to his chest, where People keep their hearts, I answered. "Grow. Let that be your answer."

"What the hell is that supposed to mean?" he roared, but I was gone, down the shingle to the sea.

"First you leave him, then you send him away!" Joreth marvels. "It's a wonder I was ever born!"

"More wonder than you can ever know," I concur.

"Well? What next?" My son stretches his long body out upon the mossy bank, as if prepared for more lengthy narrative. We are quite alone; even the pool is empty of swimmers. I do not know when Jemadar left us or why, or how much of my ancient history he has heard. Nor do I understand why I offer my story so freely when he is near. Perhaps I am grown too weary, too resigned to care. "The old man's twenty-four by my reckoning, and I'm not born until he's nearly sixty. You've a lot of years to cover still."

"As you put it, I sent him away. He stayed away. For seven years more we were apart," I offer simply. "My work as ethnographer resumed. I returned to the Mainland once again, during the so-named Era of Peace which followed upon the Second Alliance, if you know your history."

" 'When the World first held its breath,
then sighed relief,
then breathed freely for the first'

to quote a certain poet. Aye, I know my history!"

And your mother's poetry, I muse, not asking him how much more of it he knows, or where he learned it, and whether it was memorized or written. He wants me to ask; therefore I will not.

232

"Peace there may have been, but not for Redrec. He was at war with himself, struggling to prove me wrong. He was determined to fill the hollowness of his heart."

And I am grown hollow with remembering it. Enough! My son wants history, not sentiment. I am anOther; I will be Disciplined.

"He abandoned his former patrons, played only charity benefits, took no more profit than he needed to live. He fought with his publishers to wrest higher royalties from them, bestowing these on the poor as well. The house on the canal became a conservatory, filled with poor but promising students on scholarship. And he wrote; six symphonies in as many years, innumerable keyboard works—"

"Seventeen in all, actually," Joreth corrects me. I stop. Something occurs to me.

"Redrec was apolitical. I don't believe the Purists ever traced him to me. May I assume therefore his works survive?"

"Of course," Joreth answers, but he too stops. Some new thought has penetrated his consciousness; I watched him wrestle with it.

"Redrec suffered in those years," I continue. "In all respects save his growing creativity, he suffered. I do not believe he had ever before gone hungry, ever suffered anything more inconvenient than a late tram or a missed appointment. Never before wanted for anything, except in his insatiable craving for affection, which he never recognized when it was offered to him. I believe he may even have stopped drinking for a time, though his sex life resumed apace.

"Yet he suffered, and he grew, and as he grew his music grew, until at last it transcended anything which had gone before. Even the critics recognized it. And I watched, following his progress on the infonets, no matter where I was. The 'nets were global by then—the Second Alliance accom-

233

plished that much—and Redrec was ever on my screen and in my thoughts. . . ."

Something there is about an era of peace which renders it bland in description. This peace was never uniform, never progressed the same from one nation to the next, yet it endured. LamorDroghia, as Redrec had foreseen, soon came limping back to OtherWhere to ask our renewed patronage, and though by this time Mantuul as a nation was no more, its exiles accepted Others from whatever newer nation embraced them. It was safe to say that while we reached out to People because of their differences, People came to terms with Others in spite of ours.

The balance between Others on the Mainland and those free to remain in OtherWhere was still inequitable; any attempt to return our numbers to the Archipelago was met with varying degrees of resistance. The web tightened, at first painlessly, and we remained.

Nor was Redrec the only one whose prognostications began to come true. It was at about this time that I had news of Dzu.

"Praise God, you have a message incoming!"

The face which filled my screen was plump and toothy and aggressively cheerful, typical of the women of the Llellaar mountain regions, where I was stationed then. Typical, too, was the greeting; Llellaar sported a new religion behind every tree.

"Praise God," I replied by rote, surprising the comm operator, who had not expected such a response from an-Other. But, when in Llellaar . . . "Pray, let it through."

There was no real necessity for comm operators, but the Llellaar workers' unions insisted. I waited while the unnervingly jolly face dissolved into Dweneth's, as one corner of the screen automatically recorded time and place of origin:

early morning, Grenni. As always, half a World away. Dweneth was in mid yawn.

"Pardon me! Hullo. Wanted to catch you before you were for bed."

"Not for some hours yet," I answered warmly, listening to the soul-thread, which was as subliminally frantic as its holder seemed calm. "What troubles you?"

Dweneth grimaced. The screen flickered—also the Llellaar unions' doing; if things did not break down, how were People to be employed in fixing them? Resignedly, I adjusted it.

"Can't ever fool you, can I?" Dweneth sighed. "I suppose, true to form, you've not been watching the 'nets, or you wouldn't need to ask me. Dzu's been arrested."

An ascetic and tautly Disciplined Dzu had been teaching for some years in a university town in Zanti and acting as sometime consultant to the ruling Diet, a model citizen. What could have happened?

"Tell me."

Dweneth was breakfasting. She swallowed, wiped her mouth. "Pardon me again! We've been working almost round the clock. We are *this* close!"

Lacking the eager squeak in her voice, I would have known what she was talking about. Several decades of combined Othertech and People's intuitive ingenuity had advanced us far beyond the creation of superior hybrid grains. Genetic codes were being deciphered, eliminating congenital illnesses, prolonging life. Infant mortality was down to almost nil, and where a generation ago People could scarce expect to live to thirty-five, current parameters were well past eighty. It was presumed that the series of codes which warranted Dweneth's particular attention—those which would make it possible for Others and People to crossbreed—would be next.

"I rejoice with thee. But Dzu?"

Dweneth swallowed again, took a deep breath. "He was

235

of all things leading a student uprising against the very People he's been paid to advise. More details than that I haven't got, except that the Diet offered to release him into Other custody, but he refused. Said he would remain in prison until his group's demands were met—well, it's not a prison exactly; Zanti had only minimum-security detention even before Otherinfluence, which is why the very thought of a student uprising scandalizes them. They truly don't know what to do. And to make it worse, our *graax*-headed philosopher has begun a hunger strike. As if there were flesh enough on his bones to spare."

I absorbed this thoughtfully, trying to read between the facts. Dweneth finished her breakfast, put the plate aside.

"Are you with me?" she asked when the silence had gone on too long. She leaned into the screen, intense. "Jeijinn wants to go to him, even at the risk of leaving Other-Where. She must not; you understand that."

"Of course," I said. "I will go. Will you accompany me? It will be difficult to ascertain which of us he is not speaking to at present."

Dweneth laughed bitterly. "Ah, Dzu, when will you grow up?" She grew more serious. "Sorry, Dearheart, I can't. I've duties and obligations here which—s'truth, I'm beginning to sound like you! But what we're doing here simply cannot wait. I'm not good at politics, but it seems to me that if we succeed in giving People and Others this one thing in common, it may help distract them from recent unsettling events."

I knew at once what she meant. Even this so-named Era of Peace was not free of dangers. As Dzu had predicted in his youth, a manner of polarization had begun.

For some People it was only a matter of continued disquietude with the things about Others which could not be changed—our looks, our gifts, our longer lives, the things we ate or could not eat, our inability to accept the limited perspective of their customs or their gods. For some it was the changes we had wrought, the wrenching shift in the social order which resulted when those who traditionally had not—be it freedom, prosperity, or even enough to eat—gradually acquired what those of privilege had always claimed as the basis of their identity and strength.

Succinctly, religions and dietary habits loomed insignificant beside the abolition of social caste. Those who had always heretofore claimed an inherent right to power could not understand why or how the great mass of their People had now become their equals. If something had been taken away from them, as in a revolution or a coup, they might have understood it better, but the fact that they had lost nothing and in most instances had profited further, and yet the have-nots had gained everything—this was more than they could fathom. Their bafflement rendered the material things themselves meaningless, once their status as emblems of power had disappeared.

And if everyone had equal power, did power itself cease to exist? Such nihilism was terrifying. Along the fringes of People's society, the murmurs had already begun: "Well, it wasn't thus and so *before* the Others came." As if it had been we who thrust ourselves upon their shores and not conversely.

It would end we knew not where, though back in Other-Where, the Chamber, under newer supervision now that Loriel was dead and Govin gone and Frayin engaged elsewhere, continued its permutational runs in the hope of finding one single answer to a multitude of problems.

And the Council of the Matriarchy continued to propose the need for a World Governance, but the People refused.

And Dweneth and her fellow researchers counted on a generation of interbreed children to lessen the differences between us. Nothing was more important to her.

"Duties and obligations," I echoed her, troubled as always by the way the years were robbing me of her, aging her

237

twice as fast as they did me. "And what about what you want?"

"This *is* what I want!" she said fiercely. "At least, it's all I'll ever get of what I want, so leave me to it! Before long I'll be too old to bear anyone's child. So be it. Let me give the World children in the only way I can. Don't haunt me!"

"Forgive me. It was never my intention."

"But it's always your achievement. Go away! Go to Dzu before he does something irreversible. Bounce him off a wall or two in my name. Tell him if he ate a decent meal and got laid betimes, this too would pass." She passed a hand over her eyes, placed both palms on either side of her screen as if to frame my face with them. I did the same at my end. "Be careful!"

The matter of Dzu took more time than it ought, and again my cycle threatened, though this time I was prepared. A course of study at an Enclave established by invitation of the Zanti government—for this particular People's philosophies had considerable affinity with ours—gave me the proper Disciplines and meditations. And as an extra safeguard for when the time was full upon me, I had also secured the medications.

No need. The Zanti Mediators had loaned me a residence as their honored guest as I strove to wrest some reason out of Dzu and take him off their hands. Among the guesthouse's many refinements was an extensive library where a number of musical instruments were displayed.

Awakening with the dawn in a borrowed bed in a borrowed room, I heard music.

No mystery how he had gotten in. True Other, I had not locked the doors. I dared not consider what duress he might have undergone in finding me. I knew he knew when I entered the room, though he did not stay his playing. Hunched like an old man over the keys, squinting at them

238

nearsightedly though their configuration was etched upon his heart, he played, his large-knuckled hands fluid in their proficiency, though as bone-white as the keys he plied.

A flash of his father pounding the ancient Hydraulus, standing upright on its bench to reach the fist-wide keys and batter their music out of them, lasted but an instant, superceded by this gentle, plaintive caress, and the unique individual who employed it.

Farewell, Redrec long lost, I thought. And, welcome, Redrec at long last found!

He threw his head back as he played, as if in a kind of silent ecstasy. Not defiantly, not triumphantly, as his father would have done, but as one still partly bound and struggling to be free. Free of the old soft, spoiled Redrec, free to be this Redrec who could coax such beauty from unyielding ivory, wood, and wire. Hearing his soul within his music, I wept.

Wept for the presence of this no longer hollow man. He was, his music told me, now totally alone. No matter the women he had warmed and been warmed by, perhaps as late as this night now waning. Only anOther could reach within and warm his solitary soul.

I touched his shoulder on a dying chord. He remained unmoving over the keyboard until the final resonances faded, then swung about to look up into my face. He clasped my waist, I held him to my breast. This time, we chose together.

"And lots of curly hair," Nilla added. *"Or even
wavy hair. I wouldn't mind. I wouldn't care what color
his eyes were, either, as long as he was—you know.
Steady. Truthful with me, and faithful, of course. I
couldn't stand to have him fool around. And none of
your male nonsense about who feeds the kids or does
the trash."*

"Oh, so you're having kids with him already?" Till
teased as Nilla blushed. They sipped their drinks in
silence.

"Well, we would, if I found such a man," Nilla
defended herself at last. *"Why not? Wouldn't you?"*

Tilla squeezed Nilla's hand across the table. *"I
don't mean to embarrass you, dear. Go on. What does
he do, this dream man of yours?"*

Nilla thought about it. *"I'm not sure. Something
that takes more brains than brawn, I guess. A government job, maybe. That's steady, and we could travel.
I've always wanted to travel."*

Tilla gave her a pitying look. Nilla could be so
naive sometimes! *"A government job? Are there any to
be had?"*

Nilla fluttered her eyelashes before she could
speak. *"You're right. I didn't think of that. They're already taken by Other People."*

"There you go again!" Tilla scolded her. *" 'Other
People'—you keep on saying that, when you know
there's no such thing! There are People, and there are
Others, and no question who gets the better—of jobs or
anything else!"*

"You're right again," Nilla said humbly. She suddenly had no appetite. "But I thought we were talking about men."

"So we were," Tilla said brightly, pleased to see that Nilla's incorrect thinking had made her uncomfortable. She wanted to help her friend, she really did. "Let's see, now, how you've described your Dream Man: he's intelligent, steady, strong, helps with the housework. He's faithful, and he has curly hair." Tilla paused for effect. "Except for the hair, you've described an-Other."

Nilla's hands flew to her cheeks in horror. "Oh, no, I couldn't have! I didn't mean—how awful! I would never . . . ugh! You know I couldn't possibly. How strange, how freakish, how . . . incorrect!"

Tilla said nothing while Nilla babbled on, letting her friend purge her soul. Sometimes one had to be stern, even with one's friends.

Excerpt: "Portrait of a Dictator"
[from *The Partisan Press*, vol. 7, no. 23]

He is neither old nor young, and no one knows his true age. He seems not made of flesh, but carved out of some cold, unyielding stone, or rather, of some rare dense wood which has been weathered, dessicated, finally petrified, something once living become the embodiment of death.

He has no apparent vices. He indulges in neither intoxicants nor mood alterants, though rumors persist that he once trafficked in the latter. Vegetarian, celibate, he shuns all flesh. He touches no one, not even in diplomatic circumstances, nor can he bear to be touched. More than one witness has seen him demand soap and water, and wash his hands on the spot, if someone has presumed to touch him.

He rises with the dawn, eats sparingly, exercises rigorously, bathes frequently. He often works far into the night. He dresses plainly to the point of drabness and often publicly derides those who affect jewelry or any personal ornament.

He suffers no physical weakness or ailment and takes no medications, though he regularly consults a personal physician, whose sole patient he is. There are old stories of seizures, tantrums, demonic fits which required restraint and sedation, but no eyewitness lives.

His words in company are few and well chosen; his words in public are profuse, prolix, abundant, and only through them does he evidence emotion. He neither laughs nor weeps, nor succumbs to pettiness or temper. Yet men have died of his smile. Women have languished beneath his neglect. Future generations will die of his intentions.

Who is he? Where has he come from? What is it in this slight, unprepossessing figure with its burning eyes which so moves People that they will betray their spouses, deny their parents, sell their children at his word?

11

"So this time you and he were bonded at last?"

My son wants simple answers. He will not get them. "Not exactly."

"I don't believe it!" Joreth explodes, loud enough to attract the attention of passing Others, who notice by not noticing. We are at the laundry, he and I, up to our elbows, working side by side, speaking in whispers above the sound of wet cloth slapping against rock. "What was it this time? What obstacle could possibly be in the way? He had met your terms, at great personal suffering. Don't tell me you sent him away again!"

"No, I will not tell you that," I answer calmly. "We were in fact agreed thereafter to conjoin from seventh year to seventh year. Through a complex arrangement of our individual schedules we were able to live together, travel together, share the same interests and friends. I recall this as the most musical interlude of my long life, for there were concerts and entertainments almost nightly. But while we were together, we were not formally bonded, not in his World or in mine. There were considerations—for Redrec's career, but more important, for his work."

Joreth squeezes the water from a laundered shirt, his forearms corded with the effort. I wonder if he is as strong as a full Other.

"I still don't understand," he starts.

" 'Understanding comes from listening,' " I chide him. Infant school aphorisms serve those who are being childish. "Depending upon the political climate of whatever realm we visited, being officially wed to anOther might bring him unfair advantage, or overzealous censorship. You think these things new to your own time; they were not. The desire to control is innate to any ruling species, and I would not have our private life impact on Redrec's career. More to the point, I feared what the excessive psionic exchange of Other bonding might wreak upon his creativity. Surely you who have bonded with a Telepath can understand this much."

Slow recognition dawns across his People's face. He dumps the wadded wrung-out shirt into a basket, seizes the next. "All right, but even so. If you did not bond in such relatively peaceful times, why did you do so before my birth, when there was greater risk?"

"For the same reason I denied you half your parentage when the time came," I answer. The robe I am kneading on the rocks gives me ample excuse to avoid his eyes.

"But I still don't understand!" he sputters, beginning to wave his hands about; this matter of my denying him still wounds him. "You refuse to bond when it is acceptable, as if you needed to wait until there was a danger—why make it so complicated?"

I stop my kneading, sit back on my heels, shake my damp hair off my face. "Do you think it is so simple? Tell me truthfully: was it simple for you and Dwiri? Did you merely gaze into each Other's eyes and *know*? Was there no time of learning, conflict, difference? No time when edges abutted, overlapped, eroded away, and not without pain? Or did you

245

simply meet and simultaneously think: 'This is the one, the only one, and possibly forever'?''

Joreth looks at me blankly; his answer astonishes me. "Well, actually, yes. Isn't that the way it happens with everyone?''

Perhaps it does with Intermixes. By their very scarcity they are drawn to easy kinship. Or is it the old dilemma of those who mix with Telepaths and risk losing themselves? I study my son, wondering if he is the same person I abandoned a decade ago. Obviously he is not, but how much of that is Dwiri's influence? Dwiri, whom I watch grow daily in her interlink with Lerius, so much her mother's self, and yet so not.

"So you held back,'' my son muses, also sitting back on his heels, "so as not to shape his creativity, which is presumptuous enough. Who is to say how we influence someone else's life by mere proximity?''

Dweneth's argument! I want to shout, but vent my unDiscipline on the laundry.

"I suppose you will argue that you walked away from him for seven years, and seven years again, for the same reason. Simultaneously driving him mad and endangering your own life. Abandoning him in order to save him, now there's an original idea—''

He stops, slack-jawed with realization. "Just as you abandoned me, to save me.''

Do I suppress a smile? "Your tutors always said your deductive capabilities were high.''

I thrust a sopping shirt into his hands. If he should succumb to the remorse I now see working his so vulnerable face, if he should embrace me, or begin to weep, my Discipline could not bear it. I cannot bear his remorse; it was easier when he hated me. I extend a hand to stay him from whatever he would do next.

"Do not beset me with your remorse. There is nothing to be remorseful for.''

He chokes on it: "Not for hating you all these years?"

"Would you have come back to OtherWhere if you hated me?"

He wants to make some grand gesture, to throw himself at my feet perhaps, but my staying gesture holds him while he fights for Discipline.

" 'Fair for fair,' " I remind him. "I have given you Redrec. You must give me his son. Restore to me the years since I abandoned you, and that will be sufficient."

"Mother, I will!" he cries. "I will tell you every day of my life—"

"Only not today!" a familiar voice interrupts us.

AnOther would not presume to interrupt. Nor, had I thought, would this man.

"Jemadar?" I ask him archly. Clearly he must have heard enough of our words to understand we were not to be interrupted. "May I assume that this is urgent, which so disrupts anOther's privacy?"

He bows his head. "It is. Forgive me. I would not have interrupted, but . . . " He gives his attention to Joreth. "Jisra Matriarch sent me to fetch you. The radio receiver is up and functional. The news it brings is most distressing. A Council has been called—"

"I'm coming!" Joreth says at once, though not in such a rush that he cannot embrace me.

The chronicler in me longs to rush to this Council as well, but I have not been invited. And I sense as much distress in this Jemadar as in any transmission from the Mainland. Deliberately I dry my hands, roll down my sleeves. Let someone else tend the laundry from hereon. Shall I make some effort to restore order to my damp, disheveled person, if only because Jemadar watches, bemusement in his eyes?

"Mother and son reconciled?" he inquires, watching the direction Joreth has gone. My eyes must narrow at him, for he looks chagrined. "Again, forgive me. I am supposed to

247

know better. This place does redefine our given roles which has a poet reduced to doing laundry. But that does not excuse the diplomat who forgets his manners."

"Logic suggests the diplomat does not forget his manners unless he is under some extreme duress," I conjecture, sitting amid the laundry baskets, inviting him to do the same. "Tell me."

"We," he begins, "my People—Dzilbak, at any rate—wish to return to Melet. Reports on the receiver since it was activated, of a truce with the Mantuul Remnant, amnesty for those who fled, the possibility of regaining our land, now that Others are apparently no more . . ."

The diplomat is set aside, revealing only the man. It pains him to say these things, even in the abstract. He struggles for composure before he can go on.

"Dzilbak is old; he does not wish to die in exile. Old and feeble, but still the Dragon, able to sway the majority and convince them it is safe to leave this place of ice and exile for the warmer climes of home."

"And what does Jemadar think?" I ask, at the same time wondering, if Melet returns the way we have come, will they not be welcomed home by Purists, who will wonder where they've been? And whether their questions be gentle or emphasized by torture, Melet will talk, and Others, hunted down in this realm of ice, will truly be no more.

"Jemadar is ambivalent," he answers. "What he and his lord did not tell your kind when we found you on the sea is that more than half our People remained in Melet, collaborators with Mantuul and the Purists. It was these who argued for our amnesty. It will not be the same Melet we left, with Purists in control, but it is our World, where this is not. Do I think it safe? No. Yet if my lord Dzilbak dictates, I must go."

For some moments he cannot look at me; when at last he does I must force myself not to look away.

"I know what you are thinking," he says, his lined face touched with the hint of a sad smile. "And you are correct. Questioned, our children threatened, we are not Others; we will talk. You knew this when you journeyed with us, yet your Council placed no interdict upon us, to dictate we must stay. If any had asked me my opinion at the time—"

"We could not interdict any People, ever, Jemadar; you know that. It is not our way. Perhaps that is the reason we are come to this, but no matter. Do all your People follow Dzilbak?"

"All will, though one in particular wishes to remain."

"Jemadar."

"I am myself here!" he cries. "Not Dzilbak's mouthpiece, not He Who Goes Between, with no will of my own. I knew of the collaborators but did not speak it, because my first loyalty was to Dzilbak. It was my duty to Dzilbak which kept me ever at his side, when what I wanted to do from boyhood was to travel, especially to OtherWhere. But once Jemadar, always Jemadar."

"There is no disgrace in that," I offer. Duties and obligations. Strange how this man's soul reminds me of the long-dead Thrasim.

"But now I am in OtherWhere, and it gives me peace. Given my own will, I would stay. Which is why, if Dzilbak is adamant, I must go."

At first I do not understand him; once I do, I wish that I did not. "You intend to offer yourself as a forerunner, as sacrifice."

He blinks at me. "I thought only some of you were Telepaths? Or is this only Otherlogic? But consider: I am Dzilbak's right arm; what he knows, I know. I am widowed, childless, without attachments; I cannot be threatened with any death except my own. I will set myself in the Purists' path, that they might bring me in for questioning. I will, of course, refuse to talk. I have a high tolerance for pain. Only when they have wrung me to the penultimate drop shall I reluctantly surrender to them everything I know. All of which shall be the most patent of lies, you see? Content, they will leave my People unmolested, and never seek out yours.''

'' 'If the one can give what spares the hundred . . .' '' It was one of the first aphorisms of the Thousand-Year, but from this Jemadar it is disturbing. ''Why?''

''To spare my People, though some will call me traitor for it,'' he explains. ''And so that I might have an Other-Where to return to if I live.''

I cannot argue any of this, yet something puzzles me. ''Why have you told me this?''

''Only you, Lingri-one.'' He takes my hands, a People's gesture. ''Because I think you understand the difference between heroism and necessity.''

''You 'think,' but are not certain,'' I suggest.

He nods, still clasping my hands. ''That is why I sent your son away. The outriggers are already being loaded. Before I go to where I may have to die, I need to know.''

''Dzugash again.'' I gather myself. ''What do you need to know?''

''It is said . . .'' He gropes for ways to say this diplomatically. ''It is said you were once in a position to take his life, but did not.''

''Who told you this?''

He does not answer.

''Do you think it was cowardice?''

''I need for you to tell me.''

''And based upon one Other's answer, you will judge whether or not my kind are worthy of your sacrifice?''

''I make the sacrifice primarily for my People, but yes, something like.''

It had to be told eventually. I withdraw my hands from Jemadar's and tell it.

* * *

250

Dzugash knew his People well. Everything he predicted of them, while imprecise in detail, eventually came to pass. Firstly, while the Fourteen Tribes never succeeded even under the Purists' reign in entirely blurring their tribal identities, a OneWorld movement, or rather two, began to evolve as early as the First Alliance, though People's notions of what constituted a united World varied greatly.

Those who already controlled the instruments of power obviously wished to maintain such control in perpetuity; those heretofore lacking in power insisted that leadership in government and industry must be predicated, as in Other-Where, upon ability, not caste. But how, the first group countered, was such ability, derived from such a heterogeneity of background and opportunity, to be measured? Out of this quarrel arose two distinct People's parties, diametrically opposed, which called themselves One Worlders.

Opposed to OneWorldism in any form were the Ethnocentrics, whose sole definition of self lay not in the individual and her gifts, but in identification with some superceding clan or tribe. Again, some of these rose from the empowered classes, which saw their hereditary franchise threatened by the leveling potential of OneWorldism. Many banded together out of a sincere concern for the loss of their cultural folkways and traditions; I myself had labored with these in every land in my literary cataloguing and was, quite without my assent, considered to be among their champions.

The rest, the dangerous ones, were the permanent fringe elements, those like Brok'smen in Droghia or the hill brigands of Tawa, the disenfranchised, the mercenaries and arms merchants in every land, who abided not by law but self-interest enforced by brute strength. These could not stomach a World where hard work and communal benefit superceded the right to take what one wanted and fall asleep drunk nightly. Thus there were as many parties calling themselves Ethnocentrics as there had been tribes and subtribes in pre-Other times.

251

The question had always been asked: What will People do once their progress and technology equal ours? We were now beginning to learn the answers.

"This is only the surface!" Dzu announced when I returned to the Zanti holding some days after our first encounter there, to be certain he was eating. He gestured toward the vidscreen dominating one wall of his quarters; People's technology had surpassed ours in ostentation, at least. "Imagine what it implies beneath!"

The screen displayed an interactive children's game, of mazes to be run and obstacles to be overcome, where the figure of a solitary knight in strangely futuristic armor pursued foes and vanquished demons before being permitted entrance to the Palace of Self-Determination. Superficially, this was typical People's fare, fulfilling the need to sublimate aggression no longer acted out in war. Many of the threatening entities were traditional folkloric dragons and demons. But those with the most devious powers were newer, and classified as Evil Elves.

"Do you know what this one's called?" Dzu asked me. Two days before he had been comatose and wasted; now he was well enough to sit up and play this game, almost his old fervid, driven self.

"Vidgames are not my area of expertise," I demurred, though in fact I had encountered this one elsewhere in my travels.

"The makers call it The Other Place. A euphemism for Hell in most cultures, true, but don't you think it odd that they should call it that?"

I observed the game for some minutes with what objectivity I could muster. Watching me, Dzu touched the remote and deliberately turned the volume up full before obliterating ten Evil Elves as gruesomely as possible and shutting off the screen.

252

"Only the surface," he repeated, seeming strangely pleased.

He had been semiconscious for two days, the Zanti Mediators told me when they brought me to him. If I had not come, they had considered force-feeding him, though this went against their teachings. I thanked them for the meticulous care Dzu had been given thus far, and they and the gaggle of Dzu's student supporters left me alone with him.

I sat on the edge of his pallet, propped his head in the crook of my arm like an infant's, and brought water to his lips. He gagged.

"What idiocy is this?" I demanded when his eyes slitted open. Dweneth might not be with me, yet I could borrow her bullying tone.

"Lingri . . ." was all Dzu managed.

"Move over!" I ordered him, yanking him upright so that his stiff, cramp-ridden legs perforce swung to the floor. When he saw I meant to prop him up beside me, he used his last strength to support himself.

"What are you . . . doing here?" he managed to breathe rancidly, his head lolling. The Mediators had cautioned that his body was already feeding on itself.

"Joining you."

His eyes opened full. "A hunger strike? You can't! I won't permit it!"

"How do you propose to stop it?" I asked. "You will die long before I do. But rest assured that if you die, you bring me with you."

He narrowed his eyes at me. "You're bluffing!"

"Will you live long enough to be certain?"

"He wanted death. You should have let him die," Jemadar says.

"That was not for me to judge then, nor for you to judge now," I caution him. We are carrying the laundry, to spread

253

it on the volcano-warmed rocks to dry. "Further, is it not you who refutes the theory of one man as history?"

"In general," Jemadar acknowledges, "but in the case of this one man, I am forced to reconsider."

"Lingri?"

"Yes, Dzu."

"Do you know what Others' greatest weakness is?"

"Doubtless you will tell me."

Recovered, with some solid food in him, he was quick in his movements, restless, predatory. He could not sit while we shared a meal, but prowled the room, his eyes and mind and fingers working feverishly.

"It is that they cannot lie," he announced. "Hence they cannot recognize the fact that People lie habitually, whenever it will serve their needs."

I refrained from mentioning that the Chamber kept an open-ended Permutational Prevarication file, or that I had substantially contributed to it.

"Others may have improved People's temporal status, but they cannot change the People's soul," Dzu went on, prowling. "Othertech is being systematically perverted to means no Other could conceive of, much less countenance. I am aware of instances Worldwide—why do you suppose I made this gesture here in Zanti? It was one of the few places where I was reasonably certain I would not 'disappear' for my efforts." He narrowed his burning eyes at me. "You don't believe me, do you?"

"I am listening, Dzu."

"But reserving judgment, Lingri."

"Until I have all available facts? Always, Dzu. Go on."

"Fact: WeatherGlobal out of both Four Greater and the Hillpast Wastes records an increase in hydrocarbon concentrations in the valleys of the Tolay. Do Others wonder why? People lie and say it's a normal seasonal phenomenon. Stagnant air gets trapped in the lowlands during Bask, they say.

254

Yet the pollution persists, increases. Why? Because in truth it is the output of secret facturies, constructing who knows what, but pouring foulants into the air and water."

"And this was the impetus for a hunger strike? Dzu, there are proper channels—"

"Spoken like anOther!" he sneered. "I have submitted several reports to WeatherGlobal. The matter is 'under consideration.' You know how long that's apt to take! And, no, that wasn't the impetus for the hunger strike. There's more!"

"I am listening, Dzu."

"Weapons," he went on feverishly. "Do you know anything of weapons, Lingri? Refresh my flawed People's memory regarding Loriel's statement about weapons!"

"She feared the uses Kelibesh in particular might make of higher mathematics."

"And in so doing she was almost as farseeing as am I!" Dzu triumphed. "Do Others ever wonder why Tawa and Kelibesh send so many of their children to the universities for degrees in chemistry and mathematics?"

His tone grew confidential, though we were quite alone. None of what he told me was inconceivable; the Chamber and the Matriarchy labored constantly against the misuses of Othertech. But how much of what Dzu saw was happening now, and how much was only potentiality, confused by his time-defying perception?

" . . . munitions designed and factured for an impending war against the Dyr," he was saying, "to settle ancient scores, and reclaim some disputed portion of the Wastes. Weapons even Loriel could not have foreseen. Chemical gases, things to infuse into water tables. Last year there was an accident, and all the women in the surrounding villages miscarried.

"There is a research facility in Sego," he began anew, his breath coming short, his hands clawed and plucking restlessly at his borrowed clothes.

255

"I am aware of it." Dweneth had been grudgingly offered a post there even though she was a woman, to lure her
away from Grenni. She had toured the place and deemed it
"primitive."

"You are not aware of its true purpose! Behind the overt
multigenerational experiments in grain seed and livestock,
there is a secret lab whose purpose is to design a race of
superior People."

"That tale is as old as People. Dzu, how can you know
these things?"

"Rest assured—I know. Sego was chosen for the genetic
'desirability' of its females. Young girls from the countryside
are plied with gifts and promises, then inseminated from
some genetic designer's concept of a 'pure' male stock. The
newborns that result are tested. Those found 'defective' are
destroyed; the ones allowed to live are reared in some sterile,
mind-controlled environment. All this, using Other technology and techniques. Do you wonder why I grow insane? I
owe you gratitude, incidentally, for . . . saving me."

"A most unDisciplined trait I have acquired," I admitted dryly, surprised at finding Dzu capable of anything so
mundane, so vulnerable as gratitude. "If these things can be
verified, they constitute serious breaches of the Alliance.
The Matriarchy must be so informed."

"I have informed them!" Dzu cried.

"And?"

" 'Under consideration.' 'Special motions must be
made.' And 'there are proper channels'!" He mocked me
with this last, all gratitude evaporated. He stopped prowling
at last, sinking onto the pallet beside me, his head in his
hands. "A committee of WiseOnes has been commissioned
by the Council to investigate each instance I have reported,
with all deliberate speed. What say you Tolay and Sego and
the Tawa will have covered their traces well before this
committee ever arrives?"

"Quite possible, but not because your effort has been

unworthy." Seeing his torment, I understood now why Jei-jinn found such difficulty in detaching her empathy from him. Mercifully, she was now distant enough not to feel his pain. "Dzu, you cannot hold yourself responsible for the World."

He looked at me miserably. "Who else?" he pleaded, holding out hands whose fingers trembled. "Lingri, it seems as if everything Others attempt to create, People attempt to tear down. I alone can see the holes they make and try to stop them up, but I'm running out of fingers!"

I lay my own hands over his then, lacing our fingers. His stopped trembling.

"Now you have twice as many," I said.

"Now I have twice as many!" he would taunt me a decade hence, the first time he tried to kill me.

He had been in power less than a year then, calling himself simply Dzugash the Pure. Dzugash the Patriarch, Perpetual Premier of the People's Purist Praesidium, were titles heaped upon him by those who had thrust him into power. It had been clear to Others long before he gave his famous "Eternal Other" speech that Dzu and his Purists meant to exterminate us all.

To begin, to demonstrate his Plan for Purity and how he intended to implement it, he had rounded up all the Others in the Mantuul town of Freym, including myself and Jeijinn.

"It was the Great Quake, then, which changed him," Jema-dar suggests.

I have accompanied him to his People's camp, where hectic preparations for departure are under way, now that Dzilbak has his will. Peria has been summoned to read the weather; Joreth is communing with the *bRi*.

Jemadar and I are wrapped in heavy cloaks; our breath streams out before us. Yet the day is warm for this clime, and cloudless. Myriad small flowers dot the brilliant green of tundra where we tread. At the water's edge, where the outriggers are being laden, the turf is worn and churned to mud; it will take some doing—Other doing—to erase all trace of Melet once they are gone.

"The Great Quake was the impetus Dzu needed to make his thinking public," I suggest. "Lacking so dramatic an event, he would doubtless have found something else."

Between Dzu's leaving Zanti and the Great Quake, much history, public and personal, transpired.

Redrec and I brought Dzu back to OtherWhere so that I might add my voice to his before the Council and confirm the truth of his reports. Naturally, there ensued considerable debate, not surprisingly led by Govin, who had torn himself away from the tranquility of Two Greater at great personal sacrifice, if we were to take his word for it, solely for the event. Better, perhaps, that Govin had stayed where he was.

Following upon Dzu's testimony, investigations were made and policies formulated, with all deliberate Otherspeed. All aid, trade, administrative assistance, personal and cultural exchange with the entire tribe of Tawa, as well as the Llellaar cities of Tolay and Sego was suspended, until such activities as violated the Alliance in these lands were ended. The People's protests were immediate and vociferous.

". . . have not the right to dictate how we shall rule ourselves, nor the right to interfere with our self-determination!"

The commscreen in WiseFrayin's offices, wearing a Tawan face, monopolized Frayin's attention as I arrived. Dzu's findings had impacted upon my work as well; I was now reassigned to OtherWhere for the purpose of scanning all People's contemporary literatures for anti-Other sentiments. It was one thing more to separate me from Redrec, who was committed to performance tours on the Mainland.

Yet one more obstacle to bonding, which I have not mentioned to my son.

"Nor are we doing so," Frayin addressed the screen, eminently reasonable. "We are in fact removing ourselves from the equation of your self-determination. You may live your lives as you choose, as you have always done. War against your enemies, destroy your resources, oppress your minority Peoples, as you wish. But do not ask our sanction, much less our assistance, as you do so."

She turned away, shutting down the comm without the requisite departure courtesies. I must have looked surprised.

"Tawa appreciates abruptness," the Philosopher explained. She had learned much in recent years. "They will come around eventually, if only to a degree. That particular munitions plant will be shut down; the next will be constructed where we cannot as readily detect it."

"Cynicism, WiseFrayin?" I offered mildly. She had always earned my particular respect.

"Practicality, WiseLingri," she answered. "What says your current report?"

"That I and my aides have been given a task which will likely consume our lifetimes."

"Explain."

"Due to Othertech's impact upon the printing industry," I began, taking a deep breath, "every People's tribe now boasts virtual universal literacy and a flourishing publication industry. Approximately sixty-five percent of this publication is devoted to nonfictional sources. Approximately two thirds of this takes the form of periodical data sources, whose quality varies from infonet-equivalent accuracy to the most scurrilous of pseudo-journalism. The remainder consists of textbooks, archival source books, encyclopediae and compendia. . . ."

I was babbling, and stopped myself. A certain percentage of Chamber personnel had always been engaged in scanning every printed and compusystem source for the term

Other, and wherever it appeared, the text surrounding it was enhanced and cross-referenced to determine its import, positive or negative, with regard to People's beliefs, misconceptions, opinions, or "feelings" relative to Others. Until my reassignment to OtherWhere, there had been no resource to scan fictional materials with equal accuracy. As Others' only official poet, the study of fiction fell to me, and it was this Frayin was asking me about.

"As to People's fiction, it again varies in quality from the most exquisite poetry to the bawdiest of drinking songs, from high literary fiction to the most crudely written pulp."

"Do I surmise correctly," Frayin interjected, "that this fiction by its very nature cannot be scanned and categorized as readily as nonfiction?"

"Precisely, WiseFrayin. The work in question may take the form of allegory, parody, fable; any form whose subtly coded inferences may suggest Others without mentioning us by name. A children's nursery rhyme, for example, may make passing reference to Other 'differences' in a bantering, seemingly innocuous fashion, while masking great fear and loathing beneath its surface. There is the instance of the vidgames, which Dzugash has reported. In short, fiction takes many forms, and few are blatant in displaying their prejudices. It is frequently necessary to study each work in its entirety before making a determination."

"And how many such works, approximately, do you estimate exist for your study at any given time?" Frayin wanted to know.

"Inclusively, and based upon annual socioeconomic parametrical variations, between ten thousand and forty thousand new volumes are published, per nation per year."

The number took Frayin aback; she made a notation on her commscreen.

"Daunting! One does not realize, from the perspective of a species which owns no contemporary fiction, the sheer magnitude of such expression in the dominant species. One assumes you have assistance in your task?"

"I have been assigned a staff of ten, yes. But final approvals must go through me."

"Again, daunting," Frayin said. She folded her hands and weighed something before going on. "It may be of interest to you that the Council has under consideration a proposal to withdraw our presence temporarily from all People's lands, pending a possible Third Alliance."

"Indeed," I answered, refusing to think of what this might mean to Redrec and me, much less to the larger World. "But even as the Council considers, Lingri and her aides must continue to read."

"And, in sum, what is it that you read?" Frayin would not permit me the unDiscipline of self-pity.

Again I took a deep breath. "That even as some People grow in their acceptance of us, their peers grow in mistrust and fear. In my unscientific opinion, this is a condition which will always be so, until we are able to labor together for several generations. Would that we could reach into each individual's heart and whisper 'Be not afraid,' but we cannot. Thus there are no easy answers."

It need not be said that the Council ultimately decided against complete withdrawal from the People's lands. Our interaction might have remained a careful, constant rebalancing of a living equation. Remove some Others here, augment the Other presence there; increase Other involvement in a specific program in a given land, reduce our hands-on participation elsewhere. Weigh the lesser evil of denying support to a People stubbornly insistent upon using our skills and technology to implement shortsighted, greed-motivated policies against what good we might accomplish if we stayed. Judge whether more or fewer lives would be lost to untreated illness because we would not provide aid to those engaged in needless war, and all without succumbing to

261

interventionism or undue influence upon internal policy. The permutations were endless.

Where we stayed, some few condemned us for just such practices as we scrupulously avoided. Where we withdrew, some accused us of faithlessness. Yet the equation endured, precariously balanced upon the goodwill of those People who truly understood what we were doing and welcomed us where we could be useful.

But natural phenomena owe no homage to Other-wrought equations. Even as Others were reluctantly withdrawing from Tawa and Sego and Tolay, there came the Great Quake.

Ironic that the lands it struck had no previous history of violent seismic activity. Further ironic that the very lands where Others had recently departed were the hardest hit. Some few superstitious People saw this as the gods' punishment for their having abused Othertrust; far too many saw it as anOther plot, as if we had at least wished for the quake, if not caused it to happen. Most ironic of all that Others, who had only the season before transferred all Mainland seismic monitoring stations to People's less than expert hands, might have better predicted the quake had we still been in place.

Unfortunate that Two Greater Isle's Seismic Institute should be under the supervision of WiseChior at the time. A confirmed Dissenter, convinced that any interaction with People was by definition harmful, Chior took his readings from the comfort of his faraway observatory, noted the likelihood of a quake of a given magnitude in a given area, and filed a standard report, without sending his findings to the Observatory on One Greater. Following the Great Quake, Chior took further readings, as a matter of academic curiosity, to confirm the parameters of his initial observation, and also because the Observatory had received distress calls from the Mainland and was demanding to know what was going on.

Most unfortunate of all that Dzugash, hungering as always for some absolute truth, should learn what Chior had done.

Otherassistance, once the final temblors had abated, was of course immediate and boundless. Fleets of skimmers brought food and medicines, temporary shelters and personnel to help dig out, heal, rebuild—but too late. Thousands were already dead, who need not have died.

It was scarce a place for poets, but I was there, to help however I could. Redrec and his Philharmonic played for the morale of the survivors, and to raise funds from the vid sales among those lands not affected. Dweneth of course was there, to run the field hospice in the city of Freym.

"I know it sounds awful, but I welcome this!" she breathed, throwing herself into my arms, bloody scrub suit and all. "Too many years on my arse splitting chromosomes, dizzy with shoving *graaxen* through keyholes—the success rate is about the same in my work, and your arms grow just as tired. Sometimes I think there's nothing like a good disaster to bring me back to life!"

She smelled of clean sweat and someone else's blood and was more solid to the embrace than I remembered. There was more gray than gold now in her redgold curls.

"Yes, I know, I'm getting old," she answered, holding me at arm's length. "Old and fat, but there it is. Damn you, Stick, you're still so thin! We're desperately shorthanded. Had any experience in field surgery?"

"I can learn."

"Good!" She thrust a clean gown and a tray of dressings at me. "Run these and yourself through the sterifield and join me in the main tent. There's an irony there, for a former Player maid, I'm sure, but let's not go into it now!"

Surgery went on day and night, bone settings mostly, followed by amputations, internal injuries, head trauma, the occasional premature birth. To Dweneth's credit, those pulled out of the wreckage alive usually survived her instruments. I labored across the table from her, mopping up mostly, or handing her things, Other-tireless. Work shifts changed around us, and even Dweneth had to get off her feet on occasion. By the dawn of the second day, Dzugash was among us, gowned and sterile as we were.

"Chior knew!" he sputtered at me without preamble. Our next patient was being brought in, a laborer buried for two days and in need of a new set of kidneys. "I got access to Two Greater Institute's files, and there was his smug little report. If he had sent it to One Greater, Freym at least could have been warned!"

"Clamp!" Dweneth barked, already halfway into her surgery. "Warn Freym and cause a stampede—who's to say? Shut up and work or get out of my surgery! Argue on your own time!"

Strangely subdued, Dzu obeyed, though the old dangerous look slid across his eyes as we worked.

Days later, when the worst havoc was over, I sought him out on a hilltop overlooking the still-smouldering ruins of the city. I stood just behind him for a very long time, knowing he knew I was there.

He seemed most intent on the center of the city, where Otheraid was already constructing tremor-proof structures to house survivors. Once I saw him shake his head. Once I saw his shoulders quake, though he did not weep. He straightened then, turned sharply on his heel and, looking me straight in the eye, spat at my feet before he stalked away.

"Where do you suppose he's gone?" Dweneth wondered as we sat on the same hilltop days later, she, Redrec, and I, watching as the sun set, indifferent, as stars are, to what transpires beneath them.

"He is nowhere to be found in Freym, nor did he take a skimmer," I reported, having inquired. "As the countryside is still in chaos and comm is down, there is little chance he can be followed if he went on foot."

"Still, he ought to be found." Dweneth shifted beside me. A sleepy Redrec, his head in my lap as I absently stroked his hair, grunted agreement. If I could have felt anything, it would have been a perverse contentment, having these two near me. But none of us had slept of late; we worked on automatically, feeling nothing. "He's dangerous, not only to himself. This time he'll do something irreparable. You'll see!"

"He has committed no crime—"

"Yet!" Redrec remarked, taking Dweneth's side. The two were usually in far greater accord than I could achieve with either of them.

"He has the right to go where he chooses, unmolested and in peace," I argued, knowing it a lie. There was no peace for Dzu.

Dzugash the pedagogue, seeker of absolute truth, was to disappear for several decades, or perhaps forever. Dzugash the Pure, creator of absolute truths, was to take his place.

"Now I have twice as many!" he was to taunt me, throwing my words back at me as Jeijinn's lifeless body slipped to the floor, her fingers still interlaced with his. Dzu had killed her, and now intended to kill me.

It was not by accident that he chose Freym, the City the Others Might Have Spared, as the place to test the viability of his newborn Purist Party. As he had predicted so very long ago, OneWorlders and Ethnocentrics of every extreme had begun to find common cause in one thing: Others were the trouble. Root them out and all would be well.

Was Dzu the instrument of history, as some have declared, or was history Dzu's tool? Somewhere in those unaccounted exile years he had exchanged absolute truth for a series of carefully staged events designed to prove a point. His purpose, as he declared in speech after speech, was "to give the People what they want." Where what People wanted coincided with his aims, he and his followers supported them; where People did not know what they wanted, Dzugash told them. He focused their inchoate longings into a common goal, the elimination of the First Cause of all their woes, and thus he rose to power.

But being Premier of a People's Purist Party which held the majority in only a single land was insufficient, and "spontaneous" mob violence against Others in border countries took too long. Others had taught Dzu Discipline and organization; Dzu learned his lessons well.

There were fewer than one hundred Others in the vicinity of Freym when he made his move. Unbeknownst to him, I was coincidentally there, on a matter of literary research. Dzu was all but ecstatic to find me in his collection.

I was four months gone with Joreth and only hoped it did not show. Dzu needed no further ammunition.

Ostensibly as hostages under a ransom demand sent to the Council on One Greater, we were herded into the public gymnasium, rebuilt with Othertech following the Great Quake. We had been held under guard for scarce two days when our watchful silence was broken by uneasy murmur.

"WiseJeijinn," "WiseJeijinn," I heard before I saw her. My mother the Empath, here in the People's lands? "Jeijinn Matriarch . . . surely not for us? But why?"

Eyes turned toward me. Surely the Matriarch had not risked her own life solely for a long-adult offspring? Our eyes locked; we did not speak. She had not come for me.

"Where is Dzu?" she asked.

"The ransom is secondary to the conditions for release," Dzu informed his foster mother, coming directly to her when he was informed she had made the journey in person.

"And they are?"

"Chiefly a political formality," Dzu called it, toying with a compudisc he had found as if by accident in his

266

pocket, passing it deliberately from hand to hand. "A Declaration of Acknowledgment, from the senior WiseOne present . . ." He feigned to search among us. "Why, I guess that's you, Jeijinn: Declaration accepting the right of the Purist Party to rule in what was once called Mantuu, but which for some time has been wasteland, ineptly governed by a rabble of robber barons and, you must admit, any new government is preferable to such a state—"

"Blackmail," Jeijinn broke in to call it what it was. "This 'acknowledgment' would empower you to execute these Ethnocentric minority leaders whom you now hold in custody—"

"Robber barons," Dzu corrected her.

"As you wish. Call them what you will, you wish to take their lives with Others' sanction. Never!"

Dzu shrugged, continuing to toy with the compudisc. "There are of ten of them, hardened criminals all, who would as easily kill me, or you, or anyone here who got in their way. These weighed against ninety-seven useful, incorruptible Others—"

"Ninety-eight," Jeijinn corrected him, automatically including herself.

She would give him no ground now, as she had not in his growing years, striving to form his mind toward the beneficial and away from the hatred it fed on. Perhaps she sought to remind Dzu of that, to debate him to the side of good, or at least find some trace of compassion in him. It was all she could do to hold his hatred at bay; to her Empath's consciousness it radiated from him, palpable. Only I was near enough to see that she was barely ambulatory beneath the massive dose of *cleramon* she hoped would strengthen her for this confrontation.

"Ninety-eight," Dzu acknowledged, shrugging again, "if you include your grandson."

He gestured toward me and Jeijinn's eyes widened despite the *cleramon* and her Othermask. We had not been in

267

communication of late; there had been no opportunity to tell her.

"Whatever your decision, Jeijinn," Dzu added, "you yourself are free to go."

Thus the magnitude of his intention.

"Never!" Jeijinn repeated, not bothering to seek our consent; she knew she had it. "We will not treat with a regime founded on violence; we will not traffic in lives."

Dzu shrugged a third time. "I may kill the Ethnos anyway."

"Then let it be on your head, not anOther's. Do not debate me, Dzu-*la*. Remember who it was who taught you logic."

This almost reached the core of him. His head swung up, he stopped his calculated toying and gathered himself.

"I remember, Jeijinn. It was why I lured you here."

"Explain," our mother commanded evenly, though I could see the wave of nausea pass through her.

"I wanted to treat with one whose mind I knew, not some faceless functionary," Dzu explained. "Truth, I never expected you to acquiesce to my Declaration. But I wished to try you. Suppose I set you and yours free, then forge your signature? I can do that: I know it well. Thereby Others are discredited as craven and unprincipled, which is what I have told People in my speeches all along. Else I may honor the nobility of your refusal, and set you alone free once you've forfeited these ninety-odd lives. Thus are Others, through you, seen to be cold, unnatural, indifferent to death, hence the more easy to kill, which my People have always wanted to believe. Or I may pardon those you condemn, to show I am the more merciful. Or execute them, to show I am a man of my word. Whatever my course, way, Jeijinn Other, I win and you lose."

Were my mother not an Empath, we hostage Others might have moved toward her then, despite the guards and their weapons, to show our solidarity. Instead, we must do the very opposite, keep our distance and hold to our Discipline, lest any coloration of our thoughts impinge on hers. Nevertheless, she knew we would abide by whatever choice she made.

"Either way our lives are forfeit, then," she reasoned slowly, "solely because we are Others and we are found within the borders of the Purists' Mantuu."

"Exactly!" Dzu smirked, as yet suspecting nothing; he was not yet as gifted in telepathy as he was to become. "Excepting you—"

He never got to finish. Jeijinn stepped quickly across the distance separating them before Dzu or guards or Others could react, and seized Dzu's hands, interlacing her fingers with his. Dzu gasped and tried to pull away, but even at her great age, Jeijinn was stronger.

Clearly she meant to shock him into a change of heart. As leader of the Purist Party, Dzu had ordered executions, but never personally killed. Now Jeijinn clung fast to his hands and dropped her mental shields, letting his hatred flood into her empathy until hatred, or the Empath, should succumb.

Dzu shrieked as if it were he who was dying, as silently Jeijinn fell back lifeless at his feet, her fingers still locked with his, her weight nearly toppling Dzu with her. Genuine horror wrung Dzu's ordinarily tormented features, before he remembered who he was.

"Now I have twice as many!" he gloated at me, showing me Jeijinn's cold fingers interlaced with his before he pried her death grip loose. Our mother's body lay between us, her last effort failed.

Dzu gestured snarling to his guards. "Take all of them—no, wait!" He thrust one trembling hand at me. "Leave this one! Go!"

We were alone; he was not armed. I could have fended, could have run, but where, and to what end? Were there guards

269

just beyond the door to cut me down? More to the point, why had Dzu spared me? Was I to substitute for Jeijinn in determining the captive Ethnocentrics' fate? I could hear weapons in the courtyard already determining the fate of Others. Dzu held up his hand to stay me until the firing stopped.

"Now it's you who are free!" he snarled. "Go you in Jeijinn's place—but not because I'm merciful. Birth your brat and keep him hidden; never let me know his name or that he's yours. Tell Others what transpired this day in Mantuu, what will transpire in the World if I should gain control. Tell them to find allies to make war against me, for either you and yours or I and mine must die before this matter's ended!"

"You know we cannot do that. Dzu?"

Even in this state he could not help himself. "Yes, Lingri."

"What can I, or any Other, do to alter your purpose?"

I tried to reach out to him. His hand slashed sideways across my face; he flung me back.

"Kill me!" he shouted. "Or die. You and yours or I and mine. There is no Other way!"

Excerpt: "Spores of Evil"
  (from *The Partisan Press*)

The rise of the Purist Party was a phenomenon which can only loosely be compared with that of the Plalan Ascendancy nearly two thousand years before, for while both sought to unify all People under one centralized power, that was all they had in common.

The Plalan Ascendancy was based upon the "superiority" of one race—namely, the Plalans—over its subject races, who were at all times subject, enslaved, and expendable, until the Ascendancy was overthrown. There was also the religious basis of the Ascendancy, which required living sacrifice. This compares to the Praesidium's power base only in that Purist leaders are revered as godlike.

The real difference is this: the Praesidium never seeks to dominate or enslave any People. All People are "equal," the Law states, though naturally those whom the leadership smiles upon are that much more equal. The slaves, the expendables, are the Others. And while Plalas preferred to work its subjects to death, the Purists prefer simply to eliminate them, without even the alibi of god sacrifice.

How Plalas rose to power has been examined in a thousand texts; the Purists' rise is told only in their own texts, which are filled with falsehoods. How can we explain this phenomenon of Purism? How did a minority party, comprised largely of thugs and sociopaths, spring up from the soil of one barren, cultureless land and conquer the World?

In the beginning, they had no army but a few thousand mercenaries, which bore only the arms they were able to have factured in secret in Kelibesh. Their self-styled "intellectual arguments" for Purism were the basest trash, and even the simplest peasant knew it. Yet the Party flourished.

It was as if a single, malignant flower sprouted spontaneously in the tapped-out soil of Mantuu and, silently and under cover of darkness, scattered its spores from shore to shore, where they lay dormant for more than a decade in the heart of every People's land, until they took root and blossomed and set up the Law, all overnight.

First Child: *But if Others knew the People didn't want them anymore, why didn't they just go home?*

Teacher: *It was not all People, but only the Purists who did not want Others anymore, and the Purists were not always as powerful as they are today. This was one important reason why Others stayed. The good and honest People, who feared the Purists' doctrine of hate, begged them to stay so that together they would be stronger than the Purists.*

Second Child: *Did it work?*

Teacher: *For a while it did. But Others offered only justice and an opportunity to work hard; the Purists promised wealth and power even for those who did not work. And they claimed that Others knew the secret of immortality but refused to share it. The Purists were clever, and many People were easily fooled.*

First Child: *What happened then?*

Teacher: *The Purists became more and more powerful in every land. They threatened to hurt People unless they voted for the Party. If that didn't work, they wrote in false votes and changed the election results. Where all else failed, as in Zanti, they marched in with their soldiers and overthrew the government.*

Third Child: *What became of Others then?*

Teacher: *Again, the Purists were very clever. They re-membered how upset People had been when the ninety-seven Others were murdered in Mantuu. So at first they made only small laws. One law said that Others could no longer hold certain jobs. One law said Others could not eat or shop in certain places. Others gave up these things without complaint, because they always meant for People to take them back anyway. Some Others understood what was happening and tried to return to their Archipelago, and most succeeded. But the rest remained, because even after the Purists came to power, the good People begged them to stay.*

Second Child: *If so many People didn't trust the Purists, how could they take over the World?*

Teacher: *First they promised many things to the dissatisfied People, the violent People, the greedy People. When they couldn't keep these outrageous promises, they blamed it on Others. The violent People began to murder Others and said it didn't matter because Others didn't cry for their dead "the way real People do." The Purists argued that this gave them the right to kill all Others.*

Third Child: *Didn't the good People try to save the Others?*

Teacher: *Many did, and many died for their brave deeds, until the Others pleaded with them to stop. Many more Others went to their own deaths willingly, to keep good People from dying for them. This made the Purists very happy, for they could say again that Others had no feelings, if they could go to their own deaths like flockbeasts.*

First Child: *It makes us very sad that all the Others died. We wish we had been born sooner, so that we could have stopped it. . . .*

12

"Dzu had me escorted under guard, past the bodies of the slain, to the border with Dyr, where I was released. Not trusting comm, I returned as quickly as I could to Other-Where. Practicality, not heroism. So I ask, Jemadar: how do you judge me?"

"Someone once said heroism is only stubbornness in a good cause," he temporizes. "Does the lad know?"

He points with his chin toward Joreth, conferring with Peria and Dzilbak on the muddy shore; Melet canoes are already pushing off.

"He knows the facts as I knew them at the time. Only later did I learn that if I had harmed Dzu in any way, a thousand People would have been executed in Freym, and Others blamed."

"Hence you let him live, and a million Others died."

"One man as history, Jemadar? I am not a murderer. Dzu's Party held sway only in Mantuu then. There was sufficient protest in the outlying lands against the killing of the ninety-seven, and no Other died at People's hands until—"

"I know my history!" Jemadar snaps. Dzilbak has already beckoned to him, benignly but with the power of command, and he is torn. Further down the shore, the boy Yarel bids his adopted family good-bye. He cannot go with them—not now, likely not ever. Never having wept for his birth parents, his Disciplines erratically taught in these erratic times, he watches the boats go, weeping openly and unashamed. Peria goes to comfort him as we watch.

"If you understand history, Jemadar, you understand that Dzu was a known quantity. His agenda was the death of Others and the unification of his People. There were those in his Party who would have done far more harm had he been killed. Even as they do now, since he has fallen."

Peria leads Yarel away; he seems consoled if not quite comforted. Can I offer any consolation to this Jemadar, whom I may be sending to his death? I take his hands, a People's gesture, and one that he is fond of.

"Still you have not answered me. How do you judge me, Jemadar?"

He smiles bleakly; his lips brush my brow. "Honest, if nothing else. Lend me your strength of will, Lingri-one. Where I'm going, I shall need it!"

The Melet left us on the shortest night of our polar year, hoping upon Peria's advice for fog to shelter them on the going out, as it sheltered us coming in. Other lives resume their course, for as long as we may be permitted this time.

I am the only one who knows what Jemadar intends to do in Melet, and I weigh the merits of sharing my knowledge with the Matriarchs against Jemadar's privacy. He did not say it was a secret, yet he will not wish to be hailed as some manner of hero should he return.

And if he should not return—I shall not think of this. I do not think I can bear one more violent death.

★　★　★

Our polar technology is now greatly augmented, and our daily lives become that much more amenable. The carefully guised solar collector provides sufficient power to light all interior areas and keep the greenhouses flourishing even when there is no sun. As the days grow shorter, wind collectors may be added, though their visibility from the air mediates against them. Could we solve this problem, we might have sufficient power for every apparatus Joreth envisions. For now we have adequate light, three working commscreens with limited microstor, and the radio receiver.

It is a powerful device considering its size, the magnetic interference this close to the pole, and its scrounged and jury-rigged construction. It enables us to monitor radio transmissions virtually Worldwide, though we ourselves cannot transmit. At present, we have no desire to. There is no knowing who might overhear.

Thus we follow what transpires in the World almost as rapidly as it occurs, though the official news is strictly censored and the Partisan frequency's more accurate versions are seldom encouraging. There is civil war again in Kelibesh, famine in Dyr, severe volcanic disruption along the Werthan border—no doubt triggered by the unleashing of volcanos in OtherWhere—and radiation deaths in poor, beleagured Gleris. There is no word at all out of Melet.

There is irony in *The Partisan Press*'s uncensored account of what happened when the Purist Guard invaded the Archipelago and found no living Others. Did they count the corpses we left behind and think them adequate? Did they truly think we walked into the sea? Aside from the monotonous venom of the propaganda speeches, Others are seldom mentioned, and then always in the past tense. The World believes we are no more.

Perhaps this is why I have officially reopened my chronicle. Having completed my transcription of Tisra's story-chains and submitted them to those whose task it is to commit them to microstor, I am free to make use of the remaining paper for my own ends.

I have chosen as my study a broad, flat, rock shelf near a gentle spring in the quieter reaches of the deepest caverns, as near in spirit as possible to the windowless cell in the Citadel where I began this ragtag epic. One aspect our New Citadel has in common with the old is its ability to transmit sound.

The ancient Citadel's acoustic properties were designed in a time before the Thousand-Year, when rulers' ears needed to extend far beyond their physical bodies. Hence their architectures were constructed to augment every whisper, so that they might know the mood of the populace, and catch conspirators in the act. Following the Thousand-Year, the Citadel's acoustics were preserved simply for their rarity as an example of pre-Discipline genius. We no longer needed to spy on each Other.

As a bonus, Council sessions could be overheard anywhere throughout the complex system of corridors by simply listening in certain alcoves, and those same corridors echoed constantly with susurrating Othervoices as we passed daily to and fro. Toward the end, when we survivors lay hidden in every reach of the City, the Citadel became a gargantuan message drum: a code tapped on certain weight-bearing walls could directly or by relay reach any Other in the City.

Within our newfound catacomb, such subtleties are not possible, but most central arteries have been classified according to their message-bearing properties; thus as in the Old Citadel we can be summoned all at once in an emergency. And there is here, as there, the continuous murmur of Othervoices.

This is overlayered by additional subliminal sound: the pragmatic noise of domestic labor, the recitations of our few remaining children at their schooling, occasional music, the natural water sounds of the many rills and runnels which

have carved these caverns. The total is a constant soft ca-
cophony, and only deep within the rock can one escape it.

The sounds here are only trickling water, scratching
pen, and sometimes my own breathing. And still I hear
voices.

The eyewitness account I brought out of Mantuu threw the
Council into a kind of contained uproar. There were in fact
more People than Matriarchs in the Council now. In our half
century of relative amity, many People had chosen to settle
permanently in OtherWhere, to abide by our laws and Disciplines, to become coequal citizens while at the same time
retaining citizenship in their lands of origin. Represented in
our labs and universities, our industries and pastimes, at all
times integral members of Other society, even to a limited
study of telepathy, these recent citizens were also represented in the Council. Their reaction to my report was the
most vociferous.

"A protest, Mothers, signed by all our members against
these Purists and their policy of death!" they insisted, and,
"We will send representatives at once to our former lands to
raise armies against them!"

The Council as one approved the need for a formal
protest, but as to armies, the People were told "Impossible."

"What you do as People against People is your own
affair," Accolon, who was Matriarch at the time, cautioned
them, "but thereby renounce your office as Matriarch. No
life will be taken in Others' name with Others' sanction."

Baffled and frustrated by our refusal to defend ourselves,
many of these People did resign their offices, abandon their
lives in OtherWhere, and return to their former lands, in the
hope of protecting their own, at least, from this looming
menace. Thus a slow cross-exodus began—Others returning
to OtherWhere, People to their own lands—which would
continue until the arrival of the Purists' Guard upon our
shores. This Guard, having destroyed some two thirds of us

279

on the Mainland, would force the last diehard People still in OtherWhere to return with them, while dumping the last starving Others, myself among them, on the Archipelago.

We never learned what happened to those People forcibly returned. Was their fate, as "collaborators" in the Others' way of life, the same as Others'?

The cross-exodus had already begun as I concluded my report to the Council, setting off for the Industrials to find my father.

". . . and inform me of what I already know," Evere said, his voice a faded whisper.

His eyes rested on me benignly, myopic from a lifetime lost within the dimensions of a compuscreen, bewildered by the World he found beyond it whenever he reluctantly emerged. There was not even a screen in the room; Evere looked naked without one. Yet I understood. He had shut down for the last time.

There was a news blackout in Mantuu, and reports of the deaths of the ninety-seven came solely from their one survivor. Yet Evere knew. Did some tendril of Jeijinn's consciousness linger in his soul, for all their years apart?

"Have you never wondered why we found it necessary to be separated for most of our lives?" my father asked.

In fact, I had, for the greater part of my life. Only in the advent of Redrec had I begun to understand how difficult it was for men and women to live together.

"I had assumed it was a matter for your mutual privacy, Evere-*al*, and none of an offspring's concern."

"But when one parent has died, and the Other is soon to follow, it is time for total truth," Evere suggested.

He waited. I invoked the now magical incantation: "Tell me."

"Consider what it is to bond with an Empath," Evere suggested. "Consider, if you can, what it is to *be* an Empath.

280

Consider why it is that Empaths are so rare, and why they the more rarely reproduce. Yet Jeijinn risked it."

I thought of how my mother had died, remembered how she had lived: aloof, remote, utterly Disciplined whether facing a Council or a World, or the horror that was Dzu. Yet I also recalled the bursts of unDisciplined frustration with which she had sometimes reared her recalcitrant birth off-spring.

Evere leaned forward, touching his fingers to my brow. "Consider," he said, and I saw Jeijinn's life whole:

"An Empath? How? Impossible!"

Loriel's imperious voice. Eminent scientist, bonded with a scientist, aware of no Empath trait in either gene pool, she had somehow borne this most disquieting offspring. The infant at her breast, feeling Loriel's consternation through her very nerve endings, began to howl inconsolably.

Loriel clenched her eyes and chanted the Discipline, forcing herself to be calm. Gradually the child calmed also.

"Prodigious!" my grandmother breathed. "What are we to do?"

The child was reared in virtual isolation from her peers, whose unformed, unDisciplined emotions might have driven her insane. Surrounded from infancy by adults, none of whom could touch her except from necessity, never enclosed in anOther's embrace, Jeijinn grew tentatively, oddly, her intelligence increasing quadratically, her passions stunted, untested, untrusted, lest they develop to some dangerous extreme.

In time Loriel surrendered her to the few adult Em-paths, for Jeijinn was the only Empath of her generation. Her adolescent years among her own kind might be said to re-semble a state of happiness. The adult who returned to the World of normal Others was a stranger, divorced from all nonEmpaths by an ironclad Discipline, mastered for her own survival, which allowed no thought nor passion save what was needed for her task as Matriarch. Loriel's mourning for

281

a dead child could have been no greater than for this change-
ling stranger. . . .

"Ordinary Otherbonding is dilemma enough," Evere said, withdrawing his hand from my face, "as doubtless you have learned. Consider what it is for the Empath. Unlike Telepaths, who match resonance to resonance to enhance their joining, two Empaths met in psychophysical union would quite literally cancel each Other out. Yet the mating cycle must be answered. Thus the Empath chooses a nonEmpath, of specific negative traits."

He raised one hand to prevent my interrupting. Among my childhood's oft-repeated litanies had been Jeijinn's recitations of her spouse's "negative traits," perhaps in the hope of swaying me from mine.

"I do not mean what you are thinking," my father said, "though doubtless your own propensity for subsuming yourself into the task at hand without regard for food or sleep and matters Others call 'necessities' is much akin to mine. Rather, I ask you to consider what it was which made me the ideal bondmate for an Empath. Not only did I test null-empathic, the better to spare potential offspring the trait, I was also virtually devoid of any passion, save for my work. Even in the mating throes I could run equations in my head. I flatter myself this fragmentation of attention may have saved your mother's life."

Mindful of Dweneth's credo, I had to ask: "But how did this serve your needs?"

Whatever Evere was thinking then tugged at the corners of his mouth; he all but smiled. "Quite simply, I adored her," he answered finally. "Whatever her terms, I would have met them. Including siring you. That was her idea, not mine. I thought she should regret it."

How different this was from the impression I had carried all my life of two incompatible personalities, joined for the necessity of mating, then divided. Again I had to ask, "And did she?"

282

"There were 'scans upon 'scans before you were conceived," Evere explained. "Jeijinn could not bear the thought that any child might suffer as she had. And even though you emerged nonEmpath, nonTelepath and—ironically, from my perspective—nonscientist, there was no predicting the manner in which your newborn neediness would fray her empathy. Why do you suppose she so often left you in Loriel's care while she fled to the Council? In part it was to recompense Loriel for the motherhood she had sacrificed, but also Jeijinn could not bear to remain overlong in any one person's presence, not even her own child's.

"When you and Lerius joined with the Old Ones in your childhood, it was I Loriel summoned, not Jeijinn. We could not know but that this was some latent evidence of empathy in you. I wonder to this day about your affinity for People, and what this signifies."

Did he mean Dweneth or Redrec, or both? Did I dare explain that Redrec's presence often jangled my nerves in ways I imagined Jeijinn could appreciate?

"Accept one thing from me, Lingri-one." We were speaking of final things; Evere's nontelepathic ability to share Jeijinn with me had told me this from the beginning. "Let your son know both his parents, regardless of circumstance."

"Father, I will" was all I said.

He touched my face one final time; I for my part traced the burn scar on his cheek, not for the first time wishing mere touch could remove it.

I never saw him more. Lacking Jeijinn, he had no reason to live.

The voices of the past are always with me. They resonate not only in my mind, but in the voices of the story-chain tellers, which find me even in the depths of my chosen catacomb. I hear Dwiri:

". . . what it is to live always in sunshine, for I do

283

remember that, though these last years seem to be spent almost always underground. That may be my only regret in coming here, that the babe will be born in the dark season, and live half her days in night. . . ."

Dwiri walks with, confides in the Matriarch Jisra, not as part of a story-chain, but because she wishes to. Do I see some later reflection of Dweneth and myself, of countless People/Other friendships, in Jisra's listening silence? All I have wished to ask Dwiri about herself, about her mother, is about to be given me. I set aside my pen and eavesdrop.

"The Telepath Ylissa was my foster mother; it was she who brought me up until I started school. This was following the controversy over the Mayel Prizes, and the riots that spread from the Grenni clinic, when Dweneth faced down the People who demanded she hand over 'the secret of immortality,' whatever that might be. She thought it safer for me to be elsewhere, out of reach of her enemies. Thus I was reared by Ylissa, who had borne me, Dweneth being past the age.

"Mostly what I remember is endless days of breeze and sun and long, fragrant meadow grass. Holos of me showed this bleach-haired, suntanned wildling. My feet were as callused as *graax*-toes; I refused to wear shoes.

"Ylissa and I communed mostly in silence, and she taught me all the Telepaths' arts and Disciplines. I thought all children spoke with their parents in this way. Imagine how strange People's children seemed to me when I encountered them, them and their endless chattering! They would stare at me, walking with Ylissa, and that was when I began asking about my father, thinking I must get my looks from him. When Ylissa told me he was also anOther, I was understandably confused, for sheltered though I was, I knew Others did not look like me. I was still pestering Ylissa with questions when she thought to me, *Your answer is at the gate.* I thought it was a game, and so I ran. There was an old woman coming up the walk. A total stranger, yet I knew her. It was like looking at some ancient incarnation of myself. . . ."

"Promise me something?" Dweneth's voice was muffled by the surgical mask. Sterifields sometimes damaged fragile sperm or ova, and could not be used for this procedure.

"Anything," I answered immediately, watching her work on the overhead screen, fascinated.

"Die for me," Dweneth challenged, jangling the soul-thread in such close proximity. It was an old and no longer amusing joke.

"May I not rear my offspring first?" I countered dryly. "Else leave off what you're doing, unless you think a widowed Redrec equal to the task!"

"Sorry!" Dweneth grimaced behind the mask; she was growing less fond of Redrec as his self-interest increased with his years. "Just softening you up for what I really want."

"Which is?"

"Not yet. Lie still."

Crossbreeding had at last been perfected, primarily due to tireless research and well-earned breakthroughs by Dweneth and her staff at Grenni. A generation of Intermix children had begun to appear in small numbers throughout the World. It needed only to counteract the resiliency of Other chromosomes, which tended to cancel out weaker People's strains. By neutralizing all unneeded Other traits— those for blood type, hair and eye color, webtoes, for example—it was possible to cross-match with dominant People's traits, while preserving Other benefits such as strength, longevity, eidetic memory and, where found, telepathy, and an added fillip, Otherears.

Hence Intermix children were virtual physical clones of the parent from the People's side, but their "innards" comprised what Dweneth unscientifically dubbed a "merry stew" of shared traits.

The creation of this hybrid species out of the two existing ones was judged by some a blessing, by some a curse.

"What's wrong with it," Dweneth wheezed—these later years had made her short of breath—"is that it gives some People the idea we can make them immortal." She finished what she was doing, began to strip the gloves and mask off. " 'Drain my blood and give me Other blood, so I can live as long as Others!' some idiot actually challenged me at a state reception. Oh, God, I must sit down!" She did, shuddering. "I've heard worse suggestions than transfusions, too, you may believe!"

Even then, I did. In later years, the Guard in almost every death camp held rituals involving the drinking of Other blood, and even the ingestion of still-warm Other hearts.

"Idiots!" Dweneth pulled herself to her feet, set instruments in the sterilizer, began to scrub out. "I tell them bluntly, 'Take your vitamins and innoculations, eat and exercise like anOther, and that'll get you to one hundred. Want your children to live twice that? Then have them by anOther!' It shuts them up, but most would like to kill me."

"The rest speak of awarding you the Mayel Prize," I countered, offering her no sympathy. I tried to get up, she shoved me down; she was not yet so very old.

"The Mayel Prizes—oh, please! Yet something else they've got wrong. Promoting World peace and poetry and healing are all very well, but Mayel of the Thousand-Year would have protested the use of her name. And not one single Other's accepted it since it was established. All right, you may get up. He's doing fine."

" 'He'?" I repeated. "Is gender included in the technique, or do you suddenly have second sight?"

"I'm rarely wrong," she answered smugly, switching off lamps and screens.

"As you wish," I humored her. "Now, as to this promise . . ."

286

"It's two promises, really," Dweneth explained, plopping herself down on my bed in one of her guest cottages on the Grenni grounds. I was leaving in the morning. "The first is that you come back here and stay with me when he's ready to be born. I think I ought to finish what I've started. Redrec's welcome too, of course, once this World tour is over, though I know you two are no longer what you once were."

"Whatever that might have been," I answered dryly.

For all his philandering, my sometime spouse had somehow never fathered a child. He would indulge me in my Other duty to replicate, at least once, but as to his own participation . . .

"This fathering bit's not natural to me," he'd announced, playing at the provincial lad despite his receding hairline and the jowls half hidden by his graying beard. Women and music critics still found him charming. "No training, you see. Never had a father myself, except in a bully's sense. Wouldn't want to pass that legacy on to the kid, now, would I? Besides, your kind half the time raises one-parent kids, don't they? You'll be all right."

"Tell me why, for example," Dweneth demanded now, "he chooses to conduct opera in his later years, knowing it's the one form of music you can't bear, either physically or psychically. How's that for putting barriers in the way? I confess I never understood the relationship!"

"Nor I yours with Lerius," I ventured, earning her best dangerous look.

"Don't change the subject! What's done is done. It doesn't matter anymore."

She sighed, swept back her near white hair, a too familiar gesture. "Remember when we first discovered the soul-thread? We were twenty then. More than half a century ago. We swore we'd be together always, fellow adventurers, saving the World but never beholden to it, no matter what it demanded of us.

"I think those first five years in OtherWhere were all we

287

ever really had, and even those were fragmented by the Chamber, Lerius, 'duties and obligations.' " Her face and voice were stricken. "Sometimes I think without the soul-thread I would have gone mad! Were we wrong to let them use us up the way they have?"

I could not answer her.

"I have a premonition," she said finally, hugging her-self in the old way. "It's not only the upcoming elections in Mantuu, it's everything. Things are going to get very bad, for all of us—I feel it! Come back when he's due to be born? Stay as long as you can. Let me watch him grow; it's all I ask."

She gave so much, asked for so little. I could refuse her nothing.

"I have commitments in the Leeward lands," I an-swered. "A few months' research, a lecture tour or two. But most assuredly, after that . . ."

Well before that was to be Dzu in Mantuu, Jeijinn's death, Evere's. But only a Telepath can know the future, and then not always so.

"Dweneth?"

I so rarely used her name; to this day I do not know why. Certain primitive cultures held that to name a thing, even a soul, was to possess it. I subscribed to no such super-stition, yet why was I ever reluctant to use her name?

Perhaps I should have spoken it more often. It always made her smile.

"Yes, Dearheart?"

"You wanted a second promise."

She shook her head; her face grew clouded. "Not now! Let's see if we can manage the first!"

"And the second promise became me."

Dwiri's Telepath tread has brought her silently to sit beside me in my stone study. Has she read what I have written on the page or in my mind? Either way, she means to pique my Other curiosity. I put the pen aside and respond:

"Having judged your age against the year Dweneth was gone from me, I assumed as much. Will you tell me how it happened?"

"Not now," she demurs, so like her mother. "Jisra is learning my story-chain, to add it to the Others', though she does not know the beginning, for I have not told her. I thought you deserved to know it first, but I need your help."

This puzzles me. "My help? Until you came ashore in OtherWhere, I did not know you existed. You are the only secret Dweneth ever kept from me."

"She was afraid you would succeed in dissuading her." Dwiri contemplates the small, still hands in her lap. Then her white-irised eyes seek mine. "Would you have?"

At the time, I would have been convinced any contact with Lerius would mean death for her. At the time . . .

"Given the available facts, yes, I should have tried. Obviously the facts were incorrect. She joined with Lerius in some wise, yet lived. For she returned, and you are proof. I confess I still do not understand."

"Will you tell me what you do know?"

She seems to be offering me a trade. Again, as every time I speak with her, I am aware of how easily she could pluck the memory from my mind, yet she forbears. Has her father taught her politeness, or is it possible the old chronicler's tales can captivate still?

"It was two years after Joreth's birth. The Purists' influence was spreading out of Mantuu to establish a minority party in every land save Zanti. For only the second time in all our years, Dweneth asked to break the soul-thread. . . ."

"Why?" I had to ask. Desperately vibrant at that moment, the soul-thread told me she was shielding mightily. I thought at once of Lerius but also, strangely, of Dzu.

"You promised me you'd never ask!" she threw at me.

"I never had reason to, until now."

She came to me, took my face in her hands as she had

when I first reappeared out of the slaughter in Freym, as if to convince herself that I was real and whole and with her.

"Truth. How many years have you known me?"

"Fifty-seven point—"

"And still you do not trust me?"

"I trust you with my life," I answered carefully. "But not necessarily with your own."

This almost swayed her. She wrung her hands, then steeled herself. "It seems to me," she said archly, in her never quite abandoned Player's tone, "that if you truly loved me, you wouldn't have to ask. Suppose . . . suppose I told you there was an epidemic that I was being sent to cure? There is no inoculation, so I'm exposing myself to grave danger, but it's my belief I may have the cure. If not, I'm at least an extra pair of hands. Will you forbid me?"

"You are a healer," I replied, searching her People's words for their deeper truth, "and I forbid you nothing. But an epidemic would not necessitate your severing the soul-thread."

"You did, in Droghia. Without bothering to tell me why."

"That was different."

She was out of breath, and not only from age. "In all these years, I've only asked you once. You gave far readily that time, in spite of danger. Now I'm asking you again. For a year, no more. At one year to the day you will hear from me in some wise, I swear it."

"And then?" Still the soul-thread resonated; I knew there was more.

"Come for me?"

"It was that which swayed you," Dwiri suggests.

"Perhaps," I acquiesce. "She knew I had not the power to come for her beyond death. She trusted that whatever she intended to do, she would survive it. I yielded."

"Though it broke your heart."

290

"I am anOther."

"Yes, of course."

She is gone as silently as she arrived. Telepaths! I resume my pen, my memories grown prodigious.

Was it unreasonable to assume that, having held out for nearly six decades, Dweneth's destination was Lerius? I turned the facts as I knew them over and over in my mind.

Her name was legend in every land including Other-Where. She had accomplished the one thing she desired most for the World: to give it Intermix children in the hope of cementing the alliance between People and Others. Not incidentally, she had healed thousands, and her Grenni hospice was used as a model Worldwide for enlightened holistic healing. Did she see all of this as futile in light of the Purists' rise?

She spoke of being "used up," and to a great extent she had been. While she counseled Others to seek their hearts' desire, she had denied her own. Now she meant to grasp it, though it killed her.

She was going to be with Lerius.

Why then, when she sent for me, had she been with Dzu?

The past yields to the present. Joreth has summoned me to the radio room.

He spends all his waking hours here of late, my pirate son, even abandoning his music and the nightly entertainment. Does some part of him long to return to that World which is apparently tearing itself apart in our absence?

"Very busy!" he mutters, the headset on his Other ears. "I wish our pickup were better; we lose half the multiphasics. But everywhere the news is bad. Mother, it is as the WiseOnes predicted. Without us, they feed upon themselves, and with the technology we have given them!"

"Does this surprise you?" His fervor exhausts me; I

know where his mind is leading. "Jisra and the Council know?"

He hushes me while he picks up a new broadcast, frowning with concentration, his lower lip caught between his teeth. Oh, for a World that would grow quiescent long enough for me to know my son! My memories are of a wild-haired boy frolicking with *bRi*. Did it ever happen? I don't know anymore. Others are possessed of eidetic memory; I should be able to recall at once and whole everything I have ever experienced. The painful memories grow more poignant as I chronicle them. Why do the joyous ones elude me?

"The only hopeful news is out of Melet, and even that is not entirely unmixed." Joreth hands the headset over to a young Other who comes to relieve him. "There is talk of a 'new order' following some 'necessary purges.' Dzilbak the Dragon is said to have died of natural causes. We may assume Jemadar was less fortunate."

Strangely, I am less certain. Something not in my mind, not Disciplined, tells me Jemadar is still alive—a feeling? How do I dare?

"Mother? Where are you? Have you heard anything I've said?"

I touch his arm, Dweneth's gesture and, I assume, also Dwiri's. He flinches.

"I hear you," I say. "Why did you summon me, when it is Jisra and the Council who need to know?"

He shrugs, a Redrec/Joreth gesture. "I guess I needed . . . comfort? Reassurance. Sometimes I listen to these things for hours on end and think we are the fortunate ones. Let them kill themselves off, and perhaps some of us will survive to inherit what is left."

"Will there be anything left? They were already using nuclears when you were in your teens."

He cocks his head, considering. "That doesn't seem to satisfy them. They prefer to be up to their elbows in gore.

Oh, Mother, I'm so disgusted!'' He grabs two handfuls of his splendid hair and tugs on it. ''Would that Liiki and Loriel had foregone their caution and launched their spaceships! We would never know what we had left behind.''

Joreth is as little scientist as I; doubtless he thinks his ancestors so gifted they could send a million Others into space within a single generation. Moreover, where were we to go?

''Joreth-al?'' The young Other on the radio presumes to disturb us. ''There is an urgent broadcast out of Dyr Central, just beyond the farthest band. If I could boost the gain . . .''

Joreth is beside him at once, manipulating dials, listening on the spare headset. The Other nods his gratitude, begins to copy the message down.

''Computers and now radio,'' I marvel. ''Your education has been eclectic in my absence.''

''Oh, Redrec and I used to spend days on that antique set in the catacombs, broadcasting as well as receiving, the whole thing complicated by our depth underground and run-off from the canals,'' he says absently, then focuses suddenly on me. ''You don't know about that, do you? You know nothing at all after that day you walked out on us both.''

''I stand accused,'' I offer dryly. ''I thought we had come to terms with that.''

Joreth waves me off. ''Redrec did. I didn't, until I talked to you. I thought he was making excuses, covering up for you. He had developed so many masks and personalities by the time he died. . . .''

He blinks at me, then on a sudden impulse leads me out of the radio room, which is in the topmost part of our mountain, very near the Windward face, the better to pick up Worldwide signals. Any egress from this chamber is down. Joreth and I walk. He talks, pontificates. It is a family trait.

''You truly know nothing about his last years? If there's anything I could hate about Others, it's that: you close a door and walk away, never wondering about those you've left behind that door. As if you've sealed them in a stasis jar and expect to find them intact when—if—you choose to return. At least thus they remain in your memory, hmm? Frozen in whatever pose of rage or anguish you left them in."

If he only knew!

"Are you quite through?" I ask. "Or are you merely testing lyrics for a song, for this has little bearing on the actual event, whatever you remember."

"He was drunk the day you left us. Do *you* remember?"

"Betrayal!" he had shouted. "The boy means so little to you? Or is this some final way to wreak your vengeance on me? Betrayal! Hypocrisy! Cold and a hypocrite, who calls him still 'my son' and can't escape it!"

While I wondered what combination of drink or age or grief made him impermeable against any argument that he and Joreth were far better never to be associated with my name. Do I remember? It is the curse of being Other, always to remember.

"Yes."

"Well then, here's something for your memory banks: he wasn't. You were so accustomed to expect it of him, you didn't even go near him to smell it on him, much less to touch him one last time."

It was true. We had not touched, not then, not for a long time. I had approached him that day assuming I would never see him again. I never did.

We have reached my "nun's cell" now, and I would liefer be alone. Joreth will not have it. I invite him in.

"Doubtless you have a point."

Joreth sits on my sleeping shelf, looks from under his shaggy People's brows at me, wondering if he should share what he knows.

"I think you never wrote a truer word than when you divided us into four species instead of two. Men and women

294

disunderstand their opposites far more readily than People and Others.''

"No argument. Go on.''

"What did you see in him when you left? In me you saw a callow, whining boy, and no illusion. That's what I was, truly, for all your efforts at Other Discipline. But you looked at your spouse and saw a sodden wreck, a great musician gone spoiled, a ruined being. I'm going to surprise you. Ever hear of the Droghian Underground?''

Does he think I spent the last days of OtherWhere in a hole in the ground? In truth I did, but that hole had eyes and ears and pirated radio signals, bringing with often painful accuracy as much as possible of what transpired on the Mainland, until the very end.

"The Droghian Underground,'' I say after him slowly, as if to imply that one of us is mad, and I am feeling fine, "was a revival of the Trollking's network which flourished in Redrec Elder's time, primarily to service the outcasts and those skirting the law, as Redrec Elder did. The catacombs and tunnels beneath Droghia are said to be more complex and extensive than what has been built aboveground, and I can well believe this, having seen the maps of what is known, and having spent some portion of my life within those earthen walls. The Droghian Underground, in its most recent incarnation, aided some seven thousand Others in fleeing the Mainland in the final years. I have even had recourse to it myself in my comings and goings.''

"And who were its leaders?'' Joreth quizzes me, as if this were some infant school exercise.

"Doubtless they were known only to themselves. A so-called third-man scenario, in which each cell member only knew the name of the contact on his right, and took instruction from the unknown contact to his left. That way, if any were to be captured—''

"And the ringleader?''

"How am I to know?" We pause. I am no Telepath, and yet . . . "Not Redrec?"

"Why not? Who better than a musical superstar, beloved of millions, rich and seeming profligate—"

"Seeming?"

"—known to lowlife as well as the elite. . . . "

He stops. Does he think me smiling? Certainly I am amazed.

"Before you set foot on the outharbor ferry, Father was sober and busy," Joreth finishes. "Not that he was drunk to begin with. He wanted you furious with him, guilty over leaving me, and thus not likely to return. Elsewise, as he put it, you'd be 'in it up to her neck and likely to get us all killed.' "

"He had no idea what I myself was doing in those years," I muse. "You too?"

"I told you about the Tapeworm Scandal," he reminds me, "or does one's memory fail beyond one's hundredth year?"

I swing at him playfully, a People's gesture. He fends me off, anOther's. My soul is somewhat lighter than it has been these recent years, and Joreth actually laughs.

Other eyes were never meant for tears. I banish them to the backs of my hands as Dweneth might, and sit beside my son, taking his hand in both my own.

"You will have to tell me everything you did, you and he," I say.

"In time." Joreth rubs the back of his neck, an evasive gesture. "Wait until I can add newer episodes. I'm thinking of going back."

He has tried to tell me gently. Why does the information rock me? "I thought—"

"Don't think. The Council's meeting even now. It's Jisra's contention that some of us have an obligation to return—voluntarily, of course—to save the People from themselves."

"Or merely to distract them long enough to finish killing us!" I offer, though some Other-perverse corner of me understands, has pondered almost daily since we've come here the uselessness of spending my second hundred years in this realm of ice. "At any rate, if this debate be anything like Other debates I have known, your daughter will be grown before it's settled. Tell me more of Redrec. Clever of him to so mislead me, knowing I elsewise would have stayed."

"Was it Dweneth who said anOther's greatest flaw is truthfulness?" Joreth wonders. "That, being unable to tell untruth, we never expect to be lied to?"

"Something like. Joreth, tell me this one thing: what are you? People, Other, Intermix, or all of the above?"

He stops rubbing his neck. "I am whatever it suits me to be, as any Intermix has to be to stay alive and sane. Tell you about Redrec? Do you want me to tell you he risked his neck for Others because of you? Perhaps he did. But what really galvanized him was the Law."

Excerpt: The Law in All the Lands
[*Official Orders of the People's Purist Prae-sidium*]

The Law is explicit:

If you are anOther, you die.
If you harbor, shelter, or abet anOther, you die.
If you save anOther's child, your own child dies.
For every Other who eludes the Law, ten die.
If ten Others cannot be found, ten People die.

Hereby all People know the Law, and it has no exception. The choice is yours and, having made the choice, do not fault the Law for its consequences.

13

"The Law was the external thing he needed," Joreth says. "The odd thing about him was that, as an artist, he never could trust internal motives, excepting in his art. He seemed to need something outside himself to grouse about and butt his head against. You taught him that, I suspect."

"Oh, no! Not I," I answer. "Redrec was born with that. As you were. How did he die?"

"Peacefully enough. I've been less than truthful with you. He may have died drunk, but not *a* drunk, if you understand the difference.

"He caught an ague after several nights knee-deep in the canals, getting the last few boatloads of refugees out before the Purists regained control of the locks. Took to his bed with a bottle and a sly look on his face. I asked if I could help. 'Close my eyes after!' he growled. 'And write me decent press releases before the lies begin!' When I closed the door on him I could hear Gelik's *Fantasia* on the sound system. He went out smiling."

"And you mourned."

"I did. I still do. I guess I wanted ordinary parents. A

little cottage by the canalside, a lap-pet to chase about the yard. Siblings even. A sense of belonging somewhere, instead of being torn between two incompatible Worlds. The freedom to run with the wind in my hair without worrying about covering up my ears." He sighs, gets up to leave. "Self-pity is the ugliest unDiscipline of all. Give us a hug?"

I do.

"You're all bones!" he murmurs by way of endearment. "We'll have to make you eat more!"

If I sit very still beside the spring in my stone study, I can become that spring, and flow through all the caves and caverns, hearing and seeing all that is in OtherWhere.

If I stand very still and stretch out my arms cruciform, I can reach with my fingertips to the far corners of the World and perhaps, in time, beyond.

I am not a Telepath. But I have let a Telepath into my mind, and learned therefrom.

I am not People. But I have shared my body, mind, and soul with People, and thereby come to understand.

Without us, they will destroy themselves. Is this any longer our concern?

I reach my mind to the Council chamber, where I might go in person as I did from childhood, sitting in the gallery of the Old Citadel to observe and learn, but I prefer to do it thus. I am no Telepath, yet I hear and see.

Jisra speaks:

"In its simplest form, it is this: before they knew of our existence, the People preyed almost constantly upon their own, but in small, personal combats which had the effect of slowly sickening those of sensitive nature, who thereby imposed a balance upon the aggressors, causing them to cease, at least for a time. This was the normal order of things, as People understood it.

"Having interacted with us, to the extent that they believe they have destroyed us, a similar balance may occur,

300

but only if we act. Even as we debate, the aggressors triumph in our supposed annihilation. The sensitive, long sickened and powerless, have fallen into despair. The aggressors see this as weakness and prepare to annihilate the sensitive, hoping thus to eliminate sensitivity. The weapons they use are derived from things we taught them. What is our responsibility?''

And the Debate, which is older than I am, resumes.

I am not a spring, yet I can flow through caves and caverns to the Enclave. Dwiri is there, in meditation with Lerius.

What keeps you alive? I wonder, objective in my study of him. He is skeletal, wasted, skin over bones, and a mind which incandesces. *Is it only duty, the keeping of the story-chains for when Tisra dies and you become the eldest? Is it something as simple as curiosity, the need to be with your child, to see your grandchild born? Since when can temporary temporal things tempt a Telepath?*

A Telepath's lineaments were never meant for smiling. Skeletal, incandescent, Lerius smiles at me.

Come!

''. . . Thus they boasted of their conquests. Vidmaps were set up in every public place, to chart their progress in a given land, the numbers of the populace who had voted for them in the last election. . . .''

Soliah, teaching history to the young ones as I pass. Some Partisans attend her lecture. They nod, remembering.

''Later those same vidmaps were to show the invasions in Zanti and Gleris, when those lands would not countenance an elected Purist Party. Later still, they listed the numbers of Others slain in every land, their lurid colors bleeding over landscapes, sickening the People. One of the Underground's first visible actions was to sabotage those vidmaps, shorting them out or removing them entirely, and there was some popular support. . . .''

301

"Consequently we lack the permutational link to determine whether WiseJisra's proposed action be for good or ill. Suppose our reappearance only renew the killing frenzy? Suppose in so doing we not only finish ourselves, but cause the People to more violently turn upon themselves? It has been proven that the dissatisfied, thwarted in their goal of impacting upon a dominant society, will turn upon and destroy their own villages, their own People."

"The fault, WiseMerlo, lies in one's insistence upon viewing People as a childlike race, when generations of interaction clearly show . . ."

I pass the Council chamber, exhausted.

"The last to receive the Mayel Prize for music." Joreth, about Redrec, to Peria, who has asked. "At least, they were still called the Mayel Prizes then. What did they change it to ultimately, do you know?"

I do. They became the Purist Prizes, and by definition only People could be awarded them. Curious and fascinating that Redrec and Dweneth should be awarded the last of the Mayels, he for music, she for medicine—despite, the committee pointed out, her less than orthodox activities in the realm of genetic intermixing: their award was more for the number of plague innoculations administered. Or was it for something else? Either way, she refused it.

Come for me?

My activities, once the Purists' power extended from Mantuu into Hraregh, Lamora, and Tawa, became less those of a chronicler and more those of a Monitor, with variations. Monitors were best suited to evacuate those Others who could be gotten out of conquered lands, knowing as we did several tribes and their languages and mores and being more learned in disguise and subterfuge than the average Other.

Mercifully I was relatively idle at the time Dweneth's summons came.

Either way, I would have gone.

The summons breathed across the soul-thread, weak and bordering desperate. How was I to know whence it originated?

First, of course, I searched my mind for OtherWhere. Did it surprise me to find Lerius expecting me?

No! Not here!

His voice was rarely gentle in my brain.

Where, then? I thought to him, and got no answer.

Very well. I set myself apart in the quietest place I could find and listened. The answer I received was a disquieting one.

Mantuu. To be specific, Freym. Dweneth was in the very heart of the horror. How, and why? My listening yielded no duress, no confinement, no real suffering, only vast weariness and a need for me.

I went.

"Dzu's an epileptic," she informed me, as if she had seen me only yesterday.

"I did not travel half a World at your summons only to be told that!" Was I angry? Surely I was beyond Discipline.

"I'm only telling you to try to make some sense out of it myself!" she shouted, her own nerves frayed.

"They summoned me. How they found me I will never know. Dragged me out of bed, in fact, and all I'm thinking is 'Uh-oh, it's because of the Intermixes after all. Or is it because I refused the once-named Mayel Prize?' Instead, as it turned out—"

"Slow down," I commanded, surprising myself with my own imperiousness, a trace of Jeijinn at the top of her form in my voice. "For one, you're wheezing. For two, you're rambling. Try to make some sense."

She sighed, caught her breath, ran her hands through

her magnificent hair. I had never seen her look so old. Truth, she had never been so old, but was it only that?

"They were going to award me this year's Mayel for medicine. You must have known. You'd have had to be living underground not to."

"It would not be inaccurate to say I was. Go on."

She scowled at me. "I suppose I'm not allowed to ask."

" 'She who severs the soul-thread—' "

" 'Must be prepared not to know certain things.' All right. The fact is they were going to nominate me, in despite of my unorthodoxy and the fact that the sole Purist on the Committee was against me. I had a source who told me, see, before it was officially announced.

"I told them I'd save them the embarrassment, keep it off the infonets, let them nominate someone else 'cause I wouldn't take it, not since no Other was named that year. They got huffy and said I'd take it or else. Well, I didn't, and when I was asked I told them why, and the controversy raged for weeks. Your man's accepted his for music, however."

"It may be cover, for Joreth's sake," I offered, when in truth I could not know Redrec's motivation at all. "Further, music is the least political of arts."

"Says you!" Dweneth snorted. "Anyway, there I am, eighty years old and bedridden—I'd been ill, thank you for asking—thinking, 'Maybe I'll get up today,' though my own physician would have had paroxysms, when something literally lands on my roof, and two plainclothes but no mistaking 'em thugs burst in and carry me off. No one heard, no one could intervene, and the skimmer's windscreens were sealed over so I couldn't even see where we were going. Fetch us a glass of water, please; I'm fair winded!"

Half her age though just her age, I fetched her water, amazed at her lungs' capacity in spite of her disclaimers. Once a Player maid, always a Player maid.

"Better!" she gasped, after she had drunk. "So here I am in Freym, treating the Patriarch of the Purist Party for severe epileptic seizures. Think you, it may explain the whole of him, though why it never showed up in a previous scan . . . well. I still don't know why it had to be me he sent for. The old Dzu, playing at ironies? Mayhap he has so many enemies he can't trust anyone else. Or, conversely, maybe he doesn't trust me, thinks I'd like to kill him—I've been tempted, these last few days—and still desires death more than life. Or is it possible that a cure for his epilepsy could end this madness?"

"Do you believe his illness is the reason for his killing frenzy?" I asked carefully. Could it be so simple? My knowledge of People was imperfect still. "It is your hope to save the World from him with your cure?"

For the first time I understood how I had managed to arrive here unscathed, having no delusion my sea-colored eyes and carefully counterfeited identisigil could get me past the Purists' scanners if someone were to grow curious. All it needed was a drop of my blood to prove what I was, if not who. But one of Dweneth's conditions for treating Dzu must have been my safe passage. She could hardly bargain for the Others in Mantuu; there were no more.

Dweneth drank some more water, took her own pulse, frowned and shook her head.

"Cure him or kill him. I'm not decided. That's why I want you here."

"You are a healer," I began.

"Oh, rot, I don't mean literally!" she snapped. "But what would you say to a kidnapping?"

She had hatched an elaborate plot involving drugging Dzu and stealing a skimmer. She would administer the drugs, "and you can decode the skimmer access and carry him in. I know the sentries' shifts, so none will see us. You can still carry a man Dzu's size, and deprogram skimmers, can't you?"

"Not skills I have had need of recently," I suggested dryly. "Are you certain this room is safe?"

"Quite certain, with this." She showed me a device on her belt. To any but anOther such a small electrobaffler looked merely decorative.

"Well? What say you?"

"I say you don't understand the nature of the thing you're tampering with!" Dzu shrieked at both of us.

Could this creature be the Dzugash I once knew?

With what reluctance I was brought into his charnel-house presence I will not record here; say only that I was grateful for what little telepathic gift I had, to shield my mind from him. I could not shield my eyes.

His biographers would describe him as ageless; so he was. Somewhere in his thirties he had worn himself down to bone and fever and there remained, his face and person changeless, though the jet black hair might have had cosmetic help. My eyes passed over him quickly as his passed over me.

"I must confess I never thought to see you again!" he greeted me. "How fares your son? He must be nearly five by now. I trust you have him safely hid in OtherWhere?"

I did not answer.

"Why have you brought her here?" he demanded of Dweneth when his stare failed to deflect mine.

"For moral support," Dweneth said airily. "To stop my scalpel hand from slitting your throat the next time you take your sedative. You have been taking your sedative?"

He might have blanched, if bone could blanch. "I have, dutifully, and it's made all the difference. I am cured! Or do you intend to poison me now? For what? Have I harmed any People?" His eyes scanned back and forth between us rapidly; he smirked. "I smell a plot here. Shall you tell me, Lingri, or shall I put yon Dweneth's heart and health to the test? She's very old and rather frail; I doubt more than a single rack of questions would succeed in—"

"Oh, shut up!" Dweneth blustered; only I knew how frightened she was. "I saved your life; you won't harm me. Nor her, while she's here. You gave your word."

"Trust a murderer's word?" Dzu wondered coyly. "Dwen, you are naive still!"

"The murderer hasn't murdered since I saved him from the fits," she said coldly. "If we attribute your past actions to the disease, there's still time to save yourself."

" 'Save myself'?" Dzu echoed. "Is that what you say? I say you don't understand the nature of the thing you're tampering with!"

He drew closer to us, linked his arms in ours, though there were many things I would prefer to touching him.

"Do you think me the most dangerous man in the World?" His voice was shrill; he panted. "Then think again! I am the very voice of moderation compared to what would replace me should I fall."

"Which is why I didn't kill you that first night," Dweneth bluffed. "Shall I remind you?"

Linked to her through Dzu, I could see the memory in both their minds, through both their eyes: Dweneth thrust into the bright-lit room where Dzu foamed and writhed and chewed the costly carpet, soiling himself and growling; Dzu experiencing all these things and seeing Dweneth seeing him. Only a witness, I was shaken.

"All right!" Dzu shrieked, thrusting both of us away from him, trembling all over.

"Sir? Are you all right?"

The voice came from the walls. Naturally Dzu would have this conversation monitored.

"Never mind!" he barked. "Shut off the screens. Am I afeared of *women?*"

He panted like a wildcur, crouching with his hands on his knees. Dweneth put one ancient arm about his shoulders

307

and began to rub the back of his neck, leading him like a child, her eyes locked with mine above his head. She made him sit down, put his head between his knees until his breathing normalized. He emerged at last, his face hidden in his hands. We heard him sigh.

"There you have it, my one weakness—that I fear death as much as I desire it. It has been thus all my life, Dwen, yet your treatments calm me, cause me to rethink . . . Perhaps you're right, and it's been the disease driving me to act. . . . If I can be that voice of moderation, sway the Party from its current course, declare amnesty for all Others, turn it to my advantage . . . a hero . . ." He clutched both Dweneth's ancient hands in his own, sobbing like a child. "Dwen, as I owe you my life, I swear I'll try!"

She took his head upon her generous breasts and stroked him for some minutes until he calmed. Was it to be as simple as that?

"Dzu?" I had not dared speak till now.

"Yes, Lingri." His face was streaked with tears, washed clean.

"We will stay with you." I did not need to look at Dweneth to know she would acquiesce. "Our lives are yours, to help you set things right."

A shudder passed over him, but he got to his feet. Again he linked his arms with ours, and this time it was not unpleasant. I let my shields down, searching him, wishing for perhaps the only time in my life that I was a Telepath. But Dzu had studied with the Telepathy longer than I; I could read nothing.

"Thank you, but no!" he whispered, more gentle than I thought possible. "I must do this alone!"

He actually leaned to kiss us each in turn upon the cheek, then let us go.

"Go now! I will prevail, and stop the killing. Only give me time. I promise!"

* * *

308

"I'm shaking so hard, I can't make a fist!" Dweneth marveled, staring at her outsplayed hands while I piloted the skimmer. "Did it really happen, or did we dream it?"

"To the best of my knowledge, the sharing of a soul-thread does not include the sharing of dreams," I answered dryly, masking my own incredulity. "Further, I will aver that I was quite awake."

"Well then, I guess it happened!" Dweneth breathed. She scowled at the instrument panel. "Where are you going? Not to OtherWhere?"

"As we have been given Dzu's leave to journey where we will—"

"No! Take me back to Grenni! I need to rest."

I recalibrated the navcon. "As you wish." We flew in silence for some moments. "Do you believe him?"

"Do you?"

"As someone once pointed out, anOther's greatest weakness is in her inability to recognize a lie."

Dweneth laughed, wincing. "Oddly enough, I do. Or rather, I believe he believes himself. Whether he has sufficient power . . . We should have stayed."

"I think not. Dzu would not have appreciated it. He must, as he says, do this alone."

Dweneth sighed. "You're probably right. Well, here we are again! Soul-thread reestablished, neither of us much the worse for wear. Let's see how long it lasts."

"The illness Dzu's minions roused you from in Grenni," I began, studying my instruments. "Had it to do with Lerius?"

She clutched her heart dramatically. "Don't *do* that to an old woman! Why didn't I feel that coming down the soul-thread? Yes, as a matter of fact, it did. How much do you want to know?"

"How much do you wish to tell?"

She studied the landing lights on the skimmer's truncated wing. "As much as I can make sense of even now. All

309

right, yes, I went to him. I thought me, I have accomplished all that I wish to accomplish for the World, and the World's no better for it. Now it's time for my heart's desire. I'm going to confront him, demand a joining, no matter what.

"Oddly, he acquiesced almost at once, and we discovered—discovered we were wrong all these years. Or else he had mastered a level of control whereby we could join and I survive. It was . . . I have no words. Years fell away, I saw past and future whole, through his eyes. Well, I guess you experienced the same thing way back when—"

"Indeed."

She eyed me wickedly. "Only thing you missed was the physical joining—oh, my! If I could describe that I wouldn't. Wouldn't give you the satisfaction. Delicious! Enough to last a lifetime. For we have agreed, that while I keep some portion of him here"—she tapped her temple—"and he, being the Telepath, has always held me whole, that it's sufficient. We shall not meet again."

"And this satisfies you?" I asked after a very long time.

She nodded, eyes glistening with tears.

"It's why I could face a thousand Dzus. Everything is different somehow. I am complete!"

"Mercifully, there is only one Dzu," I remarked, and took my hands from the controls to clasp hers. "Dweneth, Dearheart, I rejoice with thee!"

"Even a Telepath cannot work miracles," I tell Lerius, having come at his summons. He only smiles at me. Unnerving.

I have been drawn to the Enclave by his mind, and Dwiri's. Whatever they want of me, I will have answers of them first. Dwiri is younger and, while hardly ingenuous—no Telepath ever is—at least more amenable than her father. Whether it is only my age or the fact that I am her mother's dearest friend, I believe I can move her.

"Even a Telepath cannot cause a People's woman of eighty years to conceive a child," I suggest.

"That's true," Dwiri answers for them both. "Thus, Mother had Ylissa."

I come into their half circle, kneeling as they do, though I do not drop my shields. "Please explain."

Dwiri and Lerius exchange glances; it is she who speaks.

"Mother saved Ylissa's life. Ylissa was a Telepath, studying the Dyr rites when the Purists disrupted the rites and rounded up everyone. Naturally, they were incredibly pleased to have a Telepath in their midst. Oh, the experiments they could perform!

"At any rate, I'm not quite clear on all the details, but Mother was visiting an old friend who had been a rites priestess once herself, and who then was fading quietly into death."

"Cwala," I say softly, thinking, the old acrobat would have been nearly one hundred; it was good. "Go on."

"Somehow she got Ylissa and as many Dyr released as possible. Ylissa begged to return the favor, and Mother, being pragmatic—"

"I see."

"Do you?" Dwiri wonders. "Imagine the determination of someone willing to keep her own ova in cryofreeze for nearly half a century. I'm no healer, I don't understand the process, but while Ylissa carried me, I was Dweneth's, do you see? It all had to do with going back to OtherWhere for Lerius."

"The details do not matter." I dismiss them with one hand. "That she wanted you so badly is sufficient. You are here, and doubly blessed in having two mothers."

"So I've always felt," Dwiri agrees.

"I thank you for your explanation." I get up to go. "Perhaps next time you will tell me more of your mother, of the things you remember of her growing up. I would value that."

"And how she died."

"Yes."

311

"Why not now?"

"I am needed elsewhere," I demur. Having spent most of this day woolgathering, I must return to my chronicle, if not the laundry.

"A question first?" Dwiri is winsome, having both her parents' charm. Still Lerius does not speak.

"Whatever I can answer."

"What happened to Dzu after you two left him? The killing never stopped. In fact, it became more virulent, and he more rabid in his public appearances. What went wrong?"

It is the very question the World still asks. I hold out my hands helplessly. How should I know?

"There is a theory that he tried, that he meant to keep his word. But those surrounding him were the stronger and, as he said, made him the moderate by comparison. Some say he was drugged, kept as a figurehead, made to mouth speeches he no longer understood, his brain reduced to pulp. As vulnerable as he was, it is certainly possible. Dweneth and I never got close to him again after that night. Perhaps he never meant to change. Perhaps he could not. I do not know."

"Rumor on the radio says he is still alive."

Again I hold out my empty hands. "That may be. I do not know."

Dwiri nods. "I only wondered. For a Telepath, I have an inordinate curiosity about the here and now. Most unDisciplined! Will you stay with us? Others will tend to your duties; I have told Jisra as much. And can your chronicle not wait a time?"

Lerius stirs slightly. What do they want of me?

"To join with us," Dwiri explains. "To show you Dweneth's last years, after she saved you from the leather death."

I want this more than I have wanted anything for a very long time. Yet I demur.

"Your father will tell you, if he has not already," I tell

312

Dwiri, though my eyes are for Lerius, "that I have lost a year of my life to Telepaths' whimsies. I cannot do so again. Not to two of you; I have not the strength. Not further years from my life at my age, not with the World on the brink and the Council once more in debate and Joreth restless for the Mainland and Jemadar missing. The present is all I have; I will not squander it. No!"

"I have not a year to squander, either," Dwiri answers softly, her hands framing her waist. The babe is due within the month. "We ask a day, no more."

I succumb. To have Dweneth with me once more, if only in my mind . . .

"Sometimes I can't separate your memories from mine anymore. We've traveled the same way for so long. Even if it was hemispheres apart, it was always headed in the same direction."

"Then do me one last favor? Betray me. Turn me in."

"What? I must be getting deaf. Have to change your medication; this one's making you stupid. 'Betray me.' What rot is this? Never! No!"

I have given my memories to the Telepaths and I rest now, prefatory to the final stage. I am pleasantly exhausted, with Dweneth closer to me than she has been these ten years. Somehow I do not fear the next phase, though I know it includes her death. I am at peace. I—

Someone is calling me, in the here and now. Once again, Lingri Inept becomes the indispensible. Something about the *bRi*. . . .

How strong the walls which separate us?
How dense the molecules in a stone?
Trust, and put your hand through
Touch the hand reaching from the Other side
Hold on.

How strong the ideas which divide us
Is an idea worth dying for
Also worth killing for
When living, growing, changing are the harder?
Let go.

—from *Early Poems*, by Lingri Chronicler

14

A lone canoe, a Melet outrigger, drifts against the rocks at the mouth of our passage fjord. One would think it a derelict, save that it is guarded by *bRi*. Only when I begin to trill at them does the canoe show signs of containing life.

"Mellia?"

Tangle-haired and sleepy-looking, Yarel's lost Melet companion emerges from a heap of rags amidships. Grown taller than when she left us, still rail-thin, the girl is hungry, shivering, but will not leave her boat until she speaks with me. I climb aboard and put my arms and my cloak around her; she leans into my warmth.

"Lingri-one . . . Jemadar . . . sent me. Escaped by night. A girl gone fishing, not suspicious. I knew some *bRi*-words and they . . . brought me."

"Jemadar lives?"

"Alive . . . when I left. They maimed him . . . then hailed him as a hero before they left him. He said . . . to bring Lingri."

"I will go at once. But you must rest."

She grows agitated. "No! You . . . and Joreth. 'AnOther

and an Intermix,' saith Jemadar. 'And you must return with them.' Let me eat, and sleep an hour. . . .''

"You shall eat aplenty and sleep till nightfall. Joreth and I will be with you. Did Jemadar say why?''

"Jemadar knows . . .''

The girl drowses against my shoulder for a moment. I lift her from the canoe to carry her up the fjord. The movement rouses her. "Jemadar knows 'the fate of the World,' saith he. 'If Lingri come . . . the fate of the World . . .' ''

"Nonsense!'' Joreth bellows once the girl has been fed and tucked up on my sleeping shelf and I set about to pack. "Perhaps he's only dying and he wants you to hold his hand. Worse, the Purists have turned him, and it's all a trap.''

"Be silent!'' I chide him as I should have more often when he was a child; perhaps if I had he would not shout so now. "The child has journeyed three days on the open sea. Have pity!''

He leads me out beside the cold spring and lowers his voice. "I'm sorry! But we can't know what's going on in Melet, and to go off on the say-so of Jemadar and a child—!''

"What does your precious radio say about it?'' I challenge him, understanding now the busy-ness of the Council. "Or is that information now reserved for Matriarchs?''

He grows evasive, cannot meet my eyes.

"Joreth . . .'' My tone is menacing.

"All right! The Passivists' Movement has spread to the capitals of all fourteen nations. Eight governments are at a virtual standstill, five more are wavering. Only Mantuu resists to the end, and even its Chancellor has called for what he describes as 'a miracle.' Either the Purists produce Dzu alive and well, or someone offers proof that all Others are not dead. On one of these will he decide whither his nation goes. Jisra and the Council—''

"Were preparing to go to Mantuu,'' I finished for him.

"Yes.''

316

I take him by the shoulders, mother to son. "Look me in the eye, now. The Council numbers forty-nine, all of whom are our last adults best qualified for leadership. If all die, we are left far worse than ever. We cannot even know who next should lead us, without skillscans. And forty-nine, direct to Mantuu, as opposed to two sidling in out of Melet? Is it possible Jemadar, being on the spot, knows something we cannot? Is your courage sufficient to go with me, or shall I go alone?"

"I'm going regardless!" He is on the verge of shouting. "But you'll stay here."

I arch an eyebrow at him and return to my packing. "Is this called being masterful? Even your father knew better. Mind your head!" The archway is low and he bumps his head anyway, backing out of my way as I work. "Jemadar has asked for both of us, and both of us he will get. You do not hear me arguing that you should remain here for the sake of your impending fatherhood. Or did you think this would be a day trip?"

It only now occurs to him that Dwiri comes to term within the month.

"But what if they've turned him?" he repeats helplessly. "They are capable of tortures—he is only People."

"As are some of the most courageous beings I know. At the most fundamental, my son: 'Who will be the first to trust?' "

He acquiesces, goes to pack his own things.

"Bring something warm," his mother says.

And we are on our way.

317